CLAIMED BY A DEMON KING

ETERNAL MATES BOOK 2

∽∞∾

FELICITY HEATON

Copyright © 2014 Felicity Heaton

All rights reserved. No part of this publication may be reproduced, stored in a retrieval system, or transmitted, in any form or by any means mechanical, electronic, photocopying, recording or otherwise without the prior written consent of the publisher, nor be otherwise circulated in any form of binding or cover other than that in which it is published and without a similar condition being imposed on the subsequent purchaser.

The right of Felicity Heaton to be identified as the Author of the Work has been asserted by her in accordance with the Copyright, Designs and Patents Act 1988.

First printed February 2014

First Edition

Layout and design by Felicity Heaton

All characters in this publication are purely fictitious and any resemblance to real persons, living or dead, is purely coincidental.

THE ETERNAL MATES SERIES

Book 1: Kissed by a Dark Prince
Book 2: Claimed by a Demon King
Book 3: Tempted by a Rogue Prince
Book 4: Hunted by a Jaguar
Book 5: Craved by an Alpha
Book 6: Bitten by a Hellcat
Book 7: Taken by a Dragon
Book 8: Marked by an Assassin
Book 9: Possessed by a Dark Warrior
Book 10: Awakened by a Demoness
Book 11: Haunted by the King of Death
Book 12: Turned by a Tiger
Book 13: Tamed by a Tiger
Book 14: Treasured by a Tiger
Book 15: Unchained by a Forbidden Love
Book 16: Avenged by an Angel
Book 17: Seduced by a Demon King
Book 18: Scorched by Darkness
Book 19: Inflamed by an Incubus (2022)

CHAPTER 1

Sable checked her weapons for the millionth time, a light morning breeze playing in her long black hair, causing rogue strands from her ponytail to flutter over her shoulder as she stood in the middle of the training ground in the courtyard of the elegant sandstone building that was Archangel's headquarters in London.

She ran her fingers over the twin rows of small throwing blades strapped to her ribs beneath her arms, the leather holster laying them flush against her tight black t-shirt, and expelled her breath. It wasn't a sigh. She wasn't nervous.

It wasn't. She wasn't.

She had been telling herself those two things on repeat throughout the endless briefing she had endured, trying not to let her senior, Mark, and the high-ranking staff notice her nerves.

Not that she was nervous.

Eager to get going. Excited about the prospect of taking command of a unit of hunters for the first time in her life. It was a big deal and an opportunity she wasn't going to squander. Archangel had chosen her to lead a team of fifty into Hell to the Third Realm to assist in the Third King's war against the Fifth Realm.

Thorne.

Her belly fluttered.

That was definitely nerves. Not something else. Not a reaction to just his name whispered in her mind.

An image of the brawny demon king flashed into her head, sending fire rushing through her veins. Intense dark crimson eyes. Wild russet brown hair.

Rough masculine features. Shoulders so wide that they made the biggest of her hunters look scrawny and muscles that bulged beneath bronzed tight skin.

Not to mention those rich brown horns that curled from behind his ears and that lopsided grin.

He was six-feet-seven of Heaven and ruled a realm in Hell.

Sable expelled another breath. Not a sigh. A girl had to breathe.

Several of the male hunters near the front of the group were studying her.

She cleared her throat and finished her weapons check, using it to push Thorne out of her head.

It had been growing increasingly difficult to keep the brash demon from her thoughts over the past month and almost impossible to lock him out of her dreams. Heat burned up her cheeks and she dropped her head, turning it slightly away from her team so they wouldn't notice her blushing like a schoolgirl. She checked her folded compact crossbow and the quiver of bolts attached to her belt, trying to focus on them in the hope it would shove Thorne to the back of her mind. What was wrong with her?

Get a grip.

She shut down her emotions one by one, locking them back in place and restoring order. This was a mission. Her chance to secure the rank she had desired for so long now, ever since she had joined Archangel. There were only a handful of commanders in the entire organisation and she wanted to be one of them.

Sable lifted her head and pinned her team with a deadly look. "Fall in."

They responded immediately, forming five neat rows of ten before her. They were the cream of Archangel's hunters in London. While that was a good thing, it also meant that they were highly experienced and used to working alone. If she didn't exert some authority and failed to lead them well, they would branch off and fall back into old routines. That would prove disastrous.

None of them were familiar with Hell.

She only knew the elf kingdom herself and only had Prince Loren of the elves' reports on the demon realms to go by, but he made them sound like forbidding lands filled with creatures liable to chew mortals up and spit them out before they could even think about drawing a weapon to defend themselves.

If her team didn't act like one and work together, none of them would make it out of the place alive.

She was damned if she would lose a single hunter on her first mission in charge.

"Listen up," she barked and they snapped to attention. "We don't know much about the situation we're heading into or the territory of the domain. We will need to be on our guards. We know from intelligence given to us by the elves that the kingdom known as the Third Realm has been under attack from the one known as the Fifth Realm for the past twenty-one months. The Fifth King seeks to defeat and absorb the lands of the Third King, and the Third King has asked for our assistance."

Sable pointedly looked at all her hunters in turn, ensuring she still had their attention. A few women at the back shifted foot-to-foot. She couldn't blame them for being nervous. They were all of fifty mortals heading into a demon war, but they had back up. Prince Loren was bringing a whole legion of elf warriors and they would work together on the battlefield.

"I don't need to tell you how important this mission is on many levels. This is an opportunity to form an alliance with the Third King and to gain intel on the realms and political landscape of Hell." She still couldn't get her head around that. Hell. She had popped in and out of the elf kingdom there several times over the past month, but that realm didn't look like Hell in her eyes. It looked like paradise—lush, green, and beautiful—an oasis surrounded by darkness on all sides. "Anything you think is important for Archangel to know about, you document it and report it to me or to Evan, and I'll gather the information and pass it on to Archangel. We're to assess the threat level of every species we meet. The more information we can bring back from this mission, the better we've done. Understood?"

They all nodded.

"We're leaving as soon as our transport arrives, so prepare yourselves."

Sable turned away from them and blew out another breath, trying to expel the tension cranking her muscles tight. She rolled her shoulders and flexed her fingers, and resisted the temptation to perform another weapons check.

Some of the hunters broke away from the main group, heading towards the stacks of black ribbed metal cases and luggage. She had placed Evan in charge of their equipment. As the most experienced hunter in the team, she trusted him one hundred percent with the task and with his role as her second in command.

The tall blond man motioned to the five men he had taken with him to the cases and they began checking everything against the list on his tablet one more time.

Sable paced, hoping to work off at least a little of her tension before Loren arrived with his elves. She really didn't need him noticing that she was wound tighter than he had ever been during his courtship of her best friend, Olivia.

She could do this. Mark had told her as much before she had left his office barely an hour ago. He wanted to give her the title of commander and this was her test. She wouldn't fail him and she wouldn't let anything stand in the way of her achieving that rank.

She had busted her arse over the past month, working twice as hard as normal in order to convince Mark and the senior staff that she was the perfect candidate for the role of commander on this mission.

It had absolutely nothing to do with getting a pass into Hell and seeing Thorne again.

Not at all.

She was going because she wanted the position of commander.

A familiar female voice cut off a deep male one and Sable smiled as she turned to glance across the courtyard.

Their transport was arriving. Scores of elves dressed in their tight black scale-like armour appeared before her eyes, the air shimmering around them. Prince Loren led them across the courtyard towards her, his long strides eating up the distance and his left hand resting on the hilt of the black sword sheathed at his waist. His black eyebrows knit into scowl and his purple eyes darkened.

The slight brunette beside him shook her head, causing her long chestnut hair to sway against the shoulders of her dark t-shirt, and waved him away. "I've told you a million times, Loren... I am going on this mission."

Loren's lips compressed into a thin line. Olivia was trying her mate's patience again. He looked ready to grab her and teleport her back to the realm of the elves and leave her there.

Olivia had a mean stubborn streak though and that was another reason why Sable had been eager to win this mission. Olivia was her best friend at Archangel and she didn't want her friend in the firing line during a war, but having her there was necessary. They needed a doctor on hand to take care of any injured. That and Sable needed the moral support of her friend on this mission. She would go crazy without her.

"Olivia," Loren started and then seemed to think the better of whatever he had intended to say and scrubbed a hand over his face instead. He threw Sable a pleading glance.

Sable shrugged. Helping him was above her pay grade. She couldn't overturn a decision made by Mark and the board of senior staff. Loren scowled again and turned back to his mate, speaking in a low voice now.

Sable glanced at Bleu as he strode to his prince's right, meeting his green gaze. It was strange seeing him in better control of his emotions than Loren was, able to retain a more mortal appearance, concealing his normal purple irises and pointed ears.

She smiled at Bleu as Olivia began to rant.

Bleu raked long fingers through his wild black-blue hair and gave her a warm smile in return.

"I am going whether you like it or not," Olivia snapped at Loren and then softened. "I know you're worried but I'll have you there with me, and Sable too. Archangel assigned me to this mission as the medic and to research any new species we encounter... and you know both of those things are very important to me. So I'm going and that's final."

Loren looked as if he had just lost a war. His shoulders slumped and he let out a long, weary breath. "Very well, Ki'ara."

Bleu shook his head. "Olivia, you sound more like my sister every day."

Olivia didn't look sure whether that was a compliment or not. Sable had seen Bleu often over the past few weeks. He had visited Archangel whenever Loren had and Loren was rarely away from Olivia when she was working.

The dark elf commander was a great sparring partner and had helped Sable step up her game during their training matches. She was glad he didn't hold back when he was fighting her.

Well, he didn't hold back much. She knew he wasn't going all out on her and in a way, she was glad. She had seen him fight and part of her knew she wouldn't stand a chance against him, even if her pride wouldn't allow her to admit it.

The only time Bleu hadn't been with Loren was when his sister had returned to his family home for a rare visit. Bleu had disappeared like a shot. Sable had asked about this elusive sister and Loren had informed her that Bleu had only one sibling, a younger sister, and that he was forever getting her out of scrapes, but that only seemed to make him love her more dearly.

The indulgent and amused twinkle in his eyes at times made Sable feel that he was beginning to view Olivia with similar brotherly affection. It would be nice for Olivia to have family again after everything she had been through.

Sable idly rubbed her right wrist, her thumb caressing the stylised black cross on the inside of it, and tamped down the dark thoughts that threatened to rise and ruin her mood.

"Is everyone ready?" She checked her assembled team and then the elves. Loren had finally given up trying to convince Olivia not to come on the mission and was speaking with Bleu and several of his men. He motioned towards the crates and baggage, and a group of elves broke away, heading towards them.

The rest of the elves made their way over to her team, one for each member. A few low giggles broke the silence as the female hunters in her unit met the tall, darkly beautiful male who would be teleporting them.

Sable sighed this time. "Rein it in. This is a mission, not a Club 18-30 holiday. Remember that."

Her hunters jolted to attention and nodded as one.

Sable just hoped that she could remember it. Whenever she thought about seeing Thorne again, she got the jitters. Stupid of her considering she had only met him once and for little more than a handful of hours. It hadn't stopped her from desperately trying not to hang on every word whenever Loren had spoken of the demon king. It wasn't like her, but she couldn't help herself. Something fundamental inside her had changed the moment Thorne had barged into her life.

Thorne met often with Loren to discuss their arrival and arrangements, and to keep him abreast of the situation in the Third Realm.

Loren relayed everything to her.

It hadn't satisfied her in the slightest. Loren never said how Thorne was coping with everything or how he seemed to him.

She wanted to know how he was doing and wanted to see that he was still well, and still the same brash male she had met a month ago. Of course, she refused to admit that to Olivia whenever her friend pressed her about Thorne, and her friend had pressed a lot over the long four weeks.

Sable had denied everything, refusing to admit that she couldn't stop thinking about the demon king.

She couldn't get that moment in the cafeteria out of her head. Thorne had teleported them back to Archangel after they had defeated Kordula, freeing Loren's brother Vail from the bitch-witch's spell. Thorne had stood with his hand on Sable's arm, as if he couldn't bring himself to let her go, and had stared at her for so long that she had ended up lost in his crimson gaze. He had opened his mouth to speak, had turned frustrated about something, and had teleported out of her life as quickly as he had come into it, leaving her confused and curious.

What had Thorne wanted to say to her?

Whatever had been balanced on those firm sensual lips, she wished he had just come out and said it because it had been driving her completely crazy. She had found herself pondering it at the strangest times. Dangerous times. A hunt was no place to lose track of your surroundings. That moment kept invading her head though, replaying in infinite detail, every shift in his body language and expression captured perfectly. With each replay, she found herself wanting to know more than ever what he had meant to say.

The first chance she had, she was asking him about it.

Sable grimaced and reminded herself again that she was going to Hell on a mission, not just to see Thorne. This was about the mission. This was about her future with Archangel. This wasn't about the big, rough, demon male.

She jolted when someone took hold of her arm and looked up into Bleu's eyes. Flecks of purple broke through the green, slowly taking over until not a trace of emerald remained. His violet gaze narrowed on her and he moved closer, towering over her, a vision of dark beauty and lethal grace. His lips parted, flashing white daggers at her. His fangs were down. The tips of his ears turned pointed. He had shaken off his mortal guise, revealing his true nature.

"Ready?" he murmured, his fingers lightly flexing around her arm and his gaze locked intently on her.

Sable blinked herself back the courtyard and nodded.

Her world disappeared in a swirl of cold black shadows. She closed her eyes against it. The heat of the sun on her skin gave way to the icy chill and then became a blast of moist warm air. The shrouding silence of the portal shattered under the explosion of grunts and roars and the metallic clang of weapons clashing.

The scent of morning became the odour of blood.

Sable snapped her eyes open and her heart leaped and pounded, quickening her blood and preparing her body.

The first thing she saw was Thorne shirtless and swinging his enormous broadsword at an equally massive bare-chested warrior. His opponent blocked with his own blade and growled, flashing huge fangs as he swung a meaty fist. The blow connected with Thorne's right cheek and he stumbled, grunting as he struggled to regain his footing and ready his blade to defend himself.

Sable's hand instantly went to the folded crossbow at her side and she flicked it open, pushing away from Bleu at the same time. Another immense demon attacked Thorne before he managed to right himself and the dagger sliced across the Third King's thickly muscled right shoulder.

Thorne roared and finally launched himself at the males, taking them both on at once. They weren't alone. The wide oval courtyard of the dark stone fortress was in pandemonium. Sable counted at least two dozen demons, all focused on him with their weapons drawn and at the ready. No other fought on his side.

The sight of him standing alone against so many adversaries, bleeding from multiple wounds on his torso and arms, brought a red haze down over her vision.

Sable launched herself into the fray just as one of the males attacked. Her heart raced, pumping adrenaline that made her feel high as she reached beneath her left arm, slipped her fingers into the rings on two of her throwing knives, and hurled them with deadly accuracy at the warrior. They nailed him in the left of his broad chest and his shoulder, and she didn't give him a chance to recover his focus. She loosed a barbed dart from her crossbow at him, reloaded in the space of a heartbeat, and shot the other male now attacking Thorne.

The barbed dart embedded into the demon's left thigh and he grunted, his eyes glowing crimson as he turned his attention on her. Good. She had to give Thorne a moment to recover his wits and get back in the fight.

The warrior stomped towards her, blood pulsing down his leg with each step, turning his black leathers slick and shiny. He growled, his top lip peeling back off his fangs, and shook his head. His dusky horns curled further, forming a loop and flaring forwards into twin dangerous points near his cheekbones.

Sable made a mental note to avoid them and drew the short blade strapped to her other thigh, ready to fight him. He swung the moment he was within reach and she ducked beneath the long silver blade, rolled forwards and came to her feet behind him. She slashed up his back, her knife splitting tanned flesh and scraping over bone, and grinned as he arched forwards and roared.

The thrill chasing through her blood increased, consuming her, driving her to keep going and embrace wildness it unleashed within her. She had been born to fight monsters and she felt it now more than ever as she faced off against the enormous demon males, swiftly calculating their every move before they could make it, ready for anything.

Sable grabbed a bolt with a thick cylinder on the end from her quiver pouch. Explosive dart. God she loved these things. She loaded it onto the small crossbow and swung to her left, aiming at the group of males storming towards her.

She grinned and pulled the trigger.

A large bloodstained hand clamped down on the weapon, grasping it and holding the bolt in place.

Sable growled in frustration and released her crossbow, leaving it in the demon's hand. She thrust hard with her blade, blindly stabbing at her new enemy.

The huge male grabbed her wrist before she could drive the cold steel into his flesh. The tip pressed into his muscular chest and she froze when she realised it was Thorne frowning down at her, his rough masculine features crinkled in confusion.

"You seek to harm me, Little Female? I thought we had discussed this before?"

His deep gravelly voice washed over her and his thumb caressed the inside of her wrist. Sable trembled. The hot shivery ache rolling through her increased in intensity as he tugged on her wrist, gently drawing her closer to him, his red gaze holding hers, commanding and powerful. She couldn't break its hold on her. She tilted her head right back, lost in his eyes as he towered over her, making her feel small and weak, vulnerable to him.

Sable dropped her blade, the clang of it hitting the stone slabs beneath her feet jarring in the thick silence. She breathed hard, firmly under his spell and unable to form a response.

She had forgotten just how gorgeous he was and how his presence lit her up inside like fireworks on November fifth.

"Well?" Thorne cocked his head to one side and a hank of wild red-brown hair fell down onto his bloodstained brow.

Sable slowly shook her head and forced words up her dry throat and past her lips. "I was trying to help."

A smile worked its way onto his firm lips and he flashed short fangs. "That is very kind of you... but I do not require your assistance to spar with my men."

Spar?

Sable inched her gaze towards the demon males to her left. They had all stopped and were staring at her. She looked to her other side, at her team and the elves, and cringed. None of them had moved. She alone had leapt into the fray.

A blush burned up her cheeks before she could stop it. Thorne canted his head again, raised his free hand and lightly brushed the backs of his short claws across her left cheek. She shuddered under the gentle caress, her pulse quickening for a different reason as the heat burning inside her exploded into wildfire. She had to get a grip. This was a mission.

"Did you believe me to be under attack?" he husked in a low, quiet voice that sent a fierce shiver through her, cranking up her temperature another thousand degrees.

She couldn't bring herself to look at him. She nodded, and admitting it left her feeling like a fool.

"And you came to my aid?" Had he moved closer to her? His breath washed over her cheek, moist and hot, smelling faintly of something sweet and the coppery tang of blood.

Sable nodded again.

"You are but a little mortal female… yet you desired to fight all these demon males in order to protect me?"

When he put it like that, she couldn't stop herself from blushing harder. She had reacted on instinct but the tone of his voice and the way he drew her closer still, until she could feel his heat rolling off him and over her, told her that he thought she did it because she felt something for him.

Desired him.

She cleared her throat, finally locked down her emotions and found her voice again, and even the courage to lift her gaze to his. "Not out of favouritism or anything. I'm here on a mission and that mission entails protecting you and your kingdom from demons. I saw you battling a score of demons and I did my duty."

She twisted her hand free of his grip and hated the sharp disappointed edge his eyes gained. It made her feel like a bitch. She grabbed her blade from the dark stone pavement and jammed it into its sheath, and then snatched up her crossbow and checked it over, taking her time about it, stewing under the intense heat of his gaze.

Sable kept her head bent and holstered her crossbow and the unused explosive dart. Thorne continued to stare at her. So did everyone else. She was not going to blush. She racked her brain, trying to think of something to say to make everything go back to normal, and diligently kept her gaze away from Thorne.

She had also forgotten how impossibly tight his dark mahogany leather trousers were. They clung to his muscular thighs, stretched over them like a second skin, held closed by criss-crossed lacing over his crotch.

Not staring. Not staring.

Her eyes betrayed her, leaping to the impressive bulge in his trousers, and she forced it upwards before anyone noticed. Thorne's gaze locked with hers again, holding her immobile.

"I'll need my blades and bolts back now," she muttered, not quite with the world or aware of what she was saying.

Thorne nodded. "Of course."

He signalled his men and Sable realised just what she had asked, and felt dismal as the men immediately tore the barbed darts and throwing knives from their flesh without giving a single grunt or revealing a flicker of the pain they must have experienced.

They came forwards and placed the weapons into Thorne's outstretched hand. He wiped the blood off them on his leather trousers and then held them out to her.

Sable swallowed her guilt and took them from him. She slipped the blades away beneath her arms and put the darts back in her quiver. The silence in the courtyard thickened again. She wasn't sure what to do. She had made one hell of a first impression—on her team, on the elves, on the demons.

On Thorne.

She wanted to groan and bury her head in her heads.

She needed a do-over on everything after she had appeared in the Third Realm. It really hadn't gone as planned.

Sable tossed Olivia a look and her friend wiped the smile off her face and nudged Loren. The tall, slender elf prince looked down at his mate, his black eyebrows pinned high on his forehead. Olivia gave a subtle jerk of her chin towards Sable. Loren looked her way and understanding dawned in his purple eyes.

"King Thorne." Loren broke away from his legion and Olivia, and crossed the short distance to the demon male.

Thorne's gaze finally left Sable. "Prince Loren."

Sable seized her chance to slink back unnoticed to her team. Some of them gave her funny looks. She ignored them and Bleu's inquisitive stare and checked her team over, making sure they had all arrived safely.

Thorne's focus landed back on her. She could feel it whenever it happened. A shockwave of heat rippled through her, awareness so intense that she could almost pinpoint how far he was from her and could visualise the way he was looking at her. Whenever he looked away, returning his attention to Loren, cold stole through her, fierce and frigid.

She rubbed her wrist, her actions mimicking the light stroke of Thorne's thumb over her tattoo. It ached and burned. Had she hurt it in training? Or was it a response to the way Thorne had caressed that patch of skin?

She gathered herself, squared her shoulders, turned on the spot and calmly strode back to Thorne and Loren.

The two tall men looked at her. Their height and fangs were the only things they had in common. Loren was unnaturally beautiful, lithe and held an air of darkness around him that stemmed from more than just his black hair and obsidian armour. Thorne was rugged, immense and had an aura of danger surrounding him that warned even her away.

His gaze held darkness as he finished discussing the war with Loren.

She had the answer to one of her questions at least. Thorne was troubled. The war was taking its toll on him, pushing him to his limit, wearing him down.

"King Thorne," she said without a trace of tremble in her voice and bowed her head. "I would like to introduce my team."

He ran an assessing gaze over them and then returned his attention to her. "Little Female. It is kind of Archangel to send a small contingent of your forces to assist in my demonomachy."

Sable bit her tongue, stopping herself from pointing out that she had a name and that this was a large contingent of their forces and all they could spare. She supposed that in comparison to the thousand immortal warriors that Loren had brought with him, her fifty mortal hunters did look rather pathetic.

"Sable," Loren started and frowned when Thorne bared his fangs on a growl. Thorne cast his gaze down at his boots and clenched his fists. Loren arched an eyebrow at him, sighed, and continued, "Your hunters must desire to settle themselves in their quarters."

Thorne growled again and this time Sable had the impression it was because Loren was suggesting things that he should have thought of and suggested first.

"That would be good." Sable kept her focus on Thorne, pretending he had suggested it, hoping to calm him.

"You men," Thorne barked and a group of demons near the large arched doorway of the impressive dark grey fortress saluted, pressing their hands to their bare chests. "Show the mortals and elves to their quarters."

He signalled another set of males and gestured to the elves standing guard next to the black crates and bags.

"Take their belongings and follow their instruction to ensure they all end up with their owners." Thorne glanced at her. "Come."

He turned away and walked with Loren towards the arched doorway of the large three-storey stone building that formed a wide corner in the curved courtyard. Arched windows lined the first and second floors, smaller in the longest side of the building to her right but larger and more decorative in the main part ahead of her. A balcony extended to the left of the first upper floor, giving the building a staggered appearance.

Demons patrolled the battlements at the top of the building and the walls that connected to it.

It wasn't a castle as Loren had, with towers and conical roofs, and a verdant courtyard filled with trees, grass and flowering shrubs. It was squat and heavily fortified, and bore the scars of war in many places, the stones cracked or long grooves cut into them. It had been built with defence in mind and reminded her of many of the castles in England or Wales. There was even a well in the courtyard. This place was a military stronghold.

The demons Thorne had ordered to take her team to their quarters reached her hunters and led them away, speaking in broken English to them. Loren had warned her that only the high-ranking demons could speak her language, and that many of the warriors only understood the demon tongue or could only speak a small amount of English.

The elves split into groups, some going with the mortals, some following Loren towards the doors, led by Bleu, and others going with Evan to deal with the crates.

Olivia came over and linked arms with her. "Well, that went well."

Sable scowled at her friend. "Don't start. I really hope I don't make a fool of myself any more today."

"You weren't to know he was training," Olivia whispered as they followed Thorne and Loren towards the main building of the large fortress.

The wall surrounding the courtyard was so high she couldn't see anything but a strange dark orange sky. Was it day now, or night in this realm? Whenever she left Archangel to come to the elf realm, she ended up at the opposite time of day. She had left in the morning, so this was the evening?

The elves brought light into their realm via portals. Loren had explained the demon realms had a sort of day and night because the light of the elf kingdom reached far into many of their realms. The sheer number of torches and fires blazing around the courtyard illuminated it as if it was day.

She guessed there was no shortage of fire in Hell.

She glanced back at Evan to check on him. He was already glaring at the demons. He looked her way and pointed to a square three-storey building that intersected the wall behind her, opposite the main building. An armoury? There were several buildings like it along the curving wall. Huge demon males prowled the top of the wall between each building, or loitered near their entrances, talking and laughing. Laughing. It was a little weird seeing a demon laugh. She had imagined them all to be as serious as Thorne.

But even Thorne had smile-lines bracketing his mouth and at the corners of his eyes.

"Earth... I mean, Hell to Sable?" Olivia nudged her.

Sable shook herself back to her friend. "It's a lot to take in."

She nodded to Evan and he turned back to the demons and elves assisting him. Many of the demons stared at Evan's tablet as if it were magical, their deep red eyes wide and expressions locked in lines of fascination.

A few males looked her way as they entered the main building. They grinned and bent their heads together. Whispering about her no doubt. The silly little mortal throwing herself into a battle between two dozen demons to protect their immortal king.

She groaned.

Olivia shifted her arm, wrapping it around Sable's shoulders. "It's really not that bad."

But it was. She wanted to make Bleu take her back to Archangel and find a way to undo the past hour so she could do it all over again.

"If I look like I'm about to make another tit of myself, do feel free to hit me over the head with something blunt and heavy before it happens." Sable leaned her head on Olivia's shoulder and then straightened when Thorne spoke to Loren.

"I apologise for not being ready for you." He rubbed a dark cloth over his torso, wiping the blood away. "I thought I had more time."

"No need to apologise," Loren said. "It was our fault. Archangel were eager to send their team in on the mission."

Thorne glanced over his right shoulder at Sable, his eyebrows rising. She looked away, locking her gaze on Olivia and Bleu. When had he fallen into step with them?

She couldn't look at Thorne. If she did, he was bound to see straight through her and see that she was the reason they were early. Bleu talked to Olivia about Loren and Sable drifted along beside her, not taking in the impressive carved columns that supported the vaulted ceiling in the wide hallway. She was too busy doing her best to ignore Thorne. She could block him out, keeping her eyes off him, but she couldn't ignore how she felt whenever his gaze landed on her.

Hot all over. Flushed from the intense feel of his eyes on her.

Bleu moved around Olivia and her, ending up walking beside her. "You fought well."

She shrugged off the compliment, uncomfortable with his praise, and thought of something to say to keep him around. His presence lessened the fierce reaction she had to Thorne's eyes on her and she needed that right now.

She had to find her balance again before she did something crazy.

Like kissing a demon king.

CHAPTER 2

Sable entered the main hall with Bleu and Olivia flanking her. Two rows of three thick stone columns stood on either side of them, cutting twin lines down the centre of the enormous windowless room, framing the path from the arched doorway behind her to the raised semi-circular stone platform at the opposite end of the room. Torches burned in black metal brackets around the columns, bathing the room in warm light that chased all the shadows away and flickered across the vaulted ceiling.

Loren paused with his group of elves in the centre of the room before her.

Thorne stepped up onto the stone platform at the end and turned to face them. A large elaborate black throne stood behind him and a huge tapestry depicting a war hung on the wall behind it. He handed his blood-soaked rag to another male demon. This one wore tan trousers and a cream shirt and looked more like a servant, slimmer than the muscle-bound warriors they had left in the courtyard. The man bowed his head and backed away, stepping down from the platform. She frowned at the thick torc around his neck. The twisted bands of red and black looked heavy, closed tightly around his throat.

Several of the warriors who had been fighting Thorne had worn something similar.

Bleu looked down at her and then towards the man. He was silent for a moment and then said, "They wear them when they have lost their eternal mate. It is a sign to others, a warning not to speak of females."

A widower.

"Welcome," Thorne said, his deep voice breaking into her sombre thoughts. "The others will arrive this eve and—"

A few scantily clad beautiful women came into view and Sable frowned as they fawned over him, praising his fighting and his skill. Thorne waved them away, a bored look on his face. They persisted until he growled and then they strutted away, heading towards the group of demons that had entered behind Sable. Some of the warriors from the training match. Those males lapped up the attention that Thorne had dismissed.

"As I was saying… the others will arrive this eve and there will be a feast."

What the hell did demons eat at a feast? She cast an unnerved look at the elves and then at Olivia. The elves seemed at ease and they ate vegetables and fruits. Maybe the demons did too.

She could have laughed out loud at that thought. None of the demons she had met in her long career as a hunter had looked as if they enjoyed a nourishing five-a-day. They all looked as if they lived on a protein-rich diet. Plus, elves also drank blood, so there was just as much chance that demons did too and tonight's feast would be served in cups and jugs.

"I am sure you all desire to settle into your quarters. Until the feast then." Thorne bowed his head and Loren did too, and then the elf prince was walking towards her, Olivia and Bleu.

Loren took Olivia's hand and led her away, following several demons. Sable trailed behind them, feeling Thorne's gaze on her with each step, heating her to her core.

Cold swept over her and she looked back, wondering why Thorne had stopped looking at her.

Bleu hadn't moved.

He stood in the middle of the room facing Thorne, his expression impassive but his ears pointed, flaring back against the sides of his head and tangled in his wild black hair. Thorne held his gaze, a corona of fiery red circling his darker crimson irises and his horns slowly curling around in front of his pointed ears.

Sable took a step towards both males and their focuses shattered, their gazes coming to her.

"Bleu?" she said, and then looked at Thorne, catching the fire burning in his eyes. Whatever challenge had passed unspoken between the two males, it had set alight to Thorne's temper. She needed to get Bleu away from him before the demon king did something he might regret. She shifted her gaze back to Bleu. "Are you coming?"

He looked as though he wouldn't and then nodded and began walking towards her.

Sable lingered, her focus drifting back to Thorne where he stood in the middle of the cavernous room. Bleu caught her arm, stealing her attention away from him, and she swore she heard Thorne growl.

She had seen Loren act like this around Olivia and it set her on edge.

His behaviour had all the hallmarks of a male with his mate and she didn't like it. She had never seen the point in getting serious with a man in her line of work, when every patrol might be her last, and she had seen just how serious being a mate was with her friend. Olivia was now immortal, mated to an elf prince. Their love was forever.

For a flicker of a moment, what they shared had made Sable want to try on a relationship for size, but it had only been a passing fancy. A reaction to loneliness. She liked her dalliances short and hot. Not eternal.

Sable turned away from Thorne and followed Bleu. She frowned at the elf male's hand on her arm. The jagged black claws of his armour covered his fingers and the tips pressed into her flesh. The sight of his hand on her, possessively clamped around her wrist, unnerved her too.

She took her arm back and he glanced at her, confusion reigning in his violet eyes when she scowled at him.

"I can find my own way." She picked up pace but he remained with her, his long strides making it impossible for her to lose him. She gave up trying when they caught up with Loren and Olivia.

They reached the first floor and a nice male demon showed Bleu to his room at the start of the long corridor, giving her a moment to breathe. Another led her past Olivia and Loren's quarters to the next arched dark wooden door. The man pushed it open and she thanked him with a smile before stepping inside. He muttered something in the demon tongue and closed the door behind her, leaving her alone.

Sable heaved a sigh and leaned her back against the wooden door, gazing at the large room. Her entire quarters at Archangel would fit into it four times over.

A breeze came in through the three arched windows in the wall opposite her, tousling the heavy dark red curtains. No glass.

Not much furniture either.

A large four-poster bed stood against the bare stone wall to her right, covered with thick pale furs. A dark wooden table with a speckled ancient oval mirror was to her left, beside a big wardrobe. The wall opposite the bed had a huge fireplace, with two threadbare velvet-covered armchairs in front of it. Maybe it was the lack of furniture and zero decorative touches that made the room look huge. She walked around it and decided that it wasn't. It just added to the spacious feeling.

Sable paused in front of the fireplace.

The fire in the grate burned brightly.

Strange, but she had thought it would be hot in the demon realms, even though it had always been cool and breezy whenever she had visited the elf kingdom.

How far were they from that realm? She had never asked Loren about it before. Did Thorne have a map of Hell? She wanted to see where they were in comparison to the elf kingdom and the Fifth Realm.

Maybe Loren could tell her.

Sable left her room, went to the next one and opened the door. Olivia shrieked. Loren bit out a few nasty-sounding words in the elf language.

Sable covered her eyes and scrubbed the image of Loren playing tonsil tennis with Olivia while mostly naked from her mind.

"Sorry," she muttered to the wooden floorboards. "Are you decent yet?"

"Knock next time," Olivia snapped.

"In my defence, you've been alone for all of three minutes. I didn't think you could make the leap from room orientation to sex in three minutes!" Rabbits. No. They were worse than bunnies. If Sable took her eyes off them for five seconds, they were kissing like teenagers.

Loren continued to growl dark-sounding things. She presumed they weren't complimentary and were about her because he was firmly sticking to his own language. He still refused to share knowledge of the elf language with Archangel and she supposed she could understand his reluctance. No one other than the elves could understand or speak it. It was probably handy being able to speak a language your enemy couldn't.

"Decent?" Sable asked in a small voice, fearing the elf prince was going to start directing more than insults at her.

"Yes," Olivia answered and Sable came out from behind her hand.

Their love-nest looked much like her room, but with the layout reversed, so the bed was to her left and the fireplace to her right. She looked at the dressing table near the fireplace and idly said, "You don't have a mirror."

"You have a mirror?" Olivia looked as if Sable had just announced she had cable and a fifty-inch home cinema system.

Sable shrugged.

"Well... now we know for certain who the king's favourite is."

She glared daggers at her friend, and then at Loren when his sensual lips tugged into a teasing smile.

"Ha-ha. Drop it already." Sable closed the door behind her and waited for them to look a little more serious before she continued. She decided she was going to have to wait a while.

Loren wrapped his arms around Olivia and stroked her cheek, smiling down into her eyes, looking like a lovesick fool for her friend. Olivia looked just as ridiculously sappy as she gazed up at her prince and rose on her tiptoes. Sable shifted her focus to the fireplace before she caught another eyeful of them locking lips.

Her chest ached and she ignored it.

It grew impossible when Olivia whispered sweet things to Loren and Sable found herself envying her friend.

Again.

Maybe she should have taken the time to try on a relationship for size. It did look sort of nice sometimes. Loren fussed over Olivia and Olivia did the same to him. They always had each other's backs too. And she had never seen her friend so happy.

She scratched her neck and stared into the fire, listening to their murmured conversation and the demons stomping down the hall outside the door. They didn't keep their voices low. Whatever they were discussing, it had them excited. Were they talking about the feast?

Sable closed her eyes and focused on her natural gift to sense non-humans. Their signatures came back strongly, far stronger than she had ever experienced. She could feel their excitement and the buzz running through the castle. It seeped into her as if it was her own, stirring her blood and sending a tremble of anticipation through her. She reached further, pushing herself, stretching down to the next level, seeking one strong heartbeat amidst the cacophony.

"Sable?" Olivia said, drawing her away from her pursuit of Thorne and back to the room. "You okay?"

Sable nodded. "Just fine tuning."

Concern warmed Olivia's dark brown eyes. Before her friend could go doctor on her and start asking about whether her gift was bothering her or if she had any problems with it, Sable smiled and shrugged it off.

More male voices boomed in the hallway. Talking about the feast? She had tried to learn a little of the demon tongue from Bleu but it was tricky. All she had mastered was how to greet someone depending on their status in your opinion, which mostly boiled down to various levels of insults.

"Are you sure you're okay?" Olivia asked and Sable nodded again.

"Just thinking about tonight." Before Olivia could leap in with some ridiculous mention of Thorne, Sable added, "This whole feast thing has me a little jittery. I guess first times are always like that."

"I have to admit, I haven't a clue what to expect." Olivia smiled at her and swept her wavy chestnut hair from her face, hooking it behind her ears. It was strange seeing Olivia in jeans and a black baby-doll t-shirt. She was so used to seeing her friend in her white coat with her hair pinned in a bun, looking all neat and authoritative.

Loren pulled some clothes out of thin air and Sable was never getting used to that. He could teleport whatever belonged to him from anywhere in the world, both this one and her one. He held the long elegant black jacket up and the rich elaborately detailed purple embroidery shone in the firelight.

"You are wondering what food they eat," he said in passing and picked some fluff off the jacket before laying it down over the back of one of the armchairs and pulling a pair of trousers out of the air.

Sable gaped. "Do you read minds now?"

"No, but it was on both of your faces." Loren flicked her a smile and he was charming.

Were there any ugly elves in their world? All of the ones she had met were beautiful, when their temper was in check.

When they slipped into a rage, it was a whole different matter.

She had caught Bleu in a very painful place a few times during their sparring and he always turned on her, his eyes flashing bright purple and his pointed ears flattening against the sides of his head as he hissed at her, exposing large sharp fangs.

"Demons prefer meats, but I am certain there will also be vegetables and perhaps other foods on offer, such as berries and cheeses." He paused to lay his trousers down over his jacket and his black eyebrows drew down above his crystal violet eyes. "Although, I do recommend avoiding the cheeses. Many of the animals they milk are not the same as the ones mortals would choose."

Sable didn't want to ask, not even to assuage her curiosity.

Loren pulled an elegant long dark purple dress out of the air and Sable could no longer hide her worry about the feast.

"Is there a dress code for tonight?" She looked at the beautiful gown and then Loren's fine clothing resting over the chair.

She hadn't brought anything for this sort of situation and she doubted her team had either. All of her clothes were fit for battle and nothing else. Even if she had known in advance about the feast, it wouldn't have helped. She didn't own anything as fine as the dress Loren held. She didn't own a dress period.

"I really don't want to offend Thorne," she ignored the teasing look Olivia slid her way, "but I know all of my team brought only battle clothes with them."

"That will not be a problem." Loren laid the dress down on top of his clothing and turned to her. "You represent your team so only you will be seated at the main table with the other commanding officers. Thorne will not mind if your subordinates are dressed plainly."

In other words, he would mind if she was.

Sable refused to panic about this. "Maybe there's a demon female I can borrow a dress from."

"That won't be possible," Olivia said, snatching her focus. "There are no demon females."

She gasped. "Who were those women then?"

"Witches... a vampire or two. I believe there was even a shifter amongst them," Loren replied and Sable's gaze darted back to him.

"Demons don't have females?" How had she not known that?

"No," Olivia said for him and why hadn't her friend told her about this? "The Devil put some sort of curse on seven demon species when they seized these lands to make their own realms... I guess he was pissed because he wiped out all the women and made it so the men would have to seek out their fated one. Now, demons can only mate with their fated females. The kicker is that most of them are mortal... and demons stick out like sore thumbs in our world."

Mortal.

Sable's pulse kicked up a notch. "How do they know their female?"

"They dream of her after meeting her." Loren's smile turned wicked and she didn't like the glint in his eyes.

Cold slithered through her even as her cheeks began to heat.

"You're talking... *naughty*... dreams." Could she sound any more innocent and nervous?

He nodded. "Very, very naughty."

"Loren," Olivia chided and crossed the room to him. Sable thanked her for backing her up until her friend turned to her, forming an allied front with Loren, her smile just as wicked as his was. "You're not having naughty dreams of Thorne are you, Sable?"

"No." Lie. A whopper of one. The dreams she'd had of him had been x-rated and hotter than all of her real-life encounters rolled into one. "Besides, I'm not a demon male. Why would I dream of him?"

Loren preened his jacket and casually said, "Because their female dreams of them too, and they both experience the same dream if they're sleeping at the same time."

Holy hell in a hand-basket. His triumphant smile said he had noticed the blush that had risen onto her cheeks before she had gotten the better of herself.

"Screw both of you. Stop messing with me."

"In all seriousness, demons are aggressive and it often takes their female to tame them and teach them civility, so try to avoid the unmated ones." Olivia touched Sable's arm.

She nodded, even though she didn't think they were particularly aggressive. Thorne seemed quite calm to her most of the time, and the demons she had encountered so far were not as she had pictured or how Olivia said they were.

Olivia squeezed her arm. "Why did you hurl yourself into that fight?"

Sable glared at her. Could she not have five minutes without Olivia or Loren insinuating that she fancied Thorne?

She sighed. "I honestly thought they were attacking him. What else was I to think? We were called here to help in a war and we appear in the middle of a huge fight!"

Loren smiled and she wanted to slug him. "Your clue was that the other demons in the area were merely watching events unfold and not stepping in to protect their king."

Sable loosed a ripe curse in his direction and then added, "Shut up."

"It's just like you to see a fight and want in on it," Olivia said and she was about to nod in agreement until her friend ruined it by tacking on, "Of course, if it hadn't been Thorne in the middle of that battle—"

"You can shut up too." Sable took her arm away from Olivia and scowled at both of them.

"Come, come. I believe we have teased her enough. She will use one of those crossbow bolts on us if we do not stop." Loren held his hand out to Olivia and she slipped hers into it and went to him. He pulled his mate flush against him and smiled down into her eyes before turning his gaze back on Sable. "Do not worry about the feast. Bleu will have left a dress for you in your room."

There was a knock at the door. Sable opened it and stared as a huge blond demon rolled a large wooden tub into the room and set it down by the fire. Others entered behind him, carrying pitchers of steaming water.

A bath.

Sable wanted one of those too. She needed to relax before she could even think about showing her face at the feast. She wanted to scrub away her shame and embarrassment, and unwind.

She leaned out into the hall and looked along it towards her room.

A big dark-haired male stood there with another tub and an impatient look on his rugged face.

"Got to dash." She looked over her shoulder to Loren and Olivia, at the tub and then back at them. "Try to keep the volume turned down when you're scrubbing her back, Big Guy."

Loren blushed and he blushed hard.

Sable tossed him a victorious grin and shot from the room. The demon waiting with the tub scowled at her and then something flickered in his dark red eyes and he straightened and bowed his head. She grimaced when she recognised him as one of the demons from the courtyard. Just great. She got to have her tub delivered by someone who had witnessed the whole debacle with his king.

"Roll it in, Big Guy." She pushed her door open and waved him on. He grunted something under his breath and heaved the tub forwards, picked it up with one hand on the rim, walked to the fireplace off to her left and set it down. She hadn't meant to challenge his strength but he had clearly taken her pet term and words as just that. Maybe he wasn't good with English.

He flicked her another glance, raking his gaze over her from head to toe this time, curled his lip and stalked off.

Not stalked. Limped.

Great. Not just a witness but one of the ones she had shot.

"Sorry," she called after him but he didn't stop.

He disappeared around the corner and the other demons filed in, depositing the hot water into the tub.

Water in Hell. Back at Archangel, she had wondered if they would have such things in this part of Hell. Loren's kingdom had water but then they had portals that channelled a river through their lands. Where did this kingdom get its water?

Probably through portals. Demons could teleport too.

Sable closed the door after the last demon had left and turned to the bed.

A beautiful sky-blue dress lay on top of the furs. She crossed the room to it and gazed down at the gauzy layers of fabric and the elegant silver metalwork of the corset beside it. It took her breath away. She had never worn anything so beautiful or so feminine.

A vision of her walking into the great hall and Thorne going wild for her the moment he set eyes on her rose into her mind.

She shut it out. She couldn't let things go that way. She was here on an important mission, one that would decide the fate of Thorne's kingdom. She couldn't let her desire get the better of her. She couldn't become a distraction for Thorne.

She couldn't give him the impression that she wanted him, even when she burned for him.

CHAPTER 3

Thorne was finding it impossible to concentrate. He stood in the middle of the great hall of his castle, fighting the worst case of nerves he had ever experienced. He hadn't felt this uneasy when he had gone into his first battle at the tender age of five hundred.

His father should have warned him that females were this complicated, confusing and dangerous.

He tried to focus on what Lord Van der Garde of the vampires was telling him about his latest victory on the battlefield and instead ended up wondering if the handsome, dark-haired male had much experience of females.

Thorne would bet good grog that he had much experience of the fairer sex.

Even now, some of the court females were clinging to the vampire commander, hanging on his every word as they stroked his arms through the sleeves of his crisp black knee-length jacket and teasingly caressed the shiny silver clasp on the front of the stand-up collar.

They seemed impressed by the tale he recounted, talking of the Preux Chevaliers corps and how they had decimated an entire legion of the Devil's minions in return for a handsome reward from the Seventh Realm.

If Thorne told Sable of his many victories on the battlefield, would she look upon him in such a favourable and enraptured manner? Would she stroke his muscles through his loose white shirt and tease the laces across his chest with a soft caress?

Thorne's second in command, Fargus, glanced his way as he passed by with the leader of the werewolves, Kincaid, heading towards their group on the other side of the room. Thorne desired to speak with his old werewolf friend but knew it would be unwise to bring the male to him while he was talking to the vampire commander.

The feast this eve was about breaking every species in slowly, giving them time to adjust to the presence of the others. It was a complicated, dangerous and delicate matter, and one he had been dreading since gaining pledges from the different parties.

Werewolves hated the vampires.

The elves hated the vampires.

The vampires hated the werewolves and the elves.

The vampires and werewolves looked upon the mortals with scorn, and so did many of his own men, a matter that greatly displeased him.

Lord Van der Garde laughed at something one of the females had said and looked at her in a way that left Thorne in no doubt that she would bear a pretty set of marks on her throat before the night was through.

The male certainly knew his way around females.

Thorne's thoughts wandered to one female in particular, one he would never allow this male to near.

Sable.

Just running her name through his mind, carefully intonating it to draw out the pleasure of hearing it, had him aching to see her again.

He had hungered to return to her many times over the lunar cycle. The separation had been torturous and the thought of that wretched elf male being near her had almost driven him mad, invading his dreams of his little huntress and tying him in knots.

Many times, he had come close to teleporting to her while she slumbered and bringing her to his realm. Only the knowledge that she would not understand and would fight him if he did such a thing had helped him refrain from making such a terrible move.

She was not like the mates of many of his warriors, all of which were from a time long past. Their world was different to the one Sable had grown up in. This modern mortal world had moulded her into a fierce and independent female.

It was part of the reason for his uncertainty. The other part?

He had never had a female.

Had never wooed one.

Had never lain with one.

He had waited for his eternal mate and that wait had been worth it, because it had brought him Sable.

His gaze roamed the crowded room, scouring it for her. She had been as feisty as he had remembered and just as beautiful as she had leapt into the fight at his side this day, taking on his men without thought for her own safety and without fear. Her heart had been steady, her sword hand firm.

She had been breathtaking.

A scowl drew his eyebrows together.

He had not expected her to arrive with that wretched elf touching her though, gazing at her with possessive eyes that had lingered too long upon her body. She seemed unaware of the male's attention to her, but that didn't stop Thorne from wanting to wrench his head from his body.

"King Thorne?" Lord Van der Garde said, his own scowl knitting his dark brown eyebrows and making his ice-blue eyes glitter with frost.

He was being rude. The vampire most likely thought he was angry with him over something he had said.

"My apologies. There is much on my mind this eve." Mostly a slender golden-eyed siren and a bastard unmated elf.

Putting them together in one sentence only darkened his mood. He wanted to kill the male. Thorne curled his fingers into fists, tightening them until his claws bit into his palms. It was difficult to control his mood when thoughts of Bleu and Sable plagued him.

They had appeared close this day, much closer than before. The male had laid a hand on her and she had not shirked his grip as she had in the mortal world. He feared the male had already begun to win her and that he was behind in the race to claim her.

Thorne ran a hand over his left horn, a nervous trait he could normally hide, but one that ruled him this night. He snatched a mug of mead from a passing servant and knocked it back to steady his hands and his heart. The servant waited, clearly sensing his need for more than just one. Thorne placed his empty mug down and took another. The male offered the drinks to Lord Van der Garde.

The vampire curled his lip and waved the man away. The servant moved towards the werewolves.

"I see you invited the dogs," the vampire commander said and Thorne frowned at him.

"I expect no quarrels between your men and theirs. We are here as one. I will not tolerate any fights between the gathered species."

Lord Van der Garde bent his head. "It is my turn to apologise. I will see to it that my men are informed of your wishes and will do my best to tolerate the werewolves… even if I do despise having to breathe the same air as them."

Thorne sent a prayer to the gods for patience.

He needed to keep these men in order, without stomping on the pride of their commanders, but he could already see it was going to be difficult and an added burden to the one already firmly settled on his shoulders.

He had been fighting this war for twenty-one lunar cycles and everything rested on this coming battle.

He had lost too many good warriors over those months, males he considered family, commanders who had seen many more seasons than he had. It had taken its toll on him.

So many widows to care for now.

Females he had pledged to look after as he held his friends and watched them draw their last breaths.

Many of the women lived in the castle now, but many more had decided to remain in the villages where they had lived happily with their mates.

Thorne took care of them all, ensuring they had enough food and their offspring were well, and they were all looked after by the other villagers.

He took a long drink and then frowned into the bottom of his mug. What was he doing, bringing his fated one into this war and wanting to bring her into his life?

So many widowed. So many more suffered the same fate in the war before this one, and more in the war before that. He had only lived for three thousand five hundred cycles of the Earth around the sun and had reigned for only two thousand seven hundred and fifty, yet he had witnessed over two thousand wars and had seen thousands more males die in battle and scores of kings fall across Hell.

The Fifth King was relentless too.

Every time Thorne drove him back, losing many good warriors in the process, the Fifth King always came back stronger, and with darker allies.

Recently, his army had grown too strong and had begun to attack from several points around the border with the Fifth Realm at once, making it difficult for Thorne to defend the villages closest to the frontline because he didn't have enough men to form into smaller armies.

Thorne knocked back the rest of his drink and crushed the mug in his fist. Shards of clay bit into his hand and scattered on the flagstones at his feet.

He hated being on the defensive.

He wanted to be the stronger male, the stronger kingdom, and the Fifth King was driving him towards failure, battering his pride along the way.

He opened his hand and stared at the splinters of mug embedded into his palm, feeling the vampire's gaze on it. Crimson pooled in the creases of his hand. It was foolish to allow himself to bleed around so many vampires. Especially around Lord Van der Garde.

The vampire was afflicted with bloodlust.

Thorne raised his gaze to the male. Hungry scarlet eyes locked on Thorne's palm, their narrowed elliptical pupils speaking of Lord Van der Garde's dark desires. He wanted the blood.

Thorne signalled one of the servants he knew carried blood on his tray of drinks. The male hurried over and hovered near the vampire, looking as on edge as Thorne felt. Lord Van der Garde's gaze remained rooted on Thorne's hand, transfixed, as if he had cast a spell upon him, and then the vampire blinked, shot his left hand out and snatched a cup of blood, lifted it to his lips and drank the contents in one go.

"Never bleed around me unless you are meaning to offer up your jugular to my fangs," the vampire growled, slammed the mug down on the tray, causing the others to spill, and stalked off.

Thorne plucked the shards from his hand and dropped them onto the tray, and then nodded to the servant. The male moved away, leaving him alone by his throne. He licked the blood from his palm. This was never going to work. He was fooling himself if he thought this army he had assembled could work together and save his kingdom.

He growled.

This never would have happened in his father's time. His father had been strong and powerful, and had reigned in an era of peace because of that strength. His might had driven all other demons from his realm and kept the borderlands safe. None had dared rise up against him. All had respected him.

Thorne wanted to be like his father, a good king for his people, and he was failing. More now than ever, he feared he would lose to the Fifth King and condemn his people to a brutal end.

This war was life or death to him, but he didn't care about his own life. He cared only about his people. He couldn't fail them.

He couldn't let those who viewed him as a youngling unworthy of his kingdom be proven right.

He had fought them for twenty-seven centuries and he would not give up now.

He would become the stronger male and protect his kingdom.

It was the reason he had gone to the mortal realm to seek the advice of the magic bearer, Rosalind. He had asked to see his future and had instead seen Prince Loren's, and a chance to gain a powerful ally. With the elves pledged to bring one thousand men to his realm, he had found hope again.

He had convinced the werewolves to assist him by sending two hundred men and had sought the aid of the Preux Chevaliers. They had pledged to send their First Legion, the finest in their corps. Over one hundred strong vampire males in total.

He had gathered every demon of fighting age in his kingdom and posted half of them at the border villages to protect them, and had sent his best commanders to train them. The other half had come to the castle.

He had amassed an army, a force strong enough to drive the demons of the Fifth Realm back for good. When they next attacked, he would be ready for them and he would seek out the Fifth King and claim his head and his heart as his prize.

He would end the threat to his kingdom by ending the Fifth King.

His sensitive hearing picked up some curses off to his left, at the far end of the room near the doors that led to the mortal and elf quarters. His pulse doubled as his gaze scanned the gathered humans and then settled as he realised that Sable was not among them.

The mortal hunters broadcasted fear.

Archangel had sent only fifty but it had given him something more valuable than their strength.

They had brought him Sable.

Just thinking about her lifted some of the weight from his shoulders, relaxing him yet at the same time increasing his tension. It wasn't only nerves about seeing her again. It was nerves about having her here as part of his army.

She was a warrior though, and as strange as that was to him, he had to respect it. He had witnessed how she reacted when coddled by a male during a fight and knew not to belittle her abilities as a hunter. Loren had often spoken of her during their meetings, slipping information to him, telling him of the powerful creatures that she had fought and defeated in the mortal world. She was a capable and skilled hunter, and a determined female, and he admired her for it.

He moved towards the gathered men and women, desiring to calm them and make them feel they were safe among so many species they probably viewed as enemies.

Sable would be here soon to take command of them. She would be pleased if she found him conversing with her people, putting their minds at ease.

The females among the group wore the same battle clothing they had been earlier.

Would Sable be dressed in such a manner or would she have a garment more suited to her rank and the occasion?

He tried to picture her in a dress of mortal fashion, one he had seen on females at social gatherings in the human world. The image that popped into his head was one of her in her black leather trousers, knee-high boots and tight little top that emphasised her breasts. He groaned and rubbed his mouth, fighting for control over his body as he recalled his dreams of her, lifelike visions of stripping her slowly before he claimed her as his forever.

A scuffle broke out behind him, pulling his attention away from thoughts of Sable and from her band of mortals.

He turned to see the source of the commotion. A few werewolves and vampires were engaged in a fistfight. Kincaid and Lord Van der Garde were already among them, both males looking as if they wanted to throw punches rather than stop their men from doing so. He took a step towards them, intending to intervene, and then stopped himself. It was better he allowed their commanders to deal with it so he didn't appear to be interfering in their business.

A ripple of heat travelled through his muscles, sending a shiver of awareness through him.

Sable.

He was turning before he knew it, his gaze seeking her, drawn to his little female.

When it found her, his blood chilled and then burned for a different reason.

She was beautiful, resplendent with her long black hair twirled and clasped at the back of her head and her lips rosy, but she did not wear a dress of mortal fashion.

The long flowing blue garment reached her ankles, the sheer layers parting as she walked, revealing glimpses of bare thigh through the gauzy material that made him want to growl at every male in the room who dared to look upon his female. In contrast to the loose skirt, the top was tight, the blue bands of material held in place by elaborate arcs and swirls of brushed silver metal that acted as a corset over them.

An elven dress.

The wretched elf male beside her raked an appreciative glance over her body, blatant hunger in his purple eyes.

Thorne's lips peeled back off his fangs and his horns curled in front of his ears.

He stormed through the crowd, shoving demon, elf, vampire and werewolf out of his path, picking up speed as he neared her and the male. Sable's golden eyes met his, a smile rising onto her lips. It faded when he growled low in his throat. She tensed, her eyes going wide, and backed off a step. He pushed the last obstacle aside and seized Bleu by his throat, barely registering Sable's gasp, and kicked forwards, using all of his speed to slam the male against the stone wall behind her.

Thorne's muscles ached, beginning to expand as his fury took hold of him, ruling his actions. His dragon-like wings burst from his back and tore through his shirt and his muscles strained against the now-tight white material. His horns grew, curling around themselves and flaring forwards into deadly points. His fangs descended, his lower canines sharpening to match them.

He heaved a breath and roared in Bleu's face as he hauled the male up the wall so his legs dangled above the floor.

Rage burned in his blood, the sounds around him drowned out by the rush of it in his veins and the thunderous beat of his heart.

Bleu coolly stared down at him.

Thorne cursed him for it when a familiar burn raced through him. Sable. She stared at him.

He slid his gaze to his right, looking at her out of the corner of his eye. Her horrified expression spoke of her desire to separate them.

To protect the elf.

Her male.

Thorne tightened his grip on Bleu's throat and snarled in the demon tongue, "She is not your ki'ara. You would know your fated female and would be unable to ignore the urge to fight me. How dare you dress her as your ki'ara!"

Bleu's hand calmly encircled his wrist and he looked as if he would allow his armour to transform his fingers into claws and wrest Thorne's hand from his throat, yet he made no move to fight him.

Thorne needed to fight.

His blood pumped hard and hot, and his mind screamed with fury over what this male had dared to do with his fated one. His female.

He wanted to throw him across the room, to rain blows down upon him until his temper flared and he fought back. He wanted to snag the female with his free hand, curl his claws over the metal bodice of her dress and rip the offending garment from her body.

He yearned to kiss her until she knew that she belonged to him.

He could do none of those things.

Everyone was staring at him and clarity was beginning to pierce the red haze in his mind like the rising sun drove back the darkest night, bringing calm to all those its rays touched.

He had brought these elven folk and mortals to his world because he needed their aid, and he was ruining his chance of keeping his kingdom safe.

For the sake of a female.

Thorne snarled, torn between tightening his grip around Bleu's scrawny neck and releasing him. His chest heaved with each harsh breath he sucked down into his lungs in a fight to calm himself and his fingers twitched against Bleu's flesh. The urge to press his claws in, to draw blood and ignite the male's anger was hard to ignore. He wanted to tear into him with claw and fang, to push him into responding, all to sate his need to ensure this male no longer dared to pursue his female.

He needed to kill him.

Sable moved, taking a brave step closer, and shock rippled through him when his rage lifted enough for him to realise that she looked only at him. Broken words reached his ears, filtering through the red mist clouding his senses.

She spoke to him directly and everything male in him demanded he listened to his female.

He eased his grip and turned to her. She appeared small and delicate, but formidable too as she stood with her hands braced against her hips, her bright golden gaze locked on him in a scowl.

His female was fearsome. A warrior.

He wanted to grin at that.

A female fit for a king.

"Dial it back, Tiger," she said.

He didn't understand her strange words or why she equated him with a savage animal of her world, but he knew from her gentle tone and softening expression that she meant to calm him.

Thorne could only obey.

He lowered the elf to his feet and fought to convince himself to release his throat. Sable continued to stare into his eyes, her gaze commanding his to remain rooted on her. It took a few seconds before he managed to uncurl his fingers from Bleu's neck, and only a few seconds more than that for him to notice the ragged state of his clothes, the horrified expressions of the mortals surrounding him, and the barely concealed anger flashing in the eyes of the elves.

Thorne turned away from Sable and shoved past Bleu, heading for the door beyond the mortals. They scurried out of his path, their fear tainting their scents.

He growled and tossed over his shoulder, "I will return. Prepare the feast."

He stormed out of the great hall, needing space to rein in his anger, and requiring a change of clothes. There was little point in donning a new shirt until he had his temper back under control though. He growled and snarled as he stomped along the torch-lit corridor towards his rooms, his mood degenerating again, thoughts of Sable with Bleu dragging him back towards the red mist. He female was there with the elf, no doubt checking on the male, touching his bruised throat and speaking words of concern and tenderness.

Thorne threw his head back and roared until his throat burned and he had no breath left. He dragged his claws along the stone walls, craving the pain and aching with the need to unleash his anger on something. Anything.

He reached his rooms and barged through the arched wooden door, slamming it shut behind him. He paced from one side of the expansive bedroom to the other, his gaze locked on the floor, his footfalls shaking the timbers. He snarled and tore at his ruined shirt, and only grew more frustrated as it snagged in his wings. They wouldn't go away. Not while he skirted the edge, on the brink of losing his mind to the rage pouring through him, eating away at him, filling his head with images of Bleu and Sable.

Thorne roared again and ripped the remains of the shirt from his body. He tore it to shreds, threw it to the floor and flexed his claws as he paced, his wings shifting with each step. His bones ached as his body expanded again, muscles tight against his skin, and his teeth hurt as he clamped them together. He snarled and turned on his heel to stomp back towards the door, feeling like the beast his female had called him.

A feral tiger trapped within a cage, wild and driven to pace the cramped confines to unleash his energy lest he go insane.

A soft knock sounded.

Fargus, no doubt. The fool was the only male mad enough to approach him when he was in a rage.

Thorne stopped at the door and yanked it open, ready to bite his commander's head off about the disturbance. No one was there.

His gaze dropped several inches.

He stilled right down to his heartbeat.

Sable.

Her determined expression faltered and she looked uncertain, as if she had forgotten why she had come to him.

She had come to him.

Her golden-brown eyes fell to his bare chest and his horns curled at the way she slid them over his flesh, her pupils dilating and gaze growing heated.

Could she desire him?

Was she not Bleu's?

"What do you want?" he brusquely said and cursed himself for snapping at her. Just the name of the bastard elf in his mind had been enough to sour his mood again, destroying the calm that had come over him upon seeing Sable.

She cleared her throat and inched her eyes back up to his. "I get the feeling I did something wrong and I wanted to apologise. I didn't mean to offend you."

Curious little female. "You did not offend me. The elf did."

"How?" She frowned at him and her question surprised him. No female had ever dared to question him.

Was this some sort of ruse? Perhaps she was trying to discern the truth by taking the blame for his outburst. Did she desire to know why he had lost his mind and had attacked her male?

He would tell her.

"The male attempted to claim what is rightfully mine."

Confusion flickered across her pretty face.

Thorne spelled it out for her by catching hold of her metal bodice, yanking her to him and grasping the nape of her neck to keep her still. He took a deep breath for courage and then dipped his head and claimed her mouth.

She stood frozen with her hot hands pressed against his bare chest, burning into him, and he thought she would push him away.

The moment his female's lips yielded to the hard demanding press of his and their tongues touched, pleasure nearly felled him.

He focused all of his will on holding back his strength, fearing he would hurt his little mortal with it, and tore the pins from her hair with his right hand. He sifted his fingers through the soft black strands, groaning at the feel of them slipping over his flesh. With his left, he clasped her against him.

Her dress was silk and her warm curves giving beneath his hand. He slid it lower and clutched her backside, pinning her against the full length of his body as he laid claimed to her mouth. She tensed and then melted into him, her lips parting to allow their tongues to touch again. Hers stroked his, dizzying him and driving him to kiss her harder. He gave in to the urge, unable to deny his hunger to taste her. So warm and sweet. His female tasted like ambrosia of the gods.

His knees loosened, threatening to give out as pleasure he had never experienced before flowed through every inch of him. It was stronger than he ever could have imagined, consuming and owning him, dragging him into a drugged daze where there was only fierce sensation and emotions, and the connection bursting to life between him and his little female.

Did she feel as he did? Did her limbs tremble from the pleasure overloading her and her blood run hot, thundering in her veins as desire blazed through her? He wanted to know, ached to draw back and look deep into her eyes and see that she was his now and he wasn't alone in his passion and desires, but more than that he didn't want this kiss to end.

Thorne clutched her more tightly, pulling her closer, obeying his instincts to possess her and claim her as his forever. His fangs dropped.

His female tensed, planted her hands harder against his chest and shoved him back, pinning his spine to the doorframe behind him.

She released him, wiped her mouth on the back of her hand and squared up to him, fire flashing in her eyes. His female was not pleased.

"I came here to apologise because I thought I had done something wrong again. Well, now it's your turn to apologise."

Thorne growled. "I will never apologise to the elf."

Her slap caught him off guard. His left cheek buzzed fiercely and he tasted blood. He ran his tongue around his mouth, finding the source of it on the left of his lower lip. She had struck him hard enough to cut him on his own fangs. He growled again, opened his mouth to warn her not to defend the male around him, and frowned as he realised she was storming away from him, heading back towards the great hall.

"Men," she muttered darkly. "Doesn't matter what species they are… they're all bloody idiots."

Perhaps she had not meant the elf. Perhaps she had expected him to apologise for kissing her. Strange female. Why would he apologise for kissing her? He didn't want to. He had enjoyed it.

Had she not?

Thorne grabbed a fresh shirt and managed to force his wings away. The moment they had shrunk into his back, he hurried from his room, pulling the white garment on over his head as he walked and leaving the laces down the chest undone.

He caught up with Sable before she had made it halfway along the hall, grabbed her arm and pulled her to face him. He searched her eyes but couldn't discern from them whether she had enjoyed the kiss or not.

The longer he held her, the more her gaze began to waver. After long seconds, it dropped to his mouth and her rosy lips parted. He ached to kiss them again. If he apologised, could he perhaps fulfil that desire?

Thorne muttered, "I apologise. I did not mean to cause offense."

He leaned down to kiss her and Sable snatched her arm from his grasp and stepped back.

"What the hell do you think you're doing?" she snapped and he frowned.

"I apologised. Can I not kiss you again?" Confusing little female.

"No." Her expression darkened. "Apology not accepted."

Thorne's eyebrows rose. "Why not?"

She shoved her hands onto her hips and scowled at him. "Because you didn't mean it. You're not sorry."

He huffed. "Of course I am not sorry. I wanted to kiss you and so I kissed you. Does the elf have to apologise whenever he kisses you?"

Thorne wanted to kill him. It ran around his mind, bringing pleasing images of locking the wretch in his dungeon and slowly taking his fury out on him.

Sable's eyes widened and her tone was one of pure indignation and horror. "Bleu has not kissed me!"

Thorne grinned. Something he had done that the elf had not. He liked that. Perhaps he was ahead in the fight for Sable after all.

"You will change," he commanded with a wave of his hand down her body. "I will give you a dress and you will wear it."

The way her eyes narrowed and her lips compressed into a mulish line warned that he had made a terrible mistake and was about to pay for it.

"No, I damn well will not. I like this dress… it was *given* to me, not forced upon me. I'm not one of your court whores who will do as you please without question and service your desires." She looked him over, huffed and shoved past him, heading back towards his room.

Not his room, he realised as he looked beyond her to entrance arch of the stairs up to the first floor.

"Where do you go now?" He turned on his heel to follow her.

"Home," she spat that word with such force and determination that it hit him like a punch in the gut, knocking the breath from his lungs and sending his head and heart reeling. "I'm going home. Screw your war. Screw you!"

Thorne snarled. There was no way in the seven realms he was going to let her slip out of his grasp again. He couldn't. He needed her here with him. He stomped towards her with long-legged strides, easily catching her before she could reach the stairs. He grabbed her, twisted her in his arms, ducking his head to one side to avoid the punch she aimed at him, and tossed her over his shoulder.

Sable flailed, kicking and punching, landing hard blows. "Put me down. Where are you taking me?"

The fear in her heartbeat and the tremor in her voice warned that she believed he was about to take her to his room, most likely to ravage her. Foolish female.

"Stop struggling." He grappled with her, trying to keep hold of her, determined not to let her go. "You will fall and hurt yourself. I do not mean you harm."

He turned with her, heading back along the corridor towards the great hall. She settled at last.

"Where are you taking me?" she whispered and pressed her hands against his lower back, pushing herself up. He trembled under the heat of her touch and struggled to keep his focus.

"To the feast."

He sensed the relief that flowed through her and he muttered an apology in the demon tongue. He hadn't meant to frighten her, but she had threatened to leave and he had reacted on instinct, driven to stop her.

"Please put me down... because you are hurting me." She sounded strained, hoarse. The metalwork of the corset pressed into his shoulder and no doubt bit into her supple flesh.

He cursed the elven dress and the bastard who had no doubt given it to her, carefully set her on her feet and went down on one knee before her. She remained still as he checked her over, needing to see she was unharmed to calm his turbulent emotions and keep control over his darker instincts.

Thorne stopped with his hands on her waist and looked up into her eyes.

His female was beautiful with her black hair tumbling around her shoulders but there were tears on her lashes. From the pain of the corset or fear of him?

He curled his fingers into tight fists. He wasn't sure what to do to make things better.

As an heir to a realm and later as a king, he had been trained to take action and command those below him to obey without question, demanding their fealty and expecting no argument from them.

But she was not below him.

Even a king had those above him, those he should seek to please, not command to obey his will.

The words rose up from his heart and slipped freely from his tongue this time. "I am sorry for frightening you. Would you stay... please?"

She blinked and didn't draw away as he lifted his hand to her cheek. She allowed him to brush the backs of his claws across her silky skin and it humbled him.

Sable stood silent and still for long minutes. He found it hard to wait, to remain patient and not press her for an answer. He wasn't used to being kept waiting for anything. She raised her hand, as if to touch his where it lingered against her cheek, and then lowered it to her side.

"Apology accepted. I'll stay."

Thorne released the breath he hadn't realised he held.

His female was kind too.

He smiled and rose to his feet, and paused to watch her walking ahead of him, back towards the banquet.

His queen.

He would do everything in his power to win her.

She would be his forever.

CHAPTER 4

Sable kept her head down as she entered the great hall but it didn't stop her from feeling everyone turning to stare at her.

Olivia lifted the skirt of her long dark purple dress and hurried to her. "What on Earth… why did you go dashing off after Thorne?"

She wasn't in the mood for her friend's teasing right now, but then, Olivia sounded shocked and concerned. She lifted her gaze to meet Olivia's rich brown eyes and saw the worry she had caused in them. Olivia had feared Thorne would hurt her. Sable had known better. She had known in her heart that he wouldn't hurt her, even in the deepest of his rages.

Bleu's gaze bore into her and she couldn't bring herself to look at him. He had tried to stop her when she had gone after Thorne and had looked mortified when she had told him to leave her alone and that she had to go. She hadn't meant to upset him, but it seemed she had done just that.

And she had upset Thorne too.

"I needed to apologise for whatever it was that had upset him… I thought I had done something wrong and was going to get us all kicked out." It sounded stupid when she said it aloud, but at the time, she had felt compelled to go to him and calm him, and make everything all right again.

Loren stepped forwards, a black scowl knitting his eyebrows and turning his purple eyes dark. His fangs flashed between his lips as he spoke. "It was not you who caused the king to rage."

He slid a pointed look at Bleu and she finally glanced at him. Bleu was still staring at her, barely leashed desire in his eyes.

How had she failed to notice it before?

She recalled what Thorne had said to her. Bleu had attempted to claim what was rightfully his.

Thorne believed she was his fated one.

Sable ran a hand down her face and remembered how startled he had seemed when his eyes had first fallen on her the day they had met at the Archangel facility, and how she had shivered under the scorching intensity of his gaze. Her body had come alive, as if recognising him as her counterpart, her other half.

Holy hell in a hand-basket.

Olivia and Loren were right. She had a demon king for a mate and the way he had kissed her, had looked at her with fire burning in his eyes, warned that he wasn't going to settle for anything less than eternity with her.

The familiar burn went through her and the room hushed. Sable swung to face the doors in time to see Thorne enter.

He clapped his hands, the sound sharp and startling in the silence. "To the tables."

The room erupted in murmured conversations and she couldn't help but wonder how many of them were about her and Thorne. She caught the gazes of several of her hunters as they walked to the long bench tables set out near the door to the sleeping quarters and had no doubt that they would be talking about her behaviour over dinner too.

Olivia took her arm and squeezed it, offering a consolatory smile.

"You were meant to stop me from making another idiot of myself," Sable muttered as they slowly approached the huge rectangular table on the semi-circular platform, following Loren and Bleu. Dread knotted her stomach and she glanced at the men settling themselves on the left side of it. Vampires and werewolves. At least she would be seated away from them, at the opposite end of the table.

"I didn't really get a chance. Besides, you didn't exactly make a fool of yourself… or did you? What happened between you and Thorne?"

Sable wasn't ready to admit that anything had happened so she kept her head down. She was going to keep it down until the feast was over and she was back in her room. That way, she couldn't possibly make a tit of herself and she definitely wouldn't upset Thorne or Bleu, or any other male who decided that she was a prize catch he just had to have.

Loren took Olivia from her, led her to the table and drew her seat out for her. He took the seat next to her at the end of the table. It all seemed rather civilised again until Sable went to sit between her friend and Bleu. Thorne loomed behind her and pulled her chair out, and she thought he meant to help her sit, but then he grabbed her arm in a bruising grip. He marched her along the length of the table, past all of his commanders, who stared in amazement together with the rest of the room.

Thorne growled at the male seated next to his kingly throne and the demon obediently moved along one place, forcing everyone else to do the same and making Bleu have to move next to Olivia. Thorne hauled the chair out and she half-expected him to shove her onto it.

He didn't. He towered over her, waiting.

Sable looked to Olivia, Loren and Bleu, lovingly eyeing the spot he now occupied. Her spot. A safe spot, away from the madness, where she could just keep her head down and count the minutes until she could return to her room and reflect on how insane her life had just become.

She sighed and sat on the chair. Thorne grunted something in the demon tongue and carefully eased her up to the table.

She kept very still as he took his seat beside her.

The doors burst open and servants poured in, carrying huge silver trays crammed with what she presumed was food.

Sable took a chance and leaned forwards, peering down the length of the table to Olivia, throwing her a silent plea for help.

Olivia shrugged. Loren didn't look as if he could help her either. Bleu just looked as if he wanted to kill something as he stared directly ahead, the muscle in his jaw working overtime and his ears more pointed than she had ever seen them.

The noise level in the room rose as people began helping themselves to the food as the servants set the trays down on the tables. The conversation around her was certainly flowing smoothly, which would have been a wonderful distraction from her thoughts, except they were all speaking in the demon tongue.

She didn't think Thorne or his commanders would appreciate her insulting them so she kept quiet and occupied herself by looking at the trays, finally able to assuage her curiosity about what demons served at a feast.

The servants were kind enough to fill the plates of those seated at her table.

Although, when she looked at the dark metal plate before her, she changed her mind and decided they weren't kind after all. She peered at the questionable things on her plate. Brown things. Grey things. Lumps of something charred. There was a bone or two sticking out of some of them. None of them looked appetizing and one of them definitely resembled a hoof.

Sable swallowed the bile rising into her mouth and curled her lip in disgust, despair swiftly following that emotion.

Thorne's deep rumbling voice disappeared from the conversation around her and she felt the heat of his gaze on her.

"You are not eating?" He sank his teeth into a limb of some sort and tore the dark pink flesh from it.

Sable covered her mouth, stifling her need to retch, and mumbled into her palm, "I'm not hungry."

His smile faded into a heavy scowl, his dark crimson eyes darting between her and the plate before her as she pushed it away. He pushed it back. She pushed it away. Back. Away. Back.

"You need to eat. It is good." He lifted one of the charred lumps towards her.

Sable shook her head and flicked a look of despair at Olivia, who was prodding a similar plate of meat.

Loren deftly plucked items resembling vegetables from the platters around them and offered them to Olivia. No one would do that for Sable. Perhaps Bleu would have but she really didn't want him fussing over her, and not only because it would probably send Thorne into another rage. Could she do that herself?

Thorne shoved the plate towards again.

"No, thank you." She pushed it away and risked a glance at him.

He was still scowling. He turned his frown on the servers. Was he going to blame them because she wasn't eating? He looked close to growling again and his horns were curling. He radiated anger and it was all her fault, again. *Suck it up.* She swallowed to settle her stomach and then picked at the meat with her fork, hoping to calm him and spare his servants.

Thorne snatched the plate from her, scraped everything off onto his one, and set it back down in front of her. She stared at the empty plate. Oh. She guessed she didn't get to eat after all. A low snarl escaped him and she almost smiled when she saw the frustration tightening his rough features as his crimson eyes darted around. He looked over her head towards the elves, paused and then set his jaw. Determined? To do what?

He grimaced as he skewered some things that were possibly vegetable in nature on his claws, very carefully plated them and gently nudged the plate towards her. He gave her a toothy smile when she looked up into his eyes and she had an absurd urge to pet him because he looked as if he was waiting to hear he had done good.

It was strange having a male see to her needs, let alone a king who was clearly used to not having to care for anyone in this way and was very new to it.

Sable smiled and his features softened with relief. She picked at the strange roots and greens, feeling his gaze following her every move, sensing his anxiety and anticipation. She blew out her breath and dared to nibble a grey root that could have passed for a sickly carrot.

It was surprisingly good. Definitely edible. Her smile grew.

Thorne's did too and there was a spark in his eyes that set her blood aflame. He was satisfied and she knew it was because he had pleased her. Would he look that way if she confessed that his kiss had been just as delicious?

The thought of this man looking at her with heavy-lidded eyes overflowing with satisfaction after pleasuring her made her toes curl and she had to fight to push that image away before she gave him the wrong impression. His body was magnificent though, and his kiss had been electric, and the feel of his hands on her butt when he had hauled her over his shoulder…

Thorne growled low in his throat and she realised she had been staring at his mouth, nibbling on her lower lip, while she had been lost in her thoughts. His dusky brown horns had curled again and he looked as though he was thinking about kissing her too, and she couldn't have that in front of all these people.

Sable dragged her gaze from his and focused on her food. Someone filled her clay mug with an amber liquid and she ate a bite of food and then lifted the drink to her lips to wash it down. She took a great gulp and her eyes instantly watered.

Fire blazed down her throat and combusted in her veins. Her mouth burned like acid and fumes shot up her nose, causing her to choke as she tried to gasp for air.

Whatever it was, it was stronger than the Hellfire she had tasted at Underworld, a fae-demon club in London.

She coughed, struggling to breathe, and slammed her hand on the table.

Thorne curled his hand around her left shoulder, pulled her against his side and raised another cup to her lips. She tried to refuse, didn't want more of the demon booze, but he tipped her back, forcing her to drink.

Cool water rushed past her lips, quenching the fire in her mouth and her stomach, and she lay there in his arms looking up at him, drinking it down and grateful for it.

Another memory of that night at Underworld overlaid onto the present, a moment when Bleu had held her like this while Olivia had given her water to wash away the fire in her throat. Guilt curled its claws around her heart and she wasn't sure why. She had never led Bleu on or given him the impression that she wanted him. He had been a fantastic sparring partner and a wonderful source of information, and she liked him as a friend, but he clearly thought something more could happen between them.

Thorne took the cup away, a beautiful look of concern softening his face, and she didn't stop him when he rubbed his thumb across her chin, catching the stray drops of water there.

"Thank you," she whispered, lost in his crimson eyes and the tenderness in his touch.

He smiled and he was devastating, setting fire to her blood again and making her insides flutter with need. She looked up at him, trying to force herself to focus on his ridged horns and the fangs that were a constant reminder that he was a demon, hoping they would quench the fire in her heart as the water had cooled the heat in her belly.

They didn't.

He righted her, stabbed a piece of vegetable on his claws and offered it to her. Sable leaned forwards and took it out of politeness, her head a little fuzzy from the grog. He offered another bite, his eyes brimming with curiosity and bright with interest. She took that one too, and the next, and then her reservation melted away and she began to enjoy the way he would carefully select each bite for her, mixing up what he offered, fussing over her.

He offered a smaller scrap from the plate. Sable went to take it and ended up brushing her lips over his fingertip.

He growled and her eyes leaped up to his. His gaze burned into her mouth and he looked torn between venturing further with his finger and removing it so he could kiss her.

What was she doing?

Her head twirled as she turned towards her friend and her gaze locked on Bleu. He scowled in her direction. Olivia gaped at her.

Sable blamed the booze. One mouthful had her tipsy and lightheaded, but not drunk enough.

She grabbed her mug and took smaller sips this time, hiding in it to avoid everyone.

It was empty before she knew it.

She stared into the bottom of the clay cup and then looked around the room. Everyone was eating and talking. *Boring*. This was meant to be a feast. She had always imagined they were jovial affairs, with much laughter and dancing.

Dancing. She could dance. She wanted to get up on the table and dance to the music floating around the room.

Music? She didn't recall there being music before. She looked for the musicians and found none.

Someone touched her arm and she twisted to look at them. The room whizzed past her eyes, spinning in the opposite direction to her head and her stomach, and she wanted to vomit.

She needed some air.

Sable shoved her hands onto the table, pushed herself up and turned around. She fell over her chair, landing in a twisted heap.

Thorne shot to his feet, darkness flowed into her head and ebbed away again, and she felt as if she was flying.

She opened her eyes but it wasn't the burly demon king looking down at her, gently cradling her in his arms.

Bleu.

He muttered soft things in his language while his eyes spoke volumes about murder.

Sable wanted to tell him not to be angry with Thorne but darkness swallowed her.

CHAPTER 5

You allowed her to get drunk and now she is in need of her own kind.

Those words taunted Thorne, spoken with contempt and truth that had stung him. A growl curled up his throat as an image of Bleu holding Sable in his arms, his slender female out cold, tormented him. Fury had driven him to lash out at the elf for daring to speak in such a manner to him and for daring to touch his female, but the male had clung to her, and he hadn't dared risk it in case he hurt her by mistake.

Thorne had spent the rest of the night lost in thought, his mind with Sable and his heart compelling him to go to her. His pride and sense of duty had kept him at the feast, overruling his desire to see that Sable was well, and that the bastard elf wasn't anywhere near her.

When the banquet had ended, the last guests stumbling their ways back to their rooms, Thorne had remained.

He paced the raised platform, his wings furled against his bare back, his boots heavy on the stone floor.

He should have known better than to let her partake of their mead.

He had been doing well and she had been responding to his kindness, and then she had drunk herself into oblivion. Why?

He growled and his horns curled around in front of his pointed ears.

The six guards near the main entrance of the great hall kept their eyes fixed ahead, gazes locked beyond him, as though they did not see their king in turmoil before them, his heart ripped open by a slender, small female, bleeding into the cavity of his chest. That cavity had felt empty before the night he had set eyes on her and had been a source of constant pain since.

What was he supposed to do now?

He couldn't think straight. The whole feast had been a disaster. He had attacked Bleu. Sable had passed out. On top of both of those things, another fight had broken out towards the end of the banquet, this time between the vampires and the elves.

Three vampires and one elf were now in the wing of the castle currently acting as a hospital. One table and eight chairs were also casualties of the battle and his staff were not impressed. They had limited furniture in storage and the feasts were using most of it in order to seat the visiting armies. It was a headache he didn't need. Finding quarters to house the thirteen hundred and fifty men and women, while keeping species separated and keeping the mortals safe had been difficult enough. Many of his men had had to take up residence in the outer courtyard in tents in order to accommodate their guests.

Thorne shoved his fingers through his hair. This was going to end in disaster. He was going to lose his female and then the war and his kingdom.

The doors opened and he growled, feeling sure it was the elf. The last thing he needed was Bleu coming to confront him, to blame him for Sable's poor condition and sickness.

He turned to face the bastard.

It was the prince's female.

She looked as fiery and dangerous as Sable often did and he could sense her anger as she stormed towards him, but with each step it drained a little, and by the time she reached him, she had lost her spark.

"How does Sable fare?" he asked, afraid of the answer to that question but needing to know.

Olivia stared at him in silence for long seconds, her glare cutting, and then her shoulders sagged. "She's sleeping off the booze."

"Is she sick?" He couldn't hide his fear that she was.

She shook her head, causing her wavy brown hair to dance across her shoulders. "No. The elves gave her something to settle her stomach."

Thorne growled. Why hadn't he thought of that? She might have smiled at him again if he had. He had taken his cue from Prince Loren at the feast, feeding his female vegetables more suited to her delicate palate. That had worked in his favour.

He stepped down off the platform, moving closer to Olivia. "I desire to see her."

"It might be wiser to wait until she's awake and feeling less foolish."

This female made as much sense as his did on occasion. "Why would she feel foolish?"

Olivia sighed. "On top of everything else… well… she embarrassed herself by getting drunk. Feeling like a fool around everyone the morning after is a natural human reaction."

"I will order all in this castle not to look upon her in such a fashion."

The petite female smiled. "That isn't quite what I meant. It will be Sable who is looking upon herself like a fool and I don't think you can order her to feel any other way."

No. He couldn't. He had already decided that orders didn't work on Sable and her friend was right in her observation that you could not order someone who felt foolish not to feel that emotion. He felt like a fool too and could not stop himself.

There had to be a way to smooth things over between him and Sable, and have her smile at him again. He wanted her close to him, as she had been while he had been feeding her.

"Will she be hungry when she wakes?" Food was all he knew as a method of pleasing her. Perhaps it would work again.

"Probably." Olivia shrugged. "She'll be hung over."

Thorne frowned, already putting a plan into motion in his head. "And there is a cure for this… hung over?"

The female nodded. "Bad food."

That did not make sense to Thorne. Were all human females as confusing as Sable and Olivia?

"Food she does not like or food that is decomposing?" His frown hardened. "Is this some sort of self-punishment? Because I will not allow it."

"Ah, no, you misunderstand… *again*." Olivia smiled, her brown eyes twinkling with it. "I mean food we think is bad for us. Like bacon, eggs, sausages and fried food."

He had heard of some of those things but didn't know what they looked like. That would not deter him though. His female's friend had given him a way of regaining her smiles and her kindness, and he would not fail in this mission. He focused on his wings, forcing them away, and then his horns. It was shameful to hide them, but he didn't want to cause a stir. They shrank into his head and he hoped his guards hadn't noticed. The last thing he needed was them talking about how their king had concealed his horns.

He stepped onto the semi-circular platform and picked up his white shirt from the table.

"We have not these things, but I will see to it. Thank you." He focused on the ground at his feet and dropped into the black vortex that swirled below him, catching Olivia's gasp as he disappeared.

Thorne reappeared in the mortal world in the middle of the city they called London. The bustling metropolis was dark, the streets emptying. He slipped his white shirt on and walked along the rows of bright shop fronts towards a store at the end of the road. He had visited this place in the past, when Fargus had desired what the mortals called chocolate. Thorne had tasted the sweet confection the male had purchased. It was not pleasant.

Fargus's mate craved the dark bitter variety of it and the male always found time to bring her back some whenever they made a trip to the mortal realm.

Thorne would do the same for Sable if she asked it of him. He would travel to the ends of the Earth to bring her whatever she desired. He hadn't understood Fargus's deep desire to please his female until now. He had his own female to please.

His own female to claim.

He waited for the glass doors of the brightly lit store to open and allow him entrance, and then stalked in, a demon on a mission. Mortals milled around the large shop, some in groups and others alone, pushing carts up and down the aisles. He hunted for the cold section, knowing he would find meat there. Fargus had told him that his female had not desired meat when he had pointed it out as a more suitable present for him to give to her.

The male had spoken of the things his human mate liked. Thorne tried to recount them, desiring to bring them to his female. He should have paid more attention but he had been eager to reach the magic bearer, Rosalind, and hear the future of his kingdom.

Coffee. That had definitely come up.

He racked his brain while loading his arms with the things he did know. Bacon. Sausages. Eggs. Bread. Those were easy enough. Coffee.

Fried foods?

He looked down at his bounty.

Were these fried foods? He should have asked Olivia for more information.

A brunette female passed him, dressed in an impossibly short grey skirt, heeled shoes and a tight white blouse. She glanced at him, raking her gaze over him in a way that made him want to growl at her. He hated it when the court females looked upon him in such a manner.

"Lost, Handsome?" She turned towards him and fluttered her eyelashes.

"No. Merely pausing to reflect upon what other food items constitute a cure for… hung over."

She sidled closer, clutching a basket in both hands before her. His gaze scanned the contents. Wine. Sable did not require that. Chocolate. What was it with mortal females and that infernal sweet?

"I tell you what I love to eat when I'm hung over... let's see. Fried bacon and eggs, which you happen to have right here." She stroked the packages in his arms and brushed her fingers across his skin too. Thorne barely resisted flashing his fangs at her. "Sausages are good. I love a big sausage."

He surmised that was a euphemism for a part of his anatomy. She tried to brush her leg against his and he backed off a step. It failed to deter her.

"Waffles with chocolate sauce, cream and strawberries."

Chocolate again. Perhaps it was a way into women's hearts.

"Toast with butter and jam." The female seemed to eat a lot when hung over, or she was just listing things to keep him around and keep him distracted from his mission. She edged closer again and looked up into his eyes. "You could cook it all for me tomorrow morning after we party tonight."

Insidious female. He scowled at her. "I mean this cure for my female, not for you."

He turned on his heel and stomped away from her, going in search of everything she had mentioned. When he had more than he could carry, he took it to a register, carefully bagged each item and paid for it with one of the bank cards he had teleported from his room.

Demons had long ago adjusted to travelling in the mortal world, depositing gold into the banks as they had been formed. Apparently, his people had a healthy amount of money. Unfortunately, the side effect was that banks often sent letters to the mansions he owned in England and Switzerland, desiring to meet with him to discuss better accounts, stocks, and other boring matters. He had no time for fawning mortals.

Thorne picked up the white plastic bags and carried them out into the street, checked no one was around to see him, and then dropped into the black portal that appeared beneath his feet. He rose out of it in the castle kitchen, set the bags down on the solid stone rectangular island in the middle of the large room, and let his horns back out before any of the servants could notice he had hidden them.

"Cook these items." He pointed to the bags, drawing the attention of the three young males to them.

They immediately came forwards, removed his purchases and spread them out on the counter.

And stared at them with their eyebrows pinned high on their foreheads and an increasing amount of fear in their eyes and their scents.

All three of them glanced at him and then they began whispering to each other. Thorne sighed. They did not know how to cook the food. This was a problem he had not anticipated.

"Leave," he ordered and they hurried out of the room. He approached the counter, picked up one of the packages, and read the label. It couldn't be that difficult. After a minute, he put it back down.

He was going to need help.

This food seemed to require someone with expertise and knowledge, and he had never cooked anything in his long years.

He called his portal and dropped into it, this time appearing in the elf prince's room. Bleu was there and said something about battles to Loren. Thorne spared a second to toss a vicious growl at the elf before he grabbed Olivia and teleported with her.

She gasped and shoved out of his arms as they appeared in the kitchens, turned on her heel and slapped him.

He was growing tired of females slapping him.

Loren appeared between them before Thorne could apologise and explain, his black sword drawn and at the ready, his fierce purple eyes warning him that he had made a grave mistake by taking his female.

Thorne raised both of his hands. "I am sorry for my methods but my cooks do not know how to make this 'hung over' food and I seek Olivia's assistance."

The female's gaze shifted to the goods laid out on the smooth stone counter and her lips curled into a smile that spoke of amusement but also pleasure. She was pleased that he had gone to the mortal world to gather food for Sable. It boded well. Sable may feel the same as her friend when she saw what he had done.

Loren sheathed his sword and leaned against the dark stone island. "This should be interesting."

Thorne didn't like that Bleu had remained above and knew that he would seek to visit the sleeping female.

His sleeping female.

Olivia moved forwards, distracting him from his dark thoughts, and he did his best to listen to her instructions as she opened the food and explained how to cook the items. The kitchen wasn't equipped to cook some of the items in the way she knew. He had none of the electrical appliances she asked him about because his castle and kingdom did not have the necessary power for such things. Not yet, anyway. He was working on it.

He set a broad pan over the fire and fried the bacon and sausages, eating whatever he burned by mistake, desiring to know its taste. Bacon was good. He took a small piece of the eggs after they had 'scrambled' them and set them on the bread Loren had helped to lightly toast on the flames. Thorne did not like the fruits they had prepared, but noted that mortal females seemed to enjoy them when Olivia cut them up into pieces and stole some when she thought he wasn't looking.

When they had finished, he set everything onto a large wooden tray and teleported to Sable's room.

Bleu was not there. That pleased him greatly.

Sable gasped.

"What the hell do you think you're doing?" She scrambled to cover herself with the furs and looked as pale as they were.

That did not please him.

Thorne wasn't sure what to say so he presented her with the food and waited. She stared at the tray for an excruciating length of time before raising her golden eyes to his.

"This is for me? You had this made for me?" Her gaze darted down to the food and then back to him.

"I made this for you," he rumbled and his left hand twitched against the tray, eager to stroke his horn on that side. He drew in a steadying breath instead, calming his nerves and hoping she hadn't noticed them.

Her eyes widened and a small smile touched her lips. "You made this?"

He puffed his chest out. "I gathered items Olivia said you would desire and made this 'hung over' food so you would feel better."

Sable smiled fully. "It's called a hangover. Don't demons get hangovers?"

He frowned and shook his head. "No."

He had consumed a whole barrel of mead once and had woken with a clear head the next day.

"Lucky bastard," she muttered and then froze and slowly raised her hands to her hair. She patted the tangled mess of black, her eyes grew large and she quickly raked her fingers through it. She pulled her hair back, took a piece of elastic from her wrist and tied it into a ponytail. "Do I get to eat it?"

He nodded and approached her with the tray. She shuffled backwards and settled against the pillows. When he placed the tray down on the furs covering her lap, she looked as if she might sigh.

Thorne ran an assessing gaze over the contents of the tray. A plate with the scrambled eggs on toast, sausages and bacon. A bowl with mixed fruit. Another plate with toast, next to which was a pot of jam and one of honey. Waffles with chocolate sauce. Something was missing. He growled as it struck him and teleported back to the kitchen.

The prince and his female were feeding each other fruit. He had done such a thing with his female. A bolt of pride went through him. He snagged the drink they had made and returned to Sable with it.

She gasped as he appeared in her room again, a piece of bacon hanging from her lips. Lips he had kissed. He growled low in his throat over the memory of how she had tasted and how she had responded to his kiss. She quickly pushed the bacon into her mouth, chewed and swallowed it.

"We did not have a suitable pot." He presented her with a roughly hewn jug and a clay mug.

She looked wary until he poured it. Her eyes lit up.

"Coffee?" She snatched the cup from his hand, brought it to her nose and inhaled deeply. Her shoulders relaxed and she closed her eyes and sighed.

His female liked coffee very much.

He would order his kitchen to bring more from the mortal world and learn how to brew it correctly so she could have it whenever she desired.

She sipped the drink, set it down on the tray and began to eat. She paused a moment later and looked up at him.

"Are you just going to stand there watching me eat?"

She meant for him to leave. Thorne could understand why and wouldn't refuse her request, even though he didn't want to leave. He sighed and tried to ignore the lead weight dragging his insides down, making his heart heavy. Her fine eyebrows drew together and then she did something wholly unexpected.

She patted the bed beside her. "At least sit."

She did not mean for him to leave?

He sat at the edge of the mattress before she could change her mind, a curious light feeling swirling through his veins, lifting his heart.

He looked at the bed on which he sat and the smile that had been wending its way onto his lips instantly dropped away and the light feeling turned to heat that blasted his blood and turned it into liquid fire.

A bed in which she had slumbered and still rested.

His body shot steel-hard at the thought of her curled up asleep under the furs, naked against him, her soft curves moulded against his and her body warming him. A possessive hungry growl threatened to curl up his throat but he swallowed it back down, grimaced as his leather trousers bit into his groin, and moved his left leg, concealing his hard-on.

Sable moved the tray and set it down on the bed, and shifted her legs beneath the furs, so she was sitting upright again. The covers fell down to reveal the tight black top she wore. It had thin straps and clung to her breasts. Thorne bit back a groan.

They were unfettered beneath the material and moved as she did, swaying as she leaned forwards to help herself to more coffee and to eat bites of her food. Her nipples brushed the soft cotton, puckering and stretching the material. His hands itched to knead her breasts, to weigh each warm globe in his palms and brush his thumbs over the rosy buds her top concealed.

He stared at them, his mouth going dry. Would they feel as soft as her backside had, giving beneath the gentle pressure of his touch? Would they be as warm in his hands? Would she respond sweetly as he lowered his head, drew each bud into his mouth in turn and swirled his tongue around them to taste her?

"Thorne?" Her voice jolted him and he tensed, unable to tear his gaze away from her chest and knowing from her sharp tone that she had caught him. "Yoo-hoo… I'm up here, Big Guy. You want to leave?"

"No." Why ever would he desire that when he was sitting on a bed alone in a room with her?

"Stop staring then." She waved a sausage at him and then bit into it and his mind went back to the female in the store and her euphemism.

He groaned aloud this time, unable to bear where his thoughts were taking him and Sable's teasing. She had to know that control was a tentative fragile thing for him whenever he was in her company, liable to break at any moment with only the slightest of touches. She had to know she was pushing him, no, shoving him towards the edge just by being alone with him while sitting in her bed, barely dressed, without the need for teasing.

With it, he was in danger of snapping and responding to her playfulness, and he wasn't sure she would appreciate him grabbing her shoulders, pinning her to the bed and kissing the breath out of her. He ached with a need to feel her beneath him, to possess every dangerous curve and taste every inch of her.

To stamp his name all over her, body and soul.

Sable smiled wickedly and bit into the sausage again.

Thorne dragged his hand over his mouth. She was torturing him and she knew it. Each bite of sausage, each moan she loosed as she sipped her coffee, each glance she threw his way.

All of it torture.

Was this a positive sign? Did human females torture males they desired?

Was this her way of indicating that she was open to his advances? Did that mean she wouldn't push him away or turn on him if his control did snap and he couldn't stop himself from trying to get her beneath him? Another groan spilled from his lips at the thought and his cock ached, throbbing in eagerness and anticipation. He did his best to ignore it and the urge to palm himself through his leathers, afraid his observations were wrong and she would kick him out if she noticed how she had aroused him to the point of pain.

Perhaps her teasing was a courting ritual or maybe he was reading into things, seeing them how he wanted them to be. He had done his best to study females in the short time they had been apart, trying to glean information from his mated warriors without asking outright and even going so far as to read a book on the subject of romance. He had tried to match up the information the book contained to what he knew of Sable, but none of it had seemed to fit her.

At his last meeting with Prince Loren, the elf had warned him that if he tried to apply the normal demon methods of securing their mate to Sable, he would end up empty handed and would spend the rest of his life alone. He could see now that the male was right. Sable required a different approach. He couldn't force her into a bond. She was strong, independent, and hunted his kind for a living. If he tried to follow his instincts, he would end up more than empty handed.

He would end up dead.

Thorne frowned at his knees, his desire forgotten and the warmth of being close to Sable fading away as he mulled over how easy it would be to drive her from his life before he even came close to having a chance to claim her. She had threatened to leave once already because he had forced a kiss upon her. How was he meant to win her?

It wasn't in his nature to sit back and wait for her to make a move. His instincts constantly drove him to claim her. Whenever he set eyes on her, whenever she was in the vicinity, he felt that drive beating in his heart and pounding in his blood.

It was hard to ignore it.

Right now, he wanted to kiss her again. Needed to place his mouth on hers. He wanted to crawl across the bed and kiss her, easing her down onto the mattress beneath him at the same time. He wanted her to know that she belonged to him and, no matter how strongly she fought, he would have her as his forever. No one would stand between them.

Sable stopped moving and stared at him, the heat of her gaze questioning.

Thorne shoved aside his thoughts and his desires, and focused on her instead.

"Do you still feel sick? Foolish?" he said and cast a glance at her.

The corners of her beautiful mouth turned sharply downwards and her dark eyebrows knitted together above her golden-brown eyes. Eyes that flashed with fire and told him exactly how she had taken his words. She thought he mocked her strength.

Thorne quickly added, "Your friend mentioned that you would feel foolish."

"A little." Her expression softened and a blush coloured her cheeks, skin he had caressed more than once. She had let him run his claws over her soft cheeks and he knew that was a positive sign. She pushed Bleu away whenever he tried to touch her in a gentle or tender fashion, but she had accepted his caress. Sable's colour deepened. "I didn't do anything outlandish or flash my knickers, did I?"

Thorne shook his head. Were those things she had done while drunk before? The vision of her flashing her undergarments appealed to him and had him shifting on the bed, trying to ease the growing tightness of his trousers over his groin. He glanced back down at his knees and struggled to regain his focus so she wouldn't notice the effect that she had on him.

"You didn't have to do this." She set her mug down and he lifted his head. She looked at him, right into his eyes, hers serious at last.

"I did," he countered. "I was the one who allowed you to drink our mead and I gave no thought to the strength of it. I wanted to apologise."

She smiled. "You're getting good at this apologising lark. Apology accepted."

She had taken the food as his apology. Fascinating little female.

He tried to smile but it wouldn't come.

Hers faded and her black eyebrows pinched together. "You look troubled again."

"Again?" he said, his own frown coming to the fore now.

She nodded. "You looked troubled when you were talking to Loren in the courtyard too. Is the war weighing on your mind?"

Observant little female. But it wasn't only the war that constantly pressed down on his shoulders, clouding his mood. It was her too and his need to find a way to show her that he was the only male she ever needed.

Thorne sighed. "Among other things."

Sable picked at her food, her amber gaze downcast, and silence fell over them both, heavy and thick with unspoken things. She knew what played on his mind and it played on hers too. She couldn't deny it. He had made no attempt to hide that she was his mate, his fated female, and that he intended to claim what was rightfully his. She made no attempt to hide how that unnerved her. He could see it in her whenever they were in the same room.

Hidden in the beautiful depths of her eyes there was a sliver of vulnerability that only emerged whenever she looked at him.

The tower bells rung, the sound distant through the thick stone walls. His lips quirked as he thought of that quaint mortal phrase.

Saved by the bell.

He rose and she spoke before he could, her gaze darting up to his.

"You're going somewhere?"

Did she want him to stay? He had taken her silence to mean that she wanted him to go and leave her in peace. Females were complicated little creatures, even more so than he had first imagined.

"I must attend the meeting." Yet, he couldn't bring himself to leave. If she asked him to stay, he would. He would make no excuses to his waiting guests either.

"Meeting? Shit." She threw the furs aside and Thorne froze.

His body instantly hardened back to the point of pain and he grimaced.

Sable leaped from the bed, dressed in only her small black top and a pair of tight black shorts, her long slender legs on display. A vision of her wrapping them around him as he pinned her to the wall and kissed her breathless filled his mind and his hard length ached with the need to make the dream into a reality. He palmed the bulge in his leathers and swallowed hard, his heart thundering against his ribs.

She grabbed her black combat trousers from the chair off to his left and bent to put her feet into the legs and he was done for.

The sight of her bending over before him shattered his restraint and he had taken two steps towards her before he realised what he was doing. The hunger to touch her, to fulfil his need to feel his female's flesh beneath his fingers again, warm and soft, consumed him, driving him towards her and filling his mind with a vision of stepping up behind her, clutching her hips and drawing her back against his aching shaft.

She began to tug her trousers up and Thorne growled, the thought of her concealing her delicious body displeasing him and every instinct he possessed demanding he stop her.

Sable froze.

She slowly turned her head.

Thorne forced himself to move and turn away from her before she could catch a glimpse of him. If she did, she would see the hard-on he sported for her. If that happened and she showed a glimmer of interest, a spark of desire, he wouldn't be able to hold himself back.

He would kiss her again, and a lot more besides.

"If you are unwell, you should have your second in command take your place," he said, trying to fill the room with noise so he couldn't hear the soft rustle of her clothes as she dressed. He ran his hand over his mouth again, rubbing it hard, trying not to visualise her as she covered all that tight smooth pale skin. He wanted to strip the garments from her and lick every inch of her until she begged him to tongue her sweet spot.

He had dreamed of tasting her between her thighs, pressing his tongue in hard and stroking her until she cried his name in climax.

"No way," she snapped, shattering the vision building in his mind. "He'll report back that I was absent for the initial meeting and then that's my promotion shot to hell."

Thorne realised that he had made a grave mistake in suggesting someone take her place. She prided herself on her abilities as a hunter and Loren had mentioned that she viewed her mission here as important to something she called her 'career trajectory'. She desired a promotion to a new rank.

He should have known better than to challenge her ability to lead her team, but his senses said that she was in no fit state to be out of bed and sitting through a long meeting with the other commanders and his instincts demanded he make her rest.

His darker side posed a question he couldn't easily shake. If she desired this promotion in order to improve upon her rank and better herself, would she ever consent to being his? As his queen, she would be expected to live in his realm at his side. Could she do such a thing while remaining part of Archangel, hunting his kind in her world?

Would his people accept a queen who sought to kill them the moment they stepped out of line according to mortal rules?

Sable moved around him and he brought his gaze down to her, his thoughts troubling him. He ached to lift his hand and touch her cheek, to lay his palm against her soft warm skin and look deep into her beautiful golden-brown eyes to seek the answers to the questions that plagued him.

Could Sable lay down her weapons in order to become his queen?

His forever.

She stood before him dressed for combat, with weapons strapped over her black trousers and t-shirt, even though she was going into a meeting where only allies awaited.

It gave him his answer, and that answer made his chest ache.

Sable would never give up her life with Archangel in order to forge a new one with him.

Thorne wished that knowledge gave him the power to give up his chase but it only strengthened his need to claim her. The thought of her leaving compelled him to seize hold of her with both hands and never let her go.

"Thorne?" she whispered and he blinked and looked back at her, down into her eyes. "Is something wrong?"

The fated bond between them gave her insight into his feelings. She was probably unaware of it but he doubted it would take her long to comprehend the reason why she was so attuned to him, able to detect his shifting moods. It gave her power over him, making it impossible for him to hide his true feelings from her and making it easy for her to use his emotions against him. He hoped she never did.

"There will be another gathering tonight," he said, the words distant to his ears, trying to fill the awkward silence again and avoiding answering her question.

She paled.

Thorne managed to smile at last. "I will... Olivia will keep you from the grog and I have asked the kitchen to prepare mortal food for you and your kin."

Her eyebrows rose and warmth coloured her irises, surprise and gratitude burning in them. Whenever she looked at him like that, as if he was the only male in the world, he yearned to kiss her.

He couldn't stop himself from reaching out, gently clasping her left hand and raising it to his lips. He pressed a kiss to her knuckles and breathed her in at the same time, taking her soft scent deep into his lungs. Her gaze held his, captivating him together with the fact that she allowed him to do this, and his heart took it as a positive sign.

A sign of things to come if he could rein in his need and his instincts and find the key that would unlock his little hunter's heart.

CHAPTER 6

Sable's head was killing her but the ache in her chest eclipsed it whenever she thought about Thorne's visit. She tried to concentrate on the meeting as the commanders and their selected subordinates were brought up to speed on the war between the kingdoms and discussed the plan of attack.

Thorne sat at the head of the long rectangular table in the middle of the expansive library, five places to her left. Two tall arched windows allowed dim light to filter in behind him and the lamps on the table provided a warm glow that cast the shadows back into the recesses between the bookcases lining the walls.

At the other end of the table, Loren sat with Olivia next to him. The vampires lined the side opposite her together with the elves. The werewolves had decided to sit on her side, muttering dark things about bloodsuckers in English. She supposed they meant both the elves and the vampires.

It had taken Thorne several minutes to get everyone settled and to subdue a few slanging matches between the various species present. Loren had helped settle the elves. The vampire commander had sat back with his hands clasped behind his head and let his men do as they please. The werewolf leader had at least attempted to calm his men. She said attempted because he had recited a few weak rounds of 'calm down' and 'silence' before he too had sat back and let the wolves have at the vampires across the table.

Sable had stared at Thorne the whole time. She hadn't meant to but it had been impossible to convince her eyes to leave him while he had stood at the end of the table, demanding order as his horns slowly curled, his eyes gradually brightened and his ears grew pointier.

He had been such a contrast to the gentle, quiet man who had sat with her in her room after bringing her breakfast as way of an apology.

A man who had gazed upon her with barely leashed desire in his eyes that had slowly burned through her control and pushed her towards surrendering to the wicked urges that came upon her whenever they were close to each other.

How would he have reacted if she had kissed him?

He wanted to kiss her, and the erection he had tried to hide from her while he had blatantly stared at her breasts told her that if she had kissed him, it wouldn't have ended there. He would have taken more from her this time, demanding she surrender completely to him.

That sent a thrill through her even when she knew it shouldn't.

Evan already looked as if he was waging a constant battle against spouting the words clearly balanced on the tip of his tongue. He wouldn't hesitate to remind her of what she had said back at Archangel about this not being a Club 18-30 holiday if she did give in to her desires.

Sable concentrated on the notes she had scribbled onto her pad. The plan was sound, if not a little dangerous. Luring the enemy to them meant placing many villages at the borders in danger and Thorne would be in danger too. He had made it clear that he and he alone would engage the Fifth King. Apparently, it was the done thing in demonomachies. Only kings fought kings.

She thought it was a stupid tradition and she had no qualms about agreeing to it here and now and breaking the rule later when they were on the battlefield. She was damned if she would let Thorne lose his head because he insisted on fighting solo. He was strong, powerful, and capable, but together they were stronger.

Sable pretended that thought stemmed from her mission and her duty as the commander of the Archangel team. Her heart whispered that it stemmed from her soul though and the feelings that came over her whenever she thought about Thorne fighting his enemy. She wanted to protect him. The incident in the courtyard had made it clear that he, and no doubt every other demon present, thought that a little mortal female throwing herself into battle at his side was quaint and sweet, and stupid, but it wasn't going to deter her. Every instinct she had said to protect him and she had never denied her instincts. They had saved her too many times.

Her gaze drifted back to Thorne and heat travelled through her, burning up her blood, as their eyes locked. Perhaps there were some instincts better left denied.

Like the one telling her to get up on the table and crawl the length of it to him, and to take his strong square jaw in her palms, tip his head up and gently kiss him until his restraint shattered and hers broke with it.

Thorne growled low, flashing a hint of fang, and his eyes brightened, burning crimson and setting her aflame.

"Perhaps it is time we retire to attend to our men and other business ahead of this evening's gathering?" the vampire commander said.

Her eyes darted to him, her heart skipping a beat as she realised he had been staring at her the whole time, studying her while she gazed at Thorne, and was now insinuating they needed to be left alone.

"Very well." Thorne rose from his seat and, damn, his body shifted sensually beneath his white shirt and tight dark mahogany leathers, cranking up her temperature to boiling point. He bowed his head to the assembled and then did something unexpected. Rather than looking at her, he swiftly turned to his second in command, a demon called Fargus.

Sable closed her pad and stood. Evan got to his feet beside her.

"We should run through the drills and make sure everyone is prepared." Sable turned to Evan and pretended she didn't hear the barely audible growl coming from Thorne's direction. She had to speak to her second in command and Thorne would just have to deal with it.

Loren said something and Olivia stood, and Bleu followed suit, rising to tower over her friend. Sable glanced his way, her gut twisting and heart telling her to follow him from the room and speak to him. She had to know whether they were still friends because she didn't want things between them to change.

The other elves filed out together with the members of her team. The vampires moved off to one corner of the large library beyond Thorne and his men. Their dark-haired commander looked back at her, a wicked smile curving his lips. He had enjoyed taunting her in front of the others. She stroked the blade strapped to her thigh, staring at him as she imagined acquainting him with it.

A pale slender hand curled around her arm and drew her aside. Sable glared down at it and then up into the purple eyes of its owner, expecting to find Bleu. It was Loren.

"That vampire is not one to trifle with," Loren whispered and she glanced back at the man in question, finding him still staring at her. "He is extremely vicious and dangerous, with not only a reputation but a history of carnage to back it up."

Little wonder the guy was the commander of the First Legion in the Preux Chevaliers corps.

All the more reason to keep away from him.

Since meeting Loren, she had learned about the Preux Chevaliers. They were the sons of the pureblood vampire families, or aristocrats as they loved to call themselves. Each son served centuries in Hell as a Preux Chevalier, bloodying their claws in the wars that were a constant fixture in that realm.

Because they were of pure vampire blood, they were strong enough to withstand the impact of the weak daylight in Thorne's and many of the demon realms and other kingdoms in Hell besides Loren's.

No wonder the vampires liked it in Hell. They could move around at any time without risking going crispy, could fight all they liked, and were a law unto themselves, free to drink victims dry and kill without consequences such as Archangel putting them on their naughty list.

"My prince, we should see to it that the men begin their daily training routine," Bleu said, dipping his head at the same time, and Sable wanted to slap him.

He was ignoring her and it hurt.

They had become friends and she didn't have many of those in her life. Olivia was the only person she had considered as a friend for the past ten years. Bleu and Loren had achieved that exclusive position in the short time she had known them, and now Bleu was angry with her and without reason.

She hadn't betrayed him and had never felt anything beyond friendship and a smattering of lust-filled moments. Those had been a product of loneliness. She had seen what Olivia had and she had been envious, and Bleu had been around. She had considered losing herself in him, but every time she had, Thorne had popped into her head and she had wanted him instead.

Loren nodded and escorted Olivia away, following Bleu to the doors. Bleu waited for his prince to pass him and then looked back at her. Sable stared across the room at him, lost for words and aching inside. Why had he ruined a good thing? Why couldn't he have left things the way they had been? She had liked them that way and he had wrecked them.

Bleu's purple gaze darkened and he lowered it to his feet, heaved a sigh and walked out of the door.

Sable watched him go, struggling to deny the pressing need to follow and talk to him. She wasn't sure that he would understand even if she told him that she hadn't chosen Thorne over him. She had no intention of becoming Thorne's mate.

A quiet part of her that she had buried deep reared its head and whispered that she wanted to give herself to Thorne though. She secretly wanted what Olivia and Loren shared, and none of the excuses she kept making were cutting it anymore. That part of her was growing stronger each day, with each minute that she passed in Thorne's company and came to know him better.

He was honourable, handsome, strong and could be charming when he paused to think things through rather than running with his instincts.

Her gaze sought and found him still speaking with Fargus.

"Go on and get everyone to run through the training routine. I need to speak with Olivia about something," Sable said to Evan and he nodded and left the room.

The vampires left after him and the werewolves decided to exit through the other door in the room. She couldn't blame them. She intended to avoid the vampires as much as possible too.

Sable meandered through the room to the three dimensional map she had spotted on entering the library. She stood over it, her gaze scanning the topography of Hell and the borders carefully marked on it. The Third Realm didn't occupy the best position. It shared a border with the First, Fourth, Fifth and Seventh Realms and a section of blacked-out land. That land curved around all of the demon realms. Apparently, it belonged to the Devil.

She scanned the kingdoms, moving across from right to left, from the Seventh Realm through the Third and then the First, to the elven kingdom. It was large and shared a border with the First and Second Realms and also an area labelled as the Free Kingdom. Loren had mentioned that place. Kordula had come from that land.

There were smaller kingdoms beyond it and the elven one, none of them labelled. Olivia had told her that gods and goddesses had realms in Hell, and so did other species such as fallen angels and creatures that sounded more myth than reality.

Familiar heat burned through her, but cold swept close to its heels. She looked across to her right, towards where Thorne had been, and was now gone. Fargus stood there talking to two demon males. His dark crimson gaze shifted to her.

Her wrist burned.

Sable rubbed it, trying to relieve the fierce ache. She needed to get Olivia to look at it. It had played up several times since her arrival in the Third Realm. She had a naturally fast healing ability, much quicker than all the other hunters at Archangel. If she had knocked it or injured it in a fight, it should have healed by now.

The other two demons glanced her way. The burning sensation in her wrist increased and this time her gift triggered. A prickling sensation spread through her limbs. A warning. She palmed the blade strapped to her thigh and obeyed her instincts. She turned away from the demons and exited through the door the werewolves had used.

Sable marched at double time along the long hallway and then took the steps down to the first floor two at a time, not slowing until she had placed a good distance between her and the library.

Her head ached and she rubbed her temples, hoping to alleviate it. She hadn't caught much sleep and the clarity that Thorne's gift of coffee had given her was beginning to wear off. Maybe she had been imagining the threat in the library. She had no doubt that Fargus knew she was Thorne's fated female and that meant the male wouldn't dare try anything with her.

She scrubbed a hand over her face, trying to shake her bad feeling, and turned down the hallway that led to her room.

Olivia and Loren were about to enter their quarters.

"Liv," Sable hollered and her friend paused at the threshold and smiled at her. "Wait up."

She hurried over to them and Loren looked disappointed.

"Not interrupting some afternoon delight, am I?" Sable grinned when he blushed, cleared his throat and placed his hands on Olivia's waist.

Olivia looked over her shoulder at him.

He gently squeezed her and dropped a kiss on her lips. "I will go with Bleu to see to my men."

"Wait," Sable blurted before he could turn away and then wasn't sure what to say when he looked expectantly at her. She blew out her breath and her shoulders sagged. "Tell Bleu I'm sorry."

Loren arched a single black eyebrow. "You do not need to apologise to him, Sable."

"I do. I just feel that maybe I sent out the wrong signals or something... I just don't want this to escalate. I don't want two grown men acting like idiots because of me."

Loren smiled. "Understood. I will relay your apology to him and will try to adjust his behaviour before this evening's gathering."

"Just... at least convince him to start speaking to me again. I feel like I've lost a friend... and I don't like it."

Olivia frowned and touched Sable's arm, and she was grateful for her friend's concern and comfort.

Loren heaved a sigh. "Bleu can be a handful. I will speak with him."

The dark glint in his eyes warned Sable that it wouldn't be a nice heart to heart between him and Bleu. She didn't want to get Bleu into trouble with Loren or put a strain on their relationship too.

"Go easy on him, Big Guy. Just tell him I'm sorry and that it hurts when he doesn't speak to me and acts like I don't exist." Sable held his gaze, hoping he would see in her eyes that she didn't want him to berate Bleu or force him to be nice to her.

Loren nodded. "Understood."

He pressed another kiss to Olivia's lips and then walked along the corridor towards the stairs down to the great hall.

The moment he was out of sight, Sable turned to Olivia. "I totally interrupted his afternoon delight, didn't I?"

Olivia giggled. "He can wait... I would rather hear about you and Thorne. What's happening there?"

Sable wasn't convinced her friend preferred gossip over hot sex with her mate but she followed Olivia into her room anyway. "Nothing. Nothing at all... and that's how it's going to stay."

Her friend looked disappointed now. "A wise woman once told me that I was crazy for trying to let a wonderful man walk out of my life."

"I think that woman might have been certifiably crazy herself." Sable crossed the room to the threadbare armchairs beside the large stone fireplace to her right and sat down on one. "Besides, it's a little different."

"How?" Olivia sat opposite her.

"Thorne is a demon... and then there's Bleu." She stood again, unable to keep still while she was talking about the two definitely certifiable males.

She paced the room, striding back and forth between the foot of the large four-poster bed and the armchairs.

"Ah, so you've finally noticed that Bleu has the hots for a little Sable action."

Sable tossed her a glare. "I was blind not to notice it... thinking back on it... the guy followed me around like I was a bitch in heat."

"He just likes you. He's been like it since he set eyes on you."

She froze. "He's not..."

She couldn't bring herself to say it.

Olivia shook her head and relief beat sweet and swift through Sable.

"Loren doesn't think that he's your mate. He thinks Bleu is just horny and wants more than fighting with you."

Sable groaned and flopped onto the four-poster bed on her back. She didn't want to acknowledge that Loren and Olivia had been discussing her and Bleu in that way. It was wrong on so many levels.

She stretched her arms out across the silky furs beneath her and a vision of Thorne laying her down on her bed like this, covering her body with his big muscular one, and kissing her left her aching for some afternoon delight of her own.

She really needed to get her thoughts off both men.

She tilted her head and looked at her right wrist and the tattoo on it. The ache had dulled to a throb now. She flexed her fingers and rotated her hand, trying to detect if it was still injured.

"You okay?" Olivia said and crossed the room to her.

"My wrist is bothering me. It aches from time to time." Sable sat up and rubbed it. "I probably knocked it."

Olivia sat sideways on the bed beside her and took hold of her wrist, bringing it to her. "Let me see."

Sable kept still while Olivia checked her wrist over, watching her friend carefully rotate it and feel her bones.

"No bruising and your tendons seem fine." Olivia looked up at her. "Does it hurt when I do this?"

She pressed into the delicate flesh on the inside of Sable's wrist and Sable shook her head.

"Press, prod, poke… no problem. It just aches sometimes… like a burning." Sable took her wrist back and rubbed it. "It's not so bad now, but it really hurt earlier in the meeting room."

"I'll strap it up. Could be you just banged it. I can't feel any problems with it… but keep an eye on it, okay?" Olivia rose, went to one of her black holdalls and opened it. She took out a roll of crepe bandage and came back to Sable.

Sable held her arm out and Olivia strapped it up, wrapping the cream bandage around her hand and then up her wrist and back again. She tried to keep her thoughts away from Bleu and Thorne, but it was impossible. She wanted Bleu as her friend but knew that he couldn't just let go of his desire for her and extinguish it. The way he had looked at her during the meeting warned her that he wasn't going to give up, not even if she asked him to, or begged him.

He was going to pursue her.

He was going to come to blows with Thorne again and her gut said it would be sooner rather than later, and nothing she did would stop it.

And Thorne?

Sable picked at the bandage around her wrist.

She wanted Thorne as more than a friend but she wasn't Olivia. She lived her life on the frontline and death chased her every night she went out on patrol, waiting for the moment she slipped up or took on more than she could handle. She didn't have a quiet position within Archangel as Olivia did and she didn't want one either. She didn't want to give up her career, a calling that she relished and loved, and Thorne would demand that of her if she ever consented to be his mate.

"You okay?" Olivia's soft voice broke into her dire thoughts and she shook her head and pressed her hand to it.

"Tired... having man trouble from Hell." Sable tried to smile. "Hung over."

"Get some rest." Olivia squeezed her shoulder.

Sable nodded. Maybe a nap would help clear her head and give her the strength to face the gathering tonight. Evan could handle the training sessions without her. She hated giving him any opportunity to prove himself better commander material, but she needed some rest. Just an hour would do. She would catch up with him and the others later, after her nap.

She stood, bent and hugged her friend, and then made her way back to her room. She closed the door behind her, strode to the bed and flopped onto her front, exhaling hard the moment she hit the soft furs.

Sable stared at her bandaged wrist.

Tonight was going to be a challenge and she would sooner face a legion of demons than stand in a room filled with people staring at her, and with two men who both wanted her and were willing to kill the other to possess her.

Sable groaned and closed her eyes.

She blanked her mind and waited for sleep to take her.

When it did, Thorne was waiting for her.

CHAPTER 7

Thorne was dreaming, but it was more than a dream. It was vivid. Real.

Sable lay stretched out on the huge four-poster bed before him, dressed only in the tiny black shorts she had worn when he had visited her and a matching black cotton bra. The simple underwear was erotic on her, arousing him to the point of pain. She writhed on the tawny furs, shifting sensually, a wicked dance designed to tempt him.

He stood at the foot of the bed and had been for the past five minutes or longer, watching her as she wriggled, drawing deep lungfuls of the sweet scent of her desire, drinking in the way she was looking at him as if she was on fire and only he could quench the flames.

She wanted him.

Here in this vision, she was his.

Her golden eyes implored him and her fingers tangled in the long silken black threads of her hair. She brought her knees together and swayed them side-to-side, rubbing her thighs together and entrancing him until he couldn't tear his gaze from them. She parted her legs then, slowly revealing the black cotton hiding her feminine core from his hungry eyes. His chest heaved and his horns curled, desire getting the better of him, driving him to bring his knee up onto the bed to mount it and cover her delicious, soft body with his.

Sable closed her legs, shutting them tight, stealing Heaven from view.

His heart pounded a tribal beat against his chest, a rhythm that grew in pace as she swayed her knees and gradually parted them to reveal herself again.

He growled.

Her eyes flashed with hunger in response and she licked her lips.

Wicked female.

She had never been like this in his dreams and he knew why.

She had never slept at the same time as him before. They had never shared the same vision. He had only been able to imagine what his fated one would be like, and what he had envisaged hadn't come close to reality.

She was everything he had dreamed and so much more.

Sable crooked her finger at him and he was a slave at her command.

Thorne unlaced his white shirt and pulled it over his head. Sable sucked in a sharp breath and he looked at her, catching the dark edge of desire in her gaze as it roamed his body, heating him wherever it caressed and lingered.

He drew in his own deep breath to steady himself and dropped his shirt. He stood before her, giving her time to rake her eyes over him, to study his body as he studied hers, enjoying the way desire flickered in her fiery gaze. She wanted him.

He wanted her.

Never more so than this time.

He had dreamed of her every night without fail over the past lunar cycle, and what he lacked in experience in reality, he had in abundance here in his dreams.

He would possess her, would bend his strong, beautiful female to his will, and he would claim her, and she would know that she belonged to him, body and soul.

His forever.

She would want no other.

He would see to it.

Thorne tugged the laces on his leather trousers and Sable's hungry gaze fell to his hands. She followed every move he made, her absorbed look bringing his nerves to the fore. He squashed them, reminding himself that this was a vision, not reality. Here in this dream, he was master, he was king, and his little vixen would know it.

He shoved his leathers down and her moan made his heart hitch and slam against his chest, and his length pulse with want.

Sable moved onto her knees before him and he groaned this time, the sight of her petite behind hugged by black cotton too much for him to bear.

She crawled towards him, reached out and stroked a single finger down the length of his engorged shaft. Thorne hissed through his teeth and tilted his head back, every muscle tensing as her caress scalded him.

She ran her finger back up, slowly encircling his shaft with her hand as she moved, and rubbed her thumb over the blunt head.

Thorne couldn't take it.

He dropped his head, grasped the back of her neck and dragged her up to him. She pressed against his chest, her naked flesh searing his, and moaned as he claimed her lips in a fierce, demanding kiss. Her hands settled against his pectorals and then slid upwards, coming to grasp his shoulders, fingers kneading and nails pressing in as he deepened the kiss. Their tongues tangled and he drove his into her mouth, unwilling to let her seize control.

She would know that she belonged to him.

Thorne pulled her closer. Instinct made him hold back even though he couldn't hurt her in their dreams. Sable didn't seem to care that his strength could so easily injure her.

She clawed his shoulders and groaned into his mouth, her hot tongue probing his, teasing him to the brink of madness.

Thorne growled, caught her shoulders and pushed her backwards. She fell onto the bed on her back. Her wide eyes slowly narrowed, heated desire colouring their golden depths, calling to him. His roughness had only increased her arousal. He groaned now, the thought that she wanted him to be rough with her, to be dominant, sparking every instinct he had. It was impossible to ignore them.

Not when she was daring him to let go and unleash his desire.

He shoved his trousers off and kicked them away, and she moaned as he mounted the bed. He crawled towards her and she wriggled backwards, a wicked smile curving her kiss-swollen lips. He made them his target, staring hard at them as he caught her ankle and yanked her down the bed to him. She squealed and he caught the rest of it in his kiss. Her lips played hard with his, goading him. She was trying to make him play rougher.

Thorne groaned again and gave her what she desired, kissing her so hard that he forced her down against the bed. She moaned and nipped at his lower lip with her blunt teeth. He grunted as a spear of lightning bolted through him and growled as he lost himself in the kiss. He grasped her wrists and pinned her arms above her head, shoving them hard against the soft furs.

Sable moaned low, the sound profoundly wanton. His length pulsed in response, jerking against his stomach. She arched into him and her body pressed into his, wrecking his concentration. He pulled back and stared down at her, lost in how she rocked against him, her slender body rubbing against his stomach.

"Thorne," she whispered and he was more than lost.

The sound of her uttering his name in a passion-drenched plea drove every instinct he had as a demon male to the fore.

His female needed him.

She needed release and he would give it to her.

Thorne released one of her hands and tore her black cotton bra from her, unleashing her breasts. They jiggled from the force of his actions and he swooped on one pebbled dusky nipple, pulling it hard into his mouth. Sable jerked against him and cried out, the sound of her pleasure filling the room and driving him on. He sucked hard on the pearly bud, tearing another cry of bliss from his female. She arched into him, hips rocking wildly, her actions seemingly beyond her control as she sought more pleasure to bring about her release.

He groaned against her breast and kissed downwards, his instincts screaming at him to satisfy her and end her torment, to give her the ecstasy she craved and give it to himself at the same time.

She wriggled and writhed, a frantic edge to her movements. "Thorne."

His horns curled, twisting over and flaring forwards. She moaned and he looked up to find her staring at him, or more specifically his horns.

His female brought out the demon in him, and she liked it.

He bared his fangs and growled as he shredded her panties with his claws, tearing the material from her flesh. She breathed harder, chest heaving, her breasts jutting upwards and calling him back to them. Gods, he needed her.

"Sable," he muttered and stared deep into her eyes, fighting the change as it came over him. She liked him in this state, driven wild by her, with his fangs, claws and horns on show and his eyes blazing scarlet, but she wouldn't like it if he lost control and changed completely, his wings unfurling and his body growing in size.

Sable grinned wickedly and the next few seconds were a blur as she got her legs between them, wrapped them around his neck and twisted at the middle, slamming him into his back.

Thorne stared up at her, basking in her victorious smile and her strength, and then inched his gaze downwards. Heaven.

She sat on his chest, her knees either side of his horns, a wicked goddess within his reach yet too distant at the same time.

He planted his hands on her backside and shoved her towards him. She arched and cried out as his tongue speared her soft folds and found her moist centre. She tasted delicious, ambrosia of the gods, and he wanted to feast on her until she cried his name and shattered into a thousand pieces.

He licked her and swirled his tongue around her pert nub, loving how she writhed and rocked, undulating her hips and riding his face. His female was wicked, strong, commanding. He couldn't understand why many of his kind wanted soft females. His was a goddess and the way she warred with him, the way she made him fight her for control, thrilled him.

Sable grabbed him by the horns and shoved his head hard against the mattress. She rose off him, her eyes flashing wickedly as she held him fast. He groaned as she softened her grip and stroked his horns, sending fire burning through every inch of him and ratcheting up his need for her.

She leaned down and he thought she would kiss him, craned his neck to reach her lips, but she diverted course. Her cheek pressed against his and she clutched his horns, keeping him from moving.

"You think I'm just going to lie down and let you have me?" she whispered into the shell of his ear, a husky murmur that only made him burn hotter. "You don't know me."

He didn't, he knew that, but he wanted to know her. He wanted to know what she loved and what she hated. He wanted to know everything about his future queen.

He wanted to know this in reality.

Would she be as wicked with him there? Would she be as wild and enthralling? Would she fight him for dominance as he claimed her?

He hoped so.

He loved how wild and rough she was in this vision, and how she sought to overpower him and have him at her mercy.

She nipped the pointed tip of his ear and he growled. He tried to get up, to roll her over and show her that he was determined to have her, but she shoved her hands against his chest and pushed all her weight down onto him, pinning him to the bed.

"You're going to lie down and let me have you," she murmured into his ear and licked the lobe.

Gods.

Thorne's desire to resist burned away and he could only obey her as she rose off him again, her fall of black hair cascading over her bare breasts. Her nipples poked through the inky strands, taunting him as she shuffled backwards. She raked her nails over his chest, ripping another moan from him and making his horns curl further and his claws grow sharper. Much more of that and he wouldn't be able to stop himself from changing completely.

He wasn't sure he could stop himself now.

She meant to mount him.

In all of his dreams of her, he had been on top or behind her, in control.

She was nothing as he had thought she would be, and he loved it.

Her heat brushed his hard length and he fisted the furs, groaning as she brought them into contact. She rubbed herself up and down, coating him in her warm wetness. Every inch of him tensed as he clutched the bed, fighting for control, going mad from anticipation.

Sable smiled wickedly again and raked her nails over his stomach muscles. She purred low in her throat, the sound of her approval making his cock jerk beneath her, and her purr became a moan. Her gaze turned hooded and she rocked against him again, killing him slowly with each stroke of her slick heat. He couldn't take it.

"Sable," he whispered, a plea to her this time.

She took mercy on him and rose onto her knees, and he hissed as she grasped his length.

She positioned it beneath her and inched backwards, and his hands shot to her hips as she took him into her, slowly, torturing him to the brink of insanity. Pleasure rolled through him, fierce and overwhelming. She moaned with each inch she took into her, her heat scalding him and making him throb with need, steel hard and painful. He couldn't take it. It was too much. Just the thought of her riding him had him close to coming.

"Sable."

She moaned but ignored his urgent plea, maintaining her slow pace.

He growled and her gaze met his, her lips curled at the corners and she pressed her hands into his stomach.

"Patience, Big Boy."

That sounded like a definite euphemism. He grinned, flashing fangs at her, his chest swelling with pride over the concealed compliment.

She grinned too and pressed down onto him, seating herself and forcing him deep into her. Thorne choked and his eyes widened as she flexed around him, gripping him tightly.

Sable wriggled and he moaned, inching his head side to side, warning her not to push him. He clutched her hips and held her still, giving himself a moment to find some balance. Even in a vision, it was possible to make fool of oneself, and he was damned if he was going to climax before she did.

"Holy hell... you feel good inside me."

Thorne scowled at her. She was saying naughty things on purpose, trying to drive him over the edge.

"Not as good as you feel wrapped around me." He grasped her hips and lifted her off him, and pushed her back down, ripping a harsh cry from her throat. "As tight as a glove, soft as silk and as hot as smelted steel."

She blushed.

He loved the colour red on her.

Her hands pressed harder into his stomach and she began to rock on him, wiping the smile off his face as she rode him with slow, unhurried strokes. He stared up at her, watching the pleasure flitting across her face, her expression changing with each second. Whenever she reached the height of him, close to pulling free of his shaft, she raised her eyebrows and then they would furrow as she sank back onto him, her lips parting on a breathy moan.

"Thorne," she husked and he took the hint and began to guide her on him, easily lifting her up and then curling his hips as he brought her back down. He groaned together with her every time their bodies met. The sounds of their pleasure mingled, the heat rolling off their bodies curling together around them, and he moved her harder and faster.

Sable's head fell back, her long straight black hair sticking to the fine sheen of sweat on her breasts and neck.

Thorne stared at the fluttering pulse in her throat and his fangs grew longer. Saliva pooled in his mouth.

She caught him off guard when she jerked forwards, captured his horns and yanked his head to hers. She kissed him hard, her lips mastering his as they writhed against each other, scorching him as her wet heat burned his length. He groaned and moved her harder, faster, until she was panting and trembling in his hands, moaning his name each time she broke for air.

Thorne screwed his eyes shut and rolled them over, and she wrapped her legs around him, locking them together. He grasped the nape of her neck with one hand and her hip with the other, and drove into her, making her feel every inch of him and the strength he commanded. She moaned and tugged on his horns, and his wings burst from his back, tangling in the canopy of the bed.

He didn't care.

He couldn't stop.

Not when Sable's feet were locked behind his backside, her body flexing each time he withdrew and she used her full strength to drive his cock back into her.

He growled into her mouth and bit her lower lip, drawing blood. She jerked against him as he sucked on it, every bone and muscle locking tight, and he rocked deep into her. She cried long and loud into his mouth, her body convulsing and quivering around his.

Thorne followed her over the edge, plummeting into bliss as her climax drew his from him. Seed boiled up from the base of his cock and he grunted as release exploded from him, making his whole body tremble and shake. He throbbed deep and hard, spilling himself for longer than he ever had before, and kissed her, losing himself in the moment and his female.

Thorne drew back and looked down into her beautiful, mesmerising eyes.

She smiled, a sated edge to her expression but warmth there too. Warmth that made him want to wrap his arms around her and never let go. She felt something for him.

She swam out of focus and disappeared, his room replacing her.

Thorne lay on his back on his bed, his limbs and wings tangled in the furs and his heart pounding. He tried to claw back his vision, didn't want to let it go just yet. He wanted longer with Sable as she had been in that dream world. Sleep refused to return though and he stared up at the canopy of his bed, reliving every delicious moment of the vision in his head.

He wanted to see his female again.

He needed to see Sable.

He needed to see in her eyes that she had been in that vision with him, had experienced everything as he had, and that she knew now that she was his forever.

CHAPTER 8

Sable stood in the middle of a warmly lit large room on the first floor of the main section of the castle. She leaned against one of the thick dark stone columns that supported the vaulted ceiling high above her, her gaze scanning the crowd, keeping an eye on her team as they mingled with the elves and kept their distance from the werewolves and vampires, and the demons too.

Men with trays moved through the crowd, passing drinks to everyone. She had refused all of them, fearing even a sip of the same alcohol she had drunk at the feast. People were already talking about her. Evan had reported to her after leading the training session and he had made it painfully clear that her team doubted her abilities and her reason for being here, and they weren't the only ones.

When she had first entered the gathering, she had skirted the edge of the crowd and had overheard both the werewolves and vampires discussing 'Thorne's little mortal' and that she wouldn't remain mortal for long if the big demon king had his way.

A way he would apparently get if the bets she had heard the demons placing were anything to go by. None had bet that their king would end up alone. All had bet on him claiming her within a timeframe between the next three hours and ten days.

Apparently, she was a dead cert.

She rubbed her wrist and let her gaze roam the crowd again. Besides the mortals and the elves, there wasn't much socialising happening between species. The vampires kept to the corner to her right, near the arched doorways that led onto a balcony. The werewolves remained firmly at the opposite side of the room, behind her.

The demons milled around the room, most of them following the slutty court females.

Sable looked over her left shoulder when familiar voices rose above the din and smiled at Olivia. Her friend looked beautiful in another long elven dress, this time in sky blue, with her chestnut hair twirled and pinned at the back of her head. Her flushed cheeks told Sable that Loren had got his afternoon delight after all. Sable had sort of had a little of her own in one hell of a hot dream and was having trouble shoving it out of her mind.

It had been hotter than any she'd had of Thorne before and she had awoken trembling and aching in a good way, her bones liquid and body sated, as if she had experienced everything for real. She hoped Olivia didn't ask her anything probing about Thorne tonight because she wouldn't be able to keep the blush from her cheeks and her friend would instantly know that she had been making out with the demon king either in her dreams or reality.

Loren walked beside Olivia, dressed in a mid-thigh-length elegant black jacket with sky blue embroidery and knee-high boots over his tight black trousers. They suited each other perfectly, a couple who looked as if they were made to rule the world together.

Sable pushed away from the column and tucked her long black hair behind her ears. She had opted to keep away from posh dresses tonight and had chosen to wear her favourite black leather trousers and a dark blue t-shirt with silver scroll wings on the back.

Bleu stepped out from behind Loren and Sable's palms sweated as she clenched her hands.

He approached her, his step unfaltering, each stride shifting the tails of his long black jacket but his boots silent on the stone floor. He stopped barely inches from her, close enough that she had to tilt her head right back to meet his purple gaze. His black eyebrows pinched together and then his expression softened, his eyes losing their hard edge.

"I have been rude," he whispered and she shook her head and tried to stifle the turbulent emotions that swirled through her. "I have… and I am sorry if I upset you. It was wrong of me… pathetic."

He lifted his hand as if to touch her cheek, flexed his fingers and lowered it back to his side.

His gaze darkened.

"Bleu," she said before he could speak and ruin the moment by voicing what she could see in his eyes. She couldn't change his feelings or his determination to have her, but that didn't mean she had to let him put them out there, because then he would expect a response. She couldn't respond in the way he would want her to and he would leave again, turning cold towards her and twisting the knife in her heart. She sucked at diplomacy but she was a fast learner. "I'm glad you decided to speak to me again."

He nodded and opened his mouth, and then closed it again. The action reminded her of Thorne and she realised she hadn't asked him about that night in Archangel's cafeteria yet and that she still wanted to know what he had meant to say.

Bleu's hand brushed hers and she tensed, her gaze leaping up to his.

A familiar burn went through her, the shivery ache setting her nerve endings alight. She withdrew her hand from Bleu's and turned to look across at the main entrance. Thorne strode in and her heart beat harder, her dream rising unbidden into her mind again and quickening her pulse, heating her blood.

That heat rose onto her cheeks as he stared at her and she remembered what Loren had told her.

Mates shared dreams if they were sleeping at the same time.

The hunger tinted with satisfaction in Thorne's dark crimson eyes and the way his lips curled into a wicked smile as his gaze slowly drifted over her, burning her with its intensity, said that she hadn't been the only one to see that hot vision of them together.

Was that the reason it had felt different this time? Had he been there with her, experiencing everything that she had?

Would he be so rough and delicious in reality? She shoved that thought away before it could plant roots and grow, demanding she take the risk and find out for herself.

His eyes shifted to Bleu and brightened, a corona of fire emerging around his irises. His pupils narrowed and his eyebrows knitted into a hard scowl. He flashed his fangs at Bleu. Bleu bared his own in response, the pointed tips of his ears growing as they flared back against the sides of his head.

Sable stepped into Thorne's line of sight and he huffed, his nostrils flaring, and said something in the demon language to Fargus. The male nodded and walked on ahead, and Sable rubbed her wrist as he glanced at her as he passed.

Thorne slowed and her heart beat harder, anticipation setting her on edge. He didn't stop. He raked his gaze over her again, possessing every inch of her until she ached to feel his hands on her body, and then moved on, heading towards the vampires.

Sable exhaled the breath she had been holding, her shoulders sagging with it.

Bleu muttered something in his own language and Loren responded, a sharp edge to his tone that matched the warning in his expression.

Olivia looked as if she wasn't sure what to say. She fidgeted with the silver metalwork corset over her dress.

Sable did her best to pretend that things weren't about to go south again and stepped back so she could see both Bleu and Loren, and could sneak a glance at Thorne.

He stood with the vampire leader, deep in conversation. He ran his fingers over his left horn, the action causing his white shirt to stretch tight over his biceps, and then lowered his hand. Sable itched to stroke his horns as she had in her dreams, steering him with them, forcing him to kiss her. He had liked it. No. He had *loved* it. He liked her wicked and she loved him rough.

She quickly looked away when his gaze sought her.

"So… give me intel," she said to Loren and the tall beautiful male rolled his eyes in the same way he always did whenever she tried to wheedle information out of him.

He viewed her as a nuisance but Olivia had told her to ignore it because he secretly liked feeding her snippets about his world, breadcrumbs that always had her on her tiptoes and eager to hear more. He would never dish up anything vital, but she lived in hope that one day he would slip up and tell her something major.

Besides, Loren always seemed clued up about all of the species. She supposed it was because of his position. Bleu was the same, but he was even more tight-lipped than Loren. Even her sweetest smile and best attempt had ended with Bleu telling her that he wasn't at liberty to discuss such matters. Looking back now, she thought he should have been more eager to give up some information. She was sure a man who was serious about pursuing her should have been willing to do anything to get into her good book.

Maybe he wasn't as serious about her as she thought.

Olivia had said that Bleu had the hots for her. Was he looking for a short-term deal, the sort of dalliance she used to indulge in herself?

Loren spoke, chasing away her thoughts. "You seem uneasy."

Sable looked at Olivia, catching the wary look she cast at the vampires across the room. Sable couldn't blame her for being twitchy around the vampires, not after everything her friend had been through because of that species. Loren slipped his hand into Olivia's and clasped it, and her friend lifted her eyes to meet his, a grateful warmth colouring their dark depths.

A prickle ran down her spine and she looked around, trying to find the reason her gift had thrown another warning through her. No less than six men had their eyes on her, a mixture of demons, werewolves and vampires. It was impossible to tell who was the source of danger her gift had detected.

Her eyes locked on the werewolves and the handsome man staring her way.

He appeared around her age, in his mid-thirties, but looks were deceiving with most of the non-human species. Archangel had studied werewolves, trying to determine their true age based on their appearance, but had yet to complete the data. Werewolves, like most shifter species, were reclusive, rarely making themselves known by stepping out of line amongst humans or socialising outside of their packs. On top of that, they were notoriously difficult to catch when hunters did run into a rogue one.

If she had to guess based on the data they did have, she would place the man somewhere between two hundred and three hundred years old. He was much younger than his closest companion and far older than his appearance.

The rough older man beside him appeared closer to mid-forty, his golden-brown eyes flashing with warmth and laughter curving his lips as he spoke to another male.

The two vaguely resembled each other, sharing the same rich brown hair streaked with gold, but the younger male's piercing blue eyes set them apart. Were they related?

The older male was a good two inches shorter too but he was broader, with a dusting of dark chest hair visible between the undone buttons at the top of his black shirt and stubble coating his jaw. He also looked as if he had lived through countless more fights too. Someone had busted his nose, leaving a kink in it.

The younger male continued to stare at her, scrutinising her in a way she didn't like, and hooked his thumbs into the pockets of his black jeans. The action caused his muscles to flex beneath his tight khaki t-shirt. Some of the female hunters close to her twittered in response to the sight. Sable merely looked away.

She glanced back again when a feral snarl erupted and a booming male voice followed it.

"Calm, Kyal."

The older male had hold of the younger one's arm, pulling him back. A blond male flashed fangs at the werewolves, his dark-haired companion backing him up. Sable held her breath. Thorne had certainly gathered himself a motley crew and she felt certain it was about to backfire on him.

The werewolf, Kyal, jerked his arm out of the older male's grip and stood his ground, every honed muscle tensed in preparation and his gaze pinned on the blond vampire. He bared his own fangs on a low growl.

Claimed by a Demon King

The older werewolf snapped, "Enough."

He stepped around Kyal, shoved him back towards the group of werewolves and turned on the vampires, snarling at them and revealing his fangs.

The vampires backed off and turned away, moving into the crowd.

"They will not dare to fight. The demons will quell any scuffles that may break out and Thorne will not tolerate them. Any who fight will end up in the dungeon."

Loren's announcement didn't reassure her or make her feel any less on edge around them. It seemed a war might erupt in the castle at any given moment rather than outside in Thorne's kingdom. She had heard about the 'scuffle' last night and how bloody it had been, ending with several men taken to the infirmary.

"It was a tragedy what happened to his sister's family," a man whispered as he passed and she frowned, turning her head to follow him.

Whose family?

The two men looked over towards the werewolves. Her gift said they were both of that species too. Talking about one of their kind behind their back?

Sable shifted closer, curious now and wanting to know who they were talking about.

The other male sipped his drink. "I heard she lost her entire family because of a pack feud."

The first male shook his head, causing his loose black locks to curl around his forehead. "I heard it was because her mate's cousin wanted her for himself."

A third, older male shoved the first one in the back of his head, startling him. "It's all just speculation. No one will ever know the truth. It's buried too deep now... centuries of conspiracies and theories covering everything up. The never caught the culprit... Kincaid searched for decades but turned up nothing. They say he gave up when Kyal was born and his mother died, and he needed to look after the boy."

Kincaid? Was that the older male's name? Both of them had been present in the meeting today but she hadn't learned anything about them.

He was Kyal's father, even though they looked barely ten years apart in age.

A dark-haired female with bright green eyes stopped beside the group of three males and whispered, "I heard that every cub was killed before her eyes and that she has never met Kyal because she can't bear to see him after everything she lost."

She shuddered and the older male wrapped his arms around her, drawing her close to him. He pressed a kiss to her hair. "It would never happen to our cubs. I swear it."

His words didn't seem to comfort his mate. She burrowed deeper into his embrace and Sable dragged her gaze away, wanting to give the female some privacy and unable to imagine what she must be feeling. She had never wanted kids herself, and had never intended to have a family. She couldn't imagine having a mate, let alone bringing children into her dangerous world.

Some of the court whores passing by ran their gazes over Kyal and called to him, flashing flesh his way and telling him that they couldn't wait to see him fight.

Sable glared at them and hated the whispered words that ran around her mind whenever she saw them. Had Thorne used these females as the other males were? She had witnessed several demons and some males of the other species sampling their wares and luring them away to dark corners where they thought no one would notice them.

Had Thorne done such things with them?

She shoved that thought away, her stomach turning, and focused on Kyal.

He was handsome and looked the part as he winked at the whores, throwing them a sexy grin, but there was something off about him. He might look good and honest, but she could feel the darkness within him, and it was as strong as the darkness within the vampire everyone liked to mutter about too.

Lord Van der Garde.

Her stalker.

She had caught him watching her several times tonight already. He never looked away either. He just raised his glass at her and then sipped the contents, leaving his lips bloodstained.

She palmed the blade strapped to her thigh whenever he did that, smiling at him, hoping he could see her every thought as she imagined using it to dissect him.

Apparently, he had a nickname, although everyone who had used it had whispered it, as if fearing he would hear them.

King of Death.

Sable had wanted to walk up to the vampire and ask about that, but her preservation instincts ran as deep as her marrow and she didn't fancy losing her head to his claws.

"Kincaid is Kyal's dad?" Sable said to Loren and he nodded.

"Kincaid is a respected leader of the werewolves. This is Kyal's first battle. The werewolves will hold a ceremony for him before his first fight… as a rite of passage."

"Like walking on hot coals or something?"

Loren shook his head. "He will be expected to best the ten finest werewolf warriors, sinking his fangs into their napes before they can sink theirs into his."

It sounded brutal, and stupid. "So they plan to injure their ten best fighters and possibly Kyal too just before a battle?"

Bleu nodded. Sable rolled her eyes.

"Are all traditions in your world as stupid as the ones I've been hearing over the past day?" Before Loren could respond, she jerked her chin towards the vampires. Thorne had moved away. Where had he gone? She refused to look for him. He wasn't looking at her, that was for sure. "So, what's his deal? Mr King of Death."

Loren frowned now. "He is grave."

Sable muttered, "He does seem a little grim and serious."

Loren shook his head again. "No, you misunderstand. His name is Grave. Grave Van der Garde."

Sable couldn't believe that and she couldn't stop the laugh that bubbled up her throat. She stared at the brunet vampire and he looked her way, a corona of red around his pale blue irises. Sable darted her gaze back to Loren.

"He's really called Grave?" It was too funny to be true. Loren had to have somehow grown a sense of humour.

Loren nodded, his expression deadly serious. She looked at Bleu, wanting to make sure she wasn't having the wool pulled over her eyes by his prince.

Bleu's gaze met hers.

A low growl curled over the crowd and Sable's gaze leaped straight to Thorne, as if she had instinctively known where he was all along. His eyes locked with hers, dark and commanding, and a blush crept onto her cheeks. She tore her gaze away and cursed herself for reacting to him, giving him what he wanted—her attention on him and him alone.

"He has a brother with an equally unfortunate name," Bleu said, his tone dark now and menacing, laced with the anger he radiated.

She didn't want to incite anything between him and Thorne, but she didn't want to ruin their tentative friendship by ignoring him and didn't want Thorne to think he could control her either. She bravely looked up at him.

"A worse name than Grave?"

He nodded and Loren did the same.

Oh, it only got better. No wonder the vampire had a problem with the world and everyone in it. She turned to Loren. "Lay it on me, Big Guy."

"His younger brother is called Night... although he does have an older brother called Bastian."

Olivia stifled a laugh.

Sable giggled. "Did his parents lose a bet? Grave and Night? Seriously... what were his parents on?"

Loren's expression remained grim. She glanced at Bleu and he didn't look amused either.

"Do not mention his name or show your amusement, Sable," Bleu said and she sobered immediately. He had never sounded so serious before. "He is a male afflicted with bloodlust... a terrible rage and thirst for violence and death. Do not forget that."

Sable swallowed hard and nodded. She felt so safe around Loren and Bleu, and Thorne, that it was easy to forget that the other men were dangerous and powerful, and taunting them might be the last thing she did.

She glanced at Grave.

A hot shiver tripped through her, ratcheting up her temperature again, making her burn so fiercely that she longed to step out onto the balcony and catch some air. Thorne.

Her gaze sought and found him with Fargus. He said something to his commander, nodded and walked away, heading for the arched doors onto the balcony.

He looked troubled again.

Sable's feet were moving before she even considered what she was doing.

She couldn't ignore her compulsion. She had to go to him.

She couldn't let him bear the weight of his thoughts alone.

CHAPTER 9

Thorne wasn't sure how much more he could take. Sable had looked at twenty-three other males so far in this gathering alone and had looked at some of them several times. Her golden eyes had settled on the young werewolf, Kyal, eight times, and on Kincaid at least four times. She had looked at Lord Van der Garde more times than those two males combined.

Not to mention how many times she had looked at or spoken with Bleu.

He despised that male and cursed his name, choosing the vilest one available.

It was growing impossible to keep his cool and he had sworn to himself that this evening would pass without incident. It had started off well. With a single look into Sable's eyes, he had seen that she had dreamed as he had, sharing the vision of them making love. He had wanted to go to her, to draw her into his arms and kiss her as he had in that dream, but he'd had business to attend to with the vampires.

He had meant to go to her immediately after he had finished speaking with the vampire commander, but had ended up remaining at a distance, observing how she interacted with her friends and how her gaze would roam the room, bright with curiosity. It was the fact that it only held curiosity that had spared every male she had looked at. Had she shown any hint of desire, of interest, he would have slaughtered them.

Her gaze drifted back to Grave and he growled under his breath, gaining a concerned glance from Fargus.

He was beginning to consider killing Grave and it was hard to ignore that pressing desire. Bleu first. Then Grave. And then every other male she had gazed upon this eve.

No. He clenched his fists at his sides and growled again. He needed these men. He needed every single person in this room with him in battle. He couldn't risk driving any away, especially those in command.

The instinct to claim and protect his fated one was fierce though and he wasn't sure how much longer he could deny the dark urges that claimed him whenever Sable looked at another male.

He had paced his room before coming to attend the gathering, thinking over everything he had seen in his dream of Sable and had learned about her from Loren. He was still none the wiser about how to woo her. He only had his memories of his father and mother to go on when it came to love, and a smattering of information from some of his mated warriors.

His chest ached as his thoughts returned to his mother. He had fond memories of her, ones that had only grown stronger in their centuries apart and had comforted him during the darkest times of his life. She had raised him while his father had tended to the kingdom and she had indulged him. When he had matured, she had been the one to keep his hopes strong, speaking of his fated one and encouraging him to search for her and to never give up.

She had told him that her beautiful son would have the most beautiful eternal mate the demon world had ever seen and that she would be everything he desired and all he deserved.

Thorne watched Sable speaking with Loren, studying her pale beauty and the inner strength that always shone through, keeping her back straight and head held high even when nerves flickered in the depths of her golden eyes.

His mother had been right.

Sable was the most beautiful female he had ever beheld.

She was strong, clever, amusing and caring—everything he desired and so much more.

He took a mug of grog from a passing servant and turned it in his hands. He wished his mother could have met her. She would have loved Sable. His father would have been proud.

Thorne sipped the drink, savouring the warmth it spread through him, and closed his eyes, losing himself in his thoughts.

He spoke of Sable to his parents whenever he visited their temple to bring them offerings and ease his mind. He told them much in those quiet times, lightening the burden on his heart and his shoulders, sure they were listening and offering him the comfort and strength he needed.

Thorne opened his eyes, needing the comfort that washed over him whenever he looked at Sable. He growled at the sight of her gazing at Bleu again.

"How long have you known?" Fargus said in their language and Thorne flicked him a glance.

"Known what?" Thorne knew what the male was asking and he didn't want to talk about it.

Fargus sipped his own drink, a glimmer of nerves entering his dark eyes, and then cleared his throat. "The mortal appears to be your fated one."

Thorne told himself not to answer. If he told Fargus of his worries, the male would try to find a way of fixing them, and Thorne didn't think his friend's methods of wooing would secure him Sable.

His heart had a different idea to his head and he said, "Since I met her in the mortal world one cycle of the moon ago."

Recognition dawned in Fargus's deep crimson eyes. "She was present in the demon-hunter's building when you met with Prince Loren after we had spoken with the magic bearer. Now that you mention it, I recall seeing her before you sent us away."

When he had returned to the Third Realm, Fargus had thoroughly berated him for sending him and his two other commanders away, leaving him vulnerable to the hunters and the elves. He had done what was necessary to gain Loren's trust and didn't regret his actions, and not only because he had been able to spend time with Sable.

Thorne growled when she looked at Bleu again and her gaze leaped to him. Colour climbed her cheeks and she quickly looked away.

He did not understand her. He had tried to learn the intricacies of courtship, but still knew little of what she expected or how to gain her affection, or whether he was even supposed to care about her affection and expectations.

Was he just supposed to claim her?

It was the way of most of his kind. When they found their eternal mate, they would attempt to secure her love, would quickly grow bored of trying and would simply claim her. His father had done such a thing to his mother and they had turned out well. He had never seen another pair of mates who were as loving and affectionate as they had been.

Thorne shoved aside thoughts of claiming Sable against her will. She might like it when he was rough and commanding with her, but she would hate him if he imposed a claim upon her, making her immortal without her consent.

"The female is aware that she belongs to you?" Fargus said, cutting back into his thoughts.

"She is not... or perhaps she is. I told her that she was mine." And he had kissed her, and then she had slapped him and threatened to leave. All in all, that encounter had not been a success.

"You have not stated your intention to claim her, and you allow unmated males to speak and show attention to her. Do you not want to claim the female?"

Thorne's lips peeled back on a snarl. What he wanted to do was remove Fargus's head from his body. How dare he berate him about this? He pulled the reins on his temper before it slipped beyond his control and he ended up doing something he would regret. Fargus only meant to help him with his problem.

"I wish it more than anything, but I am… she is… difficult. I do not think a normal courtship would work on her."

Mostly because a normal courtship often ended with the demon male imposing a claim and bond upon their female, binding them in restraints if necessary and doing it by force. If he did that, Sable would seek his head and he would gladly give it to her, unable to deny her anything.

Her gaze went back to Lord Van der Garde.

Thorne's temper frayed and the tethers holding his anger at bay snapped.

"I need air," Thorne said and was crossing the room towards the doors to the balcony before he did something stupid, fighting his urge to divert his course and head towards the vampire instead.

He had warned everyone that he wouldn't tolerate violence amongst the species and Grave was the commander of over one hundred men. Men that Thorne needed. If he attacked the vampire, he would leave and his men would go with him.

Thorne strode through the arched doorway and onto the wide balcony that ran the length of the room. Cooler air wrapped comforting arms around him and he breathed deep of it, seeking calm. He kept his back to the room to stave off the temptation to watch Sable and leaned his forearms on the stone balustrade, staring off into the dark distance beyond the high, wide walls of his castle and the silhouetted trees there.

He needed a moment alone, away from the other males and seeing her gaze upon them.

Each of her curious glances and lingering stares flickered through his mind, wearing his mood down and stealing his focus until the distance turned hazy and he lost awareness of the world around him.

"Is it always this dark in your land?"

Thorne's gaze shot to his left and widened.

Sable leaned there, her eyes flitting over the landscape and then the grounds below them.

He stared at her, certain that he was dreaming and that she hadn't really left the room to be here with him, alone in the dark.

The urge to gather her into his arms and kiss her came over him, stronger than ever, commanding him to obey. He could see it all playing out in his mind. He would draw her into his embrace, until she nestled against his chest, her palms pressing into his pectorals and burning him through his shirt. She would tip her head back and her lips would part, inviting him to dip towards her and claim them as his own. He would kiss her then, and wouldn't stop until she felt the same pressing and fierce need as he did. The same burning desire.

It wouldn't end well.

Would attempting to kiss her only result in her leaving?

He didn't want her to leave. He wanted her to stay and he wanted to kiss her, and he couldn't see why he couldn't have both things. She desired him. She had kissed him back in the hallway outside his quarters. She had only pushed him away and slapped him when his fangs had emerged and he had held her tighter. Perhaps he had frightened her and made her feel she wasn't the one in control.

If he kissed her softly and let her take the lead, would she kiss him again or push him away?

A touch of colour stained her cheeks. "If you keep staring at me in silence, I'm going to go back inside."

"It is always dark," Thorne rushed out, unwilling to let her carry out that threat.

She curled her lip and he had the impression that she didn't like his realm.

Thorne looked at it, trying to see it through her eyes. It was gloomy, made of rough blackened rock and soil that could support plant life, but nothing as colourful as that in her world.

"It is not so dark in the day," he said and her gaze came back to him, burning into the side of his face, making him yearn to look at her. He kept his eyes on his lands instead, letting her drink her fill of him. Did she think him handsome? Or as dark and grim as his realm? "We depend upon the elves for much of our grains, but we have improved the soil in many districts of the realm, enough to grow vegetables for the females."

He pointed towards the jagged treetops beyond the castle walls.

"There are many forests in the land, rich with green pines and animals. I saw flowers growing there once."

"Flowers in Hell?" She sounded curious.

He risked a glance at her and she looked it too, her eyes brighter than he had ever seen them.

He nodded. "This world is not as bright or colourful as yours, Sable, but there is life here and I have taken great pains to improve this realm for my people."

She looked off into the distance again and he didn't think she could see the lengths he had gone to in order to make this realm a good place for everyone who lived in it. She knew only her world, the elf kingdom and this realm, and his was meagre and grim in comparison to those bountiful lands.

It pained him.

How was he meant to win the heart of a female who looked upon his land with disgust?

"Don't you miss the sun?" she said.

Thorne shook his head and cast his gaze up at the darkness above. "You cannot miss what you do not really know."

He didn't wholly believe that. There were things that he didn't know but that he felt he missed in his life.

Female companionship.

Love.

Sable.

She glanced at him again and then looked at the lands below.

"You cannot see them in the darkness of night, but there are farms and the forest over yonder." He bit his tongue, remembering how she had mocked him when he had last used the word 'yonder', making him feel old for the first time in his long life.

He picked at the balustrade with his claws, trying to think of something he could say to make her think better of his land and of him.

Nothing came to him.

Sable didn't seem to know what to say either. She toyed with a bandage around her wrist and how had he not noticed it before? He frowned at it and reached towards her, and she stilled when he gently placed his hand under hers and lifted it.

"Did you hurt yourself?" He stroked the length of the bandage with his other hand and she shook her head, her eyes locked on his face. He raised his to meet them. They were round and beautiful, beguiling. A male could lose himself in them and never want to come back.

"Just a knock," she said but didn't seem sure.

She took her arm from him and rubbed her wrist. It wasn't the first time she had done that.

Silence fell over them again as he stared at her, the conversation dying as he struggled to find something else to say. If he spoke of his victories, would it impress her? If he asked about hers, would it please her?

She walked the fingers of her left hand along the balustrade towards him, her gaze locked on them, intent and focused. When they reached his right hand where it rested on the stone, she didn't stop. She walked her fingers over the back of it and lingered.

Thorne's heart beat harder and he burned where she touched him. He couldn't take it. It was too much. She was asking too much of him, expecting him to keep control while she touched him. He wanted to touch her too.

She sighed, took her hand away, and glanced at him. Her eyes fell back to the balustrade and the courtyard below, and he cursed himself for remaining quiet for so long. Now the silence was so thick and choking that he couldn't find his voice to break it.

Sable looked as tense as he felt and only seemed to be growing more anxious.

He opened his mouth to speak.

She whirled to face him, the swift action startling him.

"Something has been bugging me and I need to know… what had you wanted to say at the cafeteria?"

Thorne frowned. "Cafeteria?"

She sucked down a sharp breath and nodded. "After we had defeated the bitch-witch and you teleported us all back to Archangel… and you…"

She looked down at her arm and he recalled the moment she spoke of, could feel the heat of her skin on his palm just as he had that night when he had held her arm.

She raised her gaze back to his. "What had you wanted to say?"

Thorne looked over her head towards the distance, gazing out at the shadowy land.

He was a king. He was a male.

She was his female.

His fated one.

He would speak the words without hesitation or fear.

He was a king. A male. Her male.

Thorne lowered his gaze to her and looked deep into her eyes.

"I meant to ask you to come with me to my kingdom, and now you are here."

A touch of colour darkened her cheeks but she didn't look away. She bravely held his gaze and whispered, "I am."

Thorne wanted to ask her whether she would have consented had he asked her back then, but his nerve failed. Silence fell over them again, growing thicker by the second.

Sable swallowed audibly and moved a step closer to him, gaining all of his attention. He could feel her heat and with it came the desire to touch her again, to possess her beautiful curves and draw her into his embrace.

"I heard something funny… do you want to hear it?" she said and he nodded, pleased that she desired to share something with him and taking it as a positive sign. She sidled even closer and he bit back a groan as her thigh brushed his. She whispered, "There's a vampire called Grave and he has a brother called Night!"

Thorne did not find that or her carelessness amusing. "It is no laughing matter, Little Female. It would be unwise to make a joke of this male. He is liable to kill you."

"You sound like Loren," she muttered in a disappointed tone, her expression sobering, and then added, "The vampire has no sense of humour?"

Thorne shook his head. "None."

Sable shrugged, shifting her long black hair with it. "Anyone with that name should have developed a sense of humour about it. It's a stupid name."

"And what name would that be?" The deep male voice came from Thorne's left and Sable tensed.

Thorne casually turned to face Grave. "Bleu… the elf commander. What manliness is there to be found in such a weak, feminine name?"

Grave flashed partially extended fangs in a grin. "What indeed? A weak name. A strong female requires a strong name also… who might this be?"

"Mine." Thorne growled and stepped in front of Sable, shielding her from Grave's inquisitive gaze.

"Now, now. I was only making pleasant conversation, my king."

Thorne didn't like the sarcastic edge to his voice. Did he really need the vampires? He wanted to crush Grave's head in his hands and it might just be worth it.

Sable stepped out from behind him. "I don't recall being anyone's possession. My name is Sable, huntress of Archangel, slayer of vampires."

Grave tossed her a toothy smile and Thorne itched to punch him until he had no fangs to flash at his female.

"Only because you have never met a pureblood. Still, your confidence is amusing, and you certainly seem to have a way of bringing males to their knees. Perhaps you would like to test your talents on one of my men? Perhaps me? I would gladly tussle with you, Little Mortal."

Thorne growled low in his throat, his top lip peeling back off his emerging fangs. His horns curled and his muscles expanded, his rage burning through his restraint and seizing control of him.

"The female is not here to fight vampires and she falls under my protection. If you or any of your men attempt to harm her or goad her into a fight, I will personally see to it that you all die." Thorne took a step towards the vampire and rose to his full height, towering over the slender male.

Grave's smile didn't falter and he held his gaze in a calm, cold manner. Thorne didn't back down and hoped that Sable held her tongue and didn't choose this moment to throw one of her usual barbs at her enemy.

She surprised him by remaining silent and edging closer to him. Had she sensed what he could?

Grave might appear calm, but the darkness within him was rising to the fore, his terrible bloodlust slowly seizing control of him. One wrong move or word on his or Sable's part and Grave would lose his head to it, becoming a wild beast with only violence and blood on his mind.

The vampire's pupils stretched, beginning to turn elliptical, and crimson flooded his irises.

Grave tipped his chin up. "Remember, Third King, that it is better to have me on your side than as your enemy. No female is worth your kingdom. They are treacherous creatures. You think you stand on solid ground… think again."

Another male vampire emerged from the room behind Grave. "Sir, the demon commander requests your presence."

Grave held Thorne's gaze and seconds ticked by, the silence strained and more oppressive than it had ever been between Thorne and Sable. She remained tucked behind him, her heart pounding in his ears and her nerves flowing over him.

The vampire commander turned away and stalked towards the arched doorway.

Sable launched past Thorne, her blade in her hand. He grabbed her wrist and yanked her back. She growled at him and struggled to break free of his grip. He tightened it, trying not to hurt her but unwilling to let her escape and carry out her foolish plan.

He easily prised the blade from her hand. "The same goes for you, Sable. You are not to engage the vampires. You are here to perform a duty and it is best you remember that."

Sable scowled at him, darkness more formidable than Grave's bloodlust entering her eyes. She snatched the blade back and jammed it into the sheath on her thigh.

"He started it. He's been winding me up ever since he got here and I'm not having a bloodsucker saying crap about me like that!"

Thorne could understand her anger. He wanted to rearrange the vampire's face as payment for his comment about Sable being treacherous. He also knew better than to go through with it. The vampire was right and it was better to have him as an ally than as an enemy.

He looked over at the doors in time to see the other vampire enter and frowned, sure that the vampire had disappeared. No pureblood vampire possessed the ability to teleport though. It must have been a trick of the light on his sensitive eyes as they had adjusted to the sudden brightness.

He returned his attention to Sable and loosened his hold on her wrist. She didn't stop him when he stroked his thumb over the bandage around it.

He sighed down into her eyes. "Little Female, you are too eager to fight… too easy to provoke. You forget why you are here and why he is here. My kingdom depends upon the presence of both of your parties and any who break the peace in my home will find themselves in the cells. Do you understand?"

She blinked, shuttering her beautiful golden eyes, and he detected a glimmer of her fear. He didn't want to be hard on her but it was necessary. Grave was right, and not just about his need to have him as an ally.

This was about his kingdom, not him. It was about his people, both those in his army and those living in his realm.

Thorne continued to caress the inside of her wrist, surprised that she wasn't pushing him away.

She shocked him further when she spoke.

"I'm sorry. I'll remember that I'm here on a mission," the cold edge that entered her eyes chilled him to the bone and he growled when she twisted her wrist free of his grip, "not for pleasure."

Thorne reached for her but she was already walking away, heading back inside. He curled his fingers into fists, tightening them until his claws dug into his palm and he smelled blood. He hadn't meant to drive her away with his warning or make her behave coldly towards him.

He didn't understand why she'd had to draw that line between them again when it had begun to blur.

He heaved a sigh and raised his gaze to the black sky, silently asking his mother for guidance. Was he destined to mess everything up and lose his mate? Whenever she moved a step closer to him, he ended up doing something that made her move a further two steps away.

"The mortal female has spirit."

Thorne lowered his eyes to the werewolf male. Kincaid had brought his cub with him and the amused glimmer in the younger male's eyes said that they had witnessed Sable in all her confusing glory.

Thorne muttered, "Too much spirit."

Kincaid offered a consolatory smile and clapped Kyal on the back, causing the younger male to jerk forwards. "The young lad hasn't a clue what perils await him in the world."

Kyal grinned. "I've been out in the world."

Kincaid turned a frown on him. "When?"

The younger male's smile grew wider. "When, indeed."

Thorne didn't want to hear the young wolf speaking of his conquests when he had none to his name. A whelp less than a tenth of his age had more experience with females than he did. Kincaid and the others would laugh if they knew.

"It is good to meet your young cub at last, Kincaid, and to see you again. It has been many years and you wear them well." Thorne clasped the male's hand and shook it, and Kincaid covered it with his other one, tangling them together. "I fear the vampires will drive me mad."

Kyal glared at him and Thorne could sense his displeasure. He didn't like being referred to as young or a cub, even though that was what he would remain until he had been tested in battle and had gone through the rites. Thorne shifted his gaze to him and the male backed down, averting his eyes and exhaling a sigh.

Kincaid cracked a smile. "That they will. Remember the last war... we were against them that time. Those were the days."

Thorne nodded and smiled with ease as he recalled going into battle with Kincaid at his side, a cub no older than Kyal and wet behind the ears.

"I remember having to yank on your scruff to save your hide, and more than once too."

Kincaid laughed and Kyal's blue eyes lit up with interest, and Thorne was glad for their company and the distraction from his thoughts.

His gaze wandered back to the doors as he told Kyal of Kincaid's victories and failures in the last battle they had fought together.

If he couldn't win Sable over in reality, he would have to try something else.

He would show her they belonged together but would do so in a place where she felt safe and in control.

He would win her heart in their dreams.

CHAPTER 10

Sable whirled in the wet alley to face one of the three male vampires, her blade a silver arc in the darkness. It sliced through his throat and crimson flowed down his chest from the yawning cut. She quickly spun to face the remaining two and palmed the hilt of the short blade, preparing herself. She had already caught them with her throwing knives, embedding two in each thigh to slow them down, and had shot one with a specialty toxic dart.

That one was fading fast, his eyes losing focus by the second. She would take him down first, leaving only one.

Her heart pounded, adrenaline thundering through her veins. She cried out and launched herself at the poisoned vampire. He swiped at her with his claws and she ducked, skidding under his arm, and came up behind him. She swung her arm backwards, slamming the blade to its guard in his side, and then tugged it out, spun on her heel and brought it down again, clutching it in both hands.

The blade slipped between two vertebrae on his upper back and she twisted it. He unleashed an agonised roar and dropped to the ground.

The final remaining vampire moved so quickly she couldn't track him. He was behind her in an instant and she turned as fast as she could, bringing her arm up to block the attack she could sense coming.

He was too fast.

He sank his fangs into her throat before she could get her arm across his neck and she shrieked as he pulled hard on her blood and she could feel it all rushing through her veins towards him.

No.

Sable kicked and flailed and the male laughed as he released her.

Her knees gave out, hitting the wet tarmac hard enough to jar her spine, and she slapped a hand over the wound as she stared up in horror at the brunet towering over her, looming in the shadows.

The King of Death.

His crimson eyes held hers, their elliptical pupils stretched thin and irises practically glowing in the darkness. The shadows clung to him like a lover, wrapping around him and turning his pale skin stark in contrast.

The corner of his bloodstained lips tilted into a smile.

Tears stung Sable's eyes and she bit her tongue to stop herself from begging for her life.

"Pathetic mortal," Grave spat at her and grinned to reveal his fangs. "I said you could not win against me."

Sable's heart pounded and missed a beat. Blood pumped from between her fingers, streaming down her chest.

He edged a step closer and she shook her head.

"And I warned you to keep away from her." A deep voice boomed around the alley and Sable's heart missed a beat for a different reason.

Strong hands grasped the sides of Grave's head from behind and twisted it at a grotesque angle. The vampire's expression froze in one of horror. Her saviour released him and he dropped to the ground.

Sable knelt on the wet pavement, staring up as the shadows parted to reveal the most beautiful sight she had ever beheld.

Thorne.

He towered above her, immense and dangerous, his horns curled around and flaring forwards like a ram's and his leathery dragon-like wings furled against his bare back.

"Sable," he whispered and held his hand out to her. She slipped hers into it without hesitation and he gently pulled her onto her feet and into his arms.

Sable didn't have the strength to fight him. She nestled against his bare chest, using all of her strength to battle the flood of tears that threatened to burst the dam holding them back, and kept her other hand over the ragged wound on her throat.

Thorne pressed a kiss to the top of her head and she closed her eyes, shocked by the intensity of the warmth and alien feelings that flowed through her. She felt safe, protected, and loved.

"Let me see," Thorne murmured and slowly drew back.

Sable pulled down a deep breath and peeled her hand away from her throat. Thorne's dark eyebrows drew down above his glowing crimson eyes that held a beautiful look of concern.

He leaned in. "Let me make it better, my sweet."

She didn't stop him. She tilted her face to one side and closed her eyes as he licked the wound. Each careful, tender sweep of his tongue soothed her and chased away the pain radiating from the puncture marks. She mourned the loss of contact when he finally pulled back.

"There. All better." He brushed the backs of his claws across her cheek and she looked up into his eyes.

The pain was gone.

His eyebrows furrowed.

"I would never let such a thing happen to you in reality, Sable. You do not need to fear him."

In reality.

Sable frowned.

She was dreaming, and Thorne had walked into it and saved her. He was dreaming too and was here with her.

He had seen her secret fears and how the vampire haunted her.

Sable took a step back but he didn't let her get further than that. His fingers clamped around her wrist and he pulled her back to him, right against his body. She tipped her head up and found him staring down at her, no trace of anger or irritation in his eyes. They held only the deep heat of desire, the intense look she had come to crave seeing in them.

Whenever he looked at her like that, she felt beautiful and desired. She felt needed.

She felt loved.

And it frightened her.

He wanted something from her that she couldn't give him. He wanted forever.

Would he settle for now?

The sensible side of her said not to do this, not to give into the desire burning through her, the temptation that came from this being just a dream. It wasn't just a dream. It was a vision, something they shared. It was as real as reality. She couldn't keep giving herself to him in this place and expect him to keep his distance in the other.

Yet in this place, he couldn't claim her. She could do whatever she desired in this vision and there would be no physical consequences. No bruises if they were too rough. No bite marks for Olivia to question. No unwanted pregnancies.

No bond.

She could satisfy her desire for Thorne, scratch the persistent itch to have him, and keep things purely physical.

The temptation was too great to resist.

"Thorne," she whispered, looking deep into his eyes.

"I know," he murmured in response, his gaze turning hooded and dropping to her lips. "My female hungers."

She leaped and wrapped her arms around his neck as his hands caught her backside, holding her in place. Her mouth fused with his, a violent coupling that only served to set her on fire rather than satisfy her. She needed more.

Sable locked her legs around his waist and kissed him harder, and groaned as he nipped her lower lip with his fangs. He sucked it into his mouth and moved with her at the same time, slowly walking.

Where?

She groaned as her back hit the brick wall and he pinned her there, his broad muscular body pressing deliciously into hers.

He wanted to do it here, in the alley?

She moaned again, a thrill coursing through her, and she told herself it was just a dream. Not real. Thorne kissed along her jaw and down her throat, devouring it with playful nips and licks that sent fierce achy shivers through her. It certainly felt real.

"Want you naked." Those whispered words sent more than a shiver through her. She burned to give him what he desired and to feel him hard and hot against her, skin-to-skin. She ached to have him sliding deep inside her, filling her up, giving her another hit of bliss.

Sable released him and tried to pull her top up. She hit a snag when he refused to stop kissing her throat.

"Trying to get naked here, Big Guy." She tugged his little left horn to get his attention and he groaned. Her eyes widened as it grew in her hand and he flexed his hips, driving the rock hard bulge in his leathers against the apex of her thighs. "Naked. *Now.*"

Thorne practically dropped her. Sable pulled her top off and was about to tackle her leather trousers when she caught sight of Thorne opening his. She moaned, gaze lost in roaming rope after rope of muscles on his stomach and the delicious curves over his hips that led her eyes downwards to the thick pulsing shaft rising out of a nest of dark curls.

He had stopped her last time. He wouldn't have the chance this time.

Sable wrapped her hand around his length, pulled him to her and dropped to her knees. He went to speak and it came out garbled as she licked the blunt head. He slammed his hands into the wall and brick dust rained down her back.

She looked up and grinned wickedly. He leaned over her, his face screwed up and his fists buried in the wall behind her.

Sable swirled her tongue around the head of his cock and ran her hands over his powerful thighs and he groaned again, his muscles trembling beneath her touch.

"Sable," he whispered, his chest heaving and fangs flashing between his lips.

She closed her eyes and took him into her mouth, and he shuddered, moaning loudly. She smiled and moved her mouth on him, taking him as deep as she could before withdrawing. He groaned with each stroke of her mouth and swirl of her tongue, and muttered something in the demon tongue that she hoped was complimentary when she brought one hand into play, teasing his shaft and his balls. His trembling worsened and his breathing quickened.

"Sable," he implored and his hands claimed her shoulders. "No more."

He pushed her back and stared down into her eyes, his bright crimson in the low light.

"Let me touch you." He caught her arm, pulled her onto her feet, and caged her against the wall with his body. He shifted his hand, wrapping it around one wrist and then the other, and pinned them both above her head.

He had done that in their other shared dream too.

He wanted to be in control.

Or did he like how doing that made her arch against him?

The full length of her body pressed into his and he rubbed his hard shaft against her belly.

"Going to touch you now." He lowered his hand, frowned and growled when his fingers met leather. "Need you naked."

Before she could respond, he had broken the zipper of her leather trousers and had ran a claw along the stitching. He tugged and she gasped as the rest of the stitching gave, and he was lucky this was just a dream and he hadn't just ruined her favourite leather trousers by turning them into a pair of chaps.

He groaned and palmed her mound through her panties and she forgot that she was mad at him about something and gave herself over to sensation instead. His hand was hot on her, pressing, demanding, and it thrilled her. He had been rough in their last dream, battling her for control, his wickedness matching her own. She wanted him like that again.

Sable raised her legs and had them around his waist before he could notice. She locked her feet and yanked him against her, trapping his hand between them. The first flex of her hips tore a groan from his throat and the second had him pulling his hand free and forgetting his desire to touch her.

He ground against her instead, driving the full length of his shaft along her cleft. Sable pressed the back of her head into the wall and rode each thrust, moaning as the head rubbed her sensitive spot.

"Naked," she whispered, urging him into going through with the thought she could see flickering across his eyes.

He growled, ripped her cotton knickers from her, and impaled her in one deep, commanding thrust.

She cried out, the sound echoing around the alley and mingling with Thorne's grunt of bliss.

"Thorne," she moaned and he held her hip with one hand and her wrists with the other, keeping her at his mercy. She rocked on him as much as she could, urging him to let go and give her what she needed from him. Pleasure. Bliss. Ecstasy. A moment of sheer madness. "Your female needs."

He growled and his lips claimed hers in a soul-searing kiss that melted her bones and left her liquid and compliant in his arms. He pumped her hard, stroking every inch of her with his long length, each thrust taking her a little higher.

The brick was rough against her back, adding a touch of pain to her pleasure together with Thorne's tightening grip on her wrists. She moaned with each hard meeting of their hips, her breath mingling with his.

"Sable... Sable... Sable..." he chanted her name like a prayer and she found herself doing the same with his, uttering it each time their bodies met, willing him to keep going. He thrust deeper, possessing all of her, and she arched into him, using her feet to force him to roughen his strokes and take her harder.

She wanted to feel his strength.

She wanted to lose herself in him and never find herself again.

She wanted to become one with him.

Madness, but in this moment, she wanted his fangs in her throat and that ultimate connection to him.

She wanted to know what Olivia had and wanted it for herself, with Thorne.

"Thorne," Sable whispered and it was as if he had sensed her need, as if he was so attuned to her that he knew her thoughts and her feelings, and what she was afraid to ask.

He released her wrists and buried his face against her neck, kissing it hard and teasing her. She didn't want teasing. She wrapped her arms around his head and he clutched her backside, pumping harder with each stroke, adding another hint of pain to the pleasure boiling through her veins.

Just as she thought he didn't know her deepest, darkest desire after all, he sent her shooting into the stratosphere.

His fangs sank hard into her throat, pain blazed a trail across her flesh from the centre of his bite and her blood ignited, detonating the tight ball of heat in her belly.

Sable shrieked and clawed his shoulders as she convulsed against him, every inch of her on fire and tingling, trembling. A full body orgasm that left her boneless and shaking, and left her mind reeling and ears ringing.

Thorne pulled hard on her blood and another explosion rocked her as he climaxed, his length pulsing and hot jets of seed filling her. With each jet and each pull on her blood in time with them, another bomb detonated within her, ripping another cry of ecstasy from her throat. They grew in intensity until she couldn't take any more.

The pleasure overwhelmed her, overloading her senses.

She shuddered with the last one, weak and shaking in Thorne's arms. Her hands slipped down his arms. He was trembling too and breathing hard against her throat.

He whispered something in the demon language and she caught only her name, but whatever he said made the marks on her throat burn and her body come alive again, blistering hot and tingling.

"Look at me," Thorne whispered.

She tried to prise her eyes open to obey that husky command.

It was too much.

Sable slipped into darkness.

And shot up in bed.

She slapped her hand over her throat, breathing hard and fast, her eyes wide and fixed on the wall. It was blurry, her focus turned elsewhere, locked on the level below her and a room there.

A vicious roar shook the floor and she tensed.

Thorne.

She scooted from the bed and ran to the mirror on her dressing table, her heart thundering against her ribs. She dragged her hair aside and her breathing slowed as she danced her fingers over the smooth untouched skin of the left side of her throat.

The relief she had felt faded as a pair of dark red spots bloomed on her skin.

Son of a bitch.

Another roar sounded, louder this time.

Heavy footfalls joined it, growing in pace and volume.

Thorne.

Sable rushed to the door to hold it closed and had her hands on the wooden panels just as it burst open, sending her stumbling into the dressing table. Thorne's crimson gaze swung her way, wild and dangerous, and her heart slammed against her chest. She clutched the table behind her for support and glared at him.

He advanced on her, a picture of menace and determination, a man out to finish what they had started in that dream. His gaze flickered to her throat and he frowned, cocking his head to one side as he halted.

The accusation balanced on the tip of her tongue died as confusion lit his scarlet eyes.

Hadn't he known that he could claim her in their vision?

She touched her neck but felt no marks there.

Sable scrambled for the antique mirror and held it up. The marks were pale and faded into nothing as she stared at them. Why?

She had awoken before Thorne could complete the claim. Was that why the marks had now disappeared?

She didn't feel bonded to him. Not that she knew what it would feel like. Olivia said that she could feel Loren though, and maybe demon bonds were similar. She couldn't feel anything from Thorne other than confusion and a lingering touch of anger, and it was her gift telling her of those emotions.

He reached for her.

The bells tolled.

"What's happening?" Sable looked towards the arched windows lining the other wall to her left. It was pitch black outside. Still night. The bells weren't ringing for a meeting.

Thorne curled his fingers into a fist and snarled, "We are at war."

CHAPTER 11

Sable was angry with Thorne, and not just because he had almost claimed her in their shared dream. She had almost forgiven him for that, convincing herself that he hadn't realised that he could do such a thing and hadn't intended to ensnare her in a bond she didn't want.

No, what had her really angry with him was the fact that the moment she had finished dressing, he had grabbed her and teleported them both to the courtyard. The people already gathered there had drawn their conclusions about her and Thorne the second they had set eyes on them and really, she couldn't exactly be angry with them or argue that it wasn't what they thought.

Not when her hair was all over the place and Thorne was wearing only his leather trousers, and had failed to tie them up.

He tied them now as he barked orders to his men in the demon language. Didn't that look just great?

The vampires and werewolves snickered behind her. The demons looked ready to pay up on the bets that they had placed barely a few hours ago, but were eyeing her closely, paying particular attention to her neck.

Sable kept it covered and glared at them.

Thorne hadn't even given her a chance to grab her weapons.

She turned to head back to her room.

"Where do you go, Little Mortal?" Grave said from right beside her and she whirled to face him, bringing her arm up at the same time, ready to block him.

He didn't attack.

He quirked a single eyebrow at her gesture and then she sensed his focus intensify and knew he was listening to her racing heart.

"Jumpy tonight, are we not?" He reached his arms above his head, closed his eyes and loosed a low moan, as if he took great pleasure from the stretch.

It was then she realised that he was only wearing black boxer shorts.

"Jesus... put something on before I retch." Sable turned away from him, and not only because she really didn't want to see Grave mostly naked. If Thorne saw her looking at Grave, then he really would kill the vampire.

She smiled as that part of their shared dream came back to her.

"Thinking about your lover?" the vampire said as he moved around her and clearly he had chosen to ignore her and was determined to piss Thorne off.

Sable turned on the spot but he kept moving, forcing her to keep turning in order to avoid looking at him. "None of your business, Bloodsucker."

"You smell like sex... but which male seated himself twixt those lovely thighs?"

Sable refused to blush. "Back off, before I make you back off."

Grave laughed and it was haunting, a chilling sound that she prayed she never heard again. Loren and Thorne were right. He had no sense of humour. Someone had killed it and she had a feeling it had been a woman, because women were treacherous, apparently.

"You lack weapons, Little Mortal." Grave kept pace with her and she began to get dizzy.

"The female asked you to leave her alone," a deep male voice said from right in front of her and she glanced up to find Bleu towering over her, his dark purple eyes stormy and violent and his pointed ears flaring back through his wild black-blue hair. She edged her gaze to her right, to the black blade he held over her shoulder and no doubt against the throat of the vampire behind her.

Sable edged to one side, away from the sword, and bumped into Thorne. He caught her arm and pulled her against him, away from the two males, and growled, his crimson eyes flashing dangerously.

"I believe I warned you not to approach my female," he said and she wasn't sure whether he was talking to Grave or to Bleu.

Or both men.

Bleu sheathed his blade at his waist and stared hard at Thorne.

"It is unwise to take Sable from her room when she is unarmed." Bleu dropped his gaze to her and lifted his other hand, and her eyebrows rose. Her weapons. He offered the shoulder holster with her throwing knives in it, and her belt with her blade and crossbow. "When the alarm sounded, I went to my prince and Olivia, and he tasked me with bringing you down. You were not there and someone had damaged your door. I feared you had been attacked when I saw your weapons on the dressing table... but it appears I was mistaken."

She took the weapons from Bleu and shirked Thorne's grip.

"Thank you." She didn't dare tack on Bleu's name to her words of gratitude. Thorne was liable to lose his head and do something stupid. She could feel him glaring at her already.

She put her leather shoulder holster on and her hands trembled as she smoothed it down over her t-shirt and then tied her belt around her waist.

"Perhaps I was not mistaken. You seem shaken... and I do not believe the vampire is responsible." Bleu was treading on thin ice and the look in his eyes said he knew it and he wanted to push Thorne.

Men.

"Speaking of bloodsuckers. Now I'm not so unarmed..." She reached for her blade and frowned when she saw that Grave had made his exit while they had been occupied. He stood off to one side with his men, buttoning a pair of black trousers. He paused, looked over his shoulder at her, and grinned. "Bastard."

"Are you well?" Bleu said and flicked a glare at Thorne when he growled.

Sable held her hands up and stood between them, hoping to keep them both quiet for a second, preferably before they ripped each other's throats open with their fangs.

"I'm fine. I'm half asleep and need coffee—" Her eyes widened as Thorne dropped into a black portal beneath him and Bleu's expression darkened. He muttered something under his breath and green-purple light traced over his body. He disappeared too.

Double men!

Loren and Olivia appeared right in front of her and she jumped and pressed her hand to her chest.

"Holy hell... a little warning next time." Sable scowled at Loren.

Loren looked around the courtyard, as if she hadn't spoken. "Where is Bleu?"

"Don't ask me. There was a thing with Grave being an arsehole and Bleu stepped in to help me, and then Thorne showed up... and then I tried to keep them from killing each other and then they both disappeared."

Thorne reappeared right beside her and the sweet heavenly scent hit her straight away, carrying bliss through her tired bones.

Coffee.

He held the clay mug out to her and grinned, and damn she wanted to kiss him when he looked as if he might burst with male pride.

"Thank you," she said and took the mug, inhaled the delicious aroma, and sighed.

"I sent an order to the kitchen to brew some while everyone gathered. Is it to your taste?" Thorne eyed the mug.

Sable blew on it and then sipped. It tasted even better than it smelled.

"It's perfect," she said and tried to hide her smile when he puffed his bare chest out.

Bleu appeared on the other side of her.

"Oh," Olivia said and Sable looked over at him and her eyes flew wide.

He had a mug too, and a black eye and a split lip, and a very ugly bruise on his jaw.

And now that she saw him, she swung back to Thorne and noticed the bruise and cut on his jaw and the one darting across his left eyebrow.

"Seriously?" She shook her head and scowled at them both. Thorne continued to grin. He thought he had gained a victory over Bleu. Sable would see to that. She turned to Bleu and took the mug of coffee from him too. "Thank you. It was very sweet of you."

Bleu grinned now.

She knew she shouldn't encourage him, but she couldn't let either male think they could score points with her by hurting the other.

Sable poured the coffees back and forth in the two mugs, mingling the contents, and then handed one to Olivia. Loren frowned and looked as if he was considering teleporting to get his female coffee rather than letting her have one that had been brought by Thorne and Bleu. If he dared, Sable was going to scream.

Thankfully, he had better control of himself than the other two idiots standing on either side of her and didn't protest as Olivia sipped the coffee and smiled.

"It's good." She looked at both Bleu and Thorne. "Although next time, could you teleport to a Starbucks and get me a grande skimmed caramel macchiato?"

Sable laughed. Thorne and Bleu looked thoroughly unimpressed. Loren muttered something about his mate's obsession with desiring that drink every other morning.

Fargus came over and said something to Thorne in the demon language. Thorne nodded, his expression turning grave, and responded. Fargus saluted and walked away, shouting what sounded like orders.

"It does not sound good," Loren said and she looked up at him.

"What doesn't sound good?" Sable was beginning to hate her inability to understand the demon tongue. She really needed to study it. Did Rosetta Stone do a demon language course?

Maybe Loren could teach her, when he wasn't busy with Olivia or running an entire kingdom. She didn't dare ask Bleu or Thorne.

Thorne heaved a sigh and his shoulders settled lower than before, as if the weight of the world, or at least his kingdom, had just come crashing down on them.

"Demons from the Fifth Realm have breached the border again and have already killed many in a village there. We must go and force them back." Thorne went to turn away from her and she caught his wrist.

He looked back over his shoulder at her.

"They want to lure you out. You can't give them what they want. You need to stay here. If you fall… your kingdom falls, Thorne." She knew she had made a terrible mistake the moment the words left her lips.

His irises blazed crimson, burning like fire, and his horns curled. His pointed ears flared back and he growled down at her and snatched his arm from her grip.

"Do not tell me to cower in my castle, Mortal. Do not think to lecture me about the safety of my realm… I have been fighting for this realm for nearly three thousand years, as have many others here, and if I am destined to die for it, then so be it. I would sooner die on the battlefield than live in shame."

He flashed his fangs, turned his back on her and stormed away.

"Thorne." Sable reached for him and Loren grabbed her arm, pulling her back. She looked up at him, into his vivid purple eyes, and whispered, "I didn't mean to upset him."

"He knows." Loren slowly released her arm and ran his hand through his short black hair, tousling the longer lengths on top. "But you must think before you speak. You desire to protect him and his kingdom, but such words can wound."

She nodded and swore she wouldn't say such a thoughtless thing again as she sipped her coffee. She would have hated it if he had dared to tell her to remain in the castle, away from the battle, showing no faith in her abilities as a warrior or her strength.

She fought the urge to go to him and apologise, to tell him that she would never belittle him in such a manner again and search his eyes for a sign that he had forgiven her and wouldn't hold her careless words against her. They hadn't been born of a belief that he was weak. They had been born of worry, fear that he would end up hurt or worse, and the startling epiphany that she wouldn't be able to bear it if anything happened to him.

Because no matter how hard she had fought it and tried to deny it, she felt something for him, something so deep and consuming that it controlled her at times and she knew she would never be the same again.

For the first time in her life, she felt dependent upon someone, and she wasn't sure how to process it.

"Gather your men and prepare them for teleportation to the battle," Bleu said and Sable nodded again, miles away in thoughts of Thorne and how dramatically she had changed since the night he had come crashing into her life.

"I'll get ready too." Olivia took Sable's empty mug from her and went to move and Loren caught her arm.

"You, Ki'ara, are to remain here."

Olivia yanked her arm free. "Whoa, no… now wait a minute. What about that whole speech you just gave… I'm not staying in the castle. You want me to toss you a Thorne speech? I'm heading out with you all."

Sable really didn't want to do this, but she said, "Got to agree with him, Liv. We need you here, getting the infirmary ready for any wounded, and we need Loren to be able to concentrate and he sure as hell won't be able to if he thinks you're in danger."

Olivia pouted and settled her hands on her hips, pulling her dark blue t-shirt down. "I want it noted that I'm not happy about this and he," she jerked her thumb at her mate, "isn't getting sex for a week."

Loren looked horrified and Sable thought he might actually reconsider his decision.

"But you do agree it's the sensible course of action?" Sable prompted before he could speak and her friend huffed and then forced a nod. Loren growled. Olivia turned her nose up at him. The man didn't have anything to worry about. Sable had no doubt that Olivia wouldn't last five seconds when it came to refusing Loren a little naughty time. "Good. Bleu or Loren will bring you to the battlefield when we've driven the demons away and you can stabilise the wounded before they're teleported back. Now give your mate a big kiss and tell him what a wonderful warrior he is, and we'll be off."

A familiar burn went through Sable and she turned to look for Thorne.

He towered over her, barely a few inches between them. She opened her mouth to apologise and it came out as a squeak as he grabbed her, pulled her flush against him and kissed her hard. She held on to his huge biceps as she tried to catch up.

He set her back on her feet before she could and she wobbled, feeling a little dazed. He grasped her shoulders and hunkered down so they were eye level.

"You are a wonderful warrior," he whispered, his expression soft but serious, as if he truly believed what he said with all of his heart.

With that, the world rushed past her in a cold blur and she clutched hold of Thorne's arms and unleashed a barrage of demon greetings that she hoped were as rude as Bleu had told her they were.

The world reappeared and settled around her, and Thorne grinned down at her. "You have been learning my language."

She slapped his shoulder and he shrugged it off, looking pleased for some reason.

"What is *wrong* with you?" she said.

His grin widened. "You only slapped my shoulder when I kissed you this time. I call that positive progress."

Sable considered punching him and then thought the better of it when demons appeared around her, all of them with a vampire in tow. The elves appeared next, teleporting the werewolves and her team with them.

Bleu and Loren appeared last.

Their skin-tight black scaly armour flowed over their bare chests, completing itself and turning their fingers into deadly talons. Loren's helmet formed as the scales swiftly crawled up his neck. The helmet flared up from a point above his nose and swept back into serrated curved spikes like vicious dragon's horns, resembling a crown. He kept the lower half open but Sable knew that would change once he entered the battle. Slats would come out from beside his cheeks, forming a mask over his nose, mouth and jaw, completing his armour and rendering him almost invulnerable. She had learned from Bleu that their armour was only weak against the same material, meaning normal swords couldn't penetrate it.

She wanted her own set of armour just like it but lacked the psychic powers required to control it.

Bleu's lips compressed and he looked as if he was chewing hard on a wasp as his own helmet covered his head, twin horns curving from the back of it, and the mask swept down and concealed the lower half of his face.

"Prepare," Kincaid hollered and the werewolves stripped off as one.

Sable swiftly turned her back but many of the females in her team ogled them, and a couple even dared a wolf whistle.

That received a very arrogant-sounding howl in response.

Thorne stared down at her. Sable tried to ignore him but her eyes drifted to him. At least he was dressed now, wearing thick mahogany leather vambraces around his forearms over his white shirt, and heavy boots.

He held his hand out, palm facing down, and Sable knew what was coming. It had impressed her when she had first seen him do it but she had hidden it then, and tried to hide it now as the glowing red pommel of a sword rose out of the dark dirt below him. A long leather-bound hilt followed it and then a wide steel blade. It continued to rise, the blade barely tapering, as if it would never end. When the pommel reached Thorne's palm, he turned his hand and ran it down the black hilt, curled his fingers around it and pulled the point of the blade from the ground.

It stood almost as tall as his chin and he swung the heavy blade up onto his shoulder with ease.

A scream rent the silence.

Thorne growled and teleported, and many of the demons disappeared too. Loren grabbed her before Bleu could reach her and she clung to him as the world disappeared, whirling around her, and then reappeared again. Loren released her and instantly sprang into action, attacking a large male with painted black horns as he ran after a screaming female.

It was a village.

Square black stone huts with thatched roofs surrounded her, some of them on fire. More fires burned in braziers, illuminating the village but throwing the landscape around her into darkness. The ground beneath her feet was as black as night but wet, trampled into an undulating path between the buildings. It smelled of blood.

Bleu appeared beside her and swept his hand over his black blade, transforming into a long spear. He growled as he sprinted after Loren, teleporting from time to time to keep up with his prince. The elves appeared around them, dropping off her team and then flying into action. Their skin-tight black scaly armour shone in the firelight as they went to war on the demons, battling them with spears, bows, blades and telekinetic blows that sent their enemies spinning through the air in different directions.

"With me!" Sable shouted above the noise of the battle raging around them in the village and her team fell in, their weapons at the ready. "Evan, take the first squad and break through to that building."

She pointed towards a larger hut at the end of the corridor that ran between the thatched black stone ones around her. There were women gathered there, frantically fighting, and she had spotted at least one young boy with them.

Evan nodded and was moving with half the team a second later, hacking at the demons who stood in his way.

Sable scoured the battle for Thorne but couldn't find him. Smoke from the fires clouded parts of the village and made it impossible for her to get a clear view of the fight. The land banked downhill from where she stood and the buildings thinned around a hundred metres away. It was her best shot at making a swift run for the larger building, avoiding the thickest area of the battle.

"The rest of you, try to keep up. We're going around back."

She sprinted between two buildings, heading downhill, and banked right on the fourth avenue that led towards the main building. Demon males crowded the narrow corridor, busily setting fire to the thatch on the roofs of the homes.

Their heads swung her way and they grinned and said something to each other.

Sable ran straight at them, ducking as they swung huge blades at her and slashing across their calves and shins with her short sword. Her team followed her lead, disabling the demons. She didn't have time to play with them. It was imperative that they reach the main village building to assist the women and protect their children. Nothing was going to stand in her way.

A meaty hand grasped the back of her neck. Sable grimaced as claws cut into her throat and dropped her blade, her hands flying up over her shoulders to grab the demon's arms. She pulled hard on them, fighting to break free.

Several of her team turned back. She shook her head.

"Go! Get to the women and children," Sable hollered to Anais, a blonde huntress more than capable of leading the team in her stead.

Anais nodded.

Sable slipped her fingers through one of the rings on her throwing knives. She pulled it free as her men left her behind, twirled it in her grip and rammed it over her shoulder, hoping her aim was true.

The demon holding her roared and his grip loosened. Sable pressed the soles of her boots into his legs and kicked off him, breaking free. She hit the dirt, rolled and came to her feet.

A silver arc cut straight towards her. She gasped and hit the deck, landing flat on her back, and then pressed her hands into the dirt above her shoulders and flipped back onto her feet. She grabbed her blade from the ground and swung hard, cutting through the wrist of the second demon male.

He shrieked and stumbled backwards, and she silenced him by slashing his throat. The other demon lunged for her, one hand over his eye and the knife sticking out of it.

Sable spun on one heel, kicked upwards with that leg as hard as she could to launch herself off the ground and slammed her other boot into the end of the knife, driving it deeper into his head. He dropped to his knees and she rammed her blade into his chest, pressing her other palm to the end of the hilt to shove it deep enough to reach his heart.

His growl died and he fell on his side. Sable pressed her left boot against his chest and yanked her blade free. Two down, around two hundred to go.

Three werewolves rushed past her, snarling at each other and snapping at her. She flipped them off. They leaped in unison at a demon and he went down fast, screaming as the wolves mauled him. Sable made a mental note not to piss off the werewolves. Being eaten alive didn't rank high on her list of good ways to die.

She turned and ran to catch up with her team. They were miles ahead of her and had gained a few allies. The elves were fighting with them, working to take down some demons who were living up to the image most mortals had of that kind. They were huge, their eyes blazing like green fire and their wings battering her men and the elves as they fought with savage relentlessness.

Several vampires streamed past her, grinning as they fought two demons. A chocolate coloured werewolf raced into the fray and Sable frowned as it bit one of the vampires on the calf. The vampire retaliated, catching the werewolf by its hind leg, pulling it up into the air and biting down.

"You can't save it for later?" Sable shouted and threw herself into the fight, unafraid of castigating both the vampire and the werewolf. Both looked at her as she stabbed one of the demons in the thigh and then hit him in the temple with the hilt of her blade. How could they think about fighting each other when they had bad-ass demons to take down?

One of the bad-ass demons in question caught her off guard and she found herself flying through the air. No time to brace for impact. She closed her eyes and waited to hit the dirt and the inevitable pain that would follow.

Strong arms caught her and she was suddenly on her feet. Sable really didn't want to look.

She cracked one eye open and grimaced. Bleu looked pissed.

"More care," he barked and then disappeared in a flash of greenish light. He reappeared next to Loren in the village and the two of them were incredible as they led the elves, tearing through the demons with their claws and black blades, teleporting swiftly to attack unnoticed and then disappearing again before the demons could retaliate.

She couldn't keep up.

It was manic.

Sable spotted Thorne at last. He led a group of his men together with Grave, and both of them were savage and brutal as they fought, hacking their way through the enemy with little finesse. They were closing in on the main building and Thorne looked glorious, every bit a king as he fought hard to protect his people.

She shook herself. The battlefield was not the place to lose track of her surroundings.

Sable did a weapons check and then sprinted back towards the fray, feeling as if Bleu had intentionally left her nearly two hundred yards from all the action. She closed in on the fight and her gift triggered, blaring a warning through her. Sable turned on a pinhead and dropped at the same time, barely evading the blow aimed straight for her neck. She lashed out with her leg and hit the demon's knees hard. He didn't budge.

Her gift went haywire.

He wasn't alone.

Sable looked over her shoulder. One hundred yards to the battle and the nearest ally.

Her heart pounded.

The five demon males closed in.

Sable readied her blade, remaining in a crouch. Her wrist burned and she ignored it. The first male reached her. Sable launched upwards with her short sword and the male strafed backwards, grinning at her. Another male caught her arm and she slashed down the length of his forearm. He released her and she ducked beneath his arms and broke free of the circle.

One of the demons appeared right before her and she ran straight into his outstretched hand. He closed his fingers around her throat and hauled her off the floor, and she flailed, catching him hard in the thigh with her boot.

Sable narrowed her gaze on him and kicked harder, striking him before he could even think to defend.

She hit him square between the thighs and he crumpled into a heap, releasing her at the same time so he could clutch himself.

She drew her crossbow, flicked it open, and quickly loaded it with the toxic darts. They would slow down the demons but they wouldn't kill them. She didn't have a poison strong enough for that.

Sable released one bolt, quickly reloaded and released the second. She nailed two of the demons in their bare chests. They chuckled and tugged the darts free, crushing them in their fists. Their smiles twisted into grimaces as the toxin went to work.

She hooked her fingers into two of the throwing knives under her right arm and launched them at the other two demons. Both evaded perfectly, teleporting before the blades could touch them. Not a good move on her part. Sable cursed her stupidity and made a break for the main fight.

Her eyes darted around, fear making her limbs shake as she waited for the two demons to reappear. She shouldn't have forced them to teleport. It was the most effective weapon in their arsenal.

A hot prickle went through her and she dived to her left just as a sword appeared right beside her. She cried out as the tip of the blade slashed across her biceps and hit the ground hard. The pebbly surface scraped her other arm and her side as she skidded a short distance.

She growled in frustration and launched a knife at the demon. He sidestepped it and raised his blade above his head, and Sable stared at it. It dropped towards her and she rolled with everything she had, barely avoiding it. It hit the ground with a clang and the demon shifted it in his hands and came at her again as she kicked off from the dirt and broke into a dead run.

Her wrist burned hotter.

Her leg ached.

Not now. She didn't need her old injury acting up and slowing her down.

Two of the demons appeared right in front of her and she broke left, skidding on the loose ground at the same time and almost ending up flat on her face. They laughed at her and she hated them for it, knew they were amused by the little mortal fighting for her life.

Screw them.

She had been born to fight demons.

Strength surged through her and her heart steadied, and with it came a hunger she had never experienced before.

A desire to crush all the demons.

Sable ground to a halt and turned to face them.

All five sauntered towards her and began to fan out, forming a wide line.

She glanced off to her right, where her blade lay on the black ground.

Feint an attack with her remaining throwing knife. Slide for the blade. First demon attacks. Decapitate before he can swing his sword. Kick off and launch at the second male, incapacitating him before striking the third, one of the poisoned. The fourth and fifth would attack in unison. Gut the fourth, another of the poisoned, and stab the fifth, their leader, in his black heart.

Sable palmed the remaining knife strapped to her ribs.

Destroy the demons.

She feinted and the demons fell for it, all five of them bracing themselves. In the split second she had, she was across the ground and sliding in for her blade. She caught it before she slid straight past it, turned onto her belly and kicked off hard.

It all went horribly wrong at that point.

The leader disappeared and reappeared right in front of her and made her thoroughly acquainted with his boot, lodging it deep in her side. She rolled hard, pain burning through her, and struggled to breathe.

The ache in her leg grew worse.

Damned demons.

"Die," she snarled and was on her feet before she knew what was happening, running straight at the leader. He had to die. The demon filth had to die.

Darkness clouded her thoughts, the hunger to maim and kill filling every inch of her, driving her to obey.

Thorne appeared in the midst of the demons, swinging his blade and decapitating two in one go. Light broke into Sable's mind, the flash of his silver sword penetrating the darkness, and she shoved her pain down deep. He whirled to face another of the demons, beautiful in his fury as he slammed his fist into the male's face and drove him down.

Sable launched herself at the leader, catching him unawares as he watched Thorne. She slashed across his calves and he turned on her, snarling and flashing his fangs. She ducked and dodged his blows, and stabbed his sword arm. He dropped his blade and she grinned.

Too soon.

Never celebrate until your enemy is dead and you have his head in your hands.

The male's fist crashed into her arm, pain spider-webbed along her bones, and she dropped her blade.

He grinned now. She was screwed.

The darkness swirled inside her and the urge came again, the undeniable desire to destroy this demon. Wretched filth.

The pain in her arm disappeared.

He launched a hard left hook at her and Sable caught it in her right hand.

The burning in her wrist exploded into an inferno.

The demon male frowned down at his fist.

"Die," Sable whispered in a voice that was distant to her ears.

The male arched backwards and roared at the dark sky. She watched on, cold and complacent, as the skin on his hand charred, orange light breaking through cracks in it, as if lava filled him.

The darkness spread up his arm and Sable blinked, her emotions rushing back in as if a dam had burst as she yanked her hand away from him and stumbled backwards.

The demon's agonised scream tore through her and she covered her ears as he burned to ashes before her eyes.

Air shifted around her and a muffled grunt sounded behind her.

Sable turned on her heel, her eyes wide and her hands still covering her ears.

A headless male lay slumped to the ground at her feet.

Thorne stood before her, his chest heaving, covered in sweat, dirt and blood, and his blade hanging limp from his hand.

He looked beyond her to the pile of black ashes and then back into her eyes. She didn't want to look at the mess behind her. She didn't want to think about what she had just done, because it frightened her and she didn't understand it.

Thorne's face softened and he laid his sword down and took hold of her wrists on either side of her head.

He hissed and snarled, and released her.

Sable stared wide-eyed at the burns on the fingers of his left hand and shook her head. Her right wrist burned fiercely and she drew her hands away and looked at the charred bandage around it. The cross beneath shone through, bright crimson and gold when once it had been black.

She shook her head again and didn't stop this time as tears filled her eyes, her strength draining away and leaving her cold. "It's just a tattoo."

She mumbled it on repeat, trying to convince herself that she was going mad. She had got it done... when? She didn't know. It had been there for as long as she could remember. Thorne moved closer and she looked up at him, holding her wrist out to him.

"It's just a tattoo, Thorne. Isn't it?" Her words sounded weak to her ears, trembling as much as she was inside.

He looked as if he wanted to hold her and she stepped back, afraid that he might and she would hurt him again. The compulsion to destroy the demons hadn't faded, and her gift labelled him as a mark too. A demon to eradicate.

No. She didn't want to hurt Thorne.

He removed one of the leather cuffs around his forearms and she jerked backwards when he moved towards her again.

"Sable," he snapped and her gaze leaped to his. He edged closer again and she didn't stop him this time. "I will not hurt you."

"But I might hurt you," she whispered in response and tears slipped onto her cheeks. She cursed them and how uncertain and afraid she felt. She was stronger than this. She kept telling herself it even when she wanted to break down, kept clinging to the last shred of her strength and fighting the tears and the panic clogging her throat.

"You will not," he said softly and moved the cuff towards her. "You only hurt me when I touched it."

He placed the leather vambrace around her wrist. It was too large for her. He grabbed her t-shirt and she gasped as he tore a strip off around the hem, leaving it several inches shorter than before, so it showed off her midriff.

Thorne tore the piece of material in two, wrapped them around the vambrace and tied them tightly, so the leather sat flush against her arm. The pain in her wrist dulled to a throb and she looked up at Thorne. She didn't want to kill him.

Several men rushed towards them and the compulsion to slay them all didn't return.

They spoke to Thorne in the demon tongue and he nodded and then turned to her.

"The village is safe and we have some captives we can question." He stooped and picked up his broadsword and stabbed the tip into the black earth. The enormous blade slowly sank into the ground and her gaze tracked it until the red pommel disappeared and the earth healed over it. Thorne held his hand out to her. "Come."

Sable nodded and clutched her wrist to her chest as she walked. She stopped when she came across her blade, picked it up and sheathed it, and then continued walking. Thorne stayed at her side the whole time, his eyes on her. She couldn't bring herself to look at him. What had she done to that demon?

It was just a tattoo.

It had killed that demon though and had burned Thorne.

What was wrong with her?

They entered the village and she spotted Loren with Bleu, and Olivia. Her friend saw her and came rushing over.

"What's wrong… are you injured?" Olivia reached out to touch her wrist and Sable jerked away from her.

"It's fine. I don't need you to look at it, okay?" she snapped and shook her head, backing away from her friends. She didn't want them to see it glowing or discover what she had done. They wouldn't understand.

She didn't want her best friend to think she was a freak.

Olivia's face fell and she quietly said, "Okay."

Thorne looked at Sable.

Sable couldn't bring herself to face him either. He had seen what she had done and she had hurt him when he had tried to touch her. What if she would hurt everyone who touched her now or that strange urge came over her again? She shuddered and moved another step away, trying to distance herself from everyone.

"We should take the injured back to the castle," Loren said.

Bleu reached out to grab her arm. Sable slapped his hand away and clutched her wrist to her chest, her heart pounding at a sickening pace. Hurt filled his purple eyes and she shook her head and looked down at her feet.

"Maybe I can walk back," she whispered to her boots and then risked a glance at her friends.

They all looked at her as if she had gone insane.

Thorne snorted, grabbed her and dropped into a dark abyss with her.

The moment they appeared in the courtyard of his castle, she shoved away from him.

"Have you gone crazy?" she barked. "I might have hurt you again!"

Thorne growled, grabbed her and pulled her back to him. She stared up into his crimson eyes.

"I went crazy the moment I set eyes on you, my little fated one."

Sable struggled against his grip. "Don't... not right now... I can't take it."

Because she wasn't strong enough to fight him. All she wanted to do was rest her head against his chest and ask him to hold her and tell her that she had imagined everything that had happened at the battle, that she had been knocked out and dreamed all the craziness.

He released her and cold swept through her.

"True friendship is rare, and you have it with Olivia. Do not push your friend away because of this. Olivia will understand, even if you do not." He sighed and his tone softened, and she didn't stop him as he brushed the backs of his claws across her cheeks, sweeping her tears away. She looked up into his eyes and fought the urge to ask him to do more, to hold her. "Rest, Sable. You will be safe here at my home while I oversee proceedings at the border."

He disappeared before she could respond.

Now she knew how Olivia felt whenever Loren did that.

Furious.

Alone.

CHAPTER 12

Sable roamed the cold, silent corridors of the castle, slowly wending her way downwards, beneath the sleeping quarters, in search of the kitchen.

At least she had been at first.

Unable to sleep, she had wanted a drink of water to quench the burning in her throat, needing to rid herself of anything that reminded her of what had happened and what she had done.

Her tattoo had reacted to those demons and she had felt compelled to kill them.

To kill Thorne.

She shuddered, shoved that memory out of her head, and trudged onwards, following the quiet hallway. She hadn't seen anyone since leaving her quarters on the first floor. Everyone had retired to their rooms to rest after arriving back from the battle and she had avoided the main courtyard in her search for the kitchen.

Now, she wasn't sure where she was beneath the castle, but the hallways were growing narrower and gently sloping downwards, and she didn't have the energy to change her course. She walked onwards, her mind wandering as much as her feet were.

She had burned that demon to ashes.

She had hurt Thorne.

Sable wrapped her arms around herself and stroked the bandage around her right biceps. She couldn't believe she had hurt him. She hadn't meant to.

She looked down at the leather cuff still strapped around her right forearm. Her wrist had been hurting ever since she had entered this region of Hell and now she had a strange power, the ability to incinerate a demon with nothing more than a touch. Why?

Maybe she should turn back and find the kitchen after all. A healthy dose of demon grog would knock her out and she wanted to sleep, to escape this nightmare and lose herself in Thorne. She wanted to pretend nothing had happened and she was the same woman she had been barely a few days ago, a hunter with a gift, an ability to sense fae and demons.

A lamp cast pale flickering light ahead, revealing the end of the corridor.

A room.

Sable reached the threshold and paused, her breath hitching in her throat and heart clenching.

In the middle of the dark stone room stood a pure white marble statue of a couple.

A huge male demon looked down at a petite female, his expression filled with love and devotion as he gazed upon her. The woman nestled against his chest, her own gaze turned downwards and a soft smile playing on her beautiful lips. Her left hand hung away from her side, free of the incredibly detailed folds of her empire-line style gown.

That hand was worn and shiny, as if someone had slipped theirs into it many times.

Sable moved closer, entranced by the woman.

Her cheek shone in the light of the candles burning on the shelves around the walls too, as if someone had caressed it often.

Yellow roses lay at their feet in varying stages of decay. Some were completely dried and withered, brown and crisp, but others still had colour and softness.

Sable edged closer still, until she stood before the couple, and stared at them.

She had never seen such a beautiful statue before. It radiated love and tenderness, and sorrow so deep that it brought tears to her eyes.

Thorne's parents.

Loren had told her about them, that they had died almost two thousand eight hundred years ago, killed by Kordula and Loren's brother, Vail, and that Thorne had been young for a demon, only around seven hundred years old.

Sable's gaze drifted down to the woman's left hand and she reached out to it, imagining a young Thorne doing the same as he looked at his mother and father, the parents that had been taken from him.

A heavy thump echoed down the hallway behind her, followed by another, growing in volume.

Sable drew her hand back and looked around, searching for another way out. She didn't want to be caught here, in such a private place. Her heart sped up when she realised there was no other exit.

No escape.

The footsteps drew closer and with them came dread. What if it was a guard or, worse, one of the vampires? No one would find her down here.

The footsteps stopped.

Sable swiftly turned to face their owner.

Thorne stood before her, bare-chested and bedraggled. The strained lines of his face soon turned towards anger though as he looked between her and the statue behind her.

"What are you doing in this place?" he barked and frowned as he moved into the room, making it feel even smaller than it had a moment ago. "You should not be in this place."

Sable looked over her shoulder at the statue and then down at the roses.

It wasn't just a room.

It was a tomb.

Thorne had buried his parents here and still came to them often. To smooth his mother's cheek and hold her hand? To speak with his father?

Tears rose into her eyes again and threatened to spill.

She blinked them away. She had no reason to feel sorry for him. At least he had known his parents. He'd had centuries with them.

She had never known hers.

Sable looked back at Thorne and his expression softened.

"I did not mean to shout at you," he said in a gentle tone. He thought he had made her cry.

She shook her head and pinned her gaze on the floor.

"I'm sorry." She kept her head bent and hurried past him.

Thorne caught her arm and he was surprisingly gentle. She stilled, keeping her back to him, her heart beating in her throat as she waited for him to speak.

"Why were you here?"

Sable stared at the corridor. "I couldn't sleep. I was looking for the kitchen to grab some water... or maybe some booze... and I somehow ended up here. I didn't mean to intrude."

Silence fell, as oppressive as it had been when they had stood together on the balcony. Was Thorne trying to think of something to say? Was he angry with her?

He released her and sighed. "You should not wander the castle alone when so many males are present."

She had figured that out for herself when she had thought he was a vampire come to attack her or one of the demon guards.

Sable looked over her shoulder at him. He had his back to her, his gaze on the statue. He walked over to it and she felt she should leave, but she couldn't convince her feet to move.

He seemed so different tonight.

Lonely.

It made her feel lonely too.

"Why did you come down here?" she quietly said and his shoulders heaved with another sigh, his muscles expanding and relaxing, calling to her. She wanted to step up behind him and smooth her palms over them, to rest her head against his spine and hold him, because she knew that if she did, she would find her balance again.

When had she started relying on him like that? When had Thorne become her anchor, her pillar of strength? When had she become so weak?

"I could not sleep. Too much weighs on my mind." He remained with his back to her. "So I came here... to speak... you will think me a fool."

"Not at all." She turned to face him. "You came to speak with them."

She could understand that. He had probably talked to them often when they had been alive, sharing whatever burden weighed on his heart. She had done something similar a few times with Olivia and it had felt good. She wished she had been able to talk to her parents, to tell them her problems and hear them tell her that everything would be alright.

"You are sad... why?" Thorne looked over his broad shoulders at her and his revelation didn't shock her.

He could sense her feelings.

She felt a growing connection to him too, and it frightened her.

"Sad for you, I suppose," she lied and looked away when he frowned at her, as if he knew. She searched for another topic of conversation and found it in Thorne's left hand.

A single yellow rose.

"How often to demons honour their ancestors?" She had heard that most demons brought offerings of the ancestor's favourite brew or sacrificed something living to honour them.

Thorne looked down at the rose in his hand, raising it at the same time.

"Yearly, on the day of their birth and the day of their death," he said and twirled the rose stem in his fingers, slowly enough that it barely shifted the green petals and didn't affect the closed bud at all.

Sable looked at all the blooms. There were too many.

"And you only offer a single rose?" she said and he nodded. "So how often do you honour your mother?"

He was silent for a moment, and then quietly stated, "Monthly."

He cast his dark crimson gaze over the drying roses.

"More recently… I have honoured her weekly. I have needed my parents' counsel."

The lines bracketing his mouth and his eyes were visible signs of the stress he was under. Only a month had passed since she had first met him, but he seemed so different.

Weary and tired, quieter and troubled.

A little like her.

Sable edged closer to him and he lifted his gaze to her. She hated the look in his dark eyes. Her heart throbbed heavily at the sight of them glittering with so much pain, fathomless and searing, burning him up inside.

She wanted to take it all away, even when she knew she couldn't, just as he couldn't take away her hurt and her fear. He couldn't remove it but he could make her forget it for a while. He could shove the rest of the world and all of her worries aside with one single heated caress, a touch that would burn away all reason and leave her a slave to sensation and need—a slave to him and the connection blossoming between them.

He had that power over her, and a deep, longing part of her wanted him to use it. She wanted him to draw her into his thickly muscled arms and kiss away her fears, and that was a dangerous thing to desire.

Thorne heaved another sigh, his broad chest expanding with it, and then went down on one knee before the statue.

Sable watched in silence as he laid the rose at his mother's feet, looked up at the woman and spoke to her in the demon tongue. She wished she knew what he was saying as he quietly talked to her, and to his father. He gazed up at the tall male and then lowered his head. His shoulders tensed.

She moved closer to him, drawn to comforting him and unable to deny that desire, and reached out to lay her hand on his back. His head shifted towards her before she could and she withdrew her hand as he rose to his feet, standing as tall as his father.

She had to say something to break the silence before it became strained again.

"Your mother was beautiful," she whispered and he turned his head a little towards her, enough that she saw the slight smile that curved his lips.

"I have never seen a more beautiful female." He fell quiet and glanced at her out of the corner of his eye and she knew that he wanted to say more but feared how she would react if he told her that he thought her beautiful too.

She smiled to alleviate his nerves. "What were your parents like?"

"My father was brave, strong, and led this kingdom in an era of peace because of that strength. He taught me much… how to lead men… how to fight… how to do what is right, no matter the consequences. If I could be but a tenth of the male he was, the warrior he was… the king he was… I would be happy."

But clearly he thought himself less than even that small amount. Because his kingdom was at war? Loren had also told her that Thorne had been through many wars in his centuries as the Third King, and the surrounding realms constantly challenged his reign because he had been so young and inexperienced when he had ascended the throne.

But the man before her now wore the scars of those battles on his body and on his soul. He was strong and brave, and led his kingdom well, even if he couldn't see it himself.

She wished that he could or that she could make him see it.

"My mother was beautiful, and delicate, and raised me while my father dealt with the kingdom. She would walk me around the castle and laugh as I tried to fight the guards or lecture the captains and commanders. She would smile at me as I prattled on about the day I would go into battle at my father's side and we would win a great victory, and she would tell me that my greatest victory would not be a battle… it would be love." He cast his gaze down at his boots. "Sentimental, yet her words offered me comfort in our time apart. When I lost my parents, all I had to keep me going were the lessons they had taught me, the affection they had shown me, and their belief in me."

"It must have been hard for you." Hard felt like an understatement as she looked at him, at his solemn expression and the visible strain etched in every line on his handsome face and in his eyes, and then the statue behind him.

Thorne looked back at it too.

"I was not a good king… many said I was too young. I spent the first three weeks here in this room, a weeping and pathetic boy, until my father's commander came to me and told me I had mourned enough. He pulled me onto my feet, shook me hard, and turned me to face my father, and he told me that I was my father's legacy and I was king now, and I had to honour my father. I had to make him proud." Thorne brushed his hand over his father's right one and then curled his fingers into a tight fist. "I have been trying ever since."

"Thorne... I'm sure your father is proud of you."

He shrugged and faced her again. "What of your parents?"

A sore subject. Sable shrugged this time and tried to keep the biting edge of bitterness from her tone.

"What of them? I never met them."

Thorne's eyebrows pulled down over incredulous crimson eyes. "How is that possible?"

"They dropped me on an orphanage doorstep when I was a baby, barely a day old." She really didn't want to talk about this with him, or with anyone.

Sorrow and compassion coloured his eyes and she couldn't bring herself to keep looking into them. She lowered her head. Thorne lifted his hand, holding it out to her, and flexed his fingers.

Sable went to him but didn't take his offered hand or look at him. She kept her eyes on his parents.

"I often imagined what my parents were like. When I started school, sometimes we had to draw our family, and I imagined what my mother would be like. I drew what I saw in my heart... a beautiful woman like your mother... but as I grew older, I began to feel that beauty was skin deep and didn't reach her heart." Sable's dark eyebrows met in a hard frown and she clenched her fists at her sides. "She left me, and I will never know why."

She risked it and looked up at Thorne where he stood beside her, right into his eyes, drowning in the affection and concern they showed her.

"She didn't even leave a note. She just dumped me like garbage."

Thorne raised his hand and Sable didn't stop him. She needed his touch too much to push him away. She savoured it as he stroked the backs of his claws across her cheek, the soft caress melting her inside, thawing the ice around her heart and erasing some of the pain beating in it.

"I am sorry, Sable. No child deserves such a life," he whispered, his deep voice laden with tenderness.

Sable shrugged it off and tried to stifle the awkwardness running through her.

She had never spoken about her parents to anyone other than Olivia. She felt weak for spilling her sob story to Thorne, but at the same time, it felt good to share it with him and have him know the part of her she hid from the world.

He opened his hand and cupped her cheek, his large palm engulfing it, and tilted her head back, until she was looking up at him.

It suddenly hit her that he was touching her.

"You shouldn't," she said and stepped back, and he frowned, the edge of disappointment and anger in his eyes warning her that he had taken her words to mean something else. That he shouldn't kiss her. She shook her head and wrapped her hand around the leather cuff on her right wrist. "What if I hurt you again?"

Sable looked down at her arm.

"I thought it was only a tattoo, but what if I was wrong? So many demons and fae have markings… what if this is a marking like that? What if one of my parents was something non-human?" It would explain her gift and her new power, and would make her hate them even more for ditching her, leaving her to fend for herself without a clue about what she was and the world she had come from.

"It is no demon marking." Thorne wrapped his fingers around the cuff and she stared at their hands. His partially covered hers, warm and strong, steady when hers was shaking. She looked up into his eyes and he smiled. "We will find out all that we can about it, Sable. I swear it."

She dropped her gaze back to their hands and then down to his right one.

She had burned him but there were no bandages on his fingers.

Sable took her right hand back from him and reached out. She caught his hand gently in hers and raised it between them, and turned it over and tentatively stroked the tips of her fingers across his, afraid of hurting him again. The burns were gone. She had never felt so glad about anything, and had never feared as greatly as she had in that moment on the battlefield. She had thought he would burn away as the other demon had.

She had thought she would lose him.

Heat blazed through her, the intensity of it increasing as she swept her fingers over his. Her awareness of him increased with it, her heart picking up pace and her breathing following, coming faster and shorter as she toyed with his fingers. She should let go.

Should but couldn't.

Thorne's other hand brushed her cheek and it burned beneath the caress, her breath hitching in her throat. He tipped her chin up and stared down into her eyes, his blazing crimson, scorching her as they narrowed on hers and then dropped lower, taking in her lips and then her body. He raked his gaze back up and lingered on hers, and she melted under his scrutiny, aching for him to speak, to touch her, to do something other than stare into her eyes.

"You are more beautiful than my mother," he whispered in a thick, gruff voice that sent a shivery ache racing through her. His thumb played on her lower lip, the caress soft and teasing, making it tingle. "Inside and out… more beautiful than any female in existence. My mother would have adored you… and my father too. He liked spirited females… and my female has spirit, and strength, and beauty. You were born to be my queen, Sable. Mine alone. My forever."

A tiny part of her said to silence him, to make him stop, because he was starting to talk about her as if she was already his again and she didn't like it. She was too weak right now though. Her defences were down and she couldn't contain the blush that darkened her cheeks when he stepped closer, bending his head to look down into her eyes as he held her jaw, his expression more beautiful than the one his father's statue wore.

He earnestly whispered, "You are truly beautiful through and through."

Sable rose onto her tiptoes, ignoring the small voice that screamed at her to stop, to go back to her room and not do this. It was cruel to lead Thorne on but she needed to forget for a while. She needed to leave everything behind and lose herself in him.

"Kiss me... please?" she murmured and he gathered her against his chest, easily lifting her up to his lips, and gave her everything she desired.

The kiss was soft and gentle, melting her bones and burning away her reservations. She wrapped her arms around his neck and turned up the heat, sweeping her tongue across his lower lip and darting it inside when he opened to her. He moaned and slanted his head, and she mimicked him, deepening the kiss.

Thorne palmed her buttocks and she moaned into his mouth, tunnelled her fingers into the russet-brown waves of his hair and held on to him. She needed more. She wrapped her arms around his head and her hands brushed his horns.

He growled.

Sable groaned and curled her fingers around his growing horns, pulled his head back and kissed him harder.

More.

Wait.

She forced herself back and looked down into his eyes. They burned like fire, scorching her, and she wanted to kiss him again. She couldn't.

"Why are you stopping?" he husked, a pained and confused look on his handsome face. "Do you mean to slap me again?"

She would have laughed at that had her reason for stopping not been so serious.

"No... just... what if I hurt you?" Her focus switched to her wrist. It wasn't even tingling right now. It felt normal, but that didn't reassure her. It had felt normal in the moments before she had burned a demon to ashes with her bare hands too.

"Do you feel now as you did then?"

Sable shook her head. "No. Back then, I could almost feel my death coming at the hands of those demons. Right now... I feel... I feel safe."

His eyes widened and she was thankful he didn't say anything about her revelation. He did make her feel safe, and loved, but he also drove her crazy and made her want to punch him at times too.

"You will not hurt me, Sable." He craned his neck and lowered his hands, so she slid down his body.

The hard ridges of muscle on his torso rubbing against her stomach and breasts wrecked her concentration and shoved her fears out of her mind.

She would stop if her wrist hurt.

And only then.

Sable kissed Thorne again and wrapped her legs around his waist. He turned with her, and she had a flashback of their last vision. She tensed and he stopped with her back barely millimetres from the wall.

"No biting," she whispered against his lips and he groaned, the sound pained as it echoed around the small stone room. "Swear it."

"I swear it," he ground out and kissed her again, pressing her back against the wall with the force of it. He broke the kiss and rested his forehead against hers, his breath hot against her buzzing lips as he spoke. "If you want it though... if you even think about it... I will not be able to stop myself... you understand?"

She nodded. She did. His instincts said to claim her and he could sense her, knew her feelings. If she thought for a moment about the delicious feel of his fangs in her throat...

Thorne growled again, flashing fangs this time. "Sable."

"Sorry." She captured his mouth in a kiss and drove all thoughts of biting from her mind, her hands shaking against his shoulders as a small sliver of fear snaked through her.

Thorne kissed her harder and palmed her bottom, his fingers pressing deep into her flesh. She moaned and ran her hands over his arms, quivering over the feel of his muscles beneath them, all hard and straining. She wanted to kiss and lick every wicked inch of him.

He snarled at her when she broke the kiss and it became a moan as she licked his lips, teasing them. She kissed her way along his strong jaw, his whiskers scratching her lips, and then down his throat. The temptation to bite was strong but she denied it, afraid that it would only coax him into biting her and that would lead to him doing something far more damaging.

She swirled her tongue in circles instead, working her way downwards and then across his shoulder. She did bite now, little nips that tore growls from her demon king and made him hold her harder, clutching her against him and pinning her to the wall with his body.

Sable kissed over his shoulder and slowed as Thorne mimicked her, each delicious lick and nip of his teeth making her tingle. He lifted one hand from her backside and brushed the strap of her tank top aside, and paused.

"You wear no other garment beneath this top," he murmured against her skin, his moist breath fanning the flames already burning within her. She smiled at how antiquated he sounded, so noble and kingly, and oh so hot for her.

"I was in bed." She couldn't resist adding, "*Naked.*"

He groaned and ground against her, and bit out something harsh. Leather trousers could be a pain. She had thrown her combats on for comfort but he evidently didn't have looser fitting clothing.

Sable squeezed her hand between them and ran her hand over the bulge in his leather trousers.

Thorne dropped her like a hot potato and was three feet away from her in a heartbeat.

It hit Sable like a tonne of bricks.

He might be wicked in her dreams, a man made for wild nights between the sheets, but in the real world, it was a whole different matter.

So much for her worries about the court whores.

Thorne breathed hard and fast, his chest heaving with the exertion. His horns curled, flaring forwards, and his nostrils flared as he compressed his lips.

Sable sauntered over to him, swaying her hips a little for effect, luring his gaze down to them. He swallowed hard.

There was only one way she was going to do this.

Metaphorically speaking, she was going to push him in the deep end.

CHAPTER 13

Sable took hold of Thorne's hands, slipped them under her little black top and placed them over her bare breasts.

A bolt of heat lanced him and he growled, his lips peeling back off his fangs, and palmed the soft warm globes. His already aching shaft throbbed against the tight confines of his leathers, pulsing with need that pushed him, relentlessly driving him towards desperation and a point when that need would overcome him and all restraint would shatter, leaving him a slave to his baser hungers.

He wanted to see her breasts, to kiss and lick, and devour her creamy flesh and rosy buds until she cried out his name and pleasure wracked her.

He wanted to please his female.

He grabbed her around the waist with one arm, eliciting a squeal from her, leaned her backwards and shoved her top up with his other hand. His lips claimed her left nipple and her squeal became a moan as he pulled hard on it, swirling his tongue around the bud.

He had wanted to hide it from her, but the knowing look that had flickered in her golden-brown eyes when she had tried to touch him and the rigid control he had sworn to maintain had shattered beneath the weight of his inexperience, told him that she was aware of it. He cursed himself again for succumbing to the jolt of fear that had shot through him, sending his heart leaping violently into his throat and him leaping away from her.

He was inexperienced in this world, lacked knowledge that she possessed, but he would show her that he could make the dreams they had shared into reality. He would prove to her that she had no reason to doubt his abilities as a lover and as a male.

Thorne pressed his fingers into her side as he suckled, each hard tug pulling a moan from her delicious lips. He wanted to kiss them again, savour them for hours this time, but he also didn't want to leave her breasts.

Sable ran her hands over his shoulders and wriggled against him, her frustration coming through the growing link between them, a connection that they had created in their last vision. He hadn't thought it possible to claim her, not in a dream, but he had come close to doing just that. He had begun the mating process. They had begun it. She had hungered for his bite and he had been all too willing to give it to her, to penetrate her sweet pale flesh with his fangs and taste her.

He yearned to do it again and cursed his vow of restraint.

He wanted to claim her while desire maddened her and she was lost in her pleasure, before she could consider what was happening and was powerless to resist. He couldn't though. He would not do it against her will. He wanted her, ached for her to be his, but it had to be on her terms. All he could do was show her that it would be worth it.

She rubbed her legs together and he knew she sought to make the most of the pressure building between them—pressure he had created.

"Thorne," she murmured and he drew back and stared down at her. She swallowed and trembled in his arms. His beautiful female. Desire coloured her eyes, turning them into liquid pools of dark gold. Her lips parted and she husked, "Touch me."

He paused to absorb that request leaving her lips, to revel in how she responded to him now, seeking his touch and his kiss, giving herself over to him. Her expression turned frustrated and he sensed her rising need. He frowned, his own hungers coming to the fore, and ran his red gaze down her body, seeking the area that needed his attention.

He released her top and shifted to one side, keeping her bent over backwards and easily supporting her with his other arm. He skimmed his fingers down her torso and she shivered beneath the light caress.

"Thorne."

He lowered his gaze and his hand at the same time, and she arched and moaned as he covered her mound, palming her through her trousers. She rocked into his touch and he felt her need. It pounded through him, a demand he couldn't ignore. She needed more. She needed him.

"My little fated mortal needs," he growled and fisted the material blocking his way to her.

She grabbed his hand, stopping him before he could rip her trousers away.

"Reality... remember," she said in a desire-drenched whisper. "Buttons are good."

He watched as she popped them all for him, slowly revealing more smooth, toned skin for his hungry gaze. He ached to replace her hands with his own and know his female intimately at last. When she had tackled the final button, he knocked her hands away and half groaned half growled as he slid his free one into her trousers.

She wore no undergarments here too. He shot her a curious glance.

"I said I was in bed... naked." Her sultry smile hit him hard in the chest and sent heat rocketing down to his groin.

"Want you naked." He pulled her up and shoved her trousers down before she could argue.

He tore her boots off and tossed them across the room, bowling over several candles. Sable closed her eyes and turned her head slightly away. Why? She felt different, unsettled.

Was she thinking about their location? The statue honoured his parents but they were not buried here. They were in the crypt below with the rest of his ancestors.

He pulled her trousers down and threw them aside. He would take her mind off it. Before long, his little female would not be able to think at all.

Thorne lifted her again, clutching her bare backside, and growled as he walked with her to the stone wall. She was hot against him, scalding his hands, making him want to touch more of her, until she had branded her name on his flesh and they were one at last.

She tensed and shivered as he pressed her against the wall.

"It's chilly," she said and Thorne shoved her further up it and dropped to his knees at the same time. "Forget I mentioned it... don't you dare move from there."

He had no intention of moving from this spot at her feet, at least not until he had tasted his female and she had screamed his name in pleasure.

He pushed her long toned legs over his shoulders, his hands supporting her backside, and looked up at her. The desire and hunger in her eyes heated him through and he could sense that same feeling flowing through her, chasing away the chill of the stone against her back.

He stared up at her—his everything—the woman he would die without. Her expression softened and she reached down and stroked his brow and then his cheek, holding his gaze.

Thorne inhaled deeply and caught the scent of her desire rolling off the neat dark curls at the juncture of her thighs. His body hardened painfully, cock throbbing against his tight trousers. He needed to taste her. Could no longer deny that hunger.

"Want to taste you now." His tone brooked no argument, showing her that she couldn't stop him, not this time. She gasped as he delved between her thighs, plunging his tongue into her soft folds.

Sable arched away from the wall and grasped his horns, her legs falling open.

He licked her from core to nub and back again, each hard stroke followed by a soft one. She writhed against his face, her hands tugging at his growing horns and her wildness intoxicating him.

"Thorne," she murmured, her head tipped back and shoulders pressing hard into the stone. She looked delicious like that and tasted like Heaven. "Don't stop."

He growled against her. She gasped, moaned and rocked harder, lost in an urgent need for release that he could feel pounding through him, demanding he sate it. Thorne swirled his tongue around her aroused nub, teasing the bud, and her breath hitched in her throat, her body twitching as she came alive for him.

"Taste like ambrosia," he rumbled against her, holding her gaze to show her that he was serious and he had died and gone to Heaven.

She tightened her grip on his horns, a blush burning across her cheeks as she steered him lower. He growled and spread her with his thumbs, his fingers pressed deep into her buttocks.

She bit her lower lip as he speared her with his tongue, thrusting it deep into her channel, mimicking sex. Her need slammed into him through their connection, filling his head with her deepest desires and flooding him with a sense of her thoughts. She wanted him inside her.

His horns grew in her hands.

His ears flared back.

Sable looked down at him, or more precisely his back, and groaned. The skin on his back was writhing, the two long scars where his wings hid shifting. They wanted out. She moaned again, flexing against him, and he shared her thoughts, knew she relived their first joined dream and how his wings had burst free when he had been above her, inside her, possessing all of her.

"Thorne," she moaned and he licked upwards and flicked her bud with the tip of his tongue. She gasped and undulated her hips, riding his tongue, shivering with each brush and swirl. "More."

He shifted one hand lower and she stilled. "Want to be inside you."

"Be gentle," she whispered and he knew her fears too. She didn't need to worry. He would keep control and keep his claws in check for her. He would never hurt her.

"Always."

She smiled down at him, her pleasure flowing through him, telling him that his female liked to hear such things. He would tell her other sweet things if she would listen and it wouldn't drive her away from him. He would tell her of his feelings for her and how she had captivated him, and not because she was his destined mate.

He would have fallen for her beauty and spirit had she not been his fated one.

He slowly inserted one finger into her, wiping the smile from her face and replacing it with a moan of bliss. She was hot and wet, slick against him and scalding him, making him want to venture further. His own groan joined hers as he moved deeper and then withdrew, pressing his finger over her a rougher spot as he did so.

A loud moan left her lips.

"My female enjoys this."

"No shit."

Thorne grinned at her profanity and the feelings roiling within her, and within him.

He delved his tongue between her petals again as he pumped her slowly with his finger, taking her higher with each stroke and each swirl, and him with her. She tipped her head back again and rocked on him, no longer in control of her actions, her body taking the lead as she sought release. He loved that moment when it seized control and how she responded so sweetly to it, giving in to the wildness that lived within her and giving herself over to pleasure.

He groaned again and licked her harder, thrust deeper, needing more of her as his cock throbbed against his leathers, tight with a need to be inside her as his finger was. He wanted to feel her with it, to slowly bury his length in her and have her wet heat encasing him, linking them as one.

She cupped her breasts, ripping another moan from him, the sight wicked and wonderful and threatening to push him over the edge with her. She tweaked her nipples, arching into her touch and tightening around his finger.

He thrust it deep into her and suckled her at the same time and she froze, her mouth open on a silent scream as she shattered. Her body pulsed, hot around him, alive with motion even as she remained tensed and still. He slowly swept his tongue over her, his finger stationary inside her, and moaned huskily as he absorbed every shiver and flex of her body around it.

He liked to feel her climaxing.

Thorne drew back and she looked down at him.

"I want you." His gaze devoured hers and he knew it was dark with unsatisfied desire and need and that she could feel it in him.

Fear prickled across their link. "No."

His eyes darkened for a different reason and he set her down and rose to tower over her.

"I won't go that far with you." She stood her ground and he almost admired her for it because he could feel that deep inside she already thought about him being inside her, desired it as fiercely as he did.

Her growing fear calmed his rage though and had him backing down. She looked too vulnerable as she stared up into his eyes, a flicker of uncertainty in hers, and it reminded him that she had been through much this day and had been seeking comfort from him.

She had made him vow not to bite her and now her eyes and her feelings told him that she feared she would end up desiring such a thing if they took things all the way.

She was afraid that he would claim her here and now.

He wanted to, with every drop of blood in his body, but he had sworn to himself that he wouldn't claim her against her will, and if he bonded with her tonight while she was vulnerable and needed comfort, it would be just that. She would never forgive him come the morning when she was thinking straight.

He had already scored a victory tonight and would be a fool to push for more.

It took all of his willpower but he reined in his need to be inside her, but he couldn't rein in his desire. His body demanded release at his female's hand.

Thorne growled down at her, roughly took her hand and shoved it against his crotch, against the large bulge caged by his burgundy leathers.

"I will not make you… but I cannot be left like this. I need you. I need my female's caress. I gave you pleasure. You cannot deny me the same."

The look in her eyes said she couldn't deny him. She was already rubbing and caressing, and trembling with anticipation. Or was that him?

He realised he trembled too and with good reason. He was on the brink of knowing a female's touch for the first time. His female's touch.

Sable untied the laces on his trousers and pushed the snug leather down his hips, freeing his erection. He growled at the hit of cooler air and then her first caress.

He felt his eyes shine brighter scarlet as his emotions overwhelmed him and his horns curled further.

Thorne grunted as she wrapped her slender hand around him and stroked him, long slow ones that ran from root to tip, brushing the blunt head and sending hot shivers shooting down to his balls. He curled his hips into her touch, chanting her name under his breath, and pressed his hands to the wall on either side of her head.

Sable looked down at her hand on him and he looked down at her. She watched her hand intently as she stroked him, licked her lips and rubbed her thumb over the crown, smearing the pearl of moisture there. He growled and flexed his hips into her wicked caress.

She raised her hands to his chest and he scowled at her until she forced him to turn. She shoved him back against the wall and ran her hands down his body, teasingly exploring his chest and stomach as she dropped to her knees before him.

Sable took hold of his hips and pushed them into the wall, pinning him there. Thorne's breathing quickened, the rough sound filling the room, and his heart thundered. She meant to taste him as he had tasted her. He groaned at just the thought, his knees threatening to give out. She closed her eyes, leaned in and darted her tongue around the soft head of his cock.

He grunted and tensed as pleasure rolled down his length, causing his balls to draw up. She cracked her eyes open and her gaze sought his. Did she want to watch him while she pleasured him, as he had watched her?

Did she desire to see how she affected him, how little he could restrain himself around her and how her touch was bliss?

She wrapped her lips around him and took him deep into her mouth, and looked up the height of him. He stared down at her, finding it hard to keep his eyes open and keep still as she sucked him. He groaned, clenched his teeth and fought the urge to rock into her mouth, afraid that he would somehow hurt her.

Her gaze darkened and drifted over his bare torso, blazing a trail across his muscles and tearing another moan from his throat. He wanted her to rake her nails over his body, leaving fiery streaks of red on his flesh, marks for him to remember this moment by.

She sucked him harder, pressing her tongue into the ridge on the underside of his length as she withdrew and then pulling him back into her mouth, until the head brushed her throat. He grunted each time she sucked him inside, his hips flexing under her hands as he fought the need to thrust.

He didn't want to hurt her.

He had promised to be gentle.

She took one hand away from his hip and raked her nails lightly down his thigh. He shuddered and tipped his head back, his horns flaring forwards and fangs dropping as his lips parted.

The first roll of his balls in her fingers in time with her sucking had him growling. The second had his hands flying above his head and his hips pumping, a string of dark curses leaving his lips at the same time. He clawed at the stones, arching his hips towards her, and she gave up holding him back.

She used her other hand to stroke his shaft as she sucked him and swirled her tongue around the head of his cock, and rolled and tugged his balls. He grunted and growled, his face screwing up and fangs sinking deep into his lower lip. He tasted blood and he wished it was Sable's sweetness on his lips and her neck under his fangs.

Her desire flooded the link between them again, speaking of her need and that she wanted another release. She wanted him inside her. He groaned and growled at her, warning that if she continued to think such wicked things, he would be powerless to resist fulfilling her desires.

Sable tongued his slit, tasting him, and he muttered her name and clawed at the stone, leaving grooves in the dark rough rock and blunting his nails. He didn't care. The alternative was to lay his hands on Sable and he didn't trust himself right now. If he touched her, it would be hard to stop himself from pulling her up his body, turning with her and impaling her on his aching cock.

She sucked him harder, increasing her strokes, and he grew thicker, his grunts darker as he climbed towards release. She squeezed his shaft and then rubbed the spot behind his balls and his roar echoed around the small room.

His hips shoved forwards, thrusting his cock deep as he shot thick jets of seed into her mouth. She swallowed them all, gently stroking his thighs and suckling him, bringing him down slowly as he fought for breath, his heart hammering wildly against his chest and entire body quivering with release.

All the while she watched him.

He stood above her, his shoulders shoved hard against the wall and hips bowed forwards, every muscle on his body tensed and trembling. His fangs grazed his lips and the points of his horns flared close to his temples, visible in his peripheral vision.

What did she think as she gazed up at him?

Did she like how he appeared, wild and sated, lost to sensation and pleasure because of her?

She sat back, releasing him and he lowered his head and stared down at her, feeling hazy and drugged, sluggish both in mind and body.

The corners of his lips quirked into a sated smile. "I had always thought you had a wicked mouth. Now I know just how truly wicked it is."

She smiled with him.

It slowly faded as he continued to stare down at her and a sliver of fear trickled through their connection.

Sable thought he would say something else, something she didn't want to hear yet desired to know at the same time.

She was his little contradiction. His confusing little female.

She was the woman he loved with all of his heart.

CHAPTER 14

Sable's smile faded as the intensity of Thorne's gaze increased. He was going to say something foolish and make her regret what they had done, and she didn't want that.

She stood and waited for him to ruin the moment.

He tucked himself away and moved around her. Sable blinked. Not going to say something stupid, like she belonged to him now or he would make her his queen?

Or he loved her?

A bitter taste coated her tongue.

Disappointment.

Why? She didn't want him to say something so ridiculous. She really didn't.

He came back to her and held her clothes out to her. She took them from him but he remained with his hand outstretched.

"Come. I will take you back to your room."

So that was his plan. He was going to be all chivalrous and take her to her room, and once they were there, he would try to make love with her, or say something stupid to ruin the moment.

Sable righted her top and quickly tugged her trousers on. She held her boots to her chest and took Thorne's hand. The ground opened up beneath them and she closed her eyes as they dropped into it.

When the cold disappeared, she opened them again. As promised, he had taken her to her room. The fire in the grate had gone out hours ago and the room was dark, lit by a single candle on the dressing table.

Thorne gathered her closer to him, still staring down into her eyes, his striking ones enchanting her as she waited for him to say something, to do something to spoil the moment.

He lowered his head and gave her the softest kiss she had ever experienced. The barriers holding her feelings back fractured, threatening to break as his lips gently played with hers, the kiss tender and reverent, filled with soft emotions.

No one had ever kissed her like this.

As if they loved her.

As if she were their whole world.

She shivered and wanted to pull away, but found herself moving closer instead, stepping into the shelter of his embrace. He wrapped his thickly muscled arms around her, caging her against his powerful hard body, and she tiptoed, seeking a deeper kiss from him.

He refused her, keeping the kiss light and soft, playing havoc with her emotions and the dam holding them back. It fractured again and she felt she would drown in the impending flood if Thorne didn't stop kissing her, didn't stop tearing down her defences.

Why had no one kissed her like this before?

Why had she never kissed someone like this too?

The tender play of his lips against hers and the careful way he held her tucked against him left her feeling she had been missing something all her life and in all her short term relationships.

If this was how a man kissed when he was in love, then no one had ever loved her before Thorne, and she had no doubt that he felt that emotion for her.

Was this what Olivia had with Loren?

No wonder her friend had given herself to her elf prince, joining him in immortality for an eternity together.

An eternity of this?

Sable almost wanted to reach out and grab hold of it.

Thorne drew back and looked down into her eyes, his filled with affection that left her feeling that it was already too late to save herself and she was drowning now, before the dam had even burst.

She looked at him, waiting for him to do as she expected, wondering which it would be. Attempt to get inside her or say something stupid.

Thorne released her, stepping back at the same time, and then raised her hand to his lips and pressed a long kiss to it, holding her gaze.

He lingered.

She waited for the inevitable.

"Swear to me you will not wander the corridors alone again," he said in a deadly serious tone, completely not what she had expected.

"I swear." Because she had absolutely zero intention of being so stupid in the future. She didn't want to think about how badly this night might have gone if it hadn't been Thorne who had found her in that small room in the bowels of the castle.

He smoothed his hand across her cheek.

She braced herself.

He surprised her again by dipping his head and briefly brushing his lips across hers and then stepping away from her.

"Goodnight, Sable." He looked down into her eyes, his red ones overflowing with warmth and affection. The sound of her name leaving his lips warmed her inside and left her wishing he would use it more often rather than his pet name for her. "Try to get some sleep. You need to rest."

"So do you," she said and why did she want him to sleep at the same time as her? She really had no idea. It wasn't because he was clearly about to leave after being supremely chivalrous and sweet, when she had secretly wanted him to do something to make her feel he really bone-deep wanted her.

Like she wanted him.

And he had no intention of sleeping, so they couldn't pick up in their dreams where they had left off in reality.

"Do not worry yourself about me." He dropped another kiss on her lips and then he was gone, leaving only a shrinking black patch on the wooden floor behind.

That was the problem.

She did worry about him.

She worried about him, and she wanted to lift the burden on his shoulders, and wanted to keep him company in this long, sleepless night. She wanted to give him comfort, both emotionally and physically.

She bone-deep wanted him.

Holy hell.

Lust for him? Yes. The other thing? No way.

She did not love him.

CHAPTER 15

Thorne swung his broadsword up onto his shoulder and listened to the males around him as they discussed the best route to take through the land, pointing to various areas and tracks on the map he had laid out on the largest table in the library. Loren was against the idea and had voiced his opposition several times in the past fifteen minutes alone. The dark elf prince didn't like the thought of leaving his female alone in the castle.

Thorne gazed out of the arched window to his right, down to the courtyard below, quietly admitting to himself that he felt the same way. He didn't want to leave Sable alone at the castle when she was clearly struggling. He could sense her even at this distance, a sign of their growing bond, and knew her worries had yet to fade.

She had been working with her team of mortals for the past hour, commanding them to go through drills and looking every bit the powerful female and leader. He saw through her façade though. To him, she looked tired. Hadn't she slept after their encounter?

He hadn't been able to either. He had paced the courtyard and then the walls, checking on the sentries and enjoying the quiet and the comforting embrace of darkness, and the lingering warm haze from his time with Sable. He had sent several of his best warriors to the villages to check on them and all reports had come back stating that the borders were quiet. After the earlier battle, it was a weight off his mind. He had feared that the Fifth King would seek to attack again, using his numbers to overwhelm Thorne's forces and place strain on them.

Perhaps word had reached the king of Sable's ability.

Thorne's gaze tracked her, studying the luscious curves her tight black t-shirt and combat trousers only highlighted as she strode around the courtyard, watching several groups of her team as they trained with swords and other modern mortal weaponry. Her sleek black hair was up in a ponytail, something he had come to understand as a sign of intent. She meant business and he knew why.

He was one king that word had reached last night. He had overheard his men speaking of him and Sable, and when he had questioned some of them, scaring them in the process as they hadn't realised he stood nearby, they had revealed that Sable's mortals also spoke of them.

They were questioning her ability to lead them and had been hard on her after the battle.

His little female hadn't needed such behaviour from her subordinates in the aftermath of the fight, not when she had been questioning herself.

She rubbed her wrist and he noticed that she had removed the cuff he had placed around it, and had covered it with a smaller leather one.

"Thorne is miles away," Grave said in a mocking tone that told him exactly what the male thought about his desire for Sable.

Grave seemed to have a problem with females in general. Strange for a man who courted their attention, regaling them with stories of his victories and luring them back to his bedchamber.

Thorne tossed him a warning glare and went back to perusing Sable, pondering what had happened and what she had told him. She bore a mark that she believed might be fae or demonic in origin and had no parents to question about it.

She hadn't lost them, as he had lost his.

She had never known them.

He found that difficult to believe. In his world, children were cherished. No demon would think of leaving his offspring to fend for itself.

"She seems troubled today." Loren's deep voice came from nearby and he looked up at the elf in front of him, catching him gazing down at the courtyard.

Thorne suppressed his urge to growl over Loren looking at his mate, fighting his instincts to protect what was his. The male had no interest in her other than as a friend so there was little need for him to feel threatened. Loren was mated and happy. Thorne wished he could experience such a thing himself. He wanted to bind himself to Sable. He wanted to be with his love and know she loved him too.

He had made a small advance on his path to achieving that goal last night and had to keep his head and keep making those tiny leaps until she belonged to him. Allowing his instinct to claim her and drive away any male who looked upon her to take control of him would undo all of his progress. No matter how hard it became, how fiercely his need for her drove him to attack any male in the vicinity, he had to keep fighting it or risk losing Sable.

"She did not sleep last night," Thorne said quietly, hoping the others wouldn't hear him.

They were deep in discussion about the planned hunt. He didn't want to go but the men needed to bond if they were going to serve his purpose and help defend his kingdom. The vampires and werewolves in particular. His men had reported that many of those two species had been intent on attacking each other rather than fighting the demons of the Fifth Realm during the battle at the border village.

Loren stared at him, evidently expecting more information.

Thorne wanted to give it to the elf prince but it wasn't his place. If Sable discovered he had spoken with Loren about her wrist and her power, she would be angry with him. He had faith that she would tell her friend, Olivia, given enough time. She would overcome her fears.

Perhaps he could drop Loren a hint to pass on to Olivia though.

He looked up at the prince, straight into his rich purple eyes. "She is troubled by something."

"What?"

"I cannot say… but perhaps if Olivia were to ask her… perhaps she would benefit from speaking with her friend about it."

Loren's expression turned grave. "Is it about your bond?"

Thorne shook his head. "No. It is something else. Something personal. She requires a friend to speak with."

"I will speak with her." That deep male voice had Thorne growling and swinging his gaze towards the owner.

Bleu stood there, his wild black hair swept back from his forehead and his ears pointed, speaking of his emotions. He harboured feelings of aggression. Thorne did too. He wanted to tear the male's head off for interrupting him and Loren, and daring to offer to speak with his mate.

"You will do no such thing," Thorne growled, because he didn't want the wretched elf commander anywhere near Sable while she was confused and vulnerable. He would seek to take advantage of her.

The voice at the back of Thorne's mind said that many would consider what he had done last night with Sable as taking advantage of her.

Thorne shut it out.

She had initiated things. She had begged him to kiss her. He had merely complied.

Loren held his hand up as Bleu went to speak. "King Thorne is correct and it should be Olivia who speaks with her. We have discussed this, Bleu."

Bleu's violet gaze darkened and the pointed tips of his ears flared back against his head. "You spoke and I listened. There was no discussion."

"Bleu," Loren snapped and Bleu lowered his head, locking his gaze on his boots.

"Forgive me, my prince, I spoke out of turn." Bleu pressed his hand to his chest, his skin pale against the black scales of his armour that covered him from ankle to neck and to his wrists, hugging his lithe muscular body like a second skin.

Thorne wished the elves did not possess such armour. He had seen the way the female werewolves and mortals gazed upon them with desire in their eyes, clearly imagining they were nude.

That Sable had been around this male while he had been dressed in such revealing armour disturbed him. His hands twitched, claws itching to rip the black scales from Bleu's body and destroy them somehow, forcing the male to dress in less revealing clothing. His fangs lengthened and his horns began to curl around the arch of his ears, the pointed tips reaching their lobes before he drew in a deep breath and regained tentative control over his emotions.

Bleu flicked him a glare, an edge to his eyes warning that he had detected his rising anger and would fight him if he dared to attack.

Thorne wanted to provoke the male into attacking first. Only the fact that word would get back to Sable and she would be angry with him stopped him from fulfilling that desire.

Loren sighed and placed his hand on Bleu's shoulder, and spoke to him in the elf language. Thorne had tried to learn it. He had asked countless scholars about the language and none had been able to help him. The elves guarded it well, stopping any from outside of their species from knowing it.

Thorne wanted to know what Loren was telling Bleu, because the elf prince's expression was softening, the hard angles of his face becoming tinged with concern, and Thorne didn't like it. If the male wasn't telling Bleu that Sable was off limits to him, then he would come to blows with them both.

Sable belonged to him.

She had been born for him and him for her.

"Are we hunting or not?" Kincaid called out, capturing Thorne's attention and dragging it away from thoughts of accidentally swinging his broadsword at Bleu's neck to eliminate his competition. "The cub is growing restless."

"I am not… and I am *not* a cub," Kyal said in a bored tone and drummed his fingers on the wooden table, his bright blue gaze scanning the map before him. He pointed to something. "I just want to get out there."

Thorne ambled over to them and frowned at Kyal's finger where it pressed against the map.

The woods.

The lad wanted to shift form and run.

Thorne could understand that. Kyal had failed to cut his teeth in the battle yesterday. His pack members had beaten him to every demon, sometimes using rough tactics to ensure he didn't reach any enemy before them. Wolves had tried to do the same to Kincaid when he had been young, but the male had bested many of them and had torn a few throats from their enemies.

Kyal had tasted defeat, falling short of his father and likely his own expectations, and the sour look on his face said defeat tasted bitter.

"The woods are a good choice. I have seen many animals there." Thorne plotted a course with his finger, one that wouldn't take them too far from the castle and would keep their scent away from any prey before it was too late for them to flee.

"We hunt then." Grave rested his hand on the long sword sheathed at his side. "The pup might not be restless, but I am. We stand here prattling like women when we should be out there, bloodying our fangs and claws."

Grave grinned, revealing those fangs.

He had bloodied them enough yesterday at the battle and had sated himself with several of the court females too. Now he hungered to track and kill prey. The male was insatiable.

"Come." The dark-haired vampire motioned to the others.

Kincaid rolled his golden-brown eyes before muttering, "The day I follow one of your orders is the day I have died, Bloodsucker."

Kyal smirked at the irritated glare Grave shot at Kincaid.

"As you please, Dogs." Grave stormed towards the door.

Thorne looked back down at the courtyard. They would have to pass through it to reach the outer courtyard and then the main gate. He didn't want Grave passing Sable when the werewolves had fouled his mood. She was distracted, an easy target for the vampire's barbs, and liable to retaliate if she felt threatened. Vampires were training in the inner courtyard too. If she attacked their commander, they wouldn't hesitate to strike back at her and her men.

"Lord Van der Garde," Thorne called out and the male slowed before he had reached the door and looked back at him. "We will hunt, and I will lead."

The vampire's lips compressed into a thin line and he forced a nod.

Sable wasn't the only one likely to attack the vampire commander today. If Grave gave him any trouble, if he so much as looked at Sable with the intent to hurt her in his icy blue eyes, or if he failed to follow Thorne's lead, Thorne might just kill him.

Thorne swept past the vampire, led the way through the stone corridor and down to the next floor, heading towards the courtyard. He kept his broadsword resting on his shoulder, on his white shirt. He had donned his spare pair of vambraces to protect his forearms. They were worn, weaker than the one that Sable now possessed, but they would protect him against their quarry.

He stepped out of the dark interior of the castle and into the courtyard, his eyes quickly adjusting to the light. In Sable's eyes, it was probably no brighter than twilight. She likely thought it dark and grim, as unpleasant as she had thought it at night when they had been on the balcony together.

That night seemed like weeks ago now when it had been barely days. He felt as if she had been at his castle forever, her scent covering everything, filling his senses until all he could concentrate on was her.

His little female.

She pretended not to notice him but he was on to her. She had glanced his way when he had emerged from the castle and now appeared to be trying very hard not to look at him. Colour rose onto her cheeks and everything male in him demanded he go to her, gather her against him, and kiss her as he had last night before they had parted company.

That kiss had melted her more than their intimate moment that had preceded it.

He had felt her soften towards him and had sensed the rising tide of her emotions.

Her gaze leaped back to him and she frowned.

"Swap out," she hollered at her team, turned on her heel and strode towards him, catching him at the gate to the outer courtyard. "Where are you all going?"

She looked at each of his party in turn and then her golden gaze came back to him, the fiery edge to it and her emotions warning him that she had realised he had intended to leave her behind while taking all the other commanders with him.

He wanted her safe.

Protected.

That meant ignoring the part of him that wanted her constantly at his side and in his field of vision and leaving her here at the castle.

"You're all dressed for battle… so I'm going to ask again… where are you going?" She wisely kept her eyes on him while she spoke of the other men, tempering his mood. If she had looked at them, he might have been unable to ignore his constant pressing urge to maim two of them.

"We go to hunt." Loren stepped forwards, coming to stand at Thorne's side.

Sable's pretty face darkened. "Did I miss the memo… or was I not invited?"

"It is only for leaders," Grave snidely remarked and Sable shot him a deadly glare.

"Bleu is attending and so is Kyal, and neither of them are leaders… and I damned well am." She swung to face the vampire and pointed at the two men in question.

Thorne growled, unable to stop himself no matter how hard he had tried. Sable glanced at him and then turned her cheek to him, keeping her eyes on the men.

She was mad at him. Punishing him by looking at other males. Because he wanted to keep her safe?

Thorne realised his mistake.

Because she thought he was belittling her.

Grave did just that, grinning at her the whole time. "A leader of mortals. Remember that. What we go to hunt would likely kill you."

Sable clenched her fists at her sides and stood her ground, a dark look flashing in her eyes. "You're just worried that my aim might be off and I might kill you."

The vampire didn't even react. His expression remained emotionless and cold, his eyes as frosty as Antarctica as he held her gaze. "That is rather unlikely to happen. I doubt you could manage to hit me with one of your itty-bitty bolts."

Sable unleashed a noise of sheer frustration and turned on Thorne. She stepped up to him, small yet fierce, determination written in every line of her face and the taut curves of her body.

Curves he had possessed, had claimed with his hands, skin-to-skin.

"I am going on this hunt."

Thorne stared down at her, her fury and the fiery look in her striking eyes heating his blood until he burned for her. He wanted her to demand other things of him, wicked things, in that same vicious and commanding tone. He wanted her to press him to the wall as she had last night, seizing control of him, and do it all over again.

His horns curled.

Sable didn't seem to notice his growing desire for her, or if she had, she did a good job of hiding it. Not a hint of pink touched her cheeks.

"I'm coming with you whether you like it or not. I'm a hunter," she barked and turned her glare on all the men present, a challenge in her golden eyes. "I can handle myself. I'll bag the biggest, baddest monster you've ever seen."

Kincaid muttered, "You already have."

Kyal snickered.

Thorne kept staring at her, transfixed by her beauty and strength, and her determination to prove herself. She tossed a scowl at the two werewolves and turned back to him, pinning him with a black look that warned him not to refuse her.

"I'm coming too."

He imagined she might have stomped her foot had Grave not been present and ready to mock her.

Thorne nodded. "Very well."

Bleu opened his mouth and Sable held her hand up, cutting off his protest before he could voice it.

"Save it, Bleu." She turned away from him and stormed towards the arched wooden doors to the outer courtyard, her black leather boots loud on the flagstones, leaving Bleu staring after her with his mouth hanging open.

Thorne growled at him, baring his fangs, warning the male to take his eyes off her.

Bleu snarled back at him, green-purple light flickered over his black skin-tight armour, and he disappeared. Thorne clenched his molars together and turned in time to see the elf male reappearing right next to Sable.

He growled again, under his breath, silently detailing all the ways that he was going to destroy Bleu for daring to continue his pursuit of Sable.

Thorne stomped after them, tempted to unleash his darker nature and to provoke Bleu into a fight by telling the male that he had tasted twixt Sable's thighs and heard her cry *his* name as she climaxed. She belonged to him now. Her essence was within him and the bond was growing stronger. He would claim her and would have his greatest victory.

She would love him.

First, he would ensure she had eyes for only him.

He would beat Bleu to their prey and prove himself the best hunter.

He would show his female that he was the best male for her.

The only man she needed.

CHAPTER 16

Sable followed the men across the black ground outside the castle, Loren at her side. Thorne kept glancing back at her, his crimson gaze dark with emotion that she pretended she couldn't sense in him. She had made a wise bolt for Loren the moment they had reached the outer courtyard, leaving Bleu at the front of the pack with Thorne. She had tried to avoid angering Thorne and giving the two men reason to fall back on trying to outdo each other.

Her plan hadn't worked quite the way she had envisaged it.

Thorne and Bleu were determined to pick up the scent trail of some prey, both clearly wanting to beat the other to it. They bickered at times, the outbreak of angst between them always causing Loren to sigh and pinch the bridge of his nose. It amused the werewolves and the vampire.

It grated on her nerves.

Would they have behaved like this if she hadn't come?

They seemed to be getting along until she had gone to them and insisted she joined the hunting party.

Now it felt as if they were showing off and she was growing tired of the testosterone-fuelled display of masculinity they were both putting on for her.

She really had no interest in cockfights.

Sable focused on tracking the prey alone, looking for signs of life on the dark rocky barren ground. Plenty of boot prints but no animal ones.

A quarrel broke out in the demon language ahead of her. Thorne and Bleu were at it again.

Loren barked something in elvish and Bleu reeled in his idiocy, falling back and breaking away from Thorne, placing some distance between them. It seemed she wasn't the only one they were pissing off. Loren looked ready to slap Bleu.

Sable sighed and glanced ahead of them.

Her eyebrows rose.

Thorne had been right and there were trees yonder from his castle.

She smiled, remembering how mortified he had looked when he had first used that word around her and she had teased him for it. He had used it again since, and she found it a little charming, especially when he had looked uncertain, bracing himself as if he feared she would laugh at him again.

The trees resembled tall pines. They towered high on the hills, swaying in the breeze, shadowy and grim against their equally shadowy and grim backdrop.

She was beginning to miss blue skies and stars, but she felt no pressing need to leave this strange realm yet.

It fascinated her.

The pines were darker than those in her world. A product of their environment?

The wind came again, tousling her ponytail, and she tucked a few rogue strands back in place and surveyed the landscape surrounding her. She wanted to see more of this weird new world.

She couldn't fathom where this world was in comparison with hers and didn't want to think that it might really be beneath the mortal one, within the planet. It freaked her out whenever she contemplated it. Loren had told her that it was in a way, but not in others. That it existed on a different plane from her world but was connected to it via a series of pathways, and was beneath her world but not at the same time.

It was a mind fuck.

Sable frowned at her feet. There was grass. She scuffed it with her boots, amazed by it. Like the pines, it was darker than the grass in her world, verging on black. But it was definitely grass.

"Is it still bothering you?" Loren said beside her.

She turned her frown on him. "The grass?"

His black eyebrows knitted to mirror her expression. "No. Your wrist."

He nodded towards it and she realised that she had been rubbing the leather cuff around it while walking.

Sable shook her head and then admitted, "A little."

She followed the party up an incline, heading towards the treeline, and held her wrist. The urge to tell Loren about what had happened welled up within her and she squashed it, fearing the questions he would ask if she said anything.

Her gaze sought Thorne. He led the pack again, speaking with Kincaid. He fell quiet and looked over his shoulder at her, his crimson eyes questioning as he frowned. She smiled to alleviate his concern but he didn't go back to speaking with the werewolf leader. His gaze held hers and then fell, following her arm to her hand where it clutched her wrist.

He stopped and turned back and she shook her head and let go of her wrist, afraid he would come to her and make a fuss of her in front of the others. It would only lead to questions and she wanted to avoid them for as long as she could.

He hesitated, the soft look in his eyes telling her that he wanted to ignore her request and come to her anyway, and then heaved a sigh and continued up the hill, entering the forest with Kincaid at his side. Grave looked back at her, his icy eyes locking on hers, a calculating edge to them. He said something to Bleu.

Bleu instantly teleported.

Grave grinned.

Bastard.

He was trying to stir up trouble again.

Bleu reappeared right in front of her and she had to stop dead in her tracks to avoid colliding with him.

"Are you unwell?" he rushed out, concern warming his purple eyes as he ran them over her.

"I'm fine. The bloodsucker is just yanking your chain." But it was nice that Bleu had come running the moment he thought there was something wrong with her.

Sable frowned. There was something very wrong with her. She didn't want Bleu's attention, and she shouldn't find it endearing when he rushed over to her. He wasn't serious about her. She knew that deep in her heart. Olivia was right. He just wanted a little one-on-one action with her.

It had been Thorne who had noticed she was missing in the battle and had searched for her.

It had been Thorne who had bravely risked his life to teleport her back to the castle.

It had been Thorne who had kissed her with so much affection and tenderness that she had wanted to melt into a puddle.

It was Thorne who had stopped ahead of her now and was looking back at her with love in his eyes, with hope and fear, and everything that she felt colliding within her too.

"Bleu, I was speaking with Sable," Loren said and Bleu's gaze darted between them, eventually settling on his prince. "We were discussing something delicate. She is touched by your concern about her welfare, but she is well and would rather the hunt continued. You are placing her under scrutiny and exposing her to vile rumours, both from her peers and from the other species, including our own. Please return to the hunt and tracking our prey."

Bleu shifted his purple gaze to her.

"What he said." She wanted to leave it at that but the edge of irritation and hurt in his eyes made her add, "It is really nice that you were worried, but I was sort of talking to Loren, and Grave just wanted to make Thorne mad at you."

And Thorne was making his way back to them now, his horns curling and eyes beginning to glow with his fury.

Bleu lingered. "You are well though? You seem out of spirits."

"If the female says she is well, then she is well," Thorne barked and scowled as he shoved Bleu's shoulder, pushing him away from her. "She clearly does not appreciate you probing into her private life."

"This from the male who would do the same once I remove myself from her?" Bleu squared his shoulders and settled his hand on the black blade hanging at his waist.

Sable lowered her head, not wanting to watch and definitely not wanting to hear what she knew was coming, but found it impossible not to peek.

Thorne grinned. "I know her private matters. She has spoken about much with me. She has confided in me."

Bleu lips thinned and his ears flared, flattening against the sides of his head. His eyes shone vivid purple.

Loren's hand clamped down on his shoulder, holding him back.

Sable planted her hands on her hips. "Seriously, Thorne? You want to score a victory over him with something like this... because I've spoken about much with Bleu too. I've spoken about much with Loren... and with Olivia... and the list goes on. If you want me to continue to speak with you about anything, both of you, you'll grow up this second and drop this stupid rivalry."

Neither male looked inclined to agree to that.

Sable huffed. "I'm going on ahead. Be sure to ogle my fine arse as I walk away from you both because it's all you'll be seeing of me on this hunt."

She shoved past them and trudged up the hill, trying to put as much space between them as quickly as possible. Grave smiled as she passed him. Sable was tempted to punch it off his face but stopped herself. If she hit Grave, the vampire would hit back, and then all hell would break loose.

Loren bit out something harsh-sounding in the elf language.

Sable didn't slow.

Not even when Thorne appeared on her right, his dusky brown horns curled around his pointed ears and his eyes blazing scarlet fire. He shoved his fingers through his russet-brown hair and trailed them down his left horn.

"Sable," he started and she glared at him, daring him to say something stupid. She might not be foolish enough to land a punch on Grave's jaw, but she would slap Thorne in a heartbeat. "I did not mean to upset you."

"You never do," Sable spat and kept stomping up the hill. It was bigger than it had looked from the bottom and the path was rocky, bumpy underfoot. She stepped over a root and huffed. "Why can't men think before they open their mouths?"

Thorne shrugged, shifting the long blade balanced on his right shoulder. "He angered me."

"You angered him too. Does that make you feel better? Does it make you equal? I'm tired of this childish behaviour."

"I will stop then," Thorne said, his deep gravelly voice making her insides quiver and heat. She stifled that reaction and frowned at him, not convinced he could come good on that promise. "I will stop if you swear you are mine and mine alone and have no interest in Bleu."

Sable tipped her chin up and said nothing. She wasn't going to let him bully her into confessing her feelings for him, whatever they were, or that she was only interested in Bleu as a friend. If she did, she was only giving his behaviour positive reinforcement, making him think he could use this tactic on her whenever he wanted something.

"What if I just said I would stop?" he whispered and moved closer to her.

The back of his left hand brushed hers and she looked up at him, and sighed at the soft hopeful look in his beautiful eyes.

"I would like that," she admitted quietly and he nodded, turned his face forwards and walked with her.

Sable's gaze lingered on him, tracing the noble lines of his profile and the sweeping arc of his dusky ridged left horn as it arched from behind the top of his pointed ear and followed the curve around to the lobe. They didn't even bother her anymore—not in this smaller form that told her he was in control of his emotions nor in their wilder state, when they grew large and curled around like ram's horns, forming a loop and deadly points. In fact, if pressed, she would admit that she liked them. They added something to his appearance, something rugged and masculine, and alluring.

"Gods, I want you when you stare at me like that," Thorne whispered and ran his free hand over his left horn again. It grew, curving further around, the tip closer to his cheekbone. Desire. That emotion rippled through her too. "Stop it or I will whisk you into the woods before any see us disappear and take you against a tree."

Sable shivered at the thought, hot and achy inside even when she told herself not to react to his husky, naughty words. His nostrils flared and he groaned.

He raised a single dark eyebrow and looked down at her out of the corner of his eye. "You would like that? My female is a wicked little one."

"Not your female," Sable countered as she finally tore her gaze away and sauntered on ahead of him.

"Yet," Thorne said from behind her and she fought the smile that threatened to rise onto her lips at the determination in his tone.

At least he had acknowledged that he hadn't won her yet and she didn't belong to him.

He had to fight harder if he wanted more than just a swift moment of madness in a dark basement room with her.

Sable frowned at her line of thought and then at the incredible view stretched out before her beyond the brow of the hill.

The others caught up with them and Thorne led Loren forwards, to a clearing where the trees on the other side of the hill were lower. She could see for miles even in the low light and couldn't believe her eyes.

It wasn't the village nestled in the valley below that had caught her attention, or even the fenced off areas that had colourful things growing under lamps in them.

It was the huge towering white wind turbines on the hill across from her. They whirled slowly, spinning at a mesmerising pace that had her staring and losing track of her surroundings.

"I must admit, Thorne, that I admire your ingenuity. I had not thought to bring such a thing into my realm," Loren said, snapping her back to the world.

Thorne stood beside him, his back to her and his sword stabbed into the ground beside him, one hand resting idly on the guard.

"I saw them on a visit to the mortal world. I am also investigating utilising steam from the thermal vents in my kingdom to create more power stations. Then, we will be able to generate enough electricity to power special ultraviolet lamps and we will be able to grow other crops."

Sable couldn't help but admire him too. He really was trying to make his land better and she could see that he wanted to improve it for his people. He cared deeply for them.

Thorne swept his hand out across the landscape. "What you see here is only the beginning of my plans. I intend to provide farms for the widowed females and those who would like to work. They have volunteered to begin running new projects, such as farming animals of the mortal world. We are to begin with chickens and then cows. Many of the males are as pleased by this as the females. Chickens and cows means eggs and milk and other dairy produce much loved by everyone here. Those with females have grown accustomed to a broader variety of foods. Eggs were new to me until recently, but I will confess they tasted good."

His gaze darted to her and then back again. She smiled at his confession, remembering how he had made food for her when she had been hung over.

"What about pigs?" she said and he looked at her again and nodded.

"We would eventually like to bring pigs and sheep. We can use the animals for a variety of resources, not only for food."

He was thinking like a true king and she wanted to tell him so, but knew that if she mentioned that he was a good king like his father had been, that he wouldn't appreciate it. He had told her things in confidence too and she would keep them secret for him.

"We also intend to open schools," Thorne said and lifted his gaze to meet Loren's. "I would like to make a good education available to all in my land."

That made her smile. He wanted the best for his people. It was noble of him, and again she wanted to reach out and lay her hand on his arm to gain his attention and tell him that he was a good king.

Thorne's attention drifted down to her and she hid her smile, trying to hold on to her anger over what he had said to Bleu and his childish behaviour. Her anger faded and she let her smile out again when she saw in Thorne's eyes and sensed in him that he needed to know what she thought of him now. She looked up into his eyes, letting him see that she admired him for trying to make this realm a better place for his people and how strongly he fought to protect them from others.

"Educated demons. Now there is a frightening thought." Grave's snide remark went ignored. His face darkened and he bared his fangs at Kyal. Picking on the weakest in the group? Perhaps Thorne and Bleu weren't the only grown men in their party capable of childish behaviour.

Kyal ignored him too and continued stripping off, shoving his trousers down with something akin to pride. Sable averted her gaze. Seriously. Werewolves had no shame.

He growled, snarled, and when she looked to check on him, a huge tawny wolf was staring at her, his golden eyes bright in the low light. He snorted, shook all over, and then took off.

"We won't see him for a few hours. He needed a run," Kincaid said close to her elbow and she looked up at the older, brunet werewolf.

His eyes matched Kyal's wolf's golden ones, but his were bright with amusement not hunger. He gathered Kyal's clothes.

A howl sounded in the distance.

Kincaid dropped the clothes. "Kyal has a scent."

The older werewolf stripped off and had transformed before she could even look away, becoming a huge rich brown wolf.

Finally, she could fight something and prove to these irritating men that she deserved to be out on this hunt with them.

She was the best huntress at Archangel and they were going to know it.

Kincaid tore off after Kyal with Grave hot on his heels. Thorne and Bleu shot off after them.

A flaw in her plan presented itself.

Sable didn't have super-speed or the ability to teleport.

Loren offered her a consolatory smile. "We could conduct our own hunt?"

She shook her head. "Thanks for sticking with me, Big Guy, and for trying to cheer me up, but I think I'll pass."

She stared off in the direction everyone had headed, trying to convince herself that she wasn't annoyed and disappointed that everyone had left her behind, even Thorne, and that she had better things to do anyway. She should probably focus on getting her hunters ready for the next battle.

Who needed this male-bonding crap?

She continued to stare off into the distance, her senses stretching outwards, searching for Thorne.

"How would I know if I was Thorne's fated one?" Sable let the words slip out quietly, pretending that she hadn't just voiced them to Loren and that she wasn't counting the seconds until he replied.

"You already know in your heart that you are his mate, Sable. You can deny the signs if you desire, but you have dreamed of him, with him, have you not?" A blush of colour rose onto his pale cheeks when she nodded. "And you feel a connection to him?"

She nodded again and his expression said it all.

"You think I'm his mate?"

"I knew the moment I met Thorne and saw his reaction to you. He desired you greatly and looked as I had felt when I had first met Olivia… filled with a need to have you."

Sable's cheeks burned and she couldn't bring herself to look at Loren.

He looked away too. "I apologise for my crude words."

Sable shook her head. "It's okay, really. I just wanted to know if there was a chance he only fancied me like Bleu does."

Loren's face fell, his demeanour darkening with it. "What the two males are feeling are entirely different things."

She had thought as much. "Thorne says I make him crazy."

She felt a little crazy herself around him at times, driven wild with need for him but afraid of the consequences. Eternity was a long time.

Loren smiled and looked back towards the castle through the trees. "You are definitely his fated one then. Olivia made me mad with a need to claim her as my female and fight any male who tried to take her from me, even if the threat was only perceived and not real."

"Sounds like Thorne," Sable said and looked down at her wrist as it ached. She had Loren alone. Now was a perfect time to steer the conversation towards the mark on her wrist.

She tried to get the words to line up on her tongue but they wouldn't come. Why could she talk with the prince about her man trouble but couldn't talk to him about something that she desperately needed answers to? It wasn't like her to talk about personal things with anyone at all, but her relationship with Thorne certainly felt more personal than her possible non-human parentage.

Loren was five thousand years old and knew a lot about fae and demons. If anyone could tell her what the symbol on her wrist meant and where her strange powers had come from, and point her towards answers, it was him.

She had to do this.

She had to speak to him, and to Olivia, just as Thorne had told her to. They would understand. They wouldn't think she was a freak because she had a weird ability and a tattoo that had probably been there since her birth.

Sable cleared her throat.

A feral roar shattered the silence, coming from the direction the others had run.

Her nerve failed. "You should probably go and catch up with the guys. Tell them thanks for leaving me behind."

She gathered the clothes the werewolves had shed and bundled them up in her arms.

"If you are sure. It is probably best I am there. I would like to maintain good relations between the demons and my race, no matter how fiercely Bleu tries to ruin them." He held his hand out to her and smiled. "I will give you a lift back to the castle. I believe Thorne lost his head when Kyal sent out the call and rushed off without thinking about your safety, and I would lose mine if he found out I had left you to walk back alone."

Sable nodded, adjusted the clothes in her arms, and took his hand. He drew her up against him, curled his arm around her and she closed her eyes, trying not to imagine it was Thorne who held her tucked close to his chest as they teleported.

When the weird sensation of teleporting had passed, she opened her eyes, finding herself in the courtyard again. She stepped out of Loren's arms and dumped the clothes on the ground. She had been nice enough to bring them back but that was where her kindness ended. The wolves shouldn't have left them out in the woods.

Loren nodded and disappeared in a flash of blue-purple light.

Sable looked up at the hill in the far distance.

Her wrist itched and burned. Her senses blared a warning.

She looked around the courtyard, searching for the source of the disturbance in her gift. No one was looking at her, but she felt sure that someone had been a moment ago.

Her gaze met one of the vampire's and he frowned at her and then turned and walked into the castle, disappearing into the darkness.

The vampire who had come out to collect Grave that night on the balcony. He was probably wondering why she had returned and his commander hadn't.

She looked back at the hill.

A tight feeling formed in the pit of her stomach.

Sable shook it off and turned towards her men, intent on reclaiming their respect and putting both Bleu and Thorne out of her head.

CHAPTER 17

Sable stood to one side of the space they had commandeered in the courtyard of Thorne's dark castle, watching Evan as he sparred with two of the other men in her team. She studied his every move, nodding in approval at some of the ways he tricked his opponents into lowering their guards. Most of the team had retired for the day, heading back inside the castle to wash up and prepare for this evening's feast.

Her gaze drifted up to the sky. It was growing darker. She could distinguish between the day and night now, and even between those times and twilight and dawn. She was also becoming accustomed to other things, such as the constant presence of huge demon males as they went about their business, and the eerie calls that echoed in the distance at times. This realm was beginning to feel normal to her. She no longer found the grim colour of everything strange, or the wind unusual.

If they had to stay here much longer, she would probably end up feeling at home in this place and out of sorts in her own world.

Evan landed a heavy blow on the youngest of his opponents. The brunet hit the deck hard and his companion rushed over to him.

"Shit. Sorry." Evan crouched beside him and helped him into a sitting position. "You okay?"

The younger man nodded and rubbed his jaw.

"Let's call it a day." Sable ambled over to them and offered the two younger hunters a smile to show them that she meant her next words. "You both did really well. Head in and have a good soak."

The two men nodded and Evan rose to his feet and pulled the brunet onto his. He watched them heading towards the large arched doorway of the main three-storey building of the dark grey castle and then turned back to face her. His lips curved into a wicked smile.

"You want to play?" he said, his deep voice filled with a bright but teasing note.

She really shouldn't. He had been training the troops while she had been away and had been sparring for nearly thirty minutes solid with the two who had just gone inside. She had a distinct advantage over him, and she didn't like that. She preferred to play fair.

Besides, if she lost, she would never hear the end of it. Not from Evan. He wouldn't taunt her about her losing a match to him even though he had been fighting for hours. The others would find out about it though and she didn't need to give them any ammunition to make them doubt her abilities as a leader. Losing to Evan in a sparring match would be the last straw, she was sure of it.

Sable glanced at the archway to the outer courtyard. No sign of Thorne and the others returning yet. How long were they going to be away? It had been hours since Loren had teleported her back to the castle and she was beginning to worry about her friends. She couldn't care less about Grave. She wouldn't mourn if the vampire met with a grisly end. She would just be upset she had missed the show.

She decided to risk the humiliation of defeat and nodded. Sparring with Evan would take her mind off things and she didn't want to go back to her room. If she did, she would only end up worrying even more, and not only about her friends. She rubbed her wrist. The ache in it had lessened but it hadn't disappeared completely, and it bothered her.

Sable rolled her shoulders to warm up and bounced on the spot, preparing herself for the fight ahead.

Evan stood opposite her, motionless and cool, his pale hair slicked back against his head.

"Bring it." Sable crooked her finger at him, beckoning him to her.

Evan grinned.

The arched wooden doors to the outer courtyard opened.

Sable's gaze shot there and pain exploded across her jaw. She staggered right and caught Evan's muffled curse through the ringing in her ears.

She shook her head, trying to clear it, and held her hand up to stop Evan from fussing over her. He had caught her off guard.

She straightened and stared across the empty courtyard to the group of men sauntering into it.

Thorne led them. The state of him had distracted her from her fight and drove the pain from her mind now as she watched him.

A long gash cut across his cheek and streaks of blood had rolled down to his jaw and onto his neck. Blood stained his shirt too and slashes in the white material revealed a bandage beneath. The other side of his jaw bore a black bruise and had swollen, and there was a groove in his right horn.

What the hell?

The answer became clearer when Bleu stepped out from behind him, looking just as battered and bruised. Loren entered the courtyard, his expression locked in dark, grim lines.

Sable moved forwards, her gaze focused on Loren, seeking an answer from him.

Loren shook his head and pinched the bridge of his slender nose, giving Sable the feeling that she didn't want to ask and that she was witnessing the result of those feelings he had told her about—Thorne's need to deal with any male who might steal her from him and stand between him and claiming his fated one.

Thorne trudged over to her, swung his left arm and dumped a huge dead something that vaguely resembled a deer—it had antlers anyway—at her feet. He tipped his shoulders back and his chin jutted upwards.

Sable bit her tongue to hold back her desire to mention that it was rather medieval of him to bring her a dead thing and expect her to shower praise upon him. He was old, beyond medieval in years. This was probably demon courting at its finest.

Everyone stared at her. Waiting?

"Um. Thank you?"

Sable looked down at the beast. Were those claw marks on its furry black flank? And what had happened to its ravaged throat? It looked as if something had torn it out with its teeth.

She swallowed. Not something. Someone.

Her gaze lifted to Thorne and his bloodstained chin.

There were stab wounds in the carcass too, in keeping with the size of the blades on Bleu's spear. Both males had gone after the same animal with equal gusto, and she suspected that Bleu had attempted to accidentally take the king down with the beast.

How many times had he stabbed Thorne?

Sable really didn't want to know.

Her throat closed and chest tightened as polar emotions duelled in her heart, tearing her in two directions and igniting a barrage of thoughts she couldn't suppress or ignore.

One stood out amongst the torrent, driving her emotions firmly towards panic and kicking others into life that collided within her.

It was all getting out of hand.

She recalled what Grave had said to Thorne—that a woman wasn't worth his kingdom.

It hit her hard. If she stayed here, things were only going to get worse. Thorne was driven by the same deep, primal male instinct that had controlled Loren and she had seen just how out of hand it could get. Loren had tried to kill demons, vampires, and even Bleu because of his need to keep every male away from his female, Olivia.

That same madness gripped Thorne. That same drive to claim his fated one. He would lose sight of the war and lose his kingdom, and she refused to be responsible for that happening. They were meant to be at war with the demons of the Fifth Realm, not with each other.

She wanted Archangel to see her worth and her ability to lead, and bestow upon her the rank she had always desired, but not at the cost of Thorne's kingdom. It was her promotion or his realm, and she knew which she had to choose.

She drew her hand down her face and exhaled hard. She could do this. It was going to hurt them both, and she didn't want to leave, but it was for the best. She couldn't let Thorne throw away his kingdom for her.

"You are not pleased?" Thorne said in a low gravelly voice and stepped towards her.

Sable stepped back.

Thorne's expression darkened and his lips pressed together into a grim line.

"This isn't going to work." It was out of her mouth before she could stop it and her chest ached in response to the words and the flicker of hurt in Thorne's dark crimson eyes.

He growled and staggered backwards, as if her words her been a physical blow.

Sable looked to Loren for help.

The look in his purple eyes pleaded her to reconsider.

She glanced at Bleu and then at everyone else around her. More had gathered, come to watch the spectacle.

She knew what she had to do. It went against every instinct she possessed, but it was the only course of action open to her. She had come here to help save Thorne's kingdom and she was going to do just that.

Sable turned her back on Thorne.

"Where do you go?" he growled, a dark edge to his voice. His pain beat within her. He knew where she was going and it was killing him.

It was killing her too.

"You have command," she said to Evan as calmly as she could manage through the emotions clogging her throat and stinging her eyes. He nodded, his steady gaze offering her little comfort. She was giving him what he wanted and what he probably felt he deserved. She couldn't blame him for seizing the chance she was surrendering.

She began walking towards the castle.

"Sable." Thorne's deep growl rolled over her, loud in the quiet evening. "Where do you go?"

Sable closed her eyes and forced herself to keep walking when all she wanted to do was turn to him and ease his pain. "Home. If I stay here, allies will become enemies before the real enemy attacks. I won't be responsible for a war between the elves and the demons. Evan will lead Archangel's team in my place. It's for the best."

Thorne roared, the sound sending a shiver tumbling down her spine. It spoke of his fury and his pain, and she couldn't bear it.

She quickened her pace.

"You cannot leave." Thorne's heavy footfalls echoed around the courtyard and she could feel him closing in on her. "I will not allow it!"

Sable turned on him, her eyes enormous and heart pounding out a hard rhythm against her chest. "I told you before. I am *not* one of your court whores for you to order around!"

She resumed walking, faster now. She shoved through the demons gathered near the castle, watching their king fight with his little mortal, no doubt enjoying it and expecting Thorne to put her in her place.

Sable looked back and caught Loren's gaze. He shook his head, a silent warning in his purple eyes, telling her again not to do this. She knew she was on thin ice. Enraging a demon king? Not good. Not good at all.

She had to do it though and could only hope that Thorne would understand when he calmed down.

It wasn't goodbye forever. Just goodbye for now.

Sable swung her focus back to the castle and it hit on Bleu directly in front of her. Before she could open her mouth to ask what he was doing and tell him to leave her alone, he grabbed her and darkness swallowed them both.

No.

The shadows evaporated to reveal her room at Archangel headquarters.

Sable shoved Bleu away. "What the hell do you think you were doing?"

"Taking you home, as you wished." He stood over her, tall and darkly beautiful, no trace of malice in his expression. He honestly thought he had been helping.

Sable groaned. "No. All you've done is make the whole situation worse when I was trying to make it better! Now Thorne will be furious with the elves... with you. Loren is going to be pissed at you... you'll be lucky if he doesn't send you home too."

Bleu's expression shifted, revealing a flicker of concern. "I did not realise. It was not my intent. You desired to leave, were clearly distressed, and I fulfilled that wish."

She wanted to hit him. It would satisfy her immediate desire but she would only regret it later. He had been trying to help, had seen her distress and completely misinterpreted it.

"Immortal men need to get a damn clue," Sable ground out instead and looked deep into his eyes. She had hurt one man already today. Why not go for the full set? "I was upset... you're right about that... but I was upset because I didn't want to leave Thorne. I didn't want to hurt him, Bleu, and now you've made his pain worse. You've made him think I wanted to leave with you... when I didn't really want to leave him at all."

His face fell, a shadow of hurt flittering across it before he schooled his features.

"Bleu." She reached for him and he moved back a step. "Bleu... be honest with me. Do you love me?"

The muscles in his jaw flexed and he frowned down at her.

"Am I the mate you've been waiting for all your life?" She advanced a step and he backed off one, edging closer to the main door of her small apartment.

A myriad of unreadable emotions played in his eyes and then he looked away from her. "No."

"I don't want to hurt you, Bleu... and I love you as a friend... but I can never be in love with you."

"Because you are in love with the demon... with your mate?"

She wasn't going to answer that, even though it was true. She wasn't ready to voice her feelings for Thorne to anyone. Bleu lowered his head.

"I understand," he said in a quiet voice and heaved a sigh. When he looked at her, all trace of emotion was gone, erased from his face and hidden behind impassive amethyst eyes. "I am sorry, Sable. I will return and apologise to my prince and to the demon king."

"Thank you."

He lifted his hand and brushed his fingers across her cheek, staring down into her eyes. He whispered something in his own tongue, something laced with intense emotion, and then green-purple light flickered over his body and he disappeared.

She didn't need to speak elvish to know what he had said to her. It had been there in his eyes for her to read. He could have loved her. He had wanted to love her.

Sable closed her eyes and sighed.

She couldn't have loved him though.

She was in love with a demon king.

An unholy roar shook the building.

Thorne.

Sable pulled the door of her apartment open and raced towards the centre of the building, to the only place Thorne knew in it. The cafeteria.

It took her back a month to the first time she had met Thorne. She hoped he wasn't making such a grand entrance again.

She bolted down the stairs and along another corridor, the cafeteria in sight ahead of her.

Sable burst into the room and ground to a halt.

It was worse than she had anticipated.

Much worse.

Men and women hung off Thorne's arms, trying to get him under control as he fought in the middle of the room. Tables and chairs lay toppled and shoved away, forming an open space around him and the hunters fighting to subdue him.

Thorne growled and swung one big arm outwards, sending the hunters flying across the room. His wings battered others, immense and lethal, making it difficult for anyone to get close to him. His horns had curled around, flaring forwards beside his temples, and his eyes blazed crimson.

He was fully demonic and she had never seen him so far gone, or so big.

He shoved another hunter away, sending the dark-haired male to the ground, and bared huge fangs at him. The man scurried backwards as Thorne advanced on him. Blood rolled down Thorne's bare torso, pumping from gashes and from crossbow bolts still jutting out of his flesh. Hunters at the edges of the room readied more crossbows, preparing to embed more of the toxic darts into him.

"No," Sable snapped and raced forwards, every instinct she possessed screaming at her to protect Thorne. "Just back off and leave him alone."

She tore one of the hunters away from him and shoved them behind her.

"Back the hell off!" Sable pushed more hunters away. "You're making him worse. He's not a threat."

She really hoped he wasn't anyway.

Thorne snapped and snarled at the hunters closest to him, lashing out with his long talon-like claws. The hunters edged away from him as quickly as they could but many took angry blows in the process. When they were all beyond his reach, Thorne roared again, the sound laced with irritation.

Sable bravely edged closer.

Thorne whirled to face her, raising his claws to strike at the same time, and froze when his eyes met hers.

He huffed like a beast and his face twisted as he spoke to her.

In the demon tongue.

"I don't understand," Sable whispered, keeping her voice quiet in the hope it would calm him. Frustration rolled off him and over her, his emotions more tangible to her than ever. He knew she couldn't understand.

He took a step towards her, hunched over and with his dark dragon-like wings bent at awkward angles over his shoulders, scraping along the ceiling tiles. She swallowed to wet her drying throat and stood her ground, slowly tipping her head right back to keep her eyes locked on his. She hadn't expected him to be so enormous in his true demonic form. He stood over three feet taller than she was, his entire body now twice as wide as before and his muscles bulging. A formidable sight. She had never seen him like this and it scared her a little.

The hunters around the room kept their weapons directed at him. She couldn't blame them for being cautious. It wasn't every day that a fully turned demon dropped into the Archangel building. It wasn't every day that they met a demon as big and as dangerous as Thorne outside the building either.

Sable steadied her heart, not wanting to provoke him and knowing he could feel her emotions and that meant he could sense her underlying fear. She raised her hand and held it out to him. He huffed again and dropped to his knees before her. Even then, he was still taller than she was and the immense breadth of his body made her feel tiny and fragile. Weak.

Thorne leaned towards her and pressed his cheek against her palm. His glowing scarlet eyes closed. His breath heated her skin.

She stroked his cheek, her eyebrows furrowing as she studied his face. The gash from the hunt was still there on his cheek, and new ones had joined it, angry red and still seeping blood. He had come here to fight Bleu for her and instead had been faced with two dozen shocked hunters armed to the teeth.

"I have no interest in Bleu," Sable whispered and his eyes opened, locking on hers. He breathed out slowly and relaxed against her hand. "That doesn't mean I have any interest in you, either."

His red eyes brightened again, burning like coals and narrowing on her.

"I'm accustomed to battles… but those battles make sense to me. This doesn't. This is madness. I belong to neither of you. I'm not a possession for one of you to claim or a victory to be had. Can't you see that?"

His expression softened and something in his eyes spoke to her, telling her of his regret. She wanted to believe that sanity would return to the world now that she had made her feelings clear to Bleu and now that she had told Thorne that she didn't want the elf, but she knew that if the two males were around her, things would go south again. Not because Bleu would flirt with her, but because Thorne would always see him as a threat, a rival for her affection, until he had claimed her.

And she wasn't ready for anyone to claim her.

"Return," Thorne gruffly growled, great effort behind it.

He was fighting his darker nature, clawing back control so he could speak with her in a language she could understand.

Sable shook her head. "I can't go back with you. Your kingdom is at risk. I won't be responsible for your downfall."

Thorne snarled, his expression turning vicious, and then softened again.

"Return." It was pleading this time and she felt his pain, his need, beating within her.

"No. Not until this war is over or you can swear to me that you will no longer behave so rashly and ridiculously."

He shoved to his feet and turned away from her, his shoulders tensed and fists clenched. Sable's chest ached, a fierce pang lancing her.

She reached out to him, driven to reassure him and herself that this separation was only temporary.

Thorne jerked backwards, stumbled, shot a hand out to grab the table to his left and hit the deck hard. Sable gasped and looked beyond him, and frowned. Fargus stood opposite her. His eyes glowed blue. What the hell? The table legs squeaked against the linoleum as Thorne tried to pull himself up.

"Rakshasa," Thorne grumbled and made it onto his feet.

Her attention shot back to him. He stumbled forwards, swaying and meandering all over the place.

"Thorne?" Sable rushed after him as he closed in on Fargus. She had no clue what this rakshasa thing was but knew it must be bad and had something to do with Thorne's commander. She looked around her at the hunters and pointed at Fargus. "Contain him."

Fargus smiled and disappeared in a blinding flash of brilliant white light.

"No!" Thorne growled and wavered. What was wrong with him? "Everyone in... danger. Must go... back."

"Thorne?" Sable reached him as he wobbled and grabbed his arm, hoping to steady him. He collapsed, taking her down with him, landing on his back and her left leg.

She looked down at him.

Her world shattered.

A huge knife stuck out of the centre of his chest.

"Thorne!" Sable shook him but he didn't respond. His body shifted, returning to its normal size, and his wings shrank into his back. Her fingers danced over his throat, seeking his pulse. It was thready and weak against their tips and her heart beat timidly in response.

"What happened?" The familiar male voice sent a bolt of hope rushing into her heart and she looked up at Bleu.

"I thought you left."

"I tried," Bleu said and crouched beside her. He ran his purple gaze over Thorne, his black eyebrows slowly knitting. "This is not good. We will have to remove it."

Sable nodded dumbly and stared at the blade protruding from Thorne's chest. It was off centre and she prayed that meant it had missed his heart, otherwise Bleu removing it could do more damage than good.

Bleu wrapped his right hand around the hilt of the short blade and pressed his other against Thorne's chest. He leaned over Thorne, pushing his weight onto his chest, and frowned.

"Wait," Sable blurted and Bleu halted and looked up at her. "What if... won't this make it worse?"

Bleu shook his head. "Demons have extremely quick healing abilities and the blade is too low to have struck his heart directly. Thorne will heal any nick in the organ before it can bleed into his chest. My fear is that the blade is poisoned, so the entry point mattered little."

That didn't really reassure her as she had hoped it would. She stared down at the dagger, heart thumping and hands shaking, her emotions threatening to overwhelm her as tears began to line her eyes. Warmth soaked into her black t-shirt and her combat trousers where Thorne rested against her, sticking the material to her skin, the smell of his blood a stomach-turning tang in the air.

"Sable," Bleu whispered, recapturing her focus with the softness of his voice. She raised her eyes back to his, her eyebrows furrowing as she caught the warmth in his. "I swear… Thorne has a better chance if we remove the blade and tend to him. If we leave it in and it is coated in toxin, it will kill him. Believe me when I tell you that the blade has not punctured his heart. I have fought demons for four thousand years. I know where to aim to deal a deadly blow to that organ."

She didn't doubt that, and it reassured her enough that she nodded, silently asking him to go ahead and remove the blade while she held Thorne in her arms.

She sifted her fingers through Thorne's hair and stroked his cheek, hoping to soothe him. Bleu pulled the short blade from Thorne's chest and the wet sucking noise it made turned her stomach.

She caressed Thorne's brow, silently willing him to be strong and to come back to her. It was just a little knife in the chest. He could recover from that. He would recover from it.

Bleu sniffed the blade. "Poisoned. A potent one too."

Sable stared blankly at him, her mind shutting down in reaction to his announcement. She fought the weakness surging through her and focused on Bleu.

His earlier words ran through her mind and she frowned at him as a cold feeling stole through her. "What do you mean… you *tried* to leave?"

Bleu's already grim expression worsened. "I tried. I used the same pathway as we always have to enter the Third Realm. I was bounced back."

Sable's feeling worsened, weighing her insides down and chilling her flesh. "What the hell does that mean?"

Bleu held her gaze.

"Someone has blocked the path to the Third Realm."

Sable shivered and looked down at Thorne as it hit her hard.

That rakshasa thing had played them all and had won, getting what it wanted.

It had separated the king from his kingdom.

CHAPTER 18

Sable sat at the edge of her double bed, her left hand holding a cold compress to Thorne's brow and her gaze riveted on him. The apartment was quiet around her. Too quiet. The silence gave her no respite from her dark and painful thoughts.

Thorne's bare chest gently rose and fell in time with his slow breaths, his tawny skin glistening with sweat that beaded in the valleys between his muscles.

Bleu had helped her bring Thorne to her apartment and had settled him on the bed for her, and had then left to attempt to enter the Third Realm again. He had tried several times over the two days since then, all without success. He had visited the elf kingdom too and had informed his council of the problem, and they had dispatched another legion of their army. This one had teleported to the edge of the Third Realm in one of the other demon kingdoms and had attempted to enter from there.

They had failed.

For now, they couldn't contact Loren or Olivia, or anyone within the Third Realm. They were cut off and Sable had fought enough battles to know that this was the opportunity the Fifth Realm had been waiting for.

Sable's gaze drifted lower, over the taut planes of Thorne's handsome face, down his neck to his chest. The wound in the centre of it was red and angry, the skin raised around it. It was healing though, just as his other wounds were. She had gone so far as to measure it after the first few hours, needing to do something to calm her fears. The progress was slow, but it was happening. Thorne was healing.

At least on the outside.

She couldn't vouch for his condition inside.

Leads trailed across his torso, attached to pads on his chest and his left side. They linked him to one of the monitors from Olivia's lab. The steady beep reassured her and sometimes she would stare at the number on the screen, forcing herself to see that his heart was beating strong even though a fierce fever gripped him, turning his skin hot and clammy.

Sable removed the cloth from his brow, dunked it into the bowl of icy water on her nightstand, and squeezed it out before mopping his chest and face with it. He twitched wherever she laid the cloth, as if the cold hurt him. She didn't stop though. She needed to bring his temperature down.

Bleu had warned her that the toxin on the blade was one capable of killing Thorne and that she had to keep his core temperature as low as she could. She had wanted to place Thorne into an ice bath but Bleu had advised against it. Apparently, that could kill Thorne just as easily as overheating.

She had been keeping vigil at his side ever since and had lost track of exactly how many hours had passed since Fargus had shown up in the cafeteria and stabbed his king. Not Fargus. Something else. Something with glowing blue eyes and the ability to teleport.

Something that might be in the Third Realm right now, among her friends, placing them all in danger.

Sable wet the cloth and wrung it out again, and then neatly folded it and laid it across Thorne's brow. She stroked his small horns and looked down at his hand, tempted to take it in hers. She resisted and lifted her gaze back to his face. It caught on the wound on his chest. Tears threatened to well up and she cursed them and the feeling of despair that swept through her. Thorne was strong. He would wake and she would feel like a fool for doubting him.

Her stomach growled and her head ached, but she made no move to eat or rest. The blood on her black t-shirt and trousers had dried, making the material stiff in places, but she couldn't bring herself to leave him for even as long as it would take her to shower and change.

Thorne needed her, and she felt compelled to be here with him, by his side, watching over him and keeping him safe, keeping him cool. Waiting for him to wake and piece her world back together.

Someone knocked at the apartment door.

It opened a moment later and she looked over at the bedroom door. Mark stood there, his aging face awash with concern as he stared at her, and then darkening as his grey gaze dropped to Thorne where he lay on top of the dark purple covers on her double bed.

"I came as soon as I could after I had received word about the incident." Mark stepped further into the room and she nodded, grateful he had left the

Archangel conference of senior staff in Amsterdam early. She knew in her heart that restoring order amongst his hunters and checking on them weren't the only reasons he had risked displeasing the other cell leaders. He had come back to check specifically on her and Thorne too.

His eyes lingered on Thorne, a calculating and wary edge to them. She couldn't blame him for bearing a grudge against Thorne. He had come crashing into the cafeteria twice now, throwing Archangel into pandemonium and harming its hunters, sending many of them to the infirmary with minor wounds and concussions. Her superior's hand fell to his side, brushing the crisp black jacket of his suit.

Sable wished he had chosen a less sombre colour, or had at least injected one other than black or grey into his choice of clothing. The black suit with a black shirt and a charcoal tie made him appear as if he was going to a funeral. When coupled with the sense of death that hung in the air around Thorne, it sent a chill through her and slowly eroded the fragment of hope she clung to desperately.

"How is he?"

Sable looked back at Thorne. "I'm not sure. Getting better, I think. Bleu believes it might be days before he wakes."

She didn't know whether she could take many more days of this.

She didn't think she was strong enough.

Mark moved to the foot of the bed off to her left, his eyes locked on Thorne. "What happened?"

"I had to come back, and Thorne followed me. There was an incident in the cafeteria. One of his own men stabbed him in the chest with a knife coated in a toxin… at least it looked like his commander." Sable looked over her shoulder at Mark. "Thorne called it a rakshasa."

Mark's face darkened into grim lines. "His man is dead then."

She had feared as much. "What is it?"

"A type of shape-shifter." Mark ran a hand over his sandy hair, an action that painfully reminded her of how Thorne would stroke his left horn when nervous. "Think of it like a parasite or symbiotic being. It takes over its host, living as part of it at first, learning everything it can. It then kills the host and shifts into that form. It can assume the shape of any it has killed. They can replicate everything about a host. Smell, voice, everything."

Thorne had been right. Everyone was in danger. No one would know that thing was among them and had been there for God only knew how long. It might have killed any number of the people in the castle, assuming their form whenever necessary. How long ago had it killed Fargus?

"Evan will lead the team until we can find a way back into the Third Realm. Bleu is trying to get a message to Prince Loren. I'm sure he'll succeed and we can warn them about this shape-shifter." Sable wet the cloth again and pressed it back against Thorne's head. He moaned and shifted, trying to get away from the cold compress. She pressed harder, keeping him in place and murmured softly, hoping the sound would soothe him.

"Sable... I don't need to warn you how Archangel feels about relationships between humans and demons or fae."

He didn't need to remind her, and not only because she already knew Archangel frowned upon such things. He didn't need to remind her because his choice of words dredged up something she had been slowly forgetting while focused on taking care of Thorne.

There was a chance she wasn't wholly human.

She lowered her gaze to her right wrist and the leather cuff around it. It hadn't hurt since her return to the mortal world and neither had her leg. It was a relief, but she still worried that it would flare up again and she needed to know what it meant. She couldn't ask Mark about it though. If he discovered that her gift was more than they had ever thought, then the people in charge might find out, and they would want to run tests on her. She had been prodded and poked enough when she had joined Archangel.

She didn't want Mark and her bosses to look at her with that same dark, grim edge that Mark's steel-grey eyes held right now as he stared at Thorne. She didn't want them to go from looking at her with admiration and something akin to affection, to looking at her as if she was a monster. She didn't think she could handle it, not when she had been with them for most of her adult life and had come to view Archangel as her family.

"I expect you to file a full report about what happened in the Third Realm," Mark said and then softly added, "It can wait until the demon king wakes though."

"Thank you." Sable didn't take her eyes off Thorne.

She held the compress to his brow and listened to Mark withdraw from the room and then leave the apartment, quietly closing the door behind him.

Alone with Thorne again, she couldn't hold back the tide of her emotions.

She stared at his face, heart aching in her chest, hope slowly withering.

He had to wake up.

He had to come back to her.

Sable swallowed hard, lowered her trembling hand and finally took hold of his, squeezing it tightly as her strength left her.

"Fight it, Thorne," she whispered.

She stroked his brow, letting her fingers drift down to play on his cheek, reaching out to him and praying he could feel how much she needed him, could sense her hurt as she could sense his, and would listen to her plea.

"Fight for me."

CHAPTER 19

Thorne's body burned with all the fires of Hell, aflame and slowly turning to ash beneath his too-tight skin. He moaned as cool ice caressed his brow, chasing back the inferno, giving him brief respite from the heat. His bones ached, limbs too heavy to lift and muscles too weak to support them. They shook when he tried to move, clenching and trembling one moment and lax the next.

"Thorne?" Her sweet voice called to him in the dark abyss, luring him up towards her.

He clawed his way upwards, fighting the shadows that wrapped around his legs, twining tight around his ankles and trying to pull him back down.

Sable.

His female feared. Something scared her and he had to remove the source of her fear, relieving her and making her feel safe. She had told him once that she felt safe with him. He would make her feel safe again now.

He fought harder, his body shuddering as the fire swept through him, radiating outwards from a point in the centre of his chest. Each searing wave threatened to send him tumbling back into the black oblivion waiting to claim him.

"Thorne." She was distant now, little more than a wobbling reedy voice swallowed by the darkness.

Thorne grimaced and kicked at the tugging shadows clinging to his legs. He had to reach Sable. No matter how weak he felt or how tired, no matter how little energy he had, he would never stop trying to reach her. Even if it killed him.

He ground his molars and pushed onwards, shoving through the darkness, forcing himself to continue. Nothing could stop him from reaching her. Not even Death himself. He would fight the bastard and he would win. He would not give up, not until his mate's fear had ebbed and she felt safe again, and not even then. He would never give up.

Her fear trickled through the link between them, tugging at his heart, filling him with a need to reach her and pull her into his arms, and hold her close in the shield of his embrace.

His little huntress needed him.

He was coming for her.

He kept clawing his way upwards, every instinct he possessed driving him towards her.

"Fight for me," she whispered and he did, every inch of him straining as he battled the heat and the darkness, refusing to surrender to it.

His female needed him.

She shimmered into view above him, hazy and ethereal. Cold caressed his cheek and his forehead, her touch soothing the raging fires in his body, giving him the strength to keep pushing onwards.

"Wake up, Thorne."

Those words were a command to his soul, an order he couldn't ignore.

Thorne reached for her and she came into focus, her backdrop a warmly lit blanket of white and her long black hair hanging forwards, brushing her cheeks. They were reddened and damp, matching her eyes. His female had been crying. Why? What did she fear so much that it had torn down her strength and revealed this vulnerable side of her? He would destroy it, whatever it was. His female had no need to fear any longer. He was here.

A watery smile wobbled on her lips. "You awake?"

He thought he was dreaming to have his angel hovering over him as she was, her golden eyes enchanting him and her hip pressing against his bare side. She brushed her fingers over his brow and the cold came again, moist and icy.

"You look a little dazed." She moved the wet something across his forehead. A cloth? "You with me?"

He tried to nod and his neck ached. He grimaced instead, a growl rumbling up his throat as he inwardly cursed the weakness infesting him, keeping him from speaking with Sable. Her smile grew, gaining strength and emotion that flowed into him and stilled his heart. She was happy, and relieved. His female felt safe again.

"How long are you going to lay there sleeping, huh?" She mopped his brow and he frowned.

Sleeping?

Memories of his last few moments came flooding back, rewinding quickly to the point when Fargus had stabbed him in the chest with a poisoned dagger.

His hand shot to his chest and Sable gasped. Thorne realised why. She held that hand, her fingers linked with his. His gaze darted to her and her cheeks darkened. She tried to remove her hand from his but he tightened his grip, gently squeezing her fingers between his, hoping to show her that he didn't want her to let go. It pleased him that she had been holding his hand.

It did not please him that he had been poisoned, and he hated that a loathsome creature had taken his closest friend from him. He squeezed his eyes shut and drew in a deep breath to calm his emotions before they raged out of control. Any overexertion, whether physical or emotional, would send him back into the dark grip of the toxin, and he didn't want to let it take him again.

He didn't want to leave Sable or worry her.

He was the reason she feared. She had been afraid for him, and she had tended to him while he had been unconscious, watching over him like an angel. His female was kind. Beautiful. Precious.

Sable stroked his cheek. "Thorne? I'm sorry about Fargus."

He was too, and he would make the rakshasa pay for what it had done.

But to make him pay, he needed to return to his land and his people.

Prince Loren would do all that he could to lead the army should there be an attack, but they needed him. He shouldn't have left. Sable was right about that. Her words had cut him to the bone at the time, unleashing agony in his heart and his soul, but now he saw the truth of them. His place was in his kingdom, leading his men and protecting his people. By following his instincts, his deep need for Sable, and chasing after her, he had left them all exposed and in danger.

"Where is Bleu?" he said and Sable tensed, her shock rippling through him where they touched. He opened his eyes and sought her, finding her expression matched her emotions. She probably hadn't expected him to ask after the elf as the first thing he said upon waking.

Her expression shifted and he sensed guilt and other emotions awakening within her.

"Sable?"

She looked down at his chest and their joined hands, a flicker of remorse in her gaze. "There's something you need to know. Thorne... someone has... they closed the pathways to the Third Realm."

Thorne bolted up into a sitting position and immediately regretted it. His head ached, eyes stung, and chest burned. He clutched it with his free hand, fingers tugging at wires attached to his skin. A steady beep reached his ears as his faculties came back and his senses cleared. His gaze followed the wires that led from his chest to a machine off to his right. His heartbeat. The strange machine echoed it and he despised hearing the rapid rate that warned he was still in grave danger, weakened by his enemy.

He tried to tear the pads and wires off but Sable shoved him back down onto the bed.

"You're supposed to be resting." Her palm pressed into his shoulder, pinning him to the bed, as if she feared he would try to rise again and would injure himself. "Take it easy. Bleu is trying to find a way to get us back in and he's trying to get a message to Loren. It's all in hand."

That didn't make Thorne feel any better. While he had been unconscious fighting the toxin, Bleu had been taking steps to get them back into the Third Realm and had been trying to get word to Loren, and Sable clearly admired him for it.

"Your eyes are going red and your horns are curling," Sable stated and he glanced at her. She looked thoroughly unimpressed. "You had better not be seething about Bleu or thinking that I was going all gaga for him because he's trying to straighten shit out. I'm here with you, aren't I?"

She was, and judging by the dark semi-circles under her eyes and the fact she wore the same black t-shirt and combat trousers as when she had left his realm, she had been with him the whole time he had been unconscious, tending to him.

He would have found that wonderful once, a beautiful sign that she did desire him as her mate and no other, but it didn't appease him or ease his frustration this day.

He had left his kingdom in danger and had to find a way back to it.

He needed to strategize.

Sable was right. It was time to put aside his feelings and his desire to claim Sable as his fated one and to form a truce with the elf male for the sake of his kingdom. Together, they could find a way of gaining entry to his realm and he might just be able to save it, his people, and his name as their king.

"How long have I been unconscious?" he said, frowning at the ceiling and conducting a mental check of his body.

The wounds he had gained during the hunt and the fight against Archangel's people had healed. Only the one from the rakshasa's dagger remained and it was far from healed. He burned there, the fierce ache stealing some of his senses and dulling them. The poison wracked him still, infesting his body, weakening his muscles and making moving painful.

"It's been two days maybe... I lost track." Sable lowered her gaze to their joined hands and swallowed hard.

He felt her pain. Her fear. It swept through him and chased away his shock over hearing that he had left his kingdom vulnerable for two whole days, and brought his focus to rest wholly on her.

He could see the strain in her eyes and feel the fatigue that flowed through her, threatening to render her unconscious in order to force her into resting. She had weakened herself by keeping vigil at his side. He had placed her in danger.

He cursed himself and vowed never to put her through so much pain again, and that he would restore her strength, both physical and mental. He would take care of her as she had taken care of him.

He just needed to figure out what that entailed.

Thorne sat up again and pulled the pads and wires from his bare chest. Sable tried to stop him but her strength was no match for his, even when he was still fighting the toxin.

"You should rest." She pushed his chest but he refused to budge this time.

She couldn't order him to rest when she needed to do the same. He didn't think she would appreciate him telling her that so he kept it to himself.

He gently took her hand and pondered pressing a kiss to it, and then held it instead, brushing his thumb across the back of it. He couldn't allow things between him and Sable to cloud his judgement any more, or sway him from his path. He had to focus on his kingdom and his people, and put aside his need for her until both were safe.

"I need to find a way back into my kingdom, Sable. You were right, my little huntress. It is time I live up to my father's name and put an end to the war. It is time I place my kingdom before anything else." Thorne released her hand and swung his legs over the edge of the bed behind her. Her back pressed against his side. He nuzzled her hair and breathed in her scent, unable to resist lingering a moment to feel her against him, feel her warmth and softness, and then stood. His legs gave out and his backside hit the mattress. The springs creaked under his sudden weight.

"At least let me help you." Sable stood and offered her hand. "I can help you, Thorne."

He knew that. His little female was clever, skilled in strategizing and experienced in battle, and the steely look in her golden eyes told him that she was determined to get back to his realm and her friends.

Thorne took her hand and stood again. She held him steady and he slung his arm around her slender shoulders, tucking her against his side and using her as a crutch. She wrapped her right arm around his waist and settled her other hand against his chest, holding him upright.

He couldn't resist tugging her closer to him, fulfilling the need to hold her and shield her from all harm and the fear that had given him the strength to break the hold the toxin had had on him. She settled into his side and he felt her growing stronger, knew that his embrace comforted her. It humbled him. It always would. His little huntress relied upon him and he knew that she rarely depended upon anyone.

They had both stood alone for so long.

He looked around him, studying his environment. Everything smelled of Sable. Was this her home? The dark coloured fabrics and rich mahogany furniture suited his fated one. He looked back at the bed, at the crumpled dark purple sheets covering the large mattress. He had rested on her bed, alone in her room with her. His heart thumped harder, causing the wound on his chest to ache.

Sable cleared her throat. "I can sort of feel you, remember? That includes when you're getting wicked ideas that you're in no position to carry out."

Thorne's cheeks blazed and he looked down at her, catching her smiling up at him, a blush on her cheeks too.

Bleu appeared in the doorway to the rest of the curious set of small rooms and cocked a single black eyebrow.

"What is he doing out of bed?" Bleu strode into the room, scowling at Sable.

Thorne growled and bared his fangs at the elf, warning him to keep his distance and to adopt a softer tone when speaking with his female.

"Thorne would like to help figure out a way back into his realm... and you try stopping him from getting out of bed when he wants to. Besides, I'm hardly his nurse."

Thorne raised an eyebrow at the same time as Bleu. If the male's thoughts ran along the same lines as his were, imagining Sable in a small nurse's uniform, he would beat the elf into a bloody pulp, regardless of the danger of overexerting himself.

"Perverts," Sable muttered and cast a glance around. Searching for another topic to move them away from imagining her dressed rather provocatively? Thorne wouldn't say no to the change in subject. His thoughts were wreaking havoc on him, making his heart pound and blood rush southwards.

Bleu presented a change of topic. He held a small black glass vial out to Thorne.

"What is it?" Sable took it from him and popped the leaf-shaped lid off. It hit the dark carpet with a soft thud. She sniffed it and grimaced.

Bleu snatched it back. "Not for mortals. It would probably kill you, or at the very least make you sick. It is for Thorne. I took the blade to my kingdom for inspection and our chief pharmacologists believe this will negate the effects of the toxin."

Thorne was willing to try it. He reached for the vial. Sable blocked him and took it again. He frowned at her.

"How do we know it won't kill you?" The fear that came through the growing link between them flickered in her beautiful eyes too, speaking to him, demanding he reassure her.

"I have to try, Sable. My kingdom needs me, and they need me to be strong, not weak as I am now and unable to lead the army. I must try." He wrapped his hand around the one she clutched the vial in and looked deep into her eyes, studying every darker fleck among the gold, letting her feel that he was confident the liquid would cure and not kill him.

He didn't trust Bleu, but he did trust the elf's devotion to his prince. He was Bleu's best chance of reuniting with his prince before anything happened to him, and therefore Bleu needed him alive and strong too.

Besides, he believed that Sable might just kill Bleu if he dared to attempt to harm him.

His little female adored him, although she refused to admit it.

He adored her too.

She loosened her grip and he took the vial from her, lifted it to his lips and prayed to his gods that the liquid didn't kill him. He wasn't ready to die yet. Not until he had claimed Sable and spent centuries, millennia, with her.

Not even then.

He wanted to live forever with his fated one.

Thorne knocked the liquid back and grimaced as he swallowed. It tasted foul, like a sip from one of the fetid bogs in the Devil's realm within Hell, where many decaying creatures lay, melting into the water.

"Still with me?" Sable said and he forced a nod and shuddered.

"The taste leaves much to be desired." Thorne pinned Bleu with an accusatory glare. The elf smiled. Evidently, Thorne's suspicions were correct and Bleu had ensured the cure would not go down smoothly.

The effect, on the other hand, was marvellous. Cool flowed through his blood, quenching the fire and strengthening him, revitalising his tired body.

He looked down at the wound on his chest as it ached. He could feel his bones knitting together rapidly beneath his flesh. The angry redness of his skin faded and the long slash closed before his eyes. Elf medicine was incredible. He felt as if the liquid had given his natural healing abilities a mighty shove, accelerating them to an incredible speed. What would have taken him days to heal was almost gone in seconds. His ribs still ached though, his insides sore from the wound and the toxin, but he was stronger now and safe from the poison.

"Better?" Sable looked up at him, her eyes darting between his, and he nodded. "Let's go into the other room and get working then. I can whip up some food. You must be starving."

He wasn't hungry, but he knew that she was and was unlikely to eat alone in front of him and Bleu, so he nodded.

"Do you have paper and a writing implement?" Thorne said as she helped him into the other room and settled him onto a deep brown couch.

"Sure." She went to a desk in the corner. On it was a machine he knew as a computer and another that had paper sheets sticking out of it. She took some of the sheets and brought them back to him together with several pens. She laid them out on the wooden table in front of him.

Bleu settled himself in the armchair to Thorne's left and Sable hovered to his right.

"I will draw a map with the points where I know the pathways end in my kingdom and others and we shall go from there." He took up the paper and one of the pens.

"I still don't really get why you can't just teleport into the kingdom... I mean... you can teleport anywhere."

Thorne glanced up at Sable and smiled. "It is not so easy to enter each of the demon realms. Just as the elf kingdom only has a few points of access where elves and other creatures teleporting in from outside of the realm can enter it, so do the demon realms. There are even some pathways only open to me."

"It is the same for Loren," Bleu said and leaned forwards, coming to rest with his elbows on his knees. "Only the princes can use the pathways that exit directly in their quarters. The castle has another portal point where others may enter it and that is guarded at all times."

"That's why when we teleport to the elf kingdom, Loren goes to a different place?"

Bleu nodded.

"Demons within my kingdom can freely teleport anywhere within its boundaries. The exceptions being the castle and the fortresses protecting the borders at strategic points. They are protected and have only a single entry point available, which is guarded much like the one in the elf realm." Thorne leaned back on the couch, settling the paper on his lap. "Anyone teleporting in from outside of my kingdom, whether that is the mortal realm or another realm in Hell, must use a set pathway. It protects our lands and people from attack. These pathways are guarded at all times, located near fortresses. It is possible for us to close these pathways, stopping any from entering or exiting via them."

"So, someone has shut the doors to your kingdom and locked them… and we need to open them again."

"First, we need to map out all of the pathways. It is possible that there may be one that is open to us. There are some that are rarely used, almost forgotten." He reached up and brushed his fingers across the back of her palm when he caught the ripple of fatigue that travelled across her paling face. She needed to eat. They could talk more later, once she had food in her stomach. "Would you be so kind as to prepare some food while I attempt to recall all of the pathways?"

She nodded and moved around the couch. His gaze tracked her, slowly dropping to her fine backside. He wanted to touch it again, needed to grip it hard while he thrust into her, taking her and making her his.

She moved into a small area of the room that housed a kitchen and began going through the cupboards and the large metal one that kept items cold.

Thorne forced his attention back to the paper and sketched a map of all of the kingdoms with Bleu's help. The smell of food cooking set his stomach growling. Perhaps he was hungry after all. Whatever Sable was cooking, it smelled delicious, like the bacon and eggs and 'hung over' food that he had made for her.

She appeared with several plates while he was deep in discussion with Bleu. It was food similar to what he had made for her, but rather than the coffee she adored so much, she had a slender dark bottle. She sat to his right, close enough to him that he could feel her heat on his thigh, and opened the bottle.

She poured it into the first glass. Red wine. He didn't like the thought of her drinking around Bleu, but she was probably used to this alcohol and better able to handle it than she had the demon grog. Sable handed one glass to Bleu, and then filled the other two. She handed one to him and he took it from her, letting his fingers brush hers at the same time.

"I hope you like bad food." She sipped her own glass and then set it down and picked up a bread roll. She filled it with the bacon and eggs, and some sort of red sauce. When he made no move to eat, she paused and looked back at him. "I might have made this food, but don't be getting medieval ideas about me serving you. Tuck in."

Bleu ignored the food and focused on filling in the map with all the pathways he knew of in the different realms. Thorne mimicked Sable, stuffing the meat and eggs into his roll, and devoured a big bite. It tasted so delicious he almost groaned.

"You want some fruit or something, Bleu?" Sable said and the elf shook his head. She shrugged. "Suit yourself. I guess either way I would have to leave the apartment. I have zero fruit and veg on hand, and I like my blood where it is... in my body."

Thorne smiled at that.

He ate his roll while he discussed the different portals with Bleu and Sable, pinpointing the ones the elf had attempted to access. Most of them, if not all.

Sable leaned forwards, alternating between eating and drinking, working her way through both food and wine, and asking all manner of questions. He wondered how much she and Archangel knew about his world. The most basic of things seemed new to her.

"Why can't we just teleport to one of the other realms and walk across the border into yours?" She peered at the map and took another mouthful of wine.

Thorne sipped his again. "As I said earlier, Little Huntress, we could teleport to another realm but if they have closed the portals in my realm, they have a witch or several magic practitioners in their ranks. It is likely they would have sealed the borders with a spell."

"It's worth a try though, right?"

"Wrong." Bleu shook his head. "The elves the council sent to cross the border into the land could not enter that way. They met with resistance upon their return too. The First King was not pleased that they had crossed the First Realm without prior request."

"We could go and speak with this First King though, couldn't we?" Sable set her glass down on the wooden table. "That has to be worth a shot. Maybe we could find a way in then."

"No. It might be best we find a potential method of forming a hole in the barrier or restoring a pathway first." Thorne picked at a piece of bacon, craving the saltiness of the grilled meat. Sable cooked well. His female had talents he had not known of before. What other things could she do?

Sable took another mouthful of wine and then sighed. "So we need to find someone who can get us through the barrier."

He and Bleu nodded.

Her face fell again and she stared at the map.

Thorne looked down at it too, at his kingdom in particular, and the lands bordering it. The elves had chosen wisely. The First Realm was the best route back to his one, but they would have to gain an audience with the First King before attempting to breach the barrier. The First King would be less willing to allow them passage now that the elves had crossed the realm without permission.

That wasn't an insurmountable problem. He could convince the First King to grant them passage.

The problem was finding a method of breaching a barrier made by dark magic.

Thorne frowned. "Rosalind."

"Who now?" Sable glared at him and he placed his hand on her knee to reassure her, sensing her need for it.

"The little witch I came to meet with to see my future… the evening we met. You recall it?" He looked at her and she nodded, reached across the table and picked up a device similar to the one she had used that evening in the cafeteria.

She touched the screen and it came alive with colour and light, as if she was the witch and her touch was magic. She made a rapid series of taps in different places, as she had the night they had met, and then presented him with a picture of the fair-haired witch.

"This Rosalind?"

He nodded. "She is a practitioner of light magic. She may be able to help us reopen the pathway to my land."

She twisted the device to face her and studied it.

Bleu stood, catching her attention and his. "I will go and speak with my council of our plans, and will see if they have been able to make contact with my prince."

"Return at dawn. We shall leave to see the witch then." Thorne rose to his feet and Bleu nodded before disappearing.

He looked down at the hastily drawn map of the realms and the portal pathways.

Sable stood and he spared her a glance, and then his gaze slowly roamed back to her.

"We'll find a way back into your kingdom, Thorne," she said in a low voice, one that teased his ears and soothed him.

She was reassuring him?

Thorne nodded but didn't feel so certain. He had never wanted anything as much as getting back to his realm. He looked at Sable again. Perhaps there was one thing he wanted above all else.

"You seem different tonight." She glanced away. "I was listening to you talking to Bleu while I was cooking… and you were different."

Did she prefer the male she had seen this night? The one who strategized with others as an equal and didn't argue over a female? The male who took charge for the sake of his people, even going as far as giving up the one thing he desired most of all.

The one thing he might have gained by giving up.

Sable leaned closer, her body bare millimetres from his. Her hand slipped into his, her fingertips grazing his palm, and she looked up at him, brooked desire in her golden gaze.

Thorne exhaled heavily, unable to resist the lure of her beauty and the hunger in her eyes. He lowered his head, cupped the nape of her neck with his free hand, and kissed her hard.

CHAPTER 20

Thorne laid claim to Sable's sweet mouth, tangling his tongue with hers as he clasped the back of her head, holding her immobile. She moaned, the sound filled with pleasure that detonated a burst of male pride in his chest and drove him to master her and tear another breathless groan from her lips. He wanted to satisfy her, to pleasure her until she was boneless and sated, and then he wanted to crush her to his chest and sleep with her in his arms.

She tiptoed, her palms scalding his bare chest, making his blood burn and thrum in his veins. He groaned and angled his head, deepening the kiss and leaving no part of her untouched by it. He slid his free hand down to the small of her back, teased her top away from the waist of her trousers, and caressed her bare skin. It was soft beneath his touch, silky and warm, and was almost his undoing.

Thorne moaned and clutched her tighter, drawing her closer until her softness pressed against the hardness of his body.

Sable uttered another murmur of pleasure and her short nails dug into his bare chest, sending hot shivers skittering across his muscles and causing them to tense. She moaned again, deeper and more wanton this time, and he sensed her arousal spike. She liked it when she felt his muscles, felt his strength beneath her questing fingers.

She dragged them down, catching his pebbled nipples in the process, ripping another throaty groan from him. He shuddered and quaked, verged on digging his own claws into her soft flesh to anchor her and stop her from pushing him close to the edge. He wanted to give her pleasure first. He wanted his female to cry his name as she found release, experienced bliss from his touch, his kiss and his body within hers. He wanted—no, needed—to ruin her to all others and make her forever his.

His Sable.

His queen.

Thorne growled and swept her up into his arms, not breaking the kiss. She gasped into his mouth, her arms linking around his neck. He carried her back towards the bedroom, intent on laying her down on the bed and crawling on top of her, pinning her beneath him. He needed to feel her there, feel her skin-to-skin with him. The need was too strong to ignore, too fierce to resist.

She tunnelled her fingers into his hair, twining the longer strands around her slender digits as she kissed him harder, her lips clashing violently with his, speaking of the need he could sense in her. Desire, fierce and intense, unstoppable, drove her just as it rode him mercilessly, controlling his actions and urging him into giving himself over to his carnal needs.

His unquenchable thirst for Sable.

His shins hit the end of the bed and he lowered her onto it, covering her soft curvy body with his and driving her down against the mattress. She didn't release him. Her grip on his hair tightened, her kiss growing fiercer and more passionate. She rocked against him, rubbing her stomach across the steel-hard bulge in his leathers.

Thorne couldn't take it.

He groaned and arched his back, lifting his already aching shaft away from her undulating body. She whimpered and continued to rock against the air, her grip on his hair tightening until it stung his scalp.

He slowed the kiss, wanting to bring them down onto a more even keel, a place where they were no longer slaves to their need and could draw out this moment, making it everything he desired it to be.

She wriggled beneath him, a noise born of frustration grating in her throat, but loosened her grip on him too. Her fingers sifted through his hair, stroking and caressing, driving his thoughts towards her doing that to another part of his anatomy, a part that demanded her attention and craved it.

He lowered himself again, holding his weight on his elbows as they pressed into the mattress on either side of her ribs, and slowly drove his hips forwards, grinding his caged cock against her stomach. He growled, the need for more, to thrust against her soft warm skin, overriding the part of him that kept chanting to go slow.

He couldn't.

Thorne grabbed the hem of her dark t-shirt and paused at the stiff feel of it. He pushed himself up with his other hand and looked down at the material he grasped. He drew in a deep breath and caught the faint scent of blood. His blood.

He pushed the material upwards, revealing the taut plane of her stomach. Dried blood marred her soft skin too. She had been so focused on his welfare that she had neglected her own. He frowned and rose to his knees, caught her left wrist and pulled her up with him.

She looped her arms around his neck and went to kiss him again, and he turned his cheek to her.

"Wait," he said, battling his need to give in to her and claim her mouth again, struggling to focus on another desire.

The one that demanded he bathe her, washing the blood from her skin and making her feel better in the process. She needed a moment of comfort, and he intended to give her one by cleansing her, erasing all signs of what had happened to him and what she had been through, and easing her tired body with the heat of the water.

"I don't want to wait," she whispered against his cheek and peppered it with kisses that almost persuaded him that he didn't want to wait either.

He growled and swept her up into his arms.

"No, put me back down." She pushed against his chest but he held her tighter, containing her.

He began walking.

"Where are we going?" She looked ahead of him and then swiftly faced him again. Her pupils dilated, the raw need in them calling to him. She had figured out his intention and judging by the desire shining in her eyes and flowing through the connection between them, and the way she relaxed in his arms, she liked his idea.

He carried her into the bright white bathroom and set her down on the small vanity unit.

Thorne arched a brow at the glass cubicle that ran the length of the wall to his right. Not a bath as he had expected. He had thought to lay her in the hot water and sit on the edge of the tub to wash her.

His groin throbbed against his leathers, his balls tightening at the thought of stepping into the shower with her and washing her, running his hands over her soapy body while she explored his.

Would she desire to wash him too?

She was already ahead of him, hopping down from the vanity and sliding the door back so she could enter the cubicle. She reached around and turned a knob on the silver box on the wall. An electric whirring filled the silence and then water burst from the showerhead.

Sable closed the cubicle door, turned her back to it and smiled wickedly.

He was about to ask her what she was thinking when she tugged her t-shirt up, exposing the smooth plane of her stomach and her black cotton bra. He groaned as she removed the bra, revealing her beautiful pert breasts, and his cock pulsed behind his leathers at the sight of her. Everything male in him demanded he go to her and rip her clothes from her body, place her in the shower and make love with her under the water.

He took a step forwards, pulled towards her, drawn by the desire to be the one to strip her down to nothing. She paused with her hands on her belt and looked up into his eyes, her golden ones beguiling, enchanting him as they darkened with desire, need that spoke to him and silently commanded him.

He obeyed.

Thorne grasped her hands and shifted them aside, away from her belt. He unfastened it, popped the button on her combat trousers and eased the zip down. She toed off her boots, kicking them away, and her gaze remained locked on his face, her eyes darkening by degrees as he inched her trousers down, revealing the plain black cotton underwear she wore.

He groaned and pushed her trousers to her knees, falling to his before her. A gasp left her as he showered her stomach with kisses, tasting her soft skin and a trace of his own blood. She ploughed her fingers through his hair and grasped him, holding him to her stomach, as if he would ever leave. He wanted to spend hours here, exploring her with his mouth, learning all the spots that made her gasp and whimper, and quiver for more.

He kissed lower, marking a path past her navel, and ran his palms up the outside of her thighs at the same time. She trembled under his caress, her breath coming quicker, her desire heightening as it flowed through the connection between them. He listened to it, using it as his guide as he trailed his lips down her, edging closer to the waist of her underwear.

She moaned as he palmed her buttocks, gently kneading them one moment and clutching the next as he alternated between soft and hard kisses, between light nips and tender bites.

Thorne hooked his fingers into her underwear and shimmied them downwards, drawing back at the same time so he could drink his fill of her beauty as it was revealed to him. His hungry gaze devoured her, from the soft arch of lean muscle over her hipbones to the dark thatch of curls covering her mound.

The glass behind Sable shuddered as he dropped a kiss on her curls and breathed her in. Her scent drove him crazy, near blinding him with a need to rise before her and devour her mouth as he plundered her body, claiming all of her this time.

He dropped another kiss and she moaned, the sound loud in the small white tiled room, rising above the noise of the running water.

"Thorne," she husked, her fingers tugging on his hair, and a soft whimper escaped her as she arched towards him.

He growled and delved lower, thrusting his tongue between her feminine lips and tasting her desire. The sweet nectar bloomed on his tongue, flooding his mouth with her flavour and driving him onwards, filling him with a fierce need to possess all of her at last, just as he had in their dreams.

She pulled on his hair again, yanking him upwards. Thorne looked up the length of her and groaned at the beautiful sight. The curve of her back thrust her breasts upwards and their dusky dark buds called to him, making his mouth water and his cock twitch. He wanted to taste her there too. He wanted to lick and nibble her everywhere.

He rose before her and went to drop his mouth to suck the firm peak of her left breast into his mouth but she stopped him with a hand against his chest.

Thorne stared down into her eyes, captivated by the hunger shining in them and the need that echoed through their link.

He kept still as she slowly grazed her hand down his body, her dark pupils expanding as her gaze followed it, devouring his body and making him burn wherever she touched. He shuddered as she ran her fingers through the dark hair that trailed down from his navel and her gaze lifted to his, the blatant want in it ripping a moan from his throat.

Her fingers made fast work of the lacing on his trousers and he tipped his head back, moaning at the ceiling as she slipped her hand inside, running her palm down the full hard length of him. The heel of her hand rubbed the broad head and he sank his fangs into his lip, his hips thrusting forwards against his will.

Sable moaned and shoved his leathers down his hips, over his backside. She dug her nails into his buttocks, another throaty appreciative groan leaving her sweet lips.

"Hell, I love your body," she whispered and he was about to answer her with a chuckle when she pressed the first kiss to his chest, shattering his ability to speak.

She swirled her tongue downwards and around his right nipple, her fingers clutching his sides and her thumbs pressing into his hips. He groaned, sank his teeth harder into his lip, and frowned as she worked her magic on him. Each swirl, lick and kiss propelled him closer to the edge, until his need for her reached a crescendo, maddening him and pushing at his self-control.

He clamped his hand down on her head, entwining his fingers in her silky black hair, and guided her downwards, towards the place where he needed her most, ached for her attention. She giggled and wrapped her lips around his flesh, sucking the head of his cock.

Thorne growled, the sound ripping up his throat, feral and animalistic, shocking him.

He pushed her down and rocked his hips forwards, gently thrusting into her hot wet mouth.

Her moan vibrated along his hard shaft and her grip on his waist tightened. Her teeth scraped over his sensitive flesh as she withdrew and he shivered, lost in the bliss of her mouth stroking his length, teasing him towards a climax he knew would be earth-shattering, leaving him as boneless and sated as he desired to leave her. He reached for it, rocking into her mouth, giving himself over to the pleasure and letting it take him.

No.

He wanted her to feel pleasure too. He wanted her in his arms this time, their bodies as one, both of them finding bliss together.

He withdrew from her, breathing hard and fighting the urge to let her continue her ministrations, bringing him to climax.

He needed to do things right.

He needed to make Sable his.

"Thorne," she whispered huskily and tried to lick him again. He held her back, pressing a hand to her shoulder, and she looked up at him through her eyelashes.

He placed two fingers under her chin and made her rise before him, groaning low in his throat as the action revealed her breasts and then the sweet spot between her thighs.

"Want you," he murmured and caressed her hips, skimming his fingers inwards towards her mound. Her stomach quivered as he slipped two fingers between her petals. Hot moisture coated his fingers, slippery and divine, confirming what he already knew. "You want me too."

She hesitated and then nodded.

Thorne lost his head.

The shower forgotten, he pulled her to him and turned with her, pinning her against the cold tiles. She moaned and arched forwards, forcing her body against his, every delicious soft inch of her driving him wild with a need to have her, to lift her and wrap her legs around his waist and take her.

He trod on the crotch of her trousers and underwear between her feet and lifted her, pulling her free of the garments. Sable instantly wrapped her arms around his head and kissed him. Her legs looped around his waist and her feet pressed into his buttocks. He growled as she tensed her muscles and forced him towards her. His hard aching cock met soft wetness and his growl became a deep groan.

He grasped her backside, and pinned her to the wall as he kissed her and ground against her, gently rocking into her wet heat, rubbing every inch of her. She moaned whenever the head of his length swept over her sensitive bud and the heat of her increased, ratcheting up his temperature with it.

Thorne couldn't take any more.

He eased his hips back and Sable broke the kiss, her moist breath puffing against his lips and her chest heaving close to his, her nipples brushing his pectorals.

"Thorne," she murmured and he knew what she wanted to say, what she meant to ask.

He kissed her again, silencing her before she could put voice to his inexperience. He didn't need to have slept with a thousand women to know how to make love to her. It was ingrained in him, a primal knowledge that told him how to please his female and how to bring them both to the point of ecstasy.

He would make the passion and pleasure of their dreams a reality.

Thorne released her right hip and grasped his cock. He dropped his hips, raising her higher at the same time, and stared down between them as he ran the head of his length through her wet centre. His heart stuttered in his chest, breathing coming quicker, mirroring Sable's as she clutched his shoulders and moaned. He glanced at her to find her with her eyes closed and her brow furrowed, speaking of the pleasure that rippled through him.

"Thorne." It was a moan this time, a plea. A supplication.

Thorne obeyed.

He guided his length lower and his breath hitched as the head nudged into her. She moaned again, her teeth teasing her lower lip, nibbling at the tender flesh.

Thorne breathed harder, steeling himself as he fed his cock into her. She was tight around him, hot and slick. The dreams hadn't prepared him for the reality of her. His fingers tightened against her buttocks and he inched further into her, a growl rumbling up his throat as he watched his cock slowly disappearing, joining them.

His female.

His fated one.

His Sable.

He felt her gaze on him, burning into his face, and shifted his to meet it. A thousand emotions played out in her eyes and he willingly drowned in them, knowing that all he saw was mirrored in his. The fear, the trepidation, the tenderness, the passion, and the need. He felt everything that she did, experiencing it all with her as he slowly filled her, stretching her tight body to accommodate him.

He released his cock, grasped her other hip, and drove himself the rest of the way into her. A throaty gasp was his reward as she arched in his arms, her eyes closing and fingers pressing into his shoulders.

Mine.

She belonged to him now and he wanted all of her.

He grunted as he withdrew and swallowed her moan as he thrust back into her wet heat. She dug her fingers into his hair and then grasped his left horn as she clung to him. Her heels pressed into his buttocks and he growled at the delicious way she tried to control the pace of his thrusts, her wicked insistence that he move quicker. He gave her what she desired, always ready to please her, to surrender to her command.

She kissed him hard as he made love to her with long, deep strokes that drove her against the wall. Her lips clashed with his, her tongue brushing his one moment and then flickering over his fangs the next.

He groaned when she stroked one with the tip of her tongue, teasing it. His fangs lengthened, filling his mouth, awakening a dark need that he had tried to keep dormant, knowing it would only serve to push Sable away.

He wanted to bite her.

Ached to feel her soft flesh between his teeth and have her blood flowing down his throat.

Hungered to claim her.

Thorne shoved that need to the recesses of his heart and kept it there, held at bay by a more dominant need to pleasure her.

Not frighten her.

"Thorne," she murmured breathlessly against his lips, her hips rocking into his, riding his cock as much as he was riding her. She clutched him closer, her mouth warring with his as she kept up with her feet, forcing him to thrust deep into her whenever he withdrew.

He groaned, the visible display of the fierce need he could sense in her pleasuring him almost as much as being inside her at last. That she wanted him so much, needed him so intensely that she was a slave to sensation, lost in her quest for release with him, sparked a deep ache in his chest that finally confirmed everything she had told him and he had found difficult to believe.

She desired only him.

She wanted him as much as he wanted her.

He buried his face into her neck and she tensed.

"Shh," he whispered and kissed her throat. "Will not bite you."

She relaxed instantly and tilted her head away from him, trusting him with her neck. He moaned and kissed it, licking the line of her artery, feeling her pulse hammering beneath his tongue. He wanted to bite her but he wouldn't. He wouldn't force the claim upon her, no matter how fiercely he needed her, how violently he wanted to claim her as his forever.

Her breasts squashed against his chest as he drove into her, curling his hips so his pelvic bone brushed her sensitive bud. She moaned with each meeting of their bodies and held him closer, clutching him to her throat as he kissed and licked it, resisting the pressing need to sink his aching fangs into her.

She flexed and tightened around him, ripping a grunt from his lips that he couldn't contain. She moaned in answer, her restless actions warning him that she was close. He focused on her pleasure, on giving her release before he found his own, and plunged deep into her, as far as she could take him, using more of his strength in each rough thrust.

Sable tensed and jerked against him, her cry of pleasure loud in his ear. Her fingers grasped his shoulder and the back of his head, and her legs squeezed him as her body exploded with ripples of pleasure that flowed over him. She quivered around his length, her hot moisture coating him, and his balls drew up, his release rising.

He gently bit her neck, careful not to break her skin, unable to hold back his instinct as he felt her climaxing, and clutched her hips as he thrust into her. He managed only three deep plunges before his release boiled up his cock and burst from him, shattering him in the process and making his knees tremble.

Sable slowly rubbed his back and sifted her fingers through his hair, her cheek coming to rest on his shoulder.

Thorne held her in his teeth, quivering from head to toe, hazy and hot all over. He closed his eyes and focused on the feel of them joined, both of them trembling with aftershocks of pleasure. Pleasure they had found together.

Sable pressed a kiss to his shoulder and shifted backwards, forcing him to release her.

He lifted his head, unsure what to expect. His heart balanced on his tongue, fear that she would reject him keeping it trembling there, a timid thing that he cursed. He wanted to be strong, but Sable had the power to strip all of his strength from him. She left him weak. Made him vulnerable.

But she also had the power to make him feel invincible.

His eyes searched her golden ones, trying to read in them what she wanted to say.

She stroked his right horn, sending a hot shiver down from its root to his balls. His length twitched inside her.

"I thought we were going to have a shower?" She smiled wickedly.

Thorne groaned.

Grinned.

Invincible.

CHAPTER 21

Thorne knocked on the wooden door of the small thatched cottage. Sable stood behind him with Bleu, fascinated by the quaint building and the immaculate garden. Early dawn light shone on the roses that climbed over the creamy rough stone walls of the cottage, warming their red blooms.

More rosebushes lined the winding path through the garden, their blooms varying from white, to pink, to yellow and even orange. The yellow made her think of Thorne and his offering to his mother. Where did he go to in the mortal world in order to get those yellow blooms? They weren't from Hell. She was certain of that. Was there a special place that he went, perhaps one related to his mother? She wanted to ask him, but now wasn't the time.

A cold breeze blew across the roses, sweeping up the scent and swirling around her.

She rubbed her arms through her black shirt, trying to keep the chill off. She should have brought a coat. She didn't know how Thorne could happily stand there with no shirt on and just the morning sun to keep him warm.

Bleu shifted beside her, bending to smell one of the rose blooms. He looked at home surrounded by the beautiful flowers and plants, out in the countryside. He had been more relaxed ever since Thorne had announced that Rosalind lived out in the wilds of England, a short distance away from London. Sable surmised it was in Bleu's blood to feel calmed around nature when he felt a connection to it. He leaned to breathe in a different flower and the long black coat he wore over his skin-tight scaly obsidian armour fell forwards, the hem brushing the path.

The door opened.

"Elf!"

It slammed shut again.

Bleu's eyebrows shot up towards his wild black hair and he straightened.

"You have that effect on a lot of women." Sable nudged him in the ribs with her elbow and he scowled down at her.

Thorne knocked again. "We must speak with you, Rosalind."

"I'm not speaking to an elf. Make him go away." The feminine voice carried through the wooden door, a note of panic in it.

Sable moved forwards. "Why not?"

Thorne frowned at her and she shrugged it off. She wanted to know why Rosalind had a fear of elves. Besides, they needed Bleu to stick with them. He might be a royal pain in her arse at times, but he was also a skilled fighter, and they were out in the open. Who knew what other enemies might be lurking around waiting to take down Thorne, or her, or Bleu, in order to make winning the war between the two demon realms easier.

Sable lost patience. "Look, Bleu isn't going to hurt you or do anything weird. He's a friend. A good elf."

"It doesn't matter whether he's good or not. He's an elf."

"We really need your help, Rosalind. Whether that's through a door or not... although it's getting light out and I think your mortal neighbours might have concerns when they see a guy with horns and one with pointed ears." Sable edged closer to the door and told herself she was about to be necessarily cruel. They had to get inside and hidden. "Rosalind... you're a code green. That means you're not a threat. Archangel likes you. Don't make me change your status."

There was a squeak on the other side of the door.

Thorne shook his head, his expression speaking of how unimpressed he was with her behaviour. Sable shrugged again.

"She's making things difficult. I had to try something. We need to get out of the open," she hissed at him and then turned back to the door. "What is it you have against Bleu? I have a laundry list of complaints myself, and I think Thorne does too, and probably Bleu's prince has—"

The door opened a crack and Rosalind peered out at her, her dazzling blue eyes enormous. "The elf isn't a prince?"

"Um, no. He's a royal pain... but no prince. He's a commander."

Bleu growled at her.

Rosalind's eyes slowly edged towards Bleu where he stood behind her. She blinked rapidly, her fear palpable as she set eyes on him.

"I can never meet your prince," the witch blurted in one rapid stream.

Now Sable really wanted to know what Rosalind's deal was. Why couldn't she meet Loren?

"Someone predicted your future and you do not like it," Thorne said and Rosalind's blue eyes shot to him. "You do not need to meet him. You only need to listen to us and decide whether you can help us."

"We can pay you," Sable put in and Rosalind's fair eyebrows pinched tightly together, her rosy lips thinning with what looked like disgust.

"I do not accept gold. If I believe you in need of my help and feel I can assist you, I will do so." Rosalind opened the door, revealing the candlelit interior of her cottage and the rest of her. Her long black dress reached her ankles, drab and boring. The typical garb of a witch on duty.

Sable had visited a fae town once and had seen avenues of witches peddling their wares, all of them wearing a shapeless dull dress of this fashion.

"Please enter." Rosalind stepped aside, allowing Thorne to enter ahead of Sable.

He had to duck to fit into the corridor and almost banged his head on a ceiling light. Sable followed him, close to having to hunch herself in order to avoid feeling she was about to crack her head on something. She couldn't resist glancing back at Bleu.

He entered, stooping to fit his six-feet-five frame into the low hallway, and Rosalind practically flattened herself against the wall. The witch edged behind him and closed the door.

"Please go on ahead. There is a sitting room just to your right."

Sable followed Thorne down a step into a large open plan sitting room with an inglenook fireplace to her left and dark wooden beams across the pale ceiling. It was certainly cute and quaint, but she could never imagine living in such a cramped place. After her own apartment and Thorne's enormous castle, this cottage felt like a prison cell.

Thorne banged his head on a beam and growled. "Did that last time."

Sable rubbed his arm while he rubbed his forehead.

"You came before," Rosalind said as she squeezed into the room, giving Bleu yards of space, as if he had something highly contagious.

Did the witch think her bad prediction could come to pass just by being near an elf who had been near an elf prince?

"I did." Thorne took the armchair near the fireplace that she offered with a sweep of her hand. "It is not going well. I have been sealed out of my kingdom by witchcraft."

Sable went to pull up another of the dark green velvet armchairs and it moved on its own, shooting across the wooden floor towards her. She quickly edged backwards to avoid colliding with it and bumped into the arm of

Thorne's chair. He caught her around the waist, twisted her and settled her on his lap.

Sable slapped at his hands. He didn't relent.

Bleu glowered at them from the corner of the room and looked as if he might leave. She didn't want that to happen. The armchair halted next to her, another joining it. Sable pushed off Thorne's lap and sat on her own chair. She patted the one next to her. Bleu reluctantly joined them.

Rosalind moved her chair further away, knocking over a stack of books, and sat in it.

The witch had moved furniture with magic. Why not tidy the place up with it too? Sable looked around her at the small room and realised it probably wasn't possible. Books covered most of the floor, filled the bookcases, and even occupied most of the tables. Rosalind needed a bigger house.

"Excuse the mess," Rosalind said pointedly, an undertone of irritation in her voice.

"Sorry. I think this is the most books I've seen outside of Thorne's library."

"You have been to the demon realm?" Rosalind's blue eyes sparkled with interest. "Is it as grim and dark as all say?"

"Not really." Sable felt Thorne's gaze come to rest on her, intense and focused. He wanted to know what she thought of his realm. "It's actually quite nice. Admittedly, there's a monochrome colour scheme, but you get used to it."

Sable flicked her long black hair over her shoulder with her right hand and Rosalind's eyebrows rose.

"I didn't know you were an angel."

Sable's eyebrows knitted together. "Archangel? Yeah. I'm with Archangel. I'm one of their hunters. We're helping Thorne out with his war, so I have friends trapped in the Third Realm too. Friends I really need to get back to as soon as possible."

"I understand that, but you misunderstand me." Rosalind smiled, a bubble of laughter in her voice. "Although it is ironic that Archangel would in fact have an angel in its ranks."

Sable's frown hardened. Rosalind's eyes widened.

"Oh... you didn't know. I've seen that mark before." Rosalind pointed to Sable's right wrist and it shook as Sable turned it over to look at the cross.

"On who?" Sable sat up, her gaze locked on the petite ash blonde opposite her, Thorne and Bleu forgotten.

"A male. He came to me years ago... he bore that mark on his wrist. He wanted to know his future. He seemed pleased with the result."

"Why?" Sable moved to the edge of her seat, her heart pounding against her chest now and her throat going dry. An angel with a mark like hers?

She looked down at it and a shiver went through her. An angel?

"Something about a mistake he made... or was it something else... it was something like that anyway. It was a long time ago, so I forget the details." Rosalind shrugged. "I just remember that he was upset and thought he would lose his wings. He was seriously precious about those pearly white feathers of his."

"How long ago?" Sable snapped and rubbed her thumb over the mark on her wrist.

Thorne's large hand settled on her left forearm and his fingers gently curled around to hold it. She glanced back at him, nerves and anticipation exploding within her, making her tremble and feel nauseous. Thorne smiled at her and she silently thanked him for his support.

"Um. Thirty... maybe forty years?"

Sable's heart leaped into her throat. "How about thirty-five?"

Rosalind shrugged again. "It's possible."

"Sable," Thorne said in a low voice, a note of warning in it.

"I know." She really did. She couldn't just leap to conclusions but she was finding it hard to give reason a chance. She was too caught up in the thought that one of her parents was an angel and Rosalind might have met him. "This mark though, Thorne... you know I never met my parents... and I've had this for as long as I can remember... and then everything that happened during the battle."

"What happened?" Bleu said and she looked over her right shoulder at him.

His purple eyes implored her and the words slipped free.

"I burned a demon to ashes with my right hand. I just touched him, Bleu... and he turned to ashes."

"Sable... is that why you were acting so strangely?" Bleu whispered, his handsome face softening, and she nodded, her guilt rising again as she remembered how she had behaved when he had tried to help her back to the castle and how she had kept this hidden from everyone. "Have you told Olivia?"

She shook her head.

"I couldn't... I didn't want her or you guys to think I was some sort of freak." She held her hand up when he opened his mouth to speak. "I know. She would never think of me like that... and neither would you or Loren... but I was afraid. I didn't know what this mark was or where it had come from or why I had it… but I might be able to find some answers now. I swear I will tell her everything… when we get back to the Third Realm."

She looked back at Thorne, her eyebrows furrowing.

"What if I'm the mistake?" she whispered and he squeezed her arm, a tender look in his deep crimson eyes. He drew her arm towards him and she wanted nothing more than to take the comfort he desired to offer her, letting him hold her, but she couldn't. She needed answers more. She turned to Rosalind. "Is there a way to find this angel?"

Rosalind frowned. "I don't know. No mortal or immortal knows the pathway to Heaven, and even if you did, they probably wouldn't let you use it. I don't tend to ask clients about where they live or keep that sort of thing on file. They don't like it."

Dead end. How was she meant to find an angel in this world? She had never seen one in all her years with Archangel and she had never read any reports or information on them in the database.

It was impossible.

"There was a huge throw down at a vampire theatre in the city involving angels," Rosalind said and her attention snapped back to her, the embers of her hope rekindling. "Really big. Loads of angels were there. A word of warning though… I don't think this angel was looking for a kid. He looked like the kind of man who would have killed to erase a mistake and protect himself."

Sable couldn't stop herself from asking, "What did he look like?"

Rosalind stared hard at her. "Maybe a little like you… but with eyes of pure amethyst."

Sable sat back in her armchair and stared at the floor, unsure how to process all of the information or her feelings. Thorne spoke to Rosalind of his kingdom and Sable caught snippets of it, hearing enough to know that Rosalind was more than happy to help them with their problem, but her thoughts kept returning to angels.

Could she be the daughter of an angel? The result of a mistake? Did she even want to face that ugly truth?

It could be pure coincidence that she had the same tattoo as an angel.

Or not.

A man with the same tattoo had come to Rosalind around the time of her conception and asked to see his future, fearing a mistake would take away his wings?

An angel who looked like her?

It was too much.

"Are you unwell?" Thorne's deep voice roused her from her thoughts, pulling her out of the mire, and she looked into his dark crimson eyes.

She shook her head and balanced on the brink of asking him to take a detour on the way back to his realm so she could visit the theatre Rosalind had mentioned and discover whether an angel who looked like her had been there. She couldn't do that though.

Thorne's kingdom was vulnerable without him.

She also didn't think that vampires would appreciate an Archangel hunter showing up at their door asking about the angels who had attacked them.

"We should get started," Bleu said and Sable nodded.

Rosalind stared at her. So did Thorne.

His gaze left her. "Give me directions to this theatre."

"No. We don't have time," Sable said and he held his hand up.

"We will make time. This is important to you… and you need to have the answers to the questions that plague your heart, Sable." Thorne's tone brooked no argument but she opened her mouth to voice one anyway. He spoke before she could get the words out. "It is what is best for you and best for our battle. You might perhaps be able to uncover something about your power that could be useful."

Sable's shoulders sagged and she wanted to argue with him, but she didn't have the heart or the conviction, not when he looked at her with love and understanding in his eyes.

She had told him about her parents and he knew her inner fear about her power and what it meant. He wanted to help her, had even gone as far as to counter all her arguments before she could voice them, giving her no room for manoeuvre and ensuring she went along with his plan.

He wasn't really thinking about how useful she could be in the battle to save his kingdom though. She could see straight through that as an excuse to get her to agree to go to the theatre and question the vampires. He wanted her to have answers because he knew how much this revelation about herself distressed her. He wanted to take away her pain and confusion.

It touched her.

She had expected everyone to turn against her and want to treat her like a science experiment because of her new abilities, but Thorne wasn't like that and neither was Bleu. She had painted them with the Archangel brush, expecting them to be like her bosses. Thorne, Bleu and even Rosalind hadn't looked at her any differently than they had before discovering that she might be part angel. She was the only one making a big deal of it.

She supposed that powers and abilities and this kind of crazy shit was every day run of the mill stuff for them. They took it all in their stride but she couldn't. It still freaked her out.

"It will take time to find a way to reopen the pathway or get around the barrier... a couple of hours maybe," Rosalind said in a quiet voice and stood. "Come back then and hopefully I'll be close to a solution."

"Really... we should help," Sable said and Thorne growled.

"We will go to the theatre and return as soon as we can." He clutched her arm and her voice failed her when he looked down at her, the soft affection mixed with determination in his eyes stealing her breath away.

Sometimes, she was glad that he was stubborn.

Rosalind scribbled on a scrap of paper and handed it to her. She looked at the address.

"I know where this is. It's not far from Trafalgar Square in London."

"And I know where that is," Thorne said and bowed his head to Rosalind. "My thanks, Little Witch."

Rosalind nodded. "Two hours, tops."

Thorne pulled Sable closer and held his hand out to Bleu. Bleu reluctantly took it and the ground opened beneath them. Sable closed her eyes as they dropped into the black abyss, holding on tightly to Thorne.

The cold feeling passed and she opened her eyes. Wide open space surrounded her, the large square and sandstone buildings quiet in the early morning. A statue of a lion loomed over Thorne's shoulder, the sky above him a brilliant shade of blue.

Cars and red double-decker buses travelled along the main street near the square, providing the only noise.

"This way." Sable led Thorne and Bleu towards the opposite end of the square and the road that would take them to the theatre.

A vampire theatre right in the heart of London.

She couldn't believe it.

This end of the city was beautiful, the old sandstone buildings, the square and the museums attracting thousands of tourists every day, and every night. Did the vampires feed nearby? The theatre wasn't on Archangel's watch list so the vampires must have control of their patrons, and their staff, ensuring they didn't draw attention to them by openly killing.

Sable crossed the road and headed up the street towards the theatre. The elegant cream stone building stood on the right hand side of the narrow street. Steps led up to the columned porch and she tipped her head back, taking in the grandeur of the carved triangular frieze the pillars supported. The glass doors that ran the length of the portico were a modern twist to the building, out of place with the character and charm of it.

They were shuttered on the inside. She glanced at the huge windows either side of the porch and found similar black shutters beyond the glass. Definitely a home of vampires.

Thorne took the steps swiftly and was banging on the glass doors before she had caught up with him.

Would anyone answer?

Vampires were nocturnal and she didn't know how many lived in this theatre. Disturbing a nest of sleeping vampires didn't seem like a wise idea, even when she had Thorne and Bleu as back up.

Thorne kept banging, each heavy pound of his fist rattling the glass.

A smartly dressed woman passing along the street behind them stared their way. Sable really hoped that she didn't spot Thorne's horns. Bleu stood behind him, partially blocking the woman's view, but Thorne was bare-chested, and that was bound to attract some attention.

Sable began to wish the vampires *would* open the door.

The shutters on one of the doors drew back to reveal a handsome blond man.

Sable's eyes widened in recognition.

"Oh, this isn't going to be good."

CHAPTER 22

∽

"What is wrong?" Thorne's deep voice offered Sable some comfort as she stared at the grey-eyed vampire standing on the other side of the glass.

"We kinda met this vampire before… in a club… when Loren got drunk." Sable edged closer to Thorne and Bleu.

Bleu cursed in the demon tongue.

The vampire stared at them and folded his arms across his chest, causing the rolled-up sleeves of his pinstripe black shirt to tighten against his forearms. Markings tracked in a line up his arms, snagging her attention for a heartbeat. They looked fae in origin. His gaze remained locked on her at first, the dark intent in it triggering her gift and telling her to keep her distance, and then shifted to take in Bleu and then Thorne.

"Can I help you with something?" The man gave them each a look that warned he wasn't happy and she could almost hear him plotting their downfall in his head as he weighed them up in turn. His steely cold gaze lingered longer on Thorne this time. Deciding to take him on first or last?

Before Sable could answer, a young blond boy dressed in blue Thomas the Tank Engine pyjamas appeared beside the vampire, sleepily rubbing his eyes. He looked up at the man and tugged on his loose shirttails.

The sandy-haired man stooped, caught the boy under his arms and lifted him into his embrace. The smile he gave the boy caused a pang in Sable's chest. The young boy yawned again and settled his head against the vampire's shoulder, cuddling into him. The pang in her chest worsened. Before her stood the perfect image of fatherhood that she had never experienced in her life, and it came in the form of a vampire.

She had never thought of his kind, or any of the fae and demons she hunted, as being tender and capable parents with families, and she didn't want to think about it now. She had killed her share of vampires, following her orders without question, trusting Archangel and the system. How many of those vampires, demons and fae had been parents? How many families had she destroyed?

How many families had those demons, vampires and fae destroyed to put themselves onto Archangel's list?

Sable reminded herself that they had been there for a reason. Archangel only dealt with the non-humans who broke the rules and destroyed mortal lives in the process. Telling herself that didn't lift the weight from her stomach and she couldn't stop staring at the man before her and the way he clutched the boy, tucking him close to his chest in his strong arms.

Protecting him.

The pang worsened.

The vampire in question turned a red-edged glare on them. "You have three seconds to answer my question before I get Elissa down to deal with you. What do you want?"

Sable presumed Elissa wasn't a vampire and was capable of leaving the confines of the theatre in daylight and handling two immortals and a hunter on her own.

"I have a few questions... about angels."

The man's eyes burned red, his pupils beginning to turn elliptical. He covered the young boy's ears, pressing him to his chest, and growled.

"Angels," he spat and scowled at her, disgust colouring his expression. "I'm not the resident expert on those bastards. Wait here."

He disappeared.

No flash of light like the elves used or a black hole in the ground like the demons created. He just winked out of existence.

Wait a moment.

Vampires couldn't teleport.

Thorne moved closer to her and she looked up at him. His eyes glowed red, his horns curling and ears growing pointed, and it wasn't desire changing them.

"Something wrong?" She looked back at Bleu but he seemed calm enough, although he wore a look of disgust similar to the one the vampire had sported on mentioning angels. She hadn't forgotten how much Bleu hated bloodsuckers. It equalled her hatred for them. He must have been loving being around Grave and the others as much as she had been.

"The male is an incubus. I will not let him near you," Thorne growled beside her and Sable frowned at him.

"He's a vampire... although he *can* teleport. That's not normal, is it?"

"He is only a vampire in part. A large part of him is incubus. He bears the scent of one, and the markings. The boy was also an incubus." Thorne edged another step closer.

Bleu moved to stand beside her and curled his lip, flashing a hint of fang. "This whole place stinks like blood."

Sable peered closer, trying to get a good look at the foyer of the theatre. It was too dark for her to make anything out clearly, even with the weak daylight filtering in through the glass doors.

A beautiful petite raven-haired woman appeared out of the gloom, a long white dress hugging her curves. She moved into the light, close to the doors, her gaze locked on Sable. Sable couldn't tear her gaze away from the woman either. She had the most incredible eyes and Sable had never seen anything like them. They were brilliant blue around her pupils but turquoise around the edges, and the longer Sable stared into them, the calmer she felt.

"You wished to know of my kind?" the woman said, her voice a soothing melody, airy and soft.

Her kind?

"Angels." Sable looked the petite woman over. "You're an angel?"

She nodded. "I was. I gave up that life to be here."

At a vampire theatre. Sable could only guess that she had fallen in love with one of the vampires. She had heard of some pretty forbidden relationships before, but nothing on this scale.

"Did you know a male with black hair and purple eyes, and a mark like this?" Sable tugged her shirtsleeve back to reveal the stylised black cross on the inside of her right wrist.

The woman moved forwards, until daylight bathed her in a golden glow. A frown crinkled her brow. "It isn't possible... my master would not do such a thing... but my master was only one of a few angel commanders who bore this mark."

"Bore?" Past tense. Sable swallowed to wet her throat.

The angel nodded. "He is dead. Killed here in the battle. He sought to murder everyone in this place and me with them."

He sounded charming. Part of Sable hoped the homicidal angel wasn't her father.

"Is it possible that he might have been my father though?" Sable edged closer to the glass doors and the woman, her heart thumping against her chest. "Can an angel father a child?"

"It is possible. But other angels have dark hair and purple eyes. It is not uncommon."

Sable rubbed the cross with her thumb. "But none that were born with this mark?"

The angel looked at it again, her incredible eyes catching the daylight and brightening. "No. The Echelon are rare. They are born to be commanders and all are thousands of years old. Only their offspring bear it now… but you are not an angel."

Sable shook her head in agreement. "Just a regular mortal."

The woman smiled. "There is nothing regular about you."

A roar echoed through the building.

Thorne grabbed Sable, pulling her close to him, and Bleu closed ranks on her other side.

A huge ice-blond vampire male loomed behind the petite angel, immense and lethal compared with her, his pupils nothing more than tiny vertical slices in the centre of his red irises.

The angel didn't flinch or jump and her expression remained placid and serene.

The enormous bare-chested male flashed his fangs and grabbed her shoulders from behind, his claws pressing into her flesh.

She slowly lifted her hand and gently touched his left one.

She sighed. "You broke your restraints again."

The chains attached to the thick steel cuffs around his wrists rattled as the male drew her back against him and wrapped his arms around her, crossing them over her front. He bared his fangs again, aiming the threat at Thorne and then Bleu, and then pushed the woman aside. He went to step forwards, towards the doors, his gaze narrowed and calculating, claws flexing. He meant to fight them.

The petite angel stepped in front of him and stopped him with a single soft touch of his cheek.

The vampire looked down at her, the overlong white threads of his hair hanging forwards, brushing his cheeks together with her slender hand.

Sable expected him to push her aside again but he remained still, his bare chest heaving with each laboured breath.

"We were only talking, Snow," the woman whispered and stroked his cheek, "and the sun is out. These people mean me no harm. The female came to ask after her father."

"Father?" the vampire said gruffly, his voice thick and low. His silver eyebrows drew together. "Father?"

The woman nodded. "It seems my master may have committed a sin no one knew about."

Snow growled, baring his fangs. Evidently, he didn't like the woman mentioning her master, and Sable could understand why if the man had been part of the battle between the angels and vampires at the theatre.

"I'm tired of being called a mistake and a sin," Sable said and the huge male looked up at her. The softness that had entered his eyes while he had been looking down at the angel disappeared, replaced by an endless hunger for violence and blood. Sable stood her ground. "Rosalind the witch told me about the man I'm looking for information on. She said that he had wanted to know his future because he had feared he would lose his wings."

The woman turned to face Sable and smiled sadly. "It sounds like my master. He was rather precious about them."

Snow grunted and clumsily petted her dark hair.

"He's definitely dead then?" Sable wasn't sure whether she was glad to hear that or not. Had she wanted to meet her father? He probably wouldn't have wanted anything to do with her. He wouldn't have wanted to reveal his mistake to everyone.

Thorne slipped his hand into hers and gently squeezed it. She squeezed back.

The vampire stared down at their joined hands and then wrapped his arms around the woman in front of him again, tugging her back against his bare chest.

He nuzzled her black hair and turned fiery red eyes on Sable. "I killed him."

She wasn't surprised to hear that. Snow looked dangerous and a little bit crazy.

"You remind me of someone… this King of Death."

Snow's lips peeled back off his enormous fangs and he growled low in his throat. "Grave."

His demeanour changed abruptly, darkening before her eyes, and he snarled again, his fangs elongating further.

"*Grave.*" Snow set the woman aside and glared at Sable, his red eyes narrowed and filled with the hunger to maim and kill. She edged backwards, closer to Bleu and Thorne, her heart leaping high into her throat.

"Snow… no," the woman said but he ignored her this time and stepped towards them.

Another vampire appeared between Snow and the doors, a brunet male wearing a black robe that swirled around his ankles as it settled.

"Snow." The male pressed his hands to Snow's chest, holding him still as he growled and snarled and kept trying to advance, and then raised them to cup his cheeks.

Snow stilled and looked down at the new male.

"Brother? Come back to us," the brunet whispered and Snow's expression softened, losing its vicious edge. "Aurora."

The woman came forwards again to take hold of Snow's hand. She laced their fingers together and brushed her other hand over the back of his, stroking it.

The dark-haired male turned on them, his gaze as black as his brother's had been, speaking of fury and desire to shed blood.

"What the hell is going on here? Why is there a demon, a mortal and a..." He cocked an eyebrow, his expression shifting towards disgust. "An elf... on our doorstep? State your business and leave. You are upsetting my brother."

Snow grunted. "Grave."

The male's expression turned darker still and Sable could see the resemblance between the brothers. "What of that bastard?"

Sable held her hand up. "I just mentioned his name. I'm not here because of him at all. He's just helping out with King Thorne's demonomachy in Hell."

She jerked a thumb a Thorne.

It might not have been her wisest move, but then how was she to have known it would make things worse?

Snow roared, the sound deafening even through the glass, and launched forwards. The angel Aurora held him back, pulling on his left arm, and his brother shifted in front of him and pushed against his chest.

"Snow!" the male barked.

Snow growled and snarled, flashing huge fangs at Thorne.

"Demon." He pinned Thorne with a deadly glare. "Hell. Grave. Blood. Kill. Demon."

"Grave will never bother us again, Snow," the male said and Aurora kept pulling backwards.

Sable felt as if she had opened a very rotten, bad can of worms by mentioning Grave. The big vampire clearly had a problem with him, and his brother didn't seem overly fond of him either. Understandable. The guy was an arsehole.

"Snow, please?" Aurora said and Snow stopped struggling. He shoved away from his brother, turned towards her and gathered her into his arms.

He squeezed her close to his chest and petted her hair, stroking as he muttered, "Won't let Grave have you."

Aurora looked confused but she stroked his chest anyway and whispered, "I don't want anyone but you, Snow."

Sable had been wrong. The guy was crazier than Grave.

"Snow," the brother said and the larger male looked over at him, darkness back in his eyes. "Let Aurora speak with these people and then we must get you back to your room."

Snow looked reluctant to let his female go but after a few minutes more of petting her, he loosened his grip enough that she could turn to face them again.

"I am sorry I was not able to be more help. If my master was your father, then you most probably have some or all of his abilities."

"Such as being able to burn a demon to ashes by touching them?" Sable said and Aurora's face softened into a look of understanding and compassion. She nodded. "Do you know how to control this power?"

"It is a difficult one to master and not one I possess. Only the Echelon have it together with an ability to sense demons at a long distance. They were born to eradicate demons." Aurora's gaze quickly shifted to Thorne. "Sorry."

Thorne shrugged. "My kind do not tend to meet yours often these days. The angels do not like to enter Hell."

"You have been there?" Aurora looked back at Sable.

She nodded. "My power awakened there."

Aurora looked down at her wrist and then lower, taking in all of Sable. "The demon toxin in your system has hindered your power in this realm, keeping it from manifesting. It is possible that if we removed the toxin—"

"Wait? Demon toxin?" Sable really hoped Aurora wasn't about to tell her that her mother had somehow been part demon and had passed on demon traits to her too.

Aurora nodded slowly. "Were you injured once in a fight against a demon? Many species possess a toxin on their skin or claws."

Sable's eyes widened. "When I was younger, before I joined Archangel. I fought a demon punk kid and he injured my leg. It's played up ever since."

"There is still toxin in your system from that demon strike. It would be difficult to remove, a long and painful process, but if it was expunged from your body, your angelic powers would finally, fully manifest."

Sable wasn't sure she wanted the full range of angel powers available to her. She didn't want to have this one power that had awakened despite the demon toxin. On the other hand, she didn't like the thought of walking around for the rest of her life with that toxin inside her, doing God only knew what to her.

"Would I be able to come back and maybe talk more about this with you at a better time?" Sable glanced at the big vampire still petting Aurora. A better time would be one when he wasn't present, but something told her that he was unlikely to let his petite angel out of his sight, especially when she had a demon hunter visiting her.

Aurora smiled. "I would like that. Can we do that, Snow? Antoine?"

The two males sighed and then eventually nodded.

Antoine added, "The elf cannot come though."

Bleu glared at him. Antoine glared right back.

Sable wondered who would win in a fight and then shrugged it off.

"It was lovely to meet you all," Aurora said and Antoine closed the shutter across the doors before Sable could respond.

He seemed rather rude.

Sable stared at the glass doors and sighed. One of her parents had been an angel. That was the biggest mind fuck yet, bigger than trying to get her head around the fact that Hell was beneath her feet but not at the same time.

"Sable. We should return to Rosalind. I will bring you back here soon though." Thorne held his hand out to her and Sable nodded and slipped hers into it.

She took hold of Bleu's hand, forming a circle with him and Thorne, and closed her eyes as the black hole opened beneath them and they dropped into it.

She smiled.

Thorne was as protective and possessive of her as Snow was of Aurora, and she should have known that he wouldn't let her visit the theatre alone. He would be there to support her and keep her safe from harm.

He would be there for her.

Was this warm burst of happiness, comfort and relief what Olivia experienced when she was with Loren?

Was this what it was like to be deeply in love with someone and have them feel the same way about you?

If it was, Sable hoped this feeling never ended.

She wanted it to last forever.

CHAPTER 23

Thorne gently set Sable down at the front door of Rosalind's tiny home. He immediately released Bleu and swept the backs of his claws across Sable's cheek, giving her all of his attention.

She had swung from one feeling to the next while speaking with the vampires and the angel, her emotions bombarding her. They had yet to settle. She tipped her chin up, her golden gaze meeting and holding his, keeping his focus locked on her. His little female. He would take her back to the angel as soon as possible and would do all in his power to help her uncover the truth about her parents.

Sable lifted her hand and brushed her fingers across his. "I'm good. No need to look at me as if I might break at any moment."

He didn't think she would. His female was strong and brave, and far different from how she had been the night she had discovered her power. She was already growing accustomed to the change, growing more comfortable with herself. Perhaps it was only because she was in the mortal world though where her wrist no longer bothered her. She had touched it less and had given up wearing her cuff.

Thorne lowered his hand from her face to her wrist and gently clasped it, staring down at the mark on the inside of it, jet black against her skin.

If he took her back to the demon realms with him, it would bother her again.

He swept the pad of his thumb across it.

"I know that look," Sable said softly, drawing his eyes back to hers. She shook her head. "I can deal with this. It was stupid of me to leave. I put your whole kingdom in jeopardy when all I wanted to do was help save it. Well, now I'm going to do that. I'm going back with you to fight those bastards and you can't stop me. I'm not being left behind."

He never would have dared suggest such a thing, even though he felt a pressing need to do so. He knew his female better than she thought. He knew that she would be upset, angry, and feel belittled, her strength challenged, if he told her that he didn't want her in the coming battle for his kingdom.

He had learned when to step back and ignore his instinct to protect and coddle her.

She was a warrior, but it was more than that and her misplaced sense of guilt pressing her to threaten him and make it clear that she was coming with him back to the Third Realm whether he liked it or not.

She needed to feel useful and needed to keep her mind occupied, and she also needed to be there with her fellow hunters and her friends.

And him.

The soft imploring edge creeping into her eyes and her warm emotions pleaded him not to leave her behind and leave her wondering about him, fearing something would happen to him while they were apart.

His little huntress loved him, although she still would not admit it.

"I would never leave you behind, Sable. Your place is at my side." He was pushing it. He knew that. She was liable to react badly to such commanding words, ones that subtly reminded her that she was his mate and hinted that he wasn't content with their relationship as it stood.

He wanted to claim her.

He was doing his best to be patient, but now he had sampled all of her, knew her right down to her soul, and the need to mate with her and make her his forever was only growing stronger.

He wasn't sure how much longer he could deny it.

The door behind him opened. "You're back… and all in one piece. Did it go well?"

"It did. Thank you." Sable stepped away from him, turning her golden gaze on Rosalind. "Aurora believes her master might have been my father. I'm going to speak with her again about it soon, and about what powers I might have."

"Speaking of powers. I made you a present. Come on." The petite blonde witch beckoned Sable with a jerk of her chin and shuffled back into the house.

Bleu sighed, eyeing the cramped building with loathing, and followed Sable inside, hunching his shoulders to avoid banging his head.

Thorne watched him and realised that since waking in Sable's apartment at dawn, holding her tucked close against him, her bare body moulded to his, he no longer felt any animosity towards the elf male. The way she acted around Thorne, the way she looked at him, and how she responded to every touch he dared, told him that she was his now. All he had to do was somehow convince her to go through with the claiming and become his forever.

He ducked and followed the tiny corridor to the open area where Rosalind and Sable sat opposite each other in front of the fireplace, deep in discussion. Bleu stood off to one side, his rich purple eyes documenting everything in the room but never once settling on Sable. The male knew better than to risk provoking him. Perhaps Bleu's behaviour was also responsible for his lack of need to kill him. Had Sable spoken to Bleu while he had been unconscious?

Had she told him of her feelings?

Thorne wanted to ask him whether she had but held his tongue. Sable would tell him when she was ready. If he forced Bleu to tell him, she would be angry with him, and he would be another step further away from claiming her.

"I made this for you." Rosalind held something out to Sable. A silver cuff. "It's enchanted. It should help you control your power."

"Thank you." Sable took the delicate silver cuff and opened it. Thorne walked to the back of the dark green armchair and peered over her shoulder at it. The inside of the three-inch-wide metal band had symbols carved into it, covering most of the surface. Sable placed her right wrist into it and closed it. The latch clicked.

"It suits you," Thorne said and Sable looked up at him and smiled as she held her arm up and turned it this way and that, flashing the silver cuff.

"Snazzy, huh?" Sable tapped it, bringing his attention to the elegant scrollwork and the cross on the front that matched her mark. "Bonus is that if I'm ever strapped for cash, I could pawn it."

Rosalind looked mortified.

"She jests." Thorne reassured her with a smile. "Her sense of humour can be an acquired taste."

Sable frowned at him and then turned away, facing Rosalind again. "I was kidding though. I've never been one to accessorise, but this is pretty cool."

Thorne couldn't stop himself from imagining Sable dressed in nothing but the silver cuff and how it would feel cool against his skin while her flesh felt hot.

He felt her gaze come back to him, heating his blood to a thousand degrees, and shifted to relieve the tight ache in his leather trousers.

"Did you make progress on the pathways?" Thorne tried to ignore the way Sable stared at him. It was difficult, especially when he picked up a flutter of desire in her emotions.

Bleu shattered her hold on him by coming to stand beside him. "Do we have an entry point?"

Rosalind shook her head. "I probed all of the pathways into your realm but there are layers of spells in place, going deep. I can't unravel them all from here."

Thorne frowned. "Is there a better chance of breaching the barrier around my realm than reopening the portal pathways?"

"Probably. The spell would likely be single or maybe triple layer at the most. It would be quicker than attempting to negate or reverse all the spells blocking the pathways."

"Then we shall attempt to breach the barrier."

She looked uneasy. "But I can't do that from here. I need to know what spells were used... oh... you're not suggesting... you mean... I have a ticket to Hell with my name on it?"

Thorne nodded. "It is most pleasant at this time of year."

"I really don't think it is. Listen, I want to help, I really do... but going to Hell? That isn't really on my bucket list." Rosalind toyed with the black lacing down the front of her dress. "Isn't there another witch you can hit up for help?"

He shook his head this time and folded his arms across his chest, and her eyes widened. He lowered his arms to his sides again, realising that she was interpreting his body language and didn't like it one bit. He wasn't going to force her to help him, but he would not give up until she agreed to it.

"Thorne and Bleu will keep us both safe, and we'll test the barrier from the First Realm. It's okay there, apparently." Sable leaned forwards and Rosalind's gaze fell to her, her blue eyes still enormous. Sable reached over and touched Rosalind's hand on her knee. "I was pretty freaked out the first time I went to Hell too, and it wasn't by choice, but the realm I went to was nice and no one tried to hurt me."

What realm had she been forcibly taken to?

Guilt flickered in Bleu's purple eyes. Thorne growled at him, desire to throttle the male instantly surging through him, so powerful that he couldn't tamp it down or contain his rage. The male had abducted Sable, taking her against her will to the elf realm.

Sable sighed and looked over her shoulder at him. "He took me there because Loren had taken Olivia there. It was just to keep me with my friend."

Thorne still couldn't forgive him for doing such a thing and frightening Sable in the process.

Bleu muttered in the demon tongue, "I already apologised to her. I do not need to apologise to you too."

Thorne flashed his fangs at the bastard elf and folded his arms across his bare chest.

"Just ignore them. They do this a lot." Sable turned back to the witch. "The First Realm is safe, Rosalind. I promise. It's neutral and isn't at war with anyone, and it borders part of the Third Realm."

Rosalind looked up at him, her fair eyebrows raised high on her forehead. "She speaks the truth?"

Thorne nodded. "Always. We will petition the First King and ask for access to the land along the border. I swear upon my kingdom that I will keep you safe while you are in my care, Rosalind."

She still looked uneasy. She picked at the laces on her dress, looked around her small living room, and then sighed.

"Swear upon your fated one."

Thorne stiffened and growled at her. "No."

He would have gladly made such an oath once, and had done barely a few weeks ago, but now that his mate was within his grasp, he wasn't willing to risk the Fates taking her from him.

Rosalind frowned at him and then it melted away and her blue eyes fell to Sable. "I understand."

Her gaze lifted back to him and brightened. The blue swirled like a whirlpool and glittered with silver flakes. "I will take your oath upon your kingdom, King Thorne of the Third Realm. If you cross me, render me unto the wretched grasp of another or deliver me into the arms of death, I will see your kingdom suffer my eternal wrath."

Thorne's heart gave a hard painful beat and he clutched his chest, pressing his claws deep into his flesh.

He grimaced, grinding his teeth together, and fought the pain spreading through him, splintering his bones. He hadn't expected his oath to be binding and sealed by magic.

"Thorne?" Sable's soft voice filled with concern drew his focus to her. She stood beside him, her hand over his on his chest, her golden gaze warm with concern.

"I am well." He placed his other hand over her slender one, completing the tangle.

"Let's get going then, shall we?" Rosalind said, her tone bubbly and jovial again, as if she had always wanted to head to Hell and couldn't wait to get there. Confusing female. She hopped around the room, stuffing a leather satchel with vials of liquids and herbs, and several books and other implements.

Thorne breathed through the pain radiating from his heart, keeping his focus on Sable, using her presence and touch to soothe the ache and reassure himself. He didn't need to fear. He would not allow anything to happen to Rosalind. His kingdom would be safe from her wrath.

Rosalind bounced up to them. "Ready?"

He nodded and took hold of Sable's hand, clutching it tightly. She linked hands with Rosalind. Bleu took the witch's hand and then his.

Thorne focused, calling up an image of the First Realm and the white castle that towered in the centre of its black lands. The portal opened beneath his feet, expanding outwards to encompass the others, and he took a deep breath as they dropped into it, preparing himself for whatever awaited on the other side.

They landed in the inner courtyard of the white castle. Several large males immediately got to their feet, rising from the stone benches around the fountain in the centre of the curved courtyard.

They drew their swords, their pale horns curling as they readied themselves for battle.

Thorne tipped his chin up and stepped through his group, approaching the males. Their blue gazes flickered over him and they frowned and lowered their weapons.

"What business has the Third King here?" One of the males stepped forwards, an elaborate crest emblazoned in silver on the breast of his long black jacket. A commander.

Luck was with them.

Many lower ranking demons would not have recognised him and might have attacked them.

"I require an audience with the First King. It is a matter of great importance." Thorne beckoned to Sable and Rosalind and they moved closer, keeping behind him.

Bleu came up beside him, his purple gaze dark with emotion that he radiated, anger and a deep desire to harm these males.

Bleu's council had sent a contingent of elves into the First Realm to test the border and the demons had attacked them. Thorne could understand his anger, but now was not the time for acts of revenge. He looked across at Bleu, staring at the black-haired male until he drew his violet eyes away from the demons and settled them on him.

Thorne held his gaze, silently conveying everything he couldn't say aloud without upsetting the demons. If Bleu desired to avenge his fallen comrades, he could do so, but not right now. Not while Thorne needed the assistance of the First King.

The darkness in his eyes lifted and he lowered them, and gave a slight nod.

"Come." Thorne strode forwards, not waiting for the commander of the demons to speak and deny or grant them leave to continue into the building.

A commander had no power over him. All of the kings were allowed to enter another king's castle unannounced and the one they visited had to grant them a civil greeting at the very least. After that, they could do as they pleased.

He was fortunate that the First King liked him and that things were unlikely to turn violent.

He walked into the pure white building, following the arched corridor to the main hall.

The First King sat on the white spiked throne on the raised platform at the far end of the enormous room.

"What the hell?" Sable said beside him and he glanced down at her.

She scowled at the First King, her emotions buzzing in his veins. Jealousy ran rampant among them. Why?

She turned her glare on him. "The First King is a queen?"

Thorne could understand her confusion, but not her jealousy. He looked to the First King. She sat on the throne, her white corseted dress accented with pale blue that matched her eyes. Her long white hair flowed down over her shoulders, her skin almost as ashen, lending her blue eyes an ethereal look.

"Thorne," she said, a soft echo to her light voice.

She rose from her throne and drifted down the step and across the white flagstones to him, raising her hand at the same time.

Thorne took it and pressed a kiss to the back of it.

Sable seethed beside him, her glare gaining a sharp edge that cut him. She was jealous and on the verge of slapping the First King's hand from his judging by the emotions that clouded the link between them.

He stifled the smile that threatened to tug at his lips and released the First King's hand before Sable could launch an attack.

He had never imagined her to be such a possessive female. Perhaps the instincts that drove him to attack any male who gazed upon her with desire also compelled her to keep females away from him.

"Melia," he said to the First King and she smiled, blinking slowly, her face a picture of serenity and happiness.

"It has been too long." She drifted around him and ran a curious glance over Bleu, Rosalind and then Sable. "I was not expecting you to bring an elf. Has he come to apologise?"

"He was not part of the legion that crossed your lands unannounced, Melia, but those elves did so in order to assist me." Thorne suppressed a shudder as her eerie gaze returned to him. He had never liked phantoms. King Valador had given his fated one flesh and substance, freeing her of life as a wraith, but she still bore the appearance of one of her kind—strangely beautiful and enchanting, yet emitting a sense of danger and death at the same time. "The Fifth King has sealed the Third Realm, locking me out in the process. I must find a way back in."

Her face fell. "I did not know. You should have told me."

"I was unwell. The elf, Bleu, took command in my absence, attempting to breach the barrier. His prince is in my realm, no doubt defending my people in my stead. It is imperative that I return as soon as I can."

Melia drifted away and sighed. "Your visits are always too brief, Thorne. I do enjoy your company so."

Sable's anger hit him with the force of a tidal wave. "I thought all the kingdoms were ruled by demons?"

Thorne shot her a warning look. She flicked her black hair over her shoulder and tipped her chin up, keeping her profile to him. Ignoring him. Irritating little female. She meant to provoke Melia, and it was unwise to provoke a phantom. Melia still survived on souls and sucking life from her victims, turning them into phantoms too—condemning them to an incorporeal and eternal life.

He could not bear the thought of such a thing happening to Sable. To be able to see her, speak with her, but not touch her would kill him.

Melia drifted back to her white spiky throne and sank onto it. "I lost my husband in an attack from the demons under the Devil's command around a century ago… and I mourn him still. He died protecting me and his unborn heir. I rule only until my son is old enough to take the throne."

Sable's emotions shifted, her anger rapidly disappearing, replaced by guilt and sorrow. "I'm sorry for your loss."

Melia stared straight at her, her blue eyes bright and focused. "It is a lonely life to be a queen without her king… a long life."

Sable stiffened beside him and Thorne wanted to growl at Melia for daring to put ideas and fears into her head.

"The First Realm is rarely at war, and yet I lost my Valador. The other kingdoms are always at war… and the Third Realm borders many dangerous territories, including the Devil's domain." Melia continued to hold Sable under her spell, staring right into her eyes. A growl rumbled up Thorne's throat. "A weak female would not suit the Third King. If he was lost in battle—"

"That would never happen," Sable interjected and shoved her hands against her hips. Her fingers tightened against her black combat trousers. "It would never happen because I would be there by his side, fighting with him, like a woman should be—protecting him while he protected me."

Thorne grinned and stood a little taller, his gaze on Sable as she stood her ground against the First King, fire flickering in her golden eyes and anger burning through her emotions.

"She is a fiery little thing," Melia said and he felt her gaze move to him, cold and icy. "Does she truly believe that she is strong enough to fight at your side? It is not the role of a queen."

Sable took a step forwards, reclaiming Melia's attention. "Don't tell me… a queen is supposed to lay back and pop heirs out while the men do all the fighting? No, thank you. What century were you born in? Move with the times. If I ever get pregnant, I'll be giving birth on a battlefield if war came when he was due. That's how a future king should be born."

"Reckless female," Melia snapped.

Thorne couldn't take his eyes off Sable. He grinned down at her, bursting with pride as she set Melia to rights. She would make a fine queen. His queen. He exhaled softly and she looked up at him, her golden eyes widening as she caught his gaze and her anger fading.

"Brave female," Thorne murmured. "My female."

Colour blazed across her cheeks and she looked away from him and flicked her black hair over her shoulder again. "Well, it's all just theoretical. I'm just saying that a woman can fight as good as a man—or demon—and I'm more than capable of protecting Thorne's back."

Melia looked back at him.

Thorne didn't take his gaze away from Sable. He lifted his hand and brushed the backs of his claws across her cheek, feeling the heat of her blush. His horns curled, twisting around his ears as they grew more pointed. He wanted to kiss his little mortal queen.

"Does she speak true?" Melia said.

Thorne nodded. "She does. She has fought by my side twice already. My female is strong, a warrior… a female fit for a demon king."

Sable glanced up at him, her eyes searching his, as if she wanted to know whether he meant what he had said. He smiled down at her and continued to stroke her cheek, his gaze narrowing as he held hers, not hiding any of his feelings from her this time.

"I envy you," Melia whispered and Sable pulled away from him, her black eyebrows drawing together as she turned her amber gaze on the phantom queen. Melia kept her eerie eyes locked on him. "I wish you one hundred centuries together. Protect her well, Thorne."

Thorne inclined his head. "Thank you, Melia. I will."

"You may go to the boundary where our lands meet. May the gods speed your journey home."

"May they grant you better days," Thorne said.

Melia dipped her chin, her eyes closing at the same time and an air of sorrow falling over her features. She mourned her fallen king still.

Thorne took hold of Sable's hand, drawing her closer to him this time, needing to feel her against him. He would always keep her close to him and they would always have each other's backs, just as she had said. He would protect her. She would protect him. They would have one hundred centuries and more.

He led her, Rosalind and Bleu from the palace and stopped at the point where they had entered it, close to the fountain in the courtyard.

Sable took hold of Rosalind's hand and Bleu joined them, linking them together to form a circle. Thorne focused on the border between the Third Realm and the First Realm, on a small village he had visited once.

They dropped together into the portal and reappeared there. The dark huts in the village were quiet and no one roamed between them. Melia had evacuated the border villages. He could understand why. If the Fifth King claimed his realm, it was only a matter of time before the male set his sights on a bigger target.

Thorne trudged across the uneven black ground, following a path that would bring them to the border with his realm. Rosalind paused before they reached it, her enormous blue eyes fixed on the distance.

"Rosalind?" Sable touched her arm.

"I can feel it," she whispered and walked forwards, slowly raising her hands, her expression trance-like. "Mother Nature… this is some spell."

"Can you remove it?" Thorne followed her, his heart beating hard against his chest. He needed to get back into his kingdom. The moment he was in there, he could teleport to the castle.

Rosalind shook her head and his heart fell into his stomach. She looked up at him over her shoulder.

"I can't remove it, but I can tamper with it. I think I can reverse it."

"Reverse it?" He held his hand out, trying to sense the barrier that she had felt. Nothing. He pushed his hand forwards and it met with resistance.

Rosalind nodded. "We will be able to teleport or walk into the kingdom again, but no one will be able to teleport or walk out. We will all be trapped there until I can find a way to break the spell, or someone takes out the witches who cast it."

Sable's gaze shifted to him, warming his blood and soothing him. He knew what she wanted to say. It was a dangerous move. They would be able to teleport in, but so would the demons of the Fifth Realm, and then they would be trapped there with them. No one would be able to escape this time. His war with the Fifth King was about to end one way or another.

Thorne nodded.

"Make it happen."

CHAPTER 24

Thorne released Bleu and Sable the moment they appeared in the courtyard of his castle. He turned on the spot, scouring the dark grey fortress for any sign of damage. Nothing. His ears pricked as he listened for the sounds of battle raging outside the walls. Silence.

Several of his warriors rushed over, blades in hand. "King Thorne."

He nodded to acknowledge them and scanned the castle again, for a different reason this time, his blood pumping hard and hot in his veins. Where was the bastard rakshasa?

Loren appeared with Olivia. The human female pushed out of his arms and tackled Sable in a tight embrace.

"Elf!" Rosalind shrieked and was behind Thorne in a flash, pressing against his back. "Is he a prince? Make him go away."

"Thank God! I was worried sick about you," Olivia said over Rosalind and squeezed Sable tighter, until his female turned red.

"Easy," Sable squeaked and Olivia loosened her grip, grabbed her shoulders and shoved her back.

"Are you okay?"

"I was going to ask you the same thing. Something closed the pathways to the Third Realm after Thorne joined me at Archangel."

"We know. Loren tried to teleport me after you and couldn't." Olivia looked Sable over. "You sure you're okay? You seem a little on edge."

Sable placed her right hand over Olivia's on her shoulder and smiled. "I'm good. I'll tell you all about it later."

Rosalind pushed closer to Thorne, quietly chanting, "Make him go away."

Thorne cleared his throat. "This may sound a peculiar request, Prince Loren, but would you mind removing yourself from the presence of the witch?"

"Witch?" Loren cocked an eyebrow and tried to peer around him.

Rosalind squealed and moved, keeping hidden from the elf prince's curious gaze. "Make him go away."

Thorne sighed. "I believe she had an unfortunate prediction involving an elf prince."

Loren's other eyebrow joined his right one, arching high on his forehead. "I see. Very well. Bleu, I would speak with you. Come with me."

Bleu nodded and walked with Loren, heading back into the main building.

"Is he gone?" Rosalind whispered, fear lacing her voice.

"He is gone." Thorne turned to look down at her. "Although I do not think you will be able to avoid him during the entirety of your stay."

"I'm bloody well going to try." Rosalind smoothed her black dress down and blew out her breath. "I'm too young to die."

Thorne's eyebrows rose. So that was the prediction that had her on edge. An elf prince and death. He could understand her reluctance to meet Loren now.

Kyal and Kincaid strolled out of the main three-storey building of the castle, four of their men flanking them. Kyal bore several lacerations across his face and more were visible in the open V of his black shirt and on his forearms below the rolled up sleeves. They had put him through his rite of passage while Thorne had been away.

His confident swagger and the touch of pride in his blue eyes said he had passed the test, sinking his fangs into the napes of the other warriors before they could do the same to him, although the cuts he bore said he had also taken some severe blows in the process.

"I need reports," Thorne barked in the demon language and several more warriors rushed into the courtyard, heading straight for him. His elite. "Have you seen Fargus?"

They shook their heads. "Not since your disappearance."

Thorne rolled out a choice curse. It had been too much to hope that the rakshasa would make things easy on him.

"Tell me of the realm. What has been happening in my absence?" Thorne scanned the grey courtyard again, picking out all of the males, regardless of species.

One of his elite saluted. "The Fifth King has marched through much of the realm. Many of the border villages had to be abandoned. We have been meeting him whenever we can, trying to drive him back. He has passed through the eighth, seventh and sixth districts to the east."

Closing in on them. His castle stood at the centre of his realm, and outwards from it radiated bands of land, each of them numbered.

"We cannot risk more men falling. We must meet them now and end this," Thorne said in English so the mortal hunters would understand too and prepared to call his blade to him.

Sable placed her hand on his, curling her fingers around to brush his palm.

"He can't teleport out now that Rosalind flipped the spell, Thorne," she whispered and looked up into his eyes. "We need to strategize. What is the first thing your heart tells you to do?"

His heart said to claim the beautiful female before him.

He pushed that need aside and focused on the good of his kingdom.

"We must evacuate the villages that lay on the path he takes," he said to her and then turned to the warriors gathered near him, speaking to them in the demon tongue. "I need men to visit the villages between here and where the Fifth King's army entered our realm. Plot their course through the outer lands and clear any villages that he might pass through to reach the castle."

The men nodded and split up, each heading towards their small unit of warriors.

Grave ambled towards him, casually wiping blood off his lips with his thumb. It spotted the dark grey shirt he wore but the vampire showed no sign of caring about the mess he had made while feeding. Red ringed his ice-blue irises, his pupils narrow slices in their centres that gradually grew into circles.

Thorne had heard that vampires with bloodlust moderated their intake to avoid episodes and tightening its hold on them. Grave clearly didn't subscribe to that way of thinking. The male had taken blood from many of the court females, and from the cups offered at the feasts, and from their enemies during the battle at the village too. If anything, the brunet was courting his bloodlust, encouraging it to grow stronger and seize more control over him.

Thorne frowned at Grave's second in command who walked behind him. That male had come to Grave when Thorne had been on the balcony with Sable.

Perhaps the male's disappearance had not been a trick of his imagination.

Thorne launched himself at the vampire, catching him before he could react. The male struggled in his grip and his eyes slowly changed, crystal blue emerging in them.

Rakshasa.

The vampire bared his fangs and sank them deep into Thorne's wrist, tearing at his flesh. Thorne grimaced but kept hold of him, refusing to let go. He would make the bastard pay in blood for what he had done to him and to Fargus.

"What is happening here? Unhand my man!" Grave's hand closed around Thorne's throat, squeezing tightly, his claws digging in.

Sable leaped onto the vampire commander's back and wrapped her arms across his throat, using her weight to haul him backwards and choke him. "You unhand my man."

Thorne froze and swung his gaze to her, forgetting everything as those words hit him hard, knocking him and making his head reel.

Her man?

The bastard rakshasa used his distraction to his advantage. He spat blood in Thorne's face, wriggled free and teleported in a blinding white flash before Thorne could grab him again.

Grave froze now, his blue eyes wide and dark eyebrows pinned high on his forehead. Sable continued to choke him, even though he had released Thorne the moment his man had teleported. She seemed to be enjoying it and Thorne was loath to deny her her fun.

The vampire cursed, unleashing a particularly nasty oath, and then growled at Sable. "Release me, impudent female."

Sable wisely did as he bid, sliding down the male's back and landing on her feet. She sprang away from him, landing closer to Thorne. Thorne slid his arm around her waist and tugged her against his side, shielding her from the vampire, in case Grave was foolish enough to consider attacking her.

"What is happening here?" Grave turned on him, red edging his pale irises again and his pupils beginning to stretch in their centres, turning elliptical once more.

Sable shirked Thorne's grip and signalled Olivia. The mortal doctor pulled something from a bag and came to him.

"We have a rakshasa among us," Thorne bit out and scanned his surroundings again. His arm throbbed, the warm blood sliding down it turning cold as it reached his fingers. Olivia lifted his hand and bandaged the wound for him. He pulled Sable back into his embrace the moment she was within his reach, pinning her against his bare side. "It assumed the form of my commander, Fargus, and yours too. The gods only know how many others it has inhabited and could appear as. I need you all to account for your people."

"A rakshasa?" Rosalind said, her voice bright with excitement, and everyone's gazes swung her way, pinning her with looks ranging from surprise to suspicion.

Grave wore the suspicious look.

One day, Thorne would uncover why he despised females. After the things that the vampire Snow and his brother had said, Thorne was more curious about the captain of the First Legion than ever.

"I can help. I can sense a trace of the power the creature uses with…" Rosalind rifled through her leather bag, frowning down at it, her ash blond hair obscuring her face. She pulled out a spiral stick of silver metal embedded with blue and purple jewels. "This. I can locate it with this."

"And what of those it has inhabited and discarded?" Thorne hated to ask such a question but he needed to find Fargus's body so he could return it to his mate for a burial.

She nodded.

"Do that and I will be forever in your debt." He needed to kill this rakshasa and bathe his hands in the bastard's blood.

"Follow me." Rosalind closed her eyes, held the spiralling silver wand out in front of her, and started walking.

"Are you sure you're okay?" Olivia whispered and Thorne looked back at her.

Sable nodded in response to her friend and then her expression shifted, and her emotions changed with it. Thorne released her, glad that she had finally made her decision and was going to listen to him.

"We need to talk," Sable said and Olivia's expression turned concerned and then she nodded and took Sable's hand.

Thorne watched them go, his heart heavy and filled with a need to go with his mate, to be there with her and support her as she spoke to her friend about everything that had happened.

She glanced back at him, smiled and waved him towards Rosalind.

He nodded. He would do as she asked and give her some time with Olivia while he searched for the rakshasa and any the creature had killed, but as soon as he was done with his business, they were going to have a discussion of their own.

Two of his men flanked him as he followed Rosalind into the castle, Kyal, Kincaid and Grave at his back, discussing matters between themselves.

She led them downwards, through the winding narrow corridors beneath the main building and then the courtyard. Towards the dungeons.

Thorne's arm ached as he walked, his thoughts split between Sable and the rakshasa, his emotions flipping between warmth and affection, and cold fury and a pressing need for vengeance.

Rosalind muttered things beneath her breath in a strange tongue as she walked ahead of him. The torches on the walls flickered as she passed, casting golden light in her pale hair. She radiated a sense of danger that had him on edge and he blamed the cramped corridor. It concentrated everyone's power on his senses, especially hers. She had always felt mildly dangerous to him, but now she felt a thousand times more so.

She paused.

Stood still for so long that everyone behind him began to get twitchy.

"Rosalind?" Thorne said, his deep voice loud in the corridor.

She looked back at him, her eyes glowing like blue fire, stars twinkling amongst the flames.

Her fair eyebrows rose. "Something wrong?"

He wanted to ask the same thing.

She frowned and looked at her surroundings and then down at her hand and the spiral of silver she grasped. "Something interfered with the signal."

And with her too, making her forget what she had been doing, judging by the confusion in her eyes.

"This way." She pointed right.

The entrance to the dungeons.

Thorne couldn't remember the last time he had been down there. He never had any reason to visit them. No one had been sent there in years. They used most of the expansive cold room for storage these days.

Rosalind took the steps down. Thorne took one of the torches from the wall and followed close behind her, his claws at the ready should the rakshasa attack. The little witch wasn't defenceless, but he had vowed to protect her and intended to do just that.

She pushed the heavy wooden door at the end of the steps open. "Ew."

Thorne covered his nose and mouth with his hand and grunted in agreement.

Someone muttered a ripe curse behind him.

Whatever they were about to find in his dungeon, it had been there for a long time, judging by the smell.

Thorne waited for Rosalind to advance. She shook her head, her eyes watering, and gagged.

"Stay with her," he said to his two warriors in the demon tongue.

They nodded.

Thorne took slow steps into the room, his crimson gaze scanning the cells on either side of the dark space. Shadows danced wherever he swung his torch, rushing away from the light. The first three cells were empty.

The fourth.

Thorne swallowed hard and stared at the three bodies dumped in the corner of the cell behind a stack of wooden crates.

The vampire second in command was one of them.

Fargus was another. He lay with his chin on his chest, his skin and flesh wasting away, thick dark slime oozing from beneath him. He had been there months. The rakshasa had been posing as his friend for all that time, learning about him and discovering his weaknesses.

Sable.

Kincaid growled and moved past him, stricken as he stared at the third male, a young blond.

One of the werewolves.

Thorne laid his hand on Kincaid's shoulder and the werewolf commander turned to him.

"I want this creature's neck between my fangs."

Thorne nodded. "We all do, my good friend."

He turned to his two warriors who had remained at the entrance with Rosalind. "One of you, go to Fargus's mate. Check that she is safe and well."

The larger male nodded and teleported.

Rosalind took a shaky step forwards. He turned his gaze on her.

"Where is the bastard who did this?" Grave spat and approached her. She backed off, a flicker of fear in her eyes.

"Grave," Thorne barked and the vampire cast a glare his way. "We will catch him and he will pay for what he has done. Rosalind, can you locate the rakshasa?"

She closed her eyes and shook her head. "The trail ends here. I tried to locate him while you searched the room, but cannot feel him within the castle."

He had fled. Coward.

Thorne growled.

The warrior he had sent to check on Fargus's female returned, a grave look on his face. "I found her tied up with her offspring."

Thorne took a step towards him. "Are they well?"

The male nodded. "Afraid and starved, but otherwise unharmed."

"Bring them to the castle and settle them in one of the guest rooms and I will visit her."

"Already done. I brought her back with me and my mate is taking care of her."

Thorne couldn't express his gratitude to the male. He clapped him on the shoulder and squeezed it, glad to have such a thoughtful, caring male among his warriors.

"Take care of things here." Thorne released him and the male nodded, and then gestured to his comrade.

Thorne crossed the room to Rosalind and led her out, heading back up the stairs with her. The others followed, deep in discussion. Kincaid suggested waiting for the Fifth King to reach the castle before engaging him.

It would buy them valuable time to prepare, but Thorne refused to put the inhabitants of the castle at risk. He frowned and looked down at Rosalind.

"Can you create barrier spells such as the one used around my kingdom?" he said and she shrugged.

"They're difficult and require a lot of energy to create, but I can make them up to a high spec."

"Impenetrable?"

She nodded. Thorne grinned.

"Can you create one around the castle?"

She smiled now. "Of course. I can set one up for you. You'll be able to teleport out but not in though."

Thorne mulled that one over. He didn't want to have injured warriors caught outside the castle with no means of getting aid.

"You cannot leave a hole in it?" he said and she wriggled her nose, her expression turning pensive. "It would be a small space, as large as one of the concealed entrances, barely as big as me."

She looked him over and finally nodded. "I think I can do that... no, I can definitely do that. I'm as stuck in this realm as the rest of you and I would prefer to be somewhere safe. One barrier, coming right up."

Thorne was beginning to like the little witch.

"Good." He turned to the other males. "We shall remain in the castle and pick off as many as we can from the walls and then engage them once they are weakened."

And if he saw the bastard rakshasa on the battlefield, he was going to take his head.

His gaze drifted upwards, towards the courtyard, his senses reaching beyond it, searching for Sable. Was she still with Olivia? He would discuss battle plans with the others for as long as he could manage, but he needed to see her again.

He needed to feel her in his arms and feel her lips beneath his, because he feared that when he next saw her, she would have changed on him again, slipping through his grasp.

CHAPTER 25

Sable lay on the soft furs on top of Olivia's four-poster double bed, staring at the canopy draped over the frame, trying to get her thoughts into order. Her friend lingered near the foot of the bed, leaning against the ornate post there, and had been silent since they had entered the room almost ten minutes ago.

Olivia always had been a patient woman. Perhaps that was what made her a good doctor, and a good friend.

Sable sighed and toyed with the cuff around her wrist. Talking to Olivia wasn't going to get any easier the longer she took to get the ball rolling and get everything out in the open.

"So I think I might know who my father was," she said and Olivia gasped and moved closer.

Sable lowered her gaze to her friend.

Her dark eyes were enormous. "Seriously? But how? I thought there was no record of him... no clue."

"Well, about that." Sable sat up and tapped the silver cuff, took a deep breath and removed it. She turned her wrist towards Olivia. "Turns out this was a pretty big clue."

"Your tattoo?" Olivia frowned at it and then at her. "How is a tattoo a clue?"

Sable snapped the cuff shut and set it down on the furs. "It isn't a tattoo... I should have told you all of this earlier and I'm just going to get it out in the open now."

Olivia nodded.

"Remember the battle at the border village?" she said and Olivia nodded again. "I was outnumbered and Thorne saved me, but not before I thought I was going to die. I was so scared, Liv. My wrist burned worse than it had ever done."

"The burning sensation you've been having is related to this mark?"

She nodded and rubbed her fingertips over it, feeling a low thrumming in the black ink. "It got hotter and hotter, and then when I touched one of the demons, he turned to ash."

"Holy shit."

"My thoughts exactly." Sable looked down at the cross on her wrist.

"Is that why you were acting so weird?" Olivia sat beside her and took hold of her hand. She inspected her wrist, tracing the cross with her fingertips.

Sable shrugged. "I should have told you then, but I wasn't sure how. Thorne was good though. He really helped me deal. Then we met Rosalind to ask about a way back into the Third Realm and she recognised the mark… and, well… it sort of turns out that my father might have been an angel."

"Holy shit!" Olivia covered her mouth and mumbled into her palm, "Seriously?"

Sable wished she had the choice of not believing it like her friend did. She flopped back onto the bed again and ran her fingers through her hair.

"Seriously." She groaned and raised her arm above her head.

Her wrist wasn't hurting right now and there was only a faint strange sensation around the cross, which was a small relief. Rosalind's cuff seemed to be working. She picked it up off the bed and put it back on, snapping it shut around her right wrist.

She stared at the canopy again, a thousand conflicting feelings colliding inside her, making it hard to speak.

"Sable. You could have talked to me about this." Olivia settled her hand on her arm and she sighed.

"I know. I should have." She sat up again and took hold of Olivia's hands. "I just didn't know how to tell you… I was scared. I *am* scared. A month ago I thought I was human and given a gift that would help me be the best demon hunter out there so I could protect my people… now I'm half-angel and my boyfriend is a demon."

Olivia gave her a sly smile. "Boyfriend? Clearly more was happening back home than just you, Thorne and Bleu trying to make your way back here."

Sable scowled at her.

"He's a good demon though."

She had to concede that. Thorne was a good demon. A noble man. He had shown her that side of himself countless times, even when she had refused to believe it. He was a good man.

She sighed. "Why does life have to get all complicated?"

"I hear you." Olivia giggled. "Look at me. One minute I'm a doctor and the next I'm mated to an elf prince and about to become his honorary-elf princess... with all this stupid stuff to learn about customs, his world, and the nitty-gritty details of the ceremony, and things to do to make the kingdom like me as their princess."

Sable smiled now. "It sounds overwhelming."

Olivia nudged her shoulder. "Not as overwhelming as being a queen of demons."

Her smile faded. "Don't even go there."

Her friend's face fell, turning too serious for Sable's liking. "You are going to become his mate though, right?"

Sable lowered her gaze to the furs and picked at them, stifling the blush creeping onto her cheeks.

"I'm ready with the 'Sable Speech' about losing a wonderful guy. Don't make me use it."

She sighed and her shoulders sagged. She wasn't intending to make her friend use the same speech she had given her about losing a wonderful man out of fear rather than facing facts and her feelings. She knew how she felt about Thorne.

It was endless and deep, consuming her. It drove her to find him just so she could see him and have him look at her in that way that said he would never tire of seeing her too, and that he loved her with all of his heart and ached to have her as his mate.

She ached for that too, but it was complicated and confusing. It was too much to think about.

"I know," Sable said. "I'm just not sure what to do."

"My advice. Don't overthink it. You'll only make yourself crazy." Olivia patted her knee and offered a sympathetic smile that reached her dark eyes. "What you do now is the easy part. You just walk up to him, plant a huge kiss on him, and with one look into your eyes, he'll know that you've made up your mind. I knew you had the moment you said you needed to talk."

She had? Maybe Thorne knew too.

Sable smiled again. "You make it sound so easy."

"None of it is easy... but I think you're making the right decision... and not just because I'll get to have my friend as my friend forever." Olivia rose from the bed and Sable caught the flicker of relief and happiness in her dark eyes.

She hadn't thought about the fact that Olivia was immortal now, and wouldn't have aged while Sable would have grown old. Sable marked immortality and a best friend forever in the positive column of her list of pros and cons about mating with Thorne. They could gripe about having to run kingdoms together too, and share gossip and bitch about immortal men whenever one of them did something wrong.

Olivia's smile widened, as if she could hear her thoughts and they pleased her. "It's good to have you back, and you were an idiot not to tell me about the mark. All-human or half-angel, you're still my best friend and nothing will change that."

"That's because we have a true friendship."

Olivia's eyebrows rose and she hesitated before nodding, a touch of confusion in her dark eyes.

"A wise demon king once told me that," Sable said as way of an explanation for her cheesy line and Olivia smiled at her, walked to the door and opened it.

She looked back at Sable.

"Go and make him *your* demon king."

Sable's stomach somersaulted at the prospect. She took a deep breath and pulled herself together. Olivia was right and this was what she wanted with Thorne, and she didn't want to wait until war was upon them to tell him how she felt about him. He needed to know. Not only because it would bolster his strength in the coming fight, but because he had been as patient as he could, had done everything in his power to win her.

And he had.

She needed him to know that he had scored a victory and had claimed her heart, just as she knew she had won his.

Sable drew in another deep breath, smoothed her shirt over her trousers, and nodded.

She quickly walked from the room before her nerve failed, passing Loren in the corridor. He turned, his gaze tracking her for a few steps before he continued on his way. She hoped to God she didn't bump into Bleu.

Her hands shook and she curled them into fists. She breathed deep and slow, trying to steady her heart too. It pounded against her chest, fierce and strong, a beat that she walked to as she took the stone stairs down to the next floor.

Sable arrived at Thorne's heavy wooden door, raised her fist to knock and paused. She stared at the wood, fighting another wave of nerves that threatened to pull her under.

She wasn't sure how long she stood there in a daze, her mind swimming and heart racing. Before she could shake herself out of her ridiculous nervous stupor, the door swung open, revealing Thorne in all his glory.

His bare chest glistened with drops of moisture and one strong hand rubbed a piece of dark cloth over his damp russet-brown hair.

"What is wrong?" he said, his deep voice making her quiver and heat inside, evaporating some of her nerves but not chasing them off completely. He leaned towards her and looked both ways along the stone corridor and then back, his gaze resting on her again. "Are you unwell? Did your talk with Olivia not go well? Speak, Little Female… I must know what has upset you."

She should have known he would sense her outside his door, would feel her nerves and her fear rippling through the growing connection that tied them together. Now he was drawing conclusions that were all wrong, but it was sweet of him to want to know the source of her feelings, and to desire to do something to remedy them.

"I was just looking for you." Sable managed to force those words out and struggled to think of what to say next as he stared at her, his dark crimson eyes locked on her face, concern shining in them.

It didn't help that he was half-nude, evidently come straight from bathing to answer the door when he had sensed her standing there. His dark mahogany leathers were barely fastened, the lacing tied hastily over his groin.

Sable dragged her gaze away from his crotch and trailed it up his magnificent body, her own heating in response to the sight of rope after rope of honed, powerful muscles beneath bronzed tight skin.

"And so you have found me… did you need me for something?" There was a hint of desire in his thick voice, passion that began to flow through the link they shared.

Did she need him for something?

Did she ever.

She cleared her throat and drew in another fortifying breath, raised her gaze to meet his and chanted in her head that she could do this. She wanted to do this.

Before he could utter another word and throw her off course, she did exactly what Olivia had told her to do.

She tiptoed, wrapped her arms around his head and planted a huge one on him.

Thorne immediately dropped the towel and clutched her to him, his lips claiming hers in a soul-searing kiss that made her burn so hot that her fear melted under the intense heat. She groaned as he mastered her mouth, giving her no quarter, bending her to his will. Sable went willingly, a slave to the sensations bursting to life within her, bringing with it the crushing need to have more of Thorne, to never let this kiss end and never let him out of her arms.

His fingers pressed into her hips, clutching them tightly, and he groaned, the sound not born of pleasure but frustration. She fought him when he pushed her back, trying to break the kiss. Not yet. She needed more of his heat and his spice, needed to linger and slow the kiss, to awaken the deep yearning she felt within her heart in his too.

He was too strong for her though, easily pushing her back to arm's length. The softness of his expression was her undoing, the affection in it only strengthening her need to have him close to her, to hold this powerful, beautiful king in her arms and know that he was finally hers and they were together at last.

She had one hurdle to leap before she could have that dream though.

A claiming she knew nothing about.

"Is everything all right?" Thorne whispered, the dark slashes of his eyebrows furrowing as his gaze searched hers, filled with tenderness and a touch of confusion.

Sable blew out another breath. "No... yes... it will be."

The confusion in his striking crimson eyes grew, overpowering the softer emotions, and she sensed a sliver of concern go through him.

She was making a mess of this already.

Don't overthink it.

Wise words from her wise friend.

Sable sucked down another strengthening breath.

"There's no other way to say this... so I'm just going to say it."

Thorne released her, trudged into his expansive room and sank down onto his bed. He stared across the room at her, the sliver of concern she had felt in him growing into fear and other darker feelings. She cursed the way he looked at her as if she had plunged a knife into his chest. She wasn't just making a mess of things. She was making a royal mess of them and now all she wanted to do was go to him, wedge herself between his knees and stroke his horns as she looked down into his eyes. She needed to reassure him.

She knew a better way to make him see that what she wanted to say wasn't a bad thing though.

Sable closed the door to his apartments and locked it.

He frowned now, confusion surfacing again. Her big strong king, her beautiful powerful demon, looked as if he was dying inside and felt it too.

"Thorne," she murmured, unable to bring her voice above a whisper as emotions swirled through her, growing stronger by the second, becoming a maelstrom that swept her along at a dizzying pace.

She had never been good at sentimental crap. Give her a sword and a horde of bad demons and she knew exactly what to do. Give her a moment alone with the man that she loved, the one she wanted to be with for eternity, and she was struck silent, unable to think clearly or find the right words to say.

Sable crossed the room to him. He spread his thighs and she settled between his knees, placed her hands on his bare muscular shoulders, and looked down into his eyes.

She just had to say it and everything would be all right.

Sable smiled.

She *would* just say it.

"I'm in love with you."

Thorne's expression shifted from pained puppy dog to hot-blooded male demon in a heartbeat, a sexy and devastating grin curling his lips and flashing a hint of fang. He grabbed her by her hips and dragged her down to him, twisting his body at the same time so she ended up beneath him on the soft silky furs.

He growled and then his lips were on hers, capturing them in a fierce kiss that seared every inch of her and branded her with his name.

"I love you, too," he murmured between kisses, his lips brushing the words across hers, painting them with each syllable.

Sable wasn't done. She had to take the next step, had to leap and hope Thorne would catch her, and she had to do it now or she was going to chicken out.

She kissed him again, a brief hard clash of her mouth with his to boost her courage, and then pressed her forehead to his.

"Do it," she whispered, a shiver racing over her skin, turning it to goose flesh, and her heart pounding in her throat. "Claim me... I want nothing more than to be yours."

CHAPTER 26

Thorne was certain he was mistaken and that he had only imagined Sable asking him to claim her.

He pushed himself up on his hands, rising above her, and frowned into her golden eyes.

"What did you just say?" The words had left his lips before he could seek out the truth in her gaze, searching her soul through it to see if she really had just asked him to claim her.

Sable laughed and brushed her fingers through his damp hair, her palms grazing his curling horns, sending a fiery shiver down his spine. "This is a lousy start... you don't believe me?"

"I do not believe I heard you correctly... say it again."

Nerves flickered in her eyes and he realised it had taken her great courage to speak the words the first time, and now he was asking her to find the strength to put voice to them again. Was this why she had felt so scared and nervous while standing outside his door?

Had she truly come here to ask him to claim her and finally seal the bond between them, bringing her into his world as his eternal mate?

"Tell me you want me to claim you, Sable... tell me you want to be mine forever."

She hesitated still, her fingers twining in his hair, squeezing droplets of water that ran down his back, cold against his overheating flesh.

"Tell me," he pleaded, lost in her fiery eyes, in the thought that she truly had asked to be his and his fight for her was finally coming to a close.

A smile briefly danced on her lips.

"I want you to be mine... forever... Thorne. I want to claim you."

He grinned. Typical of his female that she could not give him possession of her, instead requesting possession of him. He could go along with that. He would be the first demon to let a female claim him.

He rested all his weight on his left elbow and brushed the backs of his claws on his right hand across her cheek, holding her gaze the whole time he caressed her, savouring the sight of her beneath him, her eyes sparkling with feelings he had only ever dreamed of seeing in them.

"I am yours," he husked and her cheeks heated beneath his touch, a blush rising onto them that made him smile. His little contradiction. She was strong, independent, unwilling to allow herself to be a possession of anyone, yet the simplest words from his heart could make her blush and shy away, could bring a flicker of vulnerability into her eyes that pleaded him to reassure her. He sighed, opened his hand and cupped her cheek as he swept the pad of his thumb over her lower lip. "I have always been yours… from the moment I set eyes on you… from the moment I was born."

"Thorne," Sable whispered and pulled him down to her, merging her lips with his in a kiss that spoke of her love and her need of him, and tore a groan from his throat.

She wrapped her hands around his horns and his groan became a growl of sheer pleasure as a shudder went through him. Everything male in him demanded that he strip her bare and kiss every inch of her until she trembled as he did, until she cried his name so loud and so long during the peak of her ecstasy that all in the castle would know that she now belonged to him.

Forever.

He growled again, darker this time as needs bombarded him, driving him to seize this chance that she had given him and claim her.

Thorne ripped her black shirt open, spraying buttons everywhere. They ricocheted off his bare chest. Sable gasped and he swallowed it in another demanding kiss, devouring more of her, tangling his tongue with hers so he could taste her familiar, delicious sweetness. He grabbed the hem of the t-shirt she wore beneath her shirt and yanked it up, only breaking the kiss for as long as it took the material to pass between them.

Sable wriggled her arms above her head, pulling both tops off while she continued to kiss him, her tongue stroking his now, stoking his need for her. He groaned and ran his palms down her arms and over her breasts, and it turned into a growl of frustration when his fingers met with cotton and not soft, bare flesh.

"Wait," Sable snapped but he had already used his claws to slice the thin band of fabric that held the two cups together. She huffed and then shrugged, tangled her fingers into his hair and kissed him again.

Thorne angled his head, deepening the kiss as he brought their bodies into contact, his need to feel her beneath him too great to deny any longer. He groaned into her mouth as she wrapped her legs around his waist, drawing him down into the cradle of her thighs, and thrust gently, rubbing his caged erection against her most sensitive place. She moaned, the sound divine to his ears, speaking to every instinct he possessed. She liked this, loved the feel of him rocking between her thighs, and wanted more.

He would give it to her.

"My female needs," he whispered and kissed down her neck.

She arched against him in response, a soft whimper escaping her kiss-swollen lips, and clutched his head and then his horns. She steered him lower, over her chest towards her breasts, controlling his actions in a way that would never fail to ignite his primal male instincts to dominate and subdue her. They flared up, demanding he seize control again.

"Damn straight I do," she murmured and then gasped as he wrapped his lips around her right nipple and pulled the dusky bud into his mouth. "Thorne."

He loved the way she said his name, dripping with pleasure and need, a plea for more and a praise at the same time.

He suckled her nipple, rolling it between his teeth, torturing the sweet bud until she constantly moaned and his need to dominate was satisfied. She shifted, thrusting her breasts towards him, and the action caused his right fang to nick her breast. Her expected reprimand didn't come and he groaned, sinking into her as she gasped and moaned again, her pleasure rippling through him. Wicked little female.

Thorne lapped at the tiny cut. The sweet but tangy spice of her blood dancing across his taste buds sent him shooting steel-hard in his trousers. He shuddered and moaned as she chose that moment to gyrate beneath him, rubbing his already sensitive flesh and threatening to make him spill in his leathers.

His instincts flared once more, commanding him to seize hold of her, pin her to the bed and sink his fangs into the delicate arch of her neck, initiating the claiming process and showing her that he was the one in control. He needed to strip the rest of her clothes from her and thrust into her, deep and hard, until she screamed his name and knew his strength.

Until she knew without a doubt that she was his now.

Thorne stifled those darker urges to dominate and possess her, caught her hip and pressed it down into the bed, rising off her at the same time to catch her gaze. His shifted to her neck.

She brushed her fingers across it, clearing the dark hair from her throat, and then trailed them lower, over her chest to her left breast. Her eyes fell there, drawing them down with him, and he didn't miss the naughty smile on her lips.

"Not quite the traditional place for it, my sweet little fated one," he murmured and lowered his head, flicking his tongue across her nipple and ripping a husky gasp from her throat.

He wanted to bite her neck, wanted to show the world that she belonged to him, but he wasn't averse to sinking his fangs into her breast and drinking from there too.

His cock throbbed at the thought and he eased his fangs into the soft curve of her breast. She jerked against him, her cry of pleasure loud in the quiet room, and the connection between them overflowed with her bliss. Thorne groaned and gently sucked, drawing her essence into his mouth. Warmth flowed into him, tangy yet sweet, filling his senses until he felt hazy and lost, drugged by the taste of her. He swallowed the small amount and shuddered, a bolt of pleasure shooting down his spine to his cock, tightening his balls.

Gods, he needed more.

Thorne rose over her, pushing himself up her body, and buried his head into the crook of her neck. She moaned and rocked into him, and he growled at the obstruction separating them.

Sable seemed to hate it too.

She grabbed the waist of his leathers and pushed at them, unleashing a noise of sheer frustration when they didn't budge.

Thorne reached down, never breaking contact with her neck, kissing her and teasing her with light scrapes of his fangs, and shredded the laces on his leathers with his claws. He pulled his cock free, the cool air bliss against his hot hard flesh, and Sable shoved at his leathers again, pushing them down over his hips. She wriggled beneath him, her frustration mounting, beginning to dominate her emotions that flowed through their connection.

He wanted her naked too, pressed against his flesh, bared for him. He wanted to seat himself to the hilt in her body and sink his fangs deep into her neck.

He reluctantly left her throat, swearing he would return soon enough to finish what he had started and satisfy his need to claim her, to bury his fangs into her flesh and draw all that she was into him, linking them forever.

Thorne sat back, grabbed the waist of her black combats and yanked them down without undoing them, forcing them over her hips and her thighs. She giggled and continued to wriggle, shifting her legs to help him. He pulled her boots off and then her trousers, and tossed them all on his floor.

He froze as he stared down at his beautiful female, still holding her ankles. She lay nude and glorious before him, an angel with her black hair spread across his furs and firelight flickering across her smooth skin. The bite mark on her breast dripped a teasing trail of blood that glistened, calling to him, demanding he finish what they had started.

"Naked," she whispered and every part of him wanted to obey that commanded, craved the feel of her nude against him, her soft flesh pressing into his hard.

He growled and shoved his leathers down to his knees and ended up falling rather ungracefully off the bed. Sable laughed and appeared above him on all fours, her smile contagious.

Thorne's faded when he caught sight of the twin beads of blood running down the curve of her breast, towards her nipple.

A groan tore up his throat and he kicked his leathers off, shot to his knees and sucked the bloodied bud into his mouth. Sable moaned and inhaled sharply. His horns curled, flaring forwards, and his claws lengthened, the pressing need to have her growing too strong to deny. His wings itched beneath his skin, aching to burst free, and his fangs throbbed with a need to feel her flesh beneath them again.

"Sable," he growled, low and commanding, warning her that he was close to losing control.

She rose above him, drawing him up with her, and held on to his shoulders. He devoured her breast, licking away the blood and sealing the puncture wounds, and trailed his lips upwards. He wanted her as wild and needy as he felt. Needed her maddened by desire, on the brink of losing control too.

Thorne sank his fangs into his lower lip, drawing blood, grabbed her around the waist and kissed her hard. She pushed against him at first and then moaned, her nails digging into his shoulders. A heartbeat later and she was sucking greedily on his lip, drawing him into her, and the connection that burst into existence between them was staggering, almost taking him down to his knees. He could feel all of her, every emotion that danced through her as she tasted him and experienced the same connection awaken within her, and it awed him.

Because he could feel her love for him.

And it was endless.

Beautiful.

He shivered and kissed her harder, clutching the nape of her neck to keep her in place against his lips, to keep her drawing from him. Each drop of blood solidified the connection between them, the bond that would tie them forever once she acknowledged his words.

He wanted to speak them, to complete the bond and the claiming, but needed the kiss more, needed the connection of being inside her.

He lifted her left leg, holding it tucked close to his hip, and she moaned and reached between them. Her hot hand closed around his length, sending another shiver through him, and brought him down to her core. Thorne groaned in time with her as the head of his shaft wedged into her warmth.

He grasped her hip and drove into her in one hard, deep thrust. Sable shuddered against him and bit his lip, tearing another moan from him. He clutched her as she kneeled on the bed before him and drove into her, relentless and deep, curling his hips to ensure that he reached every part of her. She grabbed his shoulders again and kissed him now, her lips clashing with his as he took her, driving them both towards release. Her breasts bounced against his chest, firm nipples rubbing his skin with each thrust of his cock into her.

Thorne shifted his grip to her backside, digging his claws in as he lost himself to his urges and fighting to hold back some of his strength so he didn't harm her. She pressed her nails into his scalp and clutched his left horn with her other hand, her kiss as fierce and relentless as his thrusts. He wedged his left knee against the bed beneath her, angling his hips, and she gasped as he plunged deeper, his pelvis slamming against her with each long stroke.

"Thorne," she whispered, a plea that she didn't have to voice because he could feel her need, feel her creeping closer to release, and wouldn't stop until he had brought her to the very edge and sent her tumbling over it with him.

The connection between them relayed everything to him, heightening his own pleasure as their blood mingled, linking them together. He couldn't take much more but neither could she.

Her nails bit into his scalp as he shoved deep into her, slamming her down onto his length, and she tipped her head back and cried out as she came, her body quivering and milking him, drawing him deeper still.

Thorne's gaze zeroed in on her neck, his eyes blazing crimson, and he roared as his wings burst from his back, spanning the room, and he sank his throbbing fangs deep into her neck, marking her as his forever.

The first touch of her blood on his tongue sent his balls clenching tight and release boiling up his length. He grunted, blinded by pleasure as he shot his seed into her welcoming body. She trembled in his arms, a high keening cry leaving her lips as she joined him, climaxing again.

The feel of her flexing and clenching around his cock, and her quivering beneath his grip tore another release from him and he groaned into her throat, shaking all over as his length throbbed within her, his seed pulsing from him. A thousand fiery sparks skittered over his flesh with each pulse, searing his bones, and he could feel Sable tremble in time with them, could sense her experiencing the same blissful release.

Thorne drank deep of her blood, drawing the life giving essence into him, ensuring the strongest bond possible existed between them. His cock continued to throb within her, spilling himself as she quivered around him, sending aftershocks of pleasure rippling through them both. His knees loosened with each one, with every tiny orgasm that detonated within him and within her.

When he finally released her and drew back, her dazed gaze met his, a broad smile playing on her bloodied lips.

His blood.

He kissed it away, mingling them once more, and then forced himself to draw back so he could say the words that would complete their bond, linking them in eternity.

Thorne cupped her cheeks and kept her gaze on his, not giving her a chance to look away as he had in their vision. He stared deep into her golden eyes and whispered the binding words in the demon tongue.

She stared blankly at him, her gaze holding his, never wavering. He could sense her nerves and uncertainty as if they were his own. He had to say it in the demon tongue, as was tradition for a mating, but now he could speak to her in her own language.

"Sable… do you consent to become my mate, to take all that I am and give all that you are, in the eyes of the gods and eternity?"

Her eyes glittered, relief and happiness pouring through their link, together with her love for him.

It took a single word to make him feel he was the luckiest, and no doubt happiest, male in all the realms.

"Yes."

CHAPTER 27

Thorne was in Heaven.

Sable lay in his arms, tucked close to his side, with her right leg hooked over his and her head on his chest. Her warm breath skittered across his pectorals and her fingertips traced patterns on his skin.

They had lain like this for hours, exhausted from their lovemaking, sated and content to share the silence. The fire burning in the grate crackled.

He wanted to stay like this forever, never leaving this cocoon of warmth and contentment.

He needed to remain here, with his fated one in his arms, held close to him. Her heart beat softly, a gentle rhythm against his side, and she wriggled closer, until every inch of her lay flush against him.

His for eternity.

"This is nice," she said on a sigh and he knew she meant every word. He could sense it in her. His female, his Sable, was enjoying this moment of quiet intimacy as much as he was.

He grazed his fingers down her arm and frowned as they reached the silver cuff around her right wrist. He angled his head to get a better look at it as he stroked his fingertips over the cool bright metal.

"Sable," he whispered and she murmured in response. His touch lingered on the cuff, his gaze remaining locked there. "What made you join Archangel?"

He hadn't wanted to bring up Archangel, knowing it would make her think about her position and that it remained an obstacle between them, but the longer he held her, the more he realised he lacked knowledge about her position and didn't know her reason for being with the demon-hunting organisation. He wanted to know everything about her.

She shifted in his arms, rolling onto her front, so her breasts pressed against his chest and her right leg slid between his, threatening to wreck his concentration and stir his hunger for her.

"I don't know." She gave a small lift of her shoulders. "I was fighting this guy… the same punk kid who got his claws into my leg."

"Why fight him?"

"Because I could sense he wasn't right. He was dangerous and he was going after a woman who didn't have a damn clue. I saved her… but some other people called the police. They hauled me in and, well… Archangel set me free." She walked her fingers over his chest, her gaze on them, a small frown marring her brow. "They asked me what happened and I told them. They realised that I could sense a faint difference between the demon and the mortals around him, and they recruited me… they convinced me I had a gift that could help them, and help people."

"You do have a gift," he said and caught the flicker of hurt in her eyes as she glanced at him and then turned her face away. He sighed and captured her hand with his, stopping it from roaming his chest, and wrapped his other arm around her, anchoring her to him. "It is a gift that you have, Sable. Your powers—"

"Came from some homicidal arsehole who ditched my mum and she ditched me. I used to like my gift. Archangel helped me. They put me through training programmes that increased that gift and I honestly believed it was a calling." She lowered her head, pressing her lips and chin against his chest, and sighed. "I never questioned where it came from… and now I wish I didn't know."

Thorne pulled her up to him and held her as he kissed her, wanting to chase away the hurt that had been in her voice and the pain he could feel beating in her heart.

"I apologise," he whispered against her lips. "I should not have asked."

She nuzzled his nose with hers and then shook her head and pushed herself up so she was looking down into his eyes.

"It's fine. I just… it's all still a little new, and raw. I guess part of me always held on to hope that I would meet my parents one day and they would be proud of me… and looking back…" She heaved a sigh. "I think this all scares me because Archangel are like my family now. I wanted to be a commander, because I wanted them… hell, I wanted them to be proud of me."

"You wanted them to be the parents you never had."

She nodded and looked away again. "It's stupid."

"There is no need to feel ashamed because you desired someone to look at you with pride in their eyes, to treat you special and tell you that you had done well and they were pleased."

She smiled and slid her gaze towards him. "Did your father ever do such a thing with you?"

It was his turn to look away now and heave a sigh. He threw one hand above his head and tucked it beneath, tangling his fingers in his hair to stop himself from stroking his left horn.

"I do not remember. He was often busy with the kingdom. I recall wanting him to be proud of me though… I still desire such a thing now."

"Thorne," she started quickly and then softened her tone. Her gaze locked on his face and her fingers stroked lines over his chest. "I'm sure he is proud of you. You're a good king… a great man. You don't need to measure yourself against him. He reigned in a time of peace, and you've lived through a time of war, and your kingdom is still here… and if I have anything to say about it, it will still be here in centuries to come, and so will you."

The belief in her words struck him hard, bringing his eyes back to hers so he could see that faith reflected in their amber depths.

"And I am certain that Archangel is proud of you—"

"I wouldn't say that," she interjected and wrinkled her nose. "Mark… my superior… sort of had an air of unimpressed father when I was tending to you. He practically laid down the law. No mortal and demon relationships allowed."

She waggled her finger and scowled, and he presumed it was meant as an impression of her senior.

"I almost mentioned that I wasn't feeling particularly human. I don't think Archangel would understand if they found out my father was probably an angel… I think they'd run experiments on me… like they wanted to run on Loren and Bleu."

He stroked her long black hair back from her face and then pinched her chin between his fingers and thumb, keeping her eyes on him.

"I am proud of you. I have never met a female as strong, brave, skilled and determined as you are. I have witnessed you fight demons, deal with events that left you shaken and yet you refused to succumb to your fears, and I have seen you stand tall when your strength is questioned and prove your worth. I would place you in the ranks of my army as a commander without a second's pause. If Archangel cannot see your worth and see that you are their ally, not their enemy, then that is their mistake, and their loss." He rubbed his thumb across her lower lip. "And I will never let them lay a finger on you."

She lifted her hand and stroked his horn, her fiery eyes glittering as she smiled down at him.

"You're becoming quite the poet, King Thorne. Maybe I should have let you closer before. You have a way of making me feel better about myself, and I like it."

"And I love you," he whispered and grasped her bare backside, pulled her up his body and kissed her. She broke away too soon, pushing herself up and looking back down into his eyes. An angel. "And you are mine... my Sable... my queen."

She smiled again, beautiful and magical, enchanting him with the way it reached her eyes and spoke to his heart.

"Your queen... just like that? No ceremony?"

"Ah, well. There is another part to the claiming. It requires a public ceremony. We must share blood and speak—"

The bells tolled.

Cold slithered down Thorne's spine and he growled.

He should have known that someone would dare to snatch this Heaven from him before he was ready to give it up and face the world.

"That isn't good, is it?" Sable pushed herself up onto her knees and he rose with her, swung his legs over the edge of the bed and stood.

"The Fifth King approaches." Thorne grabbed a new pair of thick black leather trousers from his drawers and tugged them on.

Sable rushed around his room, gathering her clothes and throwing them on as quickly as she could. "I'll need my weapons."

"We must make haste to the library and speak with the others first. There is time for us to prepare before we engage his army." Thorne's heart pounded at a sickening pace and he fought to control his nerves and the dark voices ringing in his head.

He was a great man. A good king. His little female had told him as much and she believed in him.

He paused to watch her as she struggled with her boots and she looked up at him, radiating confidence that was infectious.

"Don't be getting jittery on me now. I've seen you fight, Thorne, and I know your desire to protect your people runs deep, and I hate your traditions."

He frowned at that final one.

She straightened, crossed the room to him and ran her hands over his chest as she tiptoed and brought her mouth close to his.

"I'm fucking damned if I'm letting you fight that bastard alone. Screw your traditions. I'll have your back and I'll have my forever after with you, and you will just have to deal with it."

He grinned and swept her up into his arms, and kissed her as he dropped them through a portal, bringing them to the library. He had the impression many of the sacred traditions of his kind were going to end up ignored, overruled or altered by his fiery little fated one.

"I feel nauseous." Grave's deep voice rang out above the chatter and Thorne released Sable and set her down. "Beauty has tamed the beast it seems... I pity you, Beast."

Thorne ignored him and scanned the room, checking who was yet to arrive. Sable moved off to speak with Olivia, Loren and Bleu. Strange. He could watch his female speaking with the elf commander without even a trace of hatred or need for violence.

Bleu's dark gaze leaped to her throat and then to him. The elf scowled at him. Thorne was about to puff his chest out when Sable looked over at him too. She would want him to be the better man and not rejoice in his victory. He nodded to her and turned away from Bleu.

Rosalind stood close to him, her hands over her eyes, wearing the same black dress as before. He had been expecting her to remain in her quarters, away from the public spaces in the house. What had brought her out to the meeting?

The open book on the table and a lit candle gave him his answer.

"Do you require transport back to your room?" he asked her and she shook her head but kept her hands over her eyes.

"I think I'm good. I had finished setting up the barrier and couldn't sleep, so I came up here to see your library because Sable had mentioned you owned many books. I was reading one of them when the bells went off. Before I knew it, there was an elf in the room. I'm not sure which one it was at first... but I didn't see them... and if I don't look at him or speak to him, then I should be okay."

She sounded unsure. Thorne wanted to ease her by taking her back to her room, but the rest of him was glad that she was here. She might be able to offer valuable information to them.

"What spells have you at your disposal?" He looked towards the arched open windows at the other end of the room.

"Too many to name or number. Why?"

"Perhaps you could assist me."

She nodded and he took her arm and led her across the room, past Grave, Kyal and Kincaid, and some of their men and his. He stopped with her in front of the open window and looked out into the dimness.

"Open your eyes and tell me what you see." He placed his hands on her shoulders and made sure his body blocked her view of everyone in the room.

"If I see an elf, you're in deep trouble," she said and then slowly peeled her hands away from her face. She squinted. "I see darkness."

"Could you see the enemy from here with a spell?" He narrowed his eyes and tried to make out any movement in the early light. "Could you tell me what we are up against?"

She nodded again, muttered something under her breath and twisted her hands together. Colours sparked between her hands, bright flashes that stole some of his vision, and then she curled her fingers around, forming a cylinder with each of her hands, brought them together so they resembled binoculars he had seen in the mortal world and raised them to her eyes. Curious.

"I see... dead people. Just kidding!" She glanced up at him and her expression soured. "You need to see more movies."

He shrugged. His kingdom did not have the power required to make electronic equipment function readily available, but it was on his list of things to do to improve the lives of his people. And his queen. Sable owned many different electronic devices and he had noticed a huge number of digital discs in her small apartment and a startling lack of books. If he wanted his queen to be happy living in his kingdom, he would need to find a way to power the equipment she found necessary.

Rosalind went back to looking through her hands. "I see a problem."

That did not please him. "Tell me more."

"I see a big problem. I guessed from the spells locking down your kingdom that they had witches on their side but they have *witches*... a serious amount of witches." She lowered her hands and looked up at him again. "At least two dozen. Thorne, witches in that number... the barrier spells I've placed over your castle won't hold out long against them."

He frowned and looked off to his right, out into the early morning greyness. "You are saying we cannot attack from the walls and weaken their army before facing them on the battlefield?"

"I'm saying you can, but the barrier spell might not last long with that many witches pelting it with reversal spells and attacks. Once this barrier is down, it will take me time to construct a new one."

He couldn't risk the barrier falling. His final command to his men last night had been to move all citizens from the surrounding villages into the castle in order to keep them safe from harm. He had been relying on Rosalind's spell to do that. If he allowed the witches of the Fifth King's army to break Rosalind's spell, all of the citizens he had brought into the castle would end up exposed to danger and the attacks.

"Thorne," Sable said from beside him and he looked down into her eyes, seeing everything she wanted to say in them. He smiled and brushed his fingers across hers.

He loved her too, and he would have her back in the coming fight, just as he knew she would have his. Together, they would make it through this and would save his kingdom.

Thorne linked his fingers with hers and looked over her head to the others—to the elves, the vampires, the werewolves, and the mortals who had gathered with his demon brethren and awaited his command.

"We meet them head on."

CHAPTER 28

Sable checked her weapons for the millionth time, a light warm breeze playing in her long black hair, causing rogue strands from her ponytail to flutter over her shoulder as she stood in the middle of the central courtyard of the dark stone castle.

She ran her fingers over the twin rows of small throwing blades strapped to her ribs beneath her arms, the leather holster laying them flush against her tight black t-shirt, and expelled her breath. It wasn't a sigh. She wasn't nervous.

It wasn't. She wasn't.

She kept telling herself that, trying to shake off the bad feeling that had settled in the pit of her stomach when Thorne had announced they were going out to meet the army of the Fifth King head on. That feeling weighed her down, impossible to ignore and difficult to deny. It had hold of her, placing dreadful images in her mind, visions of Thorne falling on the battlefield before she could save him.

Sable clenched her hands at her sides and closed her eyes, reaching for the link between them that was now so strong she could almost pinpoint Thorne's location within the castle.

It was good to feel him, to know that he was safe for now, close to her even if she couldn't see him.

She smiled at the sensation of warmth that travelled outwards from her heart, unravelling along her limbs until it reached her fingertips and her toes, and left her feeling calm at last. Thorne. He was reaching for her too and it made the link stronger than she had ever felt it before, even more powerful than shortly after they had sealed their bond and had become mates.

Mates.

She still hadn't absorbed that or what it meant. She was immortal now, like Olivia. She would be queen too, if Thorne had his way. She wanted to know what lay ahead of her, needed to know the rest of what Thorne had been saying before the alarm had sounded, interrupting them. She would just have to make sure that both she and Thorne survived the coming battle so he could finish what he had been telling her.

A passing group of bare-chested demons halted their conversation and bowed their heads, lowering their gazes at the same time. They weren't the first to greet her in such a manner. Word had certainly spread quickly through the ranks of Thorne's men. She doubted there was a demon in his realm who didn't know that he had claimed her and that she would soon be their queen.

That was still a royal mind fuck.

Queen Sable.

She shook her head, pushing that thought out of it. She didn't want to be queen, but she didn't think she was going to get a choice in the matter. She had mated with Thorne, had bound herself to him, and had vowed to embrace all that he was, and that meant accepting the responsibilities that came with it.

Like being queen to a horde of demons.

Was a time when she had been happy killing their kind. Now she was going to be responsible for taking care of them.

A royal mind fuck.

A hot shiver went through her, raising the hairs on the nape of her neck, and she swung her gaze towards the source of the sensation.

Thorne strode through the massive archway that led to the great hall, his broadsword balanced on his shoulder, his bare chest shifting sensually, enticingly with each step. His focus was on Loren, Kincaid and Grave as they walked beside him, his expression locked in dark grim lines. Discussing battle plans without her?

She had half a mind to have it out with him, but she could sense his strain and the underlying current of fear that flowed through him. He wouldn't appreciate her teasing him at a time like this, when he felt the fate of his kingdom hung in the balance.

"Weapons check," she hollered to her hunters and Evan and the other two men she had placed in charge of the divisions began barking instructions.

A few of the female hunters kept glancing towards the werewolves. The shifters had been a distraction ever since they had strolled into the courtyard to prepare themselves for the battle ahead. It seemed that werewolves preferred to go into battle half-naked, dressed in just loose shorts, and were flashing an obscene amount of muscle while they waited around for Kincaid. They were worse than the demons.

Sable had diligently kept her eyes off them, even when Kyal had come to discuss tactics with her. The younger wolf was itching for a fight, eager to get out onto the battlefield and sink his fangs into some demons.

Thorne halted and spoke with some of his men, and Sable couldn't take her eyes off him. He looked magnificent in just his tight black leather trousers, his heavy boots, and his thick leather vambraces strapped to his forearms. All of the demons were bare-chested and she had figured out why. It gave their opponents less to grab hold of during the fight, making it easier for them to escape any grip or avoid being caught altogether, and also made it easier for them to make use of their wings, unleashing them or hiding them as necessary.

Thorne ran a hand over his left horn and glanced her way, and then his gaze slowly edged back to her. She smiled at him. A flutter of warmth danced in her stomach when he smiled back, flashing the tips of his fangs. The marks on her neck tingled and the ones hidden beneath her black t-shirt on her breast joined them.

His dark crimson gaze brightened, he said something to the men without taking his eyes off her, and then he was striding towards her, his long muscular legs eating up the distance between them. Clearly, it wasn't quick enough for him.

He dropped into a dark patch and she gasped as a breeze flowed across her back and his hands claimed her shoulders. He spun her to face him and before she could utter a word, his lips descended on hers, searing them with a passionate kiss that demanded all of her focus, chasing away the world around them.

Sable slipped her hands around his neck and returned the kiss, biting back a moan when his tongue tangled with hers, hot and insistent, and his fangs scraped her lip.

He drew back and the quip she had lined up on her tongue disappeared, forgotten as she stared into his striking scarlet eyes.

"Missed you," he husked, drawing another smile from her, and she twined her fingers in his hair, curling it around their tips. "Miss me too?"

She nodded and he righted her, stepped back and kept his hands on her shoulders. He looked her over, his assessing gaze falling on the blades sheathed by her ribs and then the crossbow and short sword that hung from her belt.

"You do not have enough weapons." He scowled at what she did have and she sighed.

"You have a single sword and you say I don't have a big enough arsenal?" She rolled her eyes. A frown creased her brow. "Where is your sword?"

Thorne shrugged.

Sable looked back over her shoulder to search for it and couldn't see it anywhere. She locked gazes with Thorne again. "You did that teleporting thing with it."

He nodded.

"But you don't know where it is?" She had always figured that he sent it somewhere, like the elves did with their possessions, returning them to their world.

"Demons are of the earth, are born of it, and so when we teleport we travel through it, returning to it." Thorne cocked his head and stared at the stone flags beneath her feet. "When I have no need of my sword, it too returns to the earth."

Sable frowned harder and dropped her gaze to her feet too. "So it's down there somewhere."

"Yes," he said and she tried to get her head around that, and failed.

Hell was under her world and not at the same time.

Thorne's sword existed when it was in his hand, but when it wasn't, when he sent it away, it became one with the ground.

Did that mean when he teleported, dropping into the dark circle upon the ground, that he was becoming one with the earth too?

She really didn't want to think about that.

"You are to remain here with the others." Loren's voice caught her attention and she scoured the courtyard for him, finding him a few metres away with Bleu and Olivia. Both elves wore their skin-tight black scaly armour. It covered Loren from neck to wrist, but Bleu had his helmet in place and his armour over his fingers, transforming them into vicious serrated claws.

Olivia glared up at Loren, her hands firmly planted on her hips, fingertips pressing into her dark blue jeans. "Why?"

Loren sighed and reached out to her. Olivia swatted his hand away.

"You'll need a medic on the battlefield." Her friend's expression darkened, echoing her anger. Sable could understand her upset. She would hate it if Thorne dared to tell her to remain in the castle. She wanted to support her friend and back her up, but Loren was right.

"We need a medic here, Sweet Ki'ara." Loren tried to reach out to touch her again and she huffed and slapped at his hand.

"Don't you 'sweet ki'ara' me. You need me out there."

"No," Loren said, his voice falling to a whisper. "I need you here, where I know you are safe and protected. I would die if anything happened to you, my love."

"I'm immortal now, I can—"

"You can still die," Loren interjected, his eyes flashing bright purple, and clenched his fists at his sides. The pointed tips of his ears extended, flaring back against his wild blue-black hair, and his fangs flashed between his lips as he quickly spoke. "I will hear no more on this matter. You are needed here to aid any who return injured and to set up the infirmary. This army is relying on you and others to support it, to save lives bravely given to defend this kingdom. Do you understand?"

Olivia bowed her head, her long lashes shuttering her dark brown eyes, and meekly nodded. She closed her eyes and sighed, her eyebrows pinching together, and then looked at Loren's hands. She slowly reached out and slipped her fingers into his left one, her thumb brushing his, and lifted her eyes to meet his.

"I'm sorry," she said in a low voice and her eyebrows furrowed. She stepped closer to Loren and raised her other hand, sweeping it across his cheek as he stared down into her eyes. "I didn't mean to push... I didn't mean to upset you."

The elf prince closed his eyes and leaned into her touch, swallowing hard at the same time. "I could not bear to lose you."

"I know. I couldn't bear losing you either and that's why I wanted to be out there, with you." She tiptoed and placed her arms around his neck, drawing him down to her. He lowered his head and settled it in the curve of her throat. His hands claimed her hips and drew her against him, his fingertips digging into her back. Olivia stroked the back of his head. "I'll stay here. Someone has to make sure everyone is taken care of and everyone here is safe. Right?"

He nodded but remained with his head buried in her fall of dark hair.

Olivia looked over at Sable.

Sable offered her a smile, hoping it would soothe her friend, and mouthed, "We'll take care of him."

She understood her friend's need to be with her mate, but Olivia's training was still in the early stages and that made her a liability on the battlefield, more of a nuisance than a help. They needed her in the castle, safe and protected, ready to tend to anyone who came back injured.

Sable would make sure that Loren was safe and made it through the battle, and she wouldn't be alone. She met Bleu's gaze, seeing the steadiness in it, the determination to protect not only his prince, but her and others too.

"Disgusting," Grave muttered as he strolled past with three of his men in tow, heading for Sable and Thorne, all four vampires wearing the standard black long jacket, trousers and riding boots of the Preux Chevaliers corps.

Loren lifted his head from Olivia's neck and hissed, his pointed ears flattening against the sides of his head as he bared his fangs. He growled something in the elf language that sounded dark, menacing, and a threat.

Bleu said something too, a wicked tilt to his lips that turned his visage cruel, revealing the other side of his nature that the elves often hid so well.

Grave glared at both of them, his pupils stretching thin in the centres of his ice-blue eyes, and then seemed to reconsider whatever course of action he had been preparing to take. He huffed, tilted his nose up and kept walking. He settled his hand on the hilt of the elegant sword sheathed at his waist and shoved a couple of the younger werewolves out of his way. Neither dared to growl at him. They slinked back into the pack, scowling at the dark-haired vampire as he passed with his entourage.

"Just as charming as ever," Sable muttered as Olivia, Loren and Bleu joined them.

"Keep away from him in battle, Little Female." Thorne squeezed her hand and she squeezed back to let him know that she wasn't foolish enough to fight anywhere near Grave.

He had almost lost his head to bloodlust several times when they had been here in the castle, in peaceful situations. She didn't want to imagine just how insane he would be on the battlefield.

"Is everything prepared?" Loren said, a picture of composure again, and Thorne nodded.

"I will leave men with experience in dressing wounds here at the castle with Olivia and the others. Rosalind will remain here too. She has vowed to help in any way that she can, including patching any holes in our defences if the witches at the Fifth King's disposal do attack the barrier she placed over the castle."

Sable could sense Thorne's relief about that. Keeping the people who remained in the castle safe meant a lot to him. It wasn't only civilians who would be left here while they headed out to meet the Fifth King's army. Each species were leaving a portion of their men behind, a second wave of fresh soldiers that she had no doubt they would need and who would give others a chance to rest and recuperate enough to go on fighting.

"Rosalind also informed me that the Fifth King's numbers are great, outweighing ours. It will be a difficult battle." Thorne paused and looked down at her.

Sable met his gaze, keeping her heart steady and her body still, refusing to let the flicker of nerves within her show in any way he could detect. The subtle tilt of his lips said that he was on to her and knew both her fear and her reason for hiding it from him.

"I would not dare hold you back from battle, my female. I do not wish to find myself castrated or stabbed." His smile grew and she pushed his arm, rolling her eyes at the same time.

Olivia looked as if she wanted to snipe about being held back from battle but kept quiet. Sable gave her a smile and silently promised to increase the difficulty of her training sessions. She would make a warrior out of her friend yet.

"My men are prepared," Kincaid said close beside her and she looked across at him.

Kyal stood at his side, his blue irises already transforming into their golden wolf-state. Eager as ever. She didn't know why he always wanted to rush into battle. Kincaid and the others had said he was young, calling him a cub more than once much to his chagrin, but something in his eyes said differently.

He was young physically, appearing around her age, and was rash, energetic and eager, but his eyes held a wealth of darkness and cold detachment at times. Something she couldn't name haunted them. Something he tried hard to hide behind banter, enthusiasm and empty smiles and laughter.

He had seen things in his years.

Terrible things.

And those horrors had given him purpose, a hunger and need that drove him to fight and prove himself.

If she had to put a name to that purpose, she would call it revenge.

Kyal wasn't a pup or a cub, or a werewolf to take lightly. That was just his front. His perfect feint. No. Kyal was something else. It was right there in his eyes and the cold calculating edge they gained whenever he thought no one was watching him.

Kyal was a dangerous man—the proverbial wolf in sheep's clothing.

His eyes met hers and she looked away, and wished she hadn't. Grave stood opposite her, to one side of a trio of demon males, his flunkies still guarding his back. His pale eyes slid her way and a cruel smirk tugged at one corner of his mouth.

"You smell afraid."

"Gross, and no, not afraid. Repulsed, maybe. Eager to kick some arse, possibly. Dreaming of ways to kill you while making it look like the enemy did it, *definitely*." She grinned at him and he scowled and bared his fangs.

Sable noted it still wasn't wise to piss off a vampire with bloodlust.

Unfortunately, noting it didn't stop her from blurting out, "Know a guy named Snow? Cause, man, he makes your crazy look like sane."

Grave's expression darkened, his lips thinning and the dark slashes of his eyebrows meeting above eyes rapidly turning red.

"What know you of my cousin?"

Wow. That, she had not anticipated. "You guys are related? Because when I mentioned your name, he threw a fit and his brother had to chill him out."

Grave growled at her. "Speak not of vampires above your rank, Commoner."

"Nice. I'll have you know, I'm a queen." Sable beamed at him. "That makes *you* the commoner."

"I will wait no longer. My men will walk before I stand here another second in the company of such impudence." He pinned her with a look that left her feeling he was plotting her demise, and how to make it look like the enemy did it, and then swiftly turned on his heel and swept away from them, his lackeys following him.

Thorne, Bleu and Loren sighed.

"I know. I know." Sable held her hands up. "Spare me the lecture. It's not wise to piss Grave off... blah, blah, blah. But, seriously, what is with him?"

Thorne shrugged. "I have wondered that myself upon occasion."

His tone said the occasion rose often. She tracked Grave, trying to figure out why he was so jaded and what he had against his cousins and his cousins against him.

All aristocrat born vampire males had to serve centuries as a Preux Chevalier. Had something happened between Snow and Grave in Hell?

"The bloodsucker will do as he has threatened if we do not leave now." Bleu checked his black blade over, turned to his prince, and added, "We should not hold off any longer. The drums are getting closer."

Loren nodded. "Much closer and we shall place the castle at risk. Thorne?"

Thorne closed his eyes, drew in a deep breath, and finally nodded too.

"It is time." He took hold of her hand and gave it a gentle squeeze. She looked up at him, meeting his gaze, losing herself in the rich crimson and dark pools of his pupils. "Your mortal teams will have escorts in the form of some of my men and some of the elves. I have assigned the strongest of my warriors to you. Do not hate me for it."

Sable smiled to alleviate the guilt that flickered in his eyes and the trepidation that came through their bond. She couldn't hate him for wanting to protect her. At least he wasn't trying to stop her from fighting full stop. He was certainly learning the ways to please her, and get around her too.

"I'll keep them nice and safe for you." Sable rose on her toes and caught him around the back of his head, luring him down to her. She kissed him softly, savouring it and this moment of calm before the storm. "May your gods watch over you, Thorne, or I'll kick their arses."

Thorne's sensual mouth curled into a smile and he swept his fingers across her cheek. "And may they watch over you, my queen, or suffer my eternal wrath."

He pulled her closer and then the world dropped away, and not in the way she had expected.

Thorne's huge leathery wings beat at the air, lifting them higher as he held her tucked in his arms, his crimson gaze scouring the land beyond his castle's walls.

He spread his wings and they glided lower, over the dark stone walls of both the inner courtyard and the outer one, and out above the countryside surrounding it, heading towards the ominous sound of drums that rose on the warm air.

Sable stiffened at the first glimpse of the army marching across the dark land, heading directly for the castle. She had never seen so many warriors. They swathed the land, walking in regiments, blocks of soldiers armed to the teeth.

Armed with teeth.

"Most are demons, but I see shifters among them." Thorne jerked his head to the right, towards a group that marched separately from the others, made up of mountainous bare-chested men. "Bears are here, and dragons too."

"Dragons?" Sable whispered in awe. She had heard of dragon shifters but she had never seen one. They never came to the mortal world and Archangel had marked them as extinct, just as they had the elves. "Olivia would love to study a dragon."

Thorne chuckled. "If we manage to injure one, I will have it sent to the dungeons, but do not count on it. They are notoriously robust when they shift, their scales almost impenetrable."

"You're telling me they're pretty much impervious? How are we meant to take them down?"

He grinned. "Females. A dragon is easily distracted by and fears harming females."

"I have females," Sable said and decided to bag a dragon for Olivia. It would cheer her friend up no end. "Hell, I *am* female."

Thorne growled. "And taken. If I receive word that you lured a dragon... do not test me, Sable."

The air shifted violently off to her left and Thorne muttered something in the demon tongue, banked right and flew harder, coming around and away from the army amassed below them.

Another bout of turbulence jostled her in his arms. "What the hell is happening?"

"Witches," Thorne sneered, his horns curling, and circled lower, heading back towards the army gathering several miles in front of the castle in the distance.

They landed gently near Loren, Bleu and the other leaders.

"How many?" Kincaid said the moment they touched down.

"Several thousand at my count, enough to test us." Sable was glad when her feet touched terra firma again and stepped away from Thorne. "And they have witches, dragons and bears."

"Dragons," Bleu spat and rubbed his neck.

Sable frowned. She had been around him often enough to notice the scars he had there, long slashes that had left their mark. Had a dragon left his mark on Bleu?

Loren placed a hand on his shoulder. "We shall work with Sable and her team to tackle the dragons. They are vulnerable to our weapons."

Thorne nodded. "The wolves will no doubt love to sink their fangs into the bears, would you not, old friend?"

Kincaid grinned, flashing short fangs. "Indeed. This battle is already looking up. It has been a long time since I have fought bears."

"Bears?" Kyal looked off into the distance, a note of interest in his voice. The gold in his eyes increased. Tawny fur rippled over his forearms and shoulders.

Sable looked away as he transformed, not wanting to catch an eyeful of him this time. He snarled and growled, and the sounds of bones crunching turned her stomach. She hated the thought that her father might have been an angel, but she was damned glad he hadn't been a shifter.

Kincaid transformed too, his shift far smoother than Kyal's and over in a heartbeat. The two large wolves shook all over, and then one threw his head back and unleashed a howl.

Answering howls came a heartbeat later.

And then distant roars. The bears.

Kyal and Kincaid bounded off to join their fellow warriors.

Grave drew in a deep breath and swept away from them, calling over his shoulder, "I would advise against getting in my or my men's ways."

He disappeared before she could respond and his men followed, sweeping across the dark ground behind the wolves to meet the enemy head on.

They needn't have rushed.

Sable ducked to avoid the tip of the blade that came out of nowhere.

The enemy had come to them.

CHAPTER 29

All hell had broken loose the moment the first demon had appeared amidst their ranks. Sable had found herself thrust to one side by Thorne, his broadsword catching the enemy across his throat before he could teleport, severing his head. She had rolled and come to her feet to find herself surrounded by Thorne's men and also the demons from the Fifth Realm. The battle had instantly absorbed all of her focus, the adrenaline dump quick to pass and the usual calm she experienced when fighting demons even quicker to come.

She slashed at all the demons who came too close, able to identify them by their dazzling jewel green eyes and painted black horns. A few had fallen to her blade so far, giving her confidence that she badly needed. Her demon escorts tackled any who were too strong for her but the enemy were gradually separating them and she needed to reach her team.

Sable ducked as a curved blade whizzed towards her, barely evading it, and swept her leg out, taking down the man. He pushed himself up onto his elbows and snarled at her, flashing rows of sharp teeth, his bright aquamarine eyes glinting dangerously.

Not a demon.

A handful of Sable's team reached her, aiding her in her battle against the demons closing in on them. It was pandemonium and in the midst of it sat the shirtless male warrior, a hank of wild blue hair hanging across his forehead as he stared up at her and her band of female hunters with awe in his striking eyes.

"Dragon," Sable muttered with a grin.

"Ooh, where?" Anais said and looked down at him.

He stared at the blonde huntress and swallowed hard.

"Amazons," he whispered, his deep voice laced with the wonder in his gaze. He blinked, his jewel-coloured eyes flitting from one woman to the next, but always returning to Anais, lingering longest on her.

Flecks of gold shimmered in his irises like fire as he stared up at Anais and a scowl slowly drew his dark blue eyebrows together, his lips thinning in a look that Sable could only describe as displeasure.

Sable pressed her boot against his throat, pushed him down into the dirt and cocked her head to one side. "Not Amazons... just demon-hunters. How do you feel about being studied?"

He growled now, flashing sharp teeth that she had no desire to become acquainted with, and grasped her ankle. He shoved upwards before she could adjust her weight, flipping her off him. Sable landed hard on the uneven dirt, the impact rattling her senses.

There was a shriek and a muffled grunt of pain.

Anais.

Sable pushed to her feet and one of the demons came to her aid. She swatted his hand away and turned to look for her fellow hunter.

And found an enormous blue dragon looming over her.

He roared at her, his beaked snout opening wide to flash those killer teeth that were now each as long as her hand, and reared up on his muscular hind legs. He spread his wings wide and flexed them, each easily forty feet across, sending a gust of wind down at her that knocked her backwards, and swept his long barbed tail around, catching many of his side and hers with it, toppling them.

Another shriek caught her attention. The dragon looked down at the same time as Sable did, her gaze zeroing in on Anais.

The blonde huntress repeatedly stabbed the dragon's front paw that clutched her, the blows ineffective, the dagger unable to penetrate his scales.

"Sable, get me down from here!" Anais wriggled and reached for her.

"You heard her." Sable turned to her team and the demons assisting her. "Get her away from him."

The dragon roared at that, as if her words had caused him distress, and clutched Anais closer to his chest. Sable cursed. If Anais had a blade that could pierce his armour she would have had a clean shot at his chest or his throat. What would possess the dragon to place himself at risk like that? Was he so confident that Anais didn't have a weapon that could harm him?

He answered her by tucking Anais against his scaly body, holding her with both paws as if shielding her, and beating his wings. The demons on her side attacked him, slashing at his hind legs and trying to slice through his meaty tail. He snarled and beat his wings harder, lifting off with Anais.

Abducting her.

"Give her back, you bastard!" Sable took her crossbow from her belt and loaded it with a dart. She didn't know which and didn't care. All she had to do was aim well and hit the dragon in the only vulnerable spot she could see.

His eyes.

She took aim as the huge beast rose higher into the air, each powerful beat of his wings buffeting her and making it hard to keep steady. The second she had locked on to his eye, she loosed the dart and held her breath.

He growled and jerked his head to one side, closing his eye at the same time. The dart struck, and bounced off his eyelid.

Sable unleashed a growl of frustration and ran after him.

She was damned if he was going to steal one of her team.

She hit a snag only a few metres into her sprint.

Bears.

They were too absorbed in fighting the wolves that were swarming around them to notice her. She had never seen a bear shifter and never wanted to see another in her eternal life. They were huge, towering furry behemoths that stood on their hind legs, swinging enormous clawed meaty paws at their enemies and growling the whole time. Their huge fangs dripped with blood and saliva, and several wolves lay dead or dying at their feet.

The demons caught her and pulled her back, and she could only watch as the dragon disappeared into the gloomy distance, heading in the opposite direction to the castle.

Thorne had neglected to mention that dragons had a tendency to steal that which they found fascinating.

Another shriek reached her ears and she ran in that direction.

"Each of you pick one of my huntresses and bloody well stop the dragons from stealing her!" she barked at the demons as they thundered along behind her.

They grunted and then she had the feeling she was alone.

Sable looked behind her to find all of them gone.

Not good. Her wrist ached and the low throbbing ran down to her leg. Not good at all.

Sable looked for Thorne and the others. Loren and Bleu fought nearby with their elves assisting them. They moved too quickly for her to keep up with them, appearing only long enough to attack a demon or one of the dragons in their human forms unawares before teleporting again. The demons on both sides moved in the same way, using their abilities to their advantage, but they didn't have telekinesis like the elves.

The elves used it with devastating grace, throwing their enemies hundreds of feet with just a flick of their wrists, sending them slamming into and toppling other enemies in the distance. Sable liked the elf version of bowling much more than the human one. It looked like fun and, for a flicker of a moment, she wished she had that sort of power at her disposal.

Her wrist burned again and soured her mood. She ignored it, not wanting to think that there was every chance that she might be able to hurl objects with the power of her mind or far worse, and that power had come from the angelic blood in her veins. Blood given to her by an angel who had viewed her as a mistake and a sin, something to eradicate, not love.

She shoved the bastard out of her mind and focused on finding Thorne.

She couldn't spot him among the demons nearby. Many of the demons were further ahead of her, deep in the middle of the battle. Her heart said that Thorne would be there, working his way towards the Fifth King without her aid. She needed to reach him. An invisible blast knocked her flying backwards and she landed hard, her head spinning and bones aching from the blow.

Evan appeared beside her and pulled her up onto her feet. "You okay?"

She nodded and winced as she straightened, cracking everything back into place. She huffed when she realised that she had lost her blade and grabbed the nearest one off the ground. It was heavier than her normal weapon but it would do until she spotted her own.

"Watch the women," Sable said and scanned the throng, trying to pick out any enraptured dragons. "If the guy you're fighting has blue eyes or anything other than bloody green, and doesn't have horns, he's probably a dragon shifter. One already took Anais."

"Took her down?"

"No. Took her... the son of a bitch abducted her." And hadn't he looked terribly pleased about it too? Anais could handle herself, but Sable didn't think she could handle a sixty-foot-tall dragon.

"You think they want to eat the women?"

She tossed a scowl at Evan. "I'm not asking where that sick thought came from, and no, I don't think so. The guy looked at her as if she was a goddess and Thorne says that dragons can't bring themselves to harm women. He thought we were bloody Amazons."

Sable quietly admitted she had enjoyed that. It had felt like a compliment at the time.

"You mean he probably wants to..."

Sable was glad he trailed off and didn't put out there what she had already figured out for herself.

She really hoped that Anais stuck the dragon with something pointy when he had to shift back and could fend him off until Sable could rally some troops and head out to rescue her.

"Evan, take your men and work with the demons to keep the women safe," she said and he nodded, and turned away.

And disappeared.

Sable turned in time to see him hit the deck a short distance away, landing in an awkward heap and rolling across the dark ground. She whipped her head the other way and her marrow froze.

Witches. Correction. Bitch-witches.

Three beautiful black-haired women slinked towards her, their long dresses hugging their ample breasts, accentuating a figure that most women would kill to possess.

Not her.

All Sable saw were a nightmarish repeat of a battle she wanted to forget. One bitch-witch had been bad enough. Three were that nightmare on steroids.

The one in the centre raised her hand, a glowing ball of pale blue light forming in her palm. Her dark lips curved into a sinister smile and she flipped her hand over and flicked it towards Sable, unleashing the spell.

It zoomed towards her, growing at the same time, until the orb was almost as big as she was. Sable lunged to avoid it but knew she wasn't going to be quick enough. Her legs were sluggish and unresponsive, time slowing to a trickle as she desperately tried to get out of the path of the spell.

Light exploded and the ground shook beneath her, knocking her to her knees, and she waited for the pain to come.

Nothing.

Sable looked back at the witches.

Rosalind stood there, her hands raised and palms facing the witches, and her blonde hair whipping around her shoulders and her black dress flapping against her shins. A dome of purple light flickered around her. Sparks leaped from her fingertips to the fading shield.

"What are you doing out here?" Sable shoved to her feet and readied her blade.

The witches launched another attack and Rosalind's pretty face twisted into a dark visage as she shoved forwards with her hands just as it struck the shield protecting them. The blue light bounced around the dome, crackling and sparking.

"I need to be here. I couldn't watch from the castle any longer. The witches are driving you all back towards it. You just don't know it." Rosalind's blue eyes brightened, swirling with flecks of silver that sparkled like stars.

"But you can't be here," Sable snapped. "You threatened Thorne's kingdom if you were hurt or killed or taken. You made a vow!"

And with dragons on the prowl for women, there was a high chance Rosalind would end up taken too.

Rosalind looked across at her. "I am breaking that vow. You need a witch, and I need a quick lesson in how to fight in a battle."

"Shit. You're telling me you've never fought before?" Sable's stomach dropped into her feet.

"No. But I have never been in a battle." Rosalind shrugged. "I'm not sure what I'm meant to do."

One of the witches hurled another glowing orb at them. Rosalind lowered one hand, muttered something, and then threw that hand forwards. The orb slowed as it reached her palm and then shot back at the witch who had cast it, knocking her flying.

Sable gaped. "Just keep doing that."

Rosalind nodded.

"And what should I do?" The soft female voice came from behind her and Sable squeezed her eyes shut, bit back a huff, and turned to face her friend.

Olivia crouched beside Evan, her hand on a bandage around his left arm. She adjusted the black bag slung over her shoulder and tucked the remaining crepe roll back into it.

"You should have stayed in the castle. How the hell did you get out... no... I really don't need you to tell me." Sable looked back at Rosalind, catching the guilt in her blue gaze as she launched an attack on the witches, sending a dazzling green orb hurtling towards them. It missed one and struck the other, ripping a cry from the witch that lasted only a second before the woman dropped to the ground.

"Don't be mad at her. I asked to come. I can help, Sable, if you'll just let me." Olivia picked up a short blade and tested it, swinging it in the way Sable had taught her.

Several more demons came at them and Sable really didn't have time to argue.

She formed a tight group with Olivia, Evan and Rosalind, and together they tackled the demons and the witches. Rosalind was invaluable. Her protection spell deflected most of the attacks, giving Sable and Evan the opportunities they needed to take the demons down, and she also continued to hurl twisting spheres of different colours at the witches and any group of their enemy.

Rosalind tossed three small orbs and held her hand out, her eyes focused on the distance. She twisted her hand this way and that, and the orbs obeyed each shift, changing directions and tearing through the enemy, severing limbs or punching straight through their bodies. Her hand shook and tears lined her lashes as she paled.

"Rosalind?" Sable slashed at the huge demon she was fighting to give herself an opening to reach the witch. Something was wrong. Very wrong.

Rosalind muttered to herself and the tears on her lashes spilled onto her cheeks. A huge boom shook the ground and blinding light filled the sky. Three domes of purest white erupted in the distance together with screams of agony.

Sable skewered the demon as he looked off to the distance and then tugged her blade free, spun and severed his head. He fell to the ground as she was rushing to Rosalind.

"Rosalind?" Olivia said and beat Sable to her, catching her as she collapsed and landing with her on the ground.

"What's wrong?" Sable crouched beside the two women. "Are you hurt?"

Rosalind shook her head and her watery blue gaze met Sable's.

"It hurts. I never thought it would hurt," Rosalind whispered and Sable feared she was injured after all and began checking her over. Rosalind grabbed her arm and Sable looked back into her eyes. "Is it always like this?"

"What?" Sable tried to keep her attention on Rosalind even as her focus was elsewhere, monitoring their surroundings, ensuring no one was sneaking up on them.

"Killing... war... I thought I could do this. I don't think I can."

Sable's eyes widened. Rosalind had fought in the past but she had never taken a life and it was wreaking havoc on her. Sable could remember how cold and empty she had felt when she had killed her first demon, and how she hadn't been able to sleep or eat for days, had kept replaying the fight and his death over and over again.

Rosalind had killed scores of men in barely an hour. It was little wonder she was breaking down.

"We'll take care of you," Sable said and smiled to show her that she was telling the truth and meant every word. "I won't let anything happen to you."

A bright bolt of light hit the ground in front of Rosalind and exploded, sending them all hurtling through the air in different directions.

CHAPTER 30

Sharp fire went down Thorne's side and he turned away from his opponent, expecting to find another behind him, his sword or claws bloodied from the attack. Masses of men fought there but all were engaged with each other, their focuses locked on their own fights.

Thorne growled and swung his broadsword towards his own opponent, a large male of the Fifth Realm. Their blades clashed, the fierce vibration running up Thorne's right arm, stinging his bones. The dark-haired male snarled at him, flashing bloodstained fangs, drew his sword back and swung the heavy silver blade at him again.

He blocked again, using the flat of his broadsword this time, and grimaced as pain tore up his side once more. His instincts flared and he stumbled as it hit him.

Sable.

It was her pain that he had experienced.

A sense of urgency claimed him, demanding he find her and ensure that she was safe. His female was injured somewhere amidst this pandemonium and every instinct he possessed laid the blame at his feet. He shouldn't have allowed himself to get lost in his quest to seek out the Fifth King and end him. He shouldn't have separated from her, trusting that his men could protect her.

He shoved forwards with his blade, twisted it in both hands, and brought it up in a vicious arc, severing his opponent's left arm midway down his forearm. The male roared at him, leaped back and spread his black wings. He beat them, charging Thorne, but Thorne was ready for him. He lunged towards him, clutching his blade at his side, and beat his own leathery wings, propelling him forwards, straight at the male.

The male thrust with his blade.

Thorne grinned and sidestepped, and shoved forwards with his own sword, calling on all of his strength and placing every drop of it behind his thrust. The demon roared as the blade punched through his chest, snapping bone and slicing flesh. Thorne tugged the sword upwards, bringing it in a devastating arc out of the male's torso, cutting through his heart.

He didn't wait for the male to fall. The pain came again, splintering across his side, commanding him to find his female.

Thorne cast a portal and dropped into it, reappearing a short distance away. He scanned the fray, searching for a sign of Sable among the warriors fighting with fang, blade and claw, and even among the fallen. Blood soaked the dark ground and many of his army had fallen, but many more of their enemies had lost their lives, their eyes staring unseeingly at the dark sky above.

He teleported again and again, scouring the battle for Sable each time he appeared, his senses reaching for her, trying to detect her, and his heart pounding at a sickening pace behind his breast.

Where was she?

Each teleport took him further from his foe, undoing his progress towards the Fifth King, but it was a sacrifice he willingly made. He needed to see Sable and know that she was safe from death's icy grip.

Thorne reappeared amidst a group of his enemy. The demons made the mistake of turning away from the male they had been fighting. Grave grinned, a maniacal glint in his burning red eyes, and attacked, slashing with his claws and sinking his fangs into some of the less fortunate. He drank hard, the hold of the bloodlust unmistakable as his eyes roved the demons even as he sucked down the blood of one of their allies, searching for his next victim.

Two vampires fought with him, both clean by comparison with their bloodied commander. Grave seemed to be intent on killing every demon by consuming their blood, sucking them dry. He released the male and let the body slump to the ground. The two vampires holding back the other demons growled as he shoved them aside and launched himself at another demon, tackling the larger male with ease and sinking his claws into his arms. He slashed at the male's flesh, cutting through muscle and tearing down to his bones.

The whole area stank of blood.

Blood.

Thorne backed away and focused on his, on the connection to Sable that came not only from their bond but from her blood in his body. His kind had the ability to track using blood they had tasted and it would guide him to Sable far quicker than his bond with her.

A connection blossomed within him.

Not Sable.

The feeling was weak when it should have been strong because he had taken blood from Sable recently.

Thorne frowned and looked in the direction his ability had pinpointed.

His eyes widened.

The tall elf male fought like a savage beast, tearing through his dragon enemies with ease, slashing with the vicious claws of his obsidian armour and not giving them a chance to transform into their beast-state. A wide circle of bodies surrounded him. His black helm flared into several spikes, forming a crown atop his head, and his armour hugged his lean figure.

Far leaner than when Thorne had last seen this male.

Vail.

The mad elf prince.

What was he doing here?

The answer became apparent when Vail snarled and shifted course, moving with agile grace to block another male with his bare hands. Olivia. She knelt behind Vail on the ground, clutching her left arm to her chest. Blood caked the side of her face and streamed down her arm. Vail was protecting her.

Thorne growled. What was she doing out here?

Vail twisted his opponent's arms, bending them outwards, and grinned as an audible crack sounded followed by the agonised cry of his enemy. He kicked the male hard in the stomach, sending him flying backwards into another group of warriors. The vampires turned on the injured male, taking him down.

Thorne needed to call for Loren, knew that the elf prince would want to try to capture his brother, but he couldn't leave Vail and Olivia. Loren would feel Olivia's pain as he had felt Sable's and would come to her, but would it be soon enough to arrive before his brother disappeared again?

He had been keeping an eye on his kingdom over the past lunar cycle, on the lookout for Vail, trying to help Loren bring his brother home. He knew how strongly Loren desired to reunite with him. He had no love for Vail himself, but knew in his heart that the witch Kordula had controlled him, making him do the terrible acts he committed, and he no longer held the elf to blame for the death of his parents.

He needed to find Sable too. He could sense her now, and she was on the move again and her pain was lessening, but she still hurt and he still needed to see her. If he left to seek her out, Vail could turn on any of his army who strayed too close, wanting to help him and thinking he was with the elves. Vail had already taken down at least one vampire who lay in the dead forming a circle around him. He clearly couldn't distinguish friend from foe.

"Loren. Bleu," Thorne hollered as loud as he could manage, alerting them in the only way he could without allowing Vail out of his sight.

Vail swept his claws across a male dragon's throat and stark crimson burst from the slash. The dragon gurgled and flailed, trying to cover the gaping wound with his already bloodied hands, and Vail ruthlessly shoved him away to land in a crumpled heap on top of the others.

Vail turned on Thorne.

He bared his fangs, his purple eyes near-black and not because of the low light. Vail was losing his grip, more maddened now than he had ever appeared when they had fought back in London. Shadows clung to the hollows of his cheeks beneath his helmet and darkened around his eyes, a contrast to his pale skin. His madness had turned into sickness, invading both his mind and his body, threatening to destroy him completely.

Thorne needed to bring Loren to them. Vail needed his brother's assistance.

Vail shifted his feet, bracing them shoulder-width apart. He hunched forwards, his hands dangling between his bent legs and his shoulders heaving with each heavy breath. The black slats on his helmet swiftly came forwards, forming a mask over the lower half of his face and leaving only his eyes visible in the V above. Blood rolled down his black claws and dripped to the churned earth.

Thorne laid down his broadsword at his feet and raised his hands beside his head. "I mean you no harm, Vail. Remember you met me in the mortal world. I was with your brother. I am not your enemy."

Vail twitched and his eyes narrowed.

"Vail, no," Olivia barked as the elf launched himself forwards.

Pale blue light traced over his body and he disappeared. Thorne prepared himself, knowing the elf was coming for him. The male appeared behind him and Thorne arched forwards, bellowing as cold claws cut into his side. Vail snarled close to his ear, dark-sounding things in the elf language, and ripped his claws free. A telekinetic blast hit Thorne in the back, sending him stumbling forwards. Only stumbling. Not flying through the air.

Vail wasn't fighting hand-to-hand out of choice or purely because of the sadistic pleasure he took from it, satisfaction that shone darkly in his eyes with every blow of his claws and fists that rent flesh and shattered bone.

The male was too weak to use his powers.

Thorne began to turn towards him, preparing himself for the next attack at the same time, willing to take the blows to buy Loren time to reach them. He would have sensed his brother's presence. He would be coming.

"Vail!" Olivia was on her feet, staggering towards them, reaching for him. "He is a friend."

Another dark-haired demon loomed behind her and she stilled, slowly turning her head to one side, towards the male.

Vail disappeared from before Thorne and dropped out of the air behind Olivia, landing on the demon's back and taking him down. The male knocked Olivia forwards and she hit the ground. Vail growled from his position on the demon's back and grasped the rear of the demon's head with one hand and one horn with the other, and smashed the male's face repeatedly against the stony ground. The mask of his helmet peeled back.

Vail's face twisted into a vicious, cruel visage, his fangs long between his lips and his eyes darkening by degrees.

He continued to bash the unconscious male's head into the earth, smashing it until Thorne could no longer recognise him as the demon foe who had loomed behind Olivia.

"Vail," Olivia whispered, slowly pushing herself onto her side, her face a picture of horror. "Please stop."

Vail snarled at her, shoved the demon's head into the ground with the one that clasped the back of it and yanked forwards with the other that gripped one of the demon's horns. It cracked and he ripped it free.

"Vail!" The deep male voice rang out over the battle and Vail lifted his head, his gaze narrowing on a point beyond Thorne.

Thorne turned to see Loren fighting to reach them, Bleu battling at his side. Loren threw his left hand forwards, sending a blast of telekinesis at the foes blocking his path. They flew in all directions and Loren surged forwards, using his blade to take down the next group of enemies and then teleporting closer to his brother. Bleu followed, assisting his prince and taking down any foe the male left untouched, slashing and stabbing at them with his spear. Loren held his side, growled as blood pumped from between his fingers, and gritted his teeth. He teleported again but only made it a short distance before reappearing.

Thorne had to detain Vail. Loren wouldn't reach his brother in time if he didn't.

Thorne teleported, appearing directly behind Vail. He slid his arms beneath Vail's, tightly locked his forearms against the elf's shoulders, and hauled him off the dead demon. Vail snarled and flailed, lashing out with his claws and catching Thorne's arms, leaving long gashes in his vambraces.

The male pressed his feet into the ground and launched upwards. The back of his helmet connected hard with Thorne's nose. Blood burst from it, streaming over his lips. Thorne growled at him and Vail twisted free, landing in a crouch before Olivia. The elf held his hand out behind him, towards her, and bared his fangs at Thorne.

"Vail," Loren whispered as he reached them and halted a short distance away, breathing hard. Fear flickered across his bloodstained face and he held his hand out to his brother. "Vail?"

Vail turned on him, rising to his feet at the same time, and cast him a pained and fearful look.

Olivia whimpered as she tried to move her arm and Vail's expression shifted, darkening once more, becoming savage and cruel.

He snarled something at Loren in the elf language.

Loren's purple eyes shone with something akin to guilt and he reached for Vail.

Vail hesitated.

Thorne held his breath. Would the younger elf allow his brother to help him now?

The war faded around them, the tension in the air rising by degrees as Thorne waited to see what Vail would do.

He took a step towards Loren and swallowed hard, his hands twitching at his sides, as if he wanted to reach for Loren too.

"Son of a bitch! Take this you bitches," a familiar female voice yelled from behind Thorne and a dazzling blast of purple and blue light erupted off to his left.

Vail's demeanour instantly changed. He bared his fangs and his eyes went wild, crazed as he swung to face Thorne, looking beyond him to the source of the magical attack.

Light flickered over his body.

"Vail!" Loren rushed forwards.

Vail disappeared.

Loren snarled and glared beyond Thorne, towards Rosalind where she fought behind him. And what in the gods' names was she doing out here too?

"I was so close," Loren said in a low tight voice and ground his teeth, his nostrils flaring as he narrowed his gaze on Rosalind. "If it was not for that sorceress!"

Thorne stepped into his line of sight and pressed a hand against his chest, a silent warning not to dare to attack her.

"She is not to be harmed. She has helped me twice now and I owe her much."

Loren drew in a deep breath and blew it out, and then shoved away from him. He stooped to help Olivia onto her feet and Bleu joined them.

"What did he say?" Olivia asked and Loren's expression flickered with guilt again.

He sent his armour away from his hands and gently held her face, inspecting the cut on her forehead and then the gash on her arm.

"He berated me for leaving your side," Loren said and shook his head. "I told you to stay inside, Olivia. Why did you come out here?"

"Rosalind was coming out and I have to be here, I have to help our people."

Loren growled. "Rosalind is nothing but a pain to me. She has placed you in danger, and she has driven my brother away. I wish her ill fortune."

"Don't speak like that. She protected me more than once and she's out here fighting when she's never taken a life before. She wanted to help. I wanted to help." Olivia placed her hands over Loren's, holding them to her face, and looked up into his eyes. "You're hurt. I can feel it. I hate feeling it."

"Do not worry about me, my love. I will heal."

She didn't look as if she believed him. She swept the tangled mess of her dark hair away from the left side of her throat, baring it to Loren.

"Drink. You need your strength. You need to heal. Don't give me any bullshit about being fine. I can feel you, Loren." She dropped her gaze to his side and her eyebrows furrowed as she reached out and touched the deep wound there. Tears lined her lashes and she lifted her eyes back to Loren's. "Drink. Heal. And then you can be mad at me all you want."

Loren's expression softened and he sighed, gently stroked her cheek and nodded. He lowered his head towards her neck and Thorne looked away, giving them some privacy and making sure no one attacked them while they were vulnerable. He would thank Olivia later. He needed her mate strong and capable, and her observations had been right. He had been weakening because of the wound. Bleu kept his back to them, his spear at the ready and his purple eyes locked on the battle raging around them.

Thorne reached out with his senses, needing to feel Sable and feel that she was still alive out there, somewhere. He wanted her back in his arms, held close to him as Olivia was to Loren. He wanted to ask Bleu and Loren whether they had seen her but held his tongue.

Something told him that if Bleu discovered that Sable was injured and he had lost track of her, that Loren wouldn't be the only mated male receiving harsh words from an elf.

Loren drew back from Olivia and Bleu turned to face them.

"Bleu." Loren didn't take his eyes off Olivia's, not even when Bleu halted at his side. "You are to take Olivia back to the castle. Understood?"

"But—" Olivia started.

"No!" Loren barked and frowned down at her. "This is no place for you, Olivia. I cannot fight knowing that you are out here. What if Vail had not been watching us? What then?"

She paled and looked away, tears forming on her lashes. "I would be dead."

Loren closed his eyes and pressed his lips to her forehead. "Swear to me you will not leave the castle again."

"But Sable… we were separated. I have to find her."

"I will find her. I was searching for her when I found you," Thorne put in and she looked across at him. "Men will be returning to the castle and will need your aid."

He knew better than to command her to return. She was like Sable in many respects. He needed to give her reason and a purpose, something to do to help, not order her as Loren did. Although Thorne knew the male only issued those orders to protect her and keep her safe from harm.

Olivia nodded and Loren slowly released her. He dropped another kiss on her brow and lingered there. For a man who wished his female away from battle, he seemed reluctant to let her go.

Loren took a step back and Bleu came forwards, took hold of Olivia's good arm and disappeared with her.

"I am sorry I could not stop your brother," Thorne said and picked up his broadsword.

Loren shook his head.

"I fear he is worse now than ever. I have never seen him so far gone, lost to the dark things that haunt him." Loren stared into the distance, bright colourful flashes reflecting in his violet eyes as the war raged there, the battle intensifying as men fell and fresh soldiers replaced them, boosting the dwindling numbers on both sides.

Thorne clapped a hand down on his shoulder. "One day you will reach him. I am sure of it."

Loren nodded.

Thorne hoped it would be before Vail succumbed to the madness eating away at him and Loren lost his only kin forever.

Bleu reappeared beside him, clutching his long double-bladed black spear. "I have left her at the infirmary. Many injured are returning to the castle."

Thorne knew what that meant. His already small army was growing ever smaller, weakening his chance to save his kingdom.

He scanned the battle, picking out the wolves as they bravely fought the bears off to his right, and the elves as they battled the dragons, and Rosalind and a small army of demons as they took on the witches. He could end this fight. He only needed to reach the other side of the battle and the Fifth King, and claim his head.

A slender female caught his gaze, cutting through the enemy with heart-stopping grace and beautiful determination.

Sable.

Thorne teleported in an instant, reappearing close to her side and taking down the demon she had been fighting.

She turned on him, her blade raised to attack, and froze. "I thought you would be well ahead of me."

He huffed. "I felt your pain and came back to find you."

She rubbed her side. "Just a few bruises. Hurt like a bitch at the time but I'm good now."

"Liar," Thorne said with a half-smile. He could feel her pain and still knew her fear, and it was unfounded. He wasn't going to send her away. He was going to keep her pinned to his side throughout the rest of the battle.

She shrugged and attacked another demon, ducking beneath his swing and slashing across his legs with her blade. Thorne thrust forwards with his broadsword, skewering the male on it, and then yanked his weapon free. The male dropped. Sable rose to her feet.

"So, what's the plan?" She casually loosed a dart at another demon and he roared in agony as it exploded on impact, sending him spinning through the air and landing hard on a group of demons.

Thorne pointed towards the distance.

"We go there."

He grabbed her and teleported before she could utter a word, landing them close to the point he had reached before turning back to find her. Several of his men and some of the elves teleported in beside him and fanned out, taking on the demons and dragons in their way.

Loren appeared beside him with Bleu. Thorne exchanged a look with him, nodded, and the elves disappeared, reappearing further ahead, sweeping through their enemies with black claws and blades. Some of the elves branched off and followed their prince.

Grave was already ahead of Thorne, the vampire savaging and brutally killing everything in his path, leaving a trail of bodies in his wake. His red eyes remained constantly pinned on something ahead of him. Thorne looked there and unleashed a growl when he spotted the jagged green helm of the Fifth King.

Thorne was damned if he would let the vampire reach the Fifth King first.

Two large tawny wolves rushed past Thorne, mauling the legs of their enemies with their fangs and claws. A pack followed them, streaming through their foes like shadows, moving with speed and agility that Thorne couldn't contend with. Not without teleporting anyway.

He grabbed Sable again and dropped into another portal, this one bringing them out in the battle only a few metres from the Fifth King.

The large demon male lifted his head from the neck of a female hunter and dropped her lifeless body at his feet. Blood rolled down his chin, dripping onto his broad bare chest.

"You bastard!" Sable hurled herself forwards but Thorne grabbed her arm, yanking her back to him before she could escape his reach and attempt an attack.

"Thorne," the male growled, tipping his head in greeting, and grinned.

"Frayne." Thorne drew Sable closer to him and the male's green eyes fell to her and narrowed.

Loren, Bleu and Grave reached them together with some of their men and his. Kincaid broke through the demons encircling them, his tawny fur bloodied in places and his golden eyes bright. The wolves followed him into the fray, attacking any who tried to close in on Thorne and the Fifth King, keeping them at bay.

Giving Thorne his chance, one that he was grateful for and prayed to the gods he wouldn't squander.

He would not fail his kingdom.

Not now. Not ever.

He focused, forcing his wings to shrink into his back, unwilling to give his enemy any advantage.

"You have an addition to your ranks since we last met. A pretty little one. To the victor go the spoils." Frayne licked the blood off his lips and raked a gaze over Sable, slowly taking in every inch of her. "I hope she pleases me more than the last huntress I had in my arms."

The bastard was keeping to the mortal language to frighten her and it was working. She trembled beneath his grip, her uncertainty and fear trickling through the link between them.

"Sable," Thorne said a low voice destined only for her ears and silently spoke the rest of what he needed to tell her as he looked down into her golden-brown eyes. He loved her and he would never allow this wretched male or any other to lay a hand on her.

Sable drew in a deep breath, exhaled hard and straightened her spine, her fear disappearing. She nodded, her beautiful eyes relaying the feelings that he could sense in her, the love and affection, and the blossoming confidence.

She slipped her hands beneath her arms, gave him a smile, and then flung her hands towards the Fifth King. The small ringed knives embedded in Frayne's chest and stomach before he could teleport out of their path. The large demon snarled and his horns flared forwards next to his temples, the painted white tips as sharp as the daggers Sable had launched at him.

He teleported and Sable was one step ahead of him, rolling forwards and coming to her feet behind Thorne. Thorne swung his blade with all of his might, aiming at thin air. Frayne appeared in its path and snarled as he quickly raised his right forearm. Thorne's broadsword struck the thick metal and leather vambrace he wore.

Frayne snarled and swung at him with his own sword, bringing it over his head in a fast arc.

Thorne shoved Sable back with one hand and shifted his sword in the other, spinning it in his grip so the blade ran up his arm. He went down on one knee and raised his blade, allowing it to land flat along his arm. Frayne's blade hit hard, showering sparks over Thorne and driving his knee into the dirt.

He launched upwards, using all of the strength in his legs to propel him and shove Frayne's sword up into the air. He kicked off the second the blade was above Frayne's head and barrelled into him, taking him down onto the ground. Frayne roared, his wings twisted beneath him, and grabbed Thorne's left horn, dragging him down towards him. Thorne grunted as Frayne's forehead connected with his and pain spider-webbed across his skull.

Frayne rolled and Thorne wrestled with him, determined to end up on top again, avoiding scrappy punches and trying to land a few of his own as he fought for dominance over the Fifth King.

A bolt whizzed past Thorne's head and exploded a short distance away from him.

Thorne looked across at Sable and growled when he caught sight of her. She fought her blond male hunter, Evan, her hands shaking as she struck his blade with her own and uncertainty flooding the link between them. She wasn't sure what to do and he could grasp her concern and reluctance to land a killing blow on the man who had once been her second in command.

But was no longer.

Evan's eyes flashed brilliant blue.

"Rakshasa," Thorne called and Sable's fear immediately diminished. She spun her short blade in her hand so the point was close to her elbow and slashed at the creature who had assumed the form of her friend.

Frayne sent Thorne's world spinning with a hard blow on his jaw that snapped his head to one side and Thorne grunted as he ended up on his back, pinned beneath the Fifth King.

The male grinned down at him, cracking the dried blood caking his chin.

"I will enjoy your woman and your kingdom, Thorne. I shall take great care of both of them."

Thorne roared and bucked up, hurling Frayne off him. Frayne levelled a kick at him and Thorne dropped into the darkness. He fell out of the air above Frayne, hurtling towards the Fifth King.

Frayne whipped around to face him and disappeared, dropping into his own portal. Thorne hit the ground hard, rolled and found his feet again. He grabbed the nearest weapon as he passed it and sought Frayne. The bastard had yet to appear. Sable fought off to his left, battling hard against the rakshasa. Thorne wanted to join her and make the creature pay for what it had done to Fargus but it was her fight now. The rakshasa had killed her second in command too.

Pain burst across Thorne's back and he grunted as he stumbled forwards. He twisted mid-step and raised his blade, knocking away Frayne's as the male attacked his back.

Frayne grinned at him and signalled with his free hand.

Thorne shot forwards and clashed hard with him, knocking the smile off his face as he drove him backwards, towards the centre of the circle expanding around them. He grabbed Frayne's left wing, pressed his boot into the male's stomach, and yanked hard. Frayne unleashed an agonised bellow and grasped Thorne's right arm, digging his long claws in for purchase. He twisted hard, throwing Thorne off balance and tearing a cry from his throat as his muscles protested and Frayne's claws sliced through his flesh.

"Bastard," Sable spat and a dart lodged into Frayne's right shoulder. "Enjoy that with my compliments, you prick."

Frayne snarled, yanked the bolt from his flesh and crushed it in his grip. He turned to advance on Sable and staggered, a confused frown darkening his rugged face.

Sable spun to avoid the rakshasa's swing and came to her feet nearer to Thorne.

She winked at him. "The elves make some bitching poisons."

He would have to remember to thank them. She whirled to face her opponent, bringing her short sword down at the same time, and it sliced through Evan's shoulder.

The rakshasa cried out and leaped backwards. A mistake on his part. Bleu was there, a cold smile on his face as he drove his spear forwards, skewering the creature.

Thorne punched Frayne hard on the jaw, knocking him backwards, further into the clearing. The Fifth King growled at him, sweat breaking out across his brow. It wasn't quite the victory that Thorne had desired but he wasn't about to castigate Sable for her underhand tactics on the battlefield. The Fifth King had no doubt commanded the rakshasa to poison him after all. It was only fair the bastard had a taste of his own medicine.

Frayne growled, exposing his fangs, and lashed out with his claws, slicing across Thorne's chest. Thorne ignored the sting of the lacerations and kept driving forwards, landing blow after blow on Frayne, weakening him at the same time as the toxin.

Frayne signalled again.

Who was he calling?

A tall woman with jet-black eyes appeared beside him, her long black dress hugging her curves, torn in a few places.

She attacked immediately, blasting Thorne with a glowing blue orb that exploded against his chest and sent him flying through the air. Thorne growled through the pain, unleashed his wings and spread them, halting his ascent. He shook off the agony that seared his ribs and beat his aching wings, shooting back towards the witch and Frayne.

The female threw orb after colourful orb at those around her, each one striking someone from his team. Screams rose above the din of battle and the clang of weapons clashing. He fixed his sights on her and she looked up at him, a smile curving her black lips, and tossed her hand towards him and blew across her palm. A swirling vortex of black extended from her hand, the funnel growing as it rocketed towards him.

Thorne rolled in the air and beat his wings harder, trying to evade it. Tendrils of black shot from the wide end of the vortex, reaching for him. He growled and gritted his teeth, flying as fast as he could to outstrip them before they could snag his feet and pull him into the funnel. He wasn't sure what the spell would do to him and he didn't want to find out.

He swept lower, over ranks of his enemy as they closed in on his men, and the funnel tore through them, the black tendrils grabbing any within reach and pulling them inside. Cries echoed across the battlefield and died in an instant, the moment their owner disappeared into the vortex. Blood sprayed across the untouched.

Thorne decided he definitely did not want the vortex or the tendrils to catch him, or any he cared about.

He looked back at the witch, searching for a way to take her down and destroy her spell with her.

Frayne grinned up at him and beat his own wings, gaining momentum with each powerful stroke.

Another spell hit Thorne's feet, sending him toppling heels over head. He dropped hard, landing a short distance from Sable as she fought the rakshasa with Bleu. Loren hauled Thorne onto his feet and Thorne met his steely gaze.

"I am beginning to despise witches," Loren said, a grim look on his face. "I will deal with her."

"And I will finish this." Thorne grabbed a blade from the ground and Loren disappeared.

Loren appeared close behind the witch and she lowered her hand, her spell disappearing as she turned on him. The dark elf prince grinned, flashing fangs at her, and attacked.

Thorne rushed to assist him by luring Frayne away. The Fifth King looked well again, no trace of the fever that should have gripped him on his face or in the fluid way he moved as he joined the witch in battling Loren. The witch must have cured him. He had called her to him to aid him and give him time to recuperate, distracting Thorne.

Bleu teleported to join his prince, driving Frayne back.

Frayne disappeared and the hairs on Thorne's nape rose. He turned as quickly as he could and was almost facing the Fifth King when he appeared. Frayne's claws raked down Thorne's chest, slicing deep, and Thorne roared as fire blazed through him.

Poison. The bastard had coated his claws in his own poisoned blood. The toxin wasn't enough to kill him but it would slow him down, giving Frayne the advantage.

Thorne stumbled backwards as the inferno swept through his veins, burning up his blood and making his head spin. Frayne advanced on him, his chin tipped up, looking down on Thorne as he lifted Thorne's own broadsword with both hands, raising it above his head and preparing to strike.

Thorne staggered and tried to keep upright but his heel hit a rock and he tripped, landing hard on his backside.

Victory flashed in Frayne's green eyes.

Thorne stared at the blade as it cut a silver arc through the darkness, coming straight for him.

It stopped.

Frayne roared in agony.

"Die, demon filth." The female voice was familiar but edged with cold and cruelty.

Darkness flowed through Thorne, desire to dismember the wretch towering over him, the demon scum. Hunger awakened within him, a pressing need to coat his hands with the blood of his enemies and bathe their souls in the fire of purity, sending them into the forever after to be judged.

Sable.

She stood between him and Frayne, her back to him and her hands clutching Frayne's wrists, holding them above her head. She had halted his attack. She had saved Thorne.

Orange light shone from beneath her fingers where they pressed into Frayne's flesh and the demon roared again, his agony palpable as his skin blackened and a fiery glow pierced the fractures growing in it.

Frayne threw his head back and roared.

Silence swept across the battle as all eyes turned their way, seeing Sable in all her glory.

Light burst from beneath her silver cuff around her right wrist and twin points on her shoulder-blades glowed beneath her t-shirt. The material covering them smouldered and smoke rose, curling upwards. The twin points stretched into glowing lines.

Sable grunted and wavered, and agony tore through the link between them, throbbing in his bones and where his wings joined his back.

She was hurting herself.

Her grip loosened.

Frayne's blade fell, cutting straight towards her.

Thorne threw himself at her, his heart pounding as he raced to reach her in time and every inch of him on fire as he battled the poison weakening his body. Her knees hit the dirt and he kicked off, launching himself forward with every ounce of strength he could muster, reaching for her. He placed his right forearm above his head as he covered her with his body. The sword struck hard, slicing through his leather vambrace and deep into his forearm.

He didn't wait for Frayne to pull the blade free. He released Sable, grasped the blade with his free hand, and shot upwards, knocking his broadsword from Frayne's grasp.

Thorne growled as he felt Sable's pain, heard her moan as she held herself. It drove him on and red filled his vision, a haze descending that purged the weakness from his body and drowned out the world, leaving only Frayne behind.

He would take the bastard's head.

He grabbed the hilt of his sword and it singed his palm, hot from where Frayne had held it in his burning flesh. He dragged the blade free of his right arm and let the useless limb fall to his side as he spun on his heel and swung hard at Frayne.

Frayne raised his blackened forearms to protect himself and the metal vambraces shattered beneath Thorne's blow. The sword sliced through his arms and straight through his neck, sending it bouncing across the dirt. Frayne's body slumped sideways and crumbled to ash as Sable's gift consumed it.

A call went out, rising long and loud above the battle.

Thorne dug the point of his broadsword into the earth, breathing hard as it hit him. Months of fighting had come to an end. His kingdom was safe at last.

None of it mattered to him as he stood there on the battlefield, bathed in the blood of his enemies, every laceration on his body stinging like cold fire and the weakness from the poison returning.

All that mattered was Sable.

He dropped to his knees beside her, rolled her over, and gathered her into his arms. Tears streaked her dirty cheeks and her eyes fluttered open. Bright gold shone in her irises, dazzling him.

"Don't touch... I'll burn..." She tried to push away but he held her closer, slipping one arm beneath her knees and the other around her back, grimacing as the deep wound on his right arm burned.

He paused and frowned as something tickled that arm and leaned to one side.

Feathers.

They were small and grey, coating delicate arches of bone and muscle that protruded from her shoulders.

"Don't," she whispered and swallowed hard. "Don't let them—"

"Shh. Save your strength," he murmured and pressed a long kiss to her forehead.

His female didn't need to speak for him to know what she desired. He could feel it in her, knew her well enough to understand what she wanted him to do without her even asking. He carefully tucked the newly born wings inside her t-shirt. They trembled beneath his touch and shrank, slowly disappearing into her back.

Sable moaned and clutched him with both hands, gripping his shoulders. "Hurts."

He could remember the first time his wings had emerged and how painful it had been, and how he had felt sick to his stomach, ready to vomit as the new tender bones grew. They had been sensitive to the slightest touch, aching whenever anything brushed them. He waited for Sable's to disappear and then rose with her, holding her in his arms and only stumbling a little as his knees threatened to give out.

He sucked in a sharp breath and exhaled hard, trying to shut down the pain lancing his bones and refusing to let the toxin render him unconscious. Sable needed him strong. He would be strong for her.

He grew aware of everyone around him. Loren and Bleu were closest, with Kincaid in mortal form behind them, tugging on a pair of trousers he had stolen from one of the dead demons. Grave stood off to one side, barking orders at his men to search for survivors. Several of his demons were working with him, scouring the fallen for their injured comrades and teleporting with them whenever they found one. The remaining elves joined them in their search.

Thorne held Sable closer as Bleu and Loren approached him.

"Is she hurt?" Bleu said with concern in his purple eyes and Thorne shook his head.

"She is still unused to her new abilities. Using it to protect me while wearing the cuff that dampens her powers only served to awaken more of them. The strain was too much for her, but she will be well soon." Thorne looked down at his fierce little female. His queen. "Will you not?"

Sable muttered something dark in his language.

Thorne smiled.

His little angel had a demon's tongue.

He looked around the battlefield, taking a moment to check on those he could see and ensure that those who needed aid received it. He had scored one victory, seeing his kingdom safe for now, but he feared his greatest battle remained unfinished.

Thorne looked down at Sable.

Would she stay with him and take her rightful place at his side as his queen?

Or would she desire to return to her world and Archangel?

CHAPTER 31

Sable sat on the bench in the infirmary and grimaced as fire blazed a trail across her chest. Thorne growled on the bed beside her, his anger directed at Olivia. Olivia ignored him and continued to clean his wounds, each one she tended hurting Sable too. This was part of the bond that she could definitely live without, and Olivia had told her that she shared that opinion.

Sable reached up and took Thorne's hand in hers, staring at it as she tried to ground herself again, using him as her anchor. Her world had tilted on its axis again and her footing felt unstable, liable to drop out from beneath her at any given moment. Her stomach somersaulted whenever she thought about what had happened on the battlefield.

"Olivia, a moment." Thorne's deep voice curled around Sable, comforting her and chasing the chill from her bones.

Olivia moved off to check on her other patients and Thorne sat up, swinging his legs over the edge of the low bed. He shuffled closer to her and she kept her gaze on their joined hands, avoiding his inquisitive look.

"When I was young," he whispered in a low voice and moved closer still, until he was all she could feel, smell, see and hear, capturing all of her attention. She looked up into his eyes, seeking the calm she felt whenever she stared into their rich crimson depths, the steadiness that she needed now more than ever. He leaned down, bringing his face close to hers, and continued, "When I was young, and my wings first emerged, I vomited."

That made her smile.

It was strange having someone who knew what she was going through but it also made her feel blessed to have Thorne in her life, to have someone by her side who had experienced what she had on the battlefield.

"I was close to being sick," Sable admitted and then wrinkled her nose. "But I manned up and kept my shit together."

Thorne frowned now, his handsome visage darkening with it. "I was very young."

"Younger than thirty-five?"

His expression soured. "Very well. You are more of a man than I... for now."

The look in his crimson eyes said he was tempted to say more than that. He wanted to tease her, saying she would likely throw up at some point before she was used to her wings emerging.

Wings.

Mind fuck.

"Guess we know who my dad was now. Not really much room for doubt anymore." She toyed with Thorne's hand and he settled his other one over hers, clasping it between his.

"There is still much for us to learn though. I mean to keep my promise, Sable. I will go with you to meet the angel female again and together we shall discover more about your lineage and what it will mean for you." The earnestness in his eyes and his tone touched her and she smiled again, letting him see it even though she knew he could feel it within her through their bond.

At least someone was on her side. She wasn't sure Archangel would feel the same.

If she returned to them.

That was still up in the air, the topic of a constant debate in her mind.

Loren hobbled past and paused, backtracking to them. He looked down at her. "Have you seen Olivia?"

Sable nodded. "She was just torturing Thorne. She went that way."

He went to leave and then stopped again as Olivia bustled over to them and caught him in a tight hug. He flinched and Olivia loosed a muffled grunt.

"Sometimes, this bond thing sucks." Olivia pushed back and sighed at a long gash running from Loren's right thigh up over his hipbone. She pointed to the bed Thorne sat on. "Sit."

Loren did as he was told, settling himself next to Thorne. "It seems I am due some torture."

"Telling her that you are immortal and will heal seems to have little effect," Thorne said and Loren stifled a smile, and so did Sable.

"I can hear you," Olivia muttered and set about cleaning Loren's wound through the cut in his armour.

"Where's Bleu?" Sable said because she wanted to thank him for helping her with the rakshasa. She only wished she could have made the son of a bitch suffer more as payment for what it had done.

Loren flinched again as Olivia dabbed at the wound on his side with cotton wool. "Returned to the mortal world. A messenger was able to teleport into the castle and delivered a request for Bleu's assistance elsewhere. I granted him leave since it was Kyter and the communication stated that the jaguar male had an elf in need of assistance."

"The pathways are open again?" Sable tried to keep her thoughts off Bleu and wondering whether he had been eager to go because he liked the jaguar bar-owner or whether he had gone because of her and Thorne.

Olivia slid her a knowing smile. "Don't worry. I'm sure that a little time spent in Kyter's company and a few shots of Hellfire will have Bleu forgetting his troubles."

Sable smiled at her friend's poor attempt to make her feel better about the whole situation.

Loren's attempt only made her laugh aloud, drawing a few odd looks from the men and women in the infirmary.

"Bleu will be fine and will find himself a female to slake his urges on and then he will be back to normal and his regular visits to the mortal world when the mood strikes him."

Olivia slapped his arm. "You've been around demons for too long. You're becoming uncouth."

Loren frowned at her and then a smile worked its way across his lips. "You have been around me too long, Sweet Ki'ara, if you are beginning to use words such as uncouth."

Sable grinned. "Next thing you know it, you'll be saying yonder."

Thorne arched an eyebrow at her. Loren did too.

"Yonder is a perfectly good word," Loren said and grimaced as Olivia went back to tending to his wound.

"Never said it wasn't." Sable played with Thorne's fingers again and sidled closer, until her knees brushed his. "I sort of like the word yonder."

A sexy smile tugged at Thorne's lips. He slipped his arm around her waist, hauled her onto his lap and kissed her. Sable melted into it, losing herself in how good it felt to be in his arms and know that he was safe now, and so was his kingdom.

He drew back too quickly and she pouted and tried to kiss him again. Thorne made a very weak effort to stop her and then he was kissing her again, clutching her closer this time, his fingers pressing into her sides. The possessiveness of the kiss thrilled her, sending a shiver down her limbs, and she leaned into him, capturing his shoulders with her palms and holding him in place.

Someone cleared their throat.

He groaned and broke the kiss, pressing his forehead against hers for a second before turning to speak with the demon who had arrived beside them.

Sable moved to sit on the bench and tuned him out as he talked in the demon tongue. She looked over at Loren. The handsome elf scanned the room, his frown growing.

"Who are you looking for?" Olivia said and stood, tossing the bloodied cotton wool onto the pile at her feet.

"I desire a word with the sorceress." Loren kept scanning the long room and Sable joined him.

The demon left and Thorne gave her a quizzical look.

"Have you seen Rosalind?" she said and he shook his head.

"Not since she frightened Vail away with her magic."

Sable's eyebrows shot up. "Vail was here?"

Was that why Loren wanted to speak with her, because she had scared him off?

Olivia nodded. "He came out of nowhere to defend me after we were all separated by that spell. Loren tried to reach him and we think he was close to getting through to him, but then Rosalind launched an attack on the witches again, and he teleported."

Thorne raised his hand, calling his man back. "Keep an eye open on the battlefield for the witch Rosalind. She is missing and may be injured."

The man nodded and teleported.

"She is not injured. She was taken."

Sable frowned up at Grave as he loitered off to her left, nursing his arm and covered in dried blood and lacerations.

"Taken?" Thorne shot to his feet. "Explain yourself."

His fear washed through her and she slipped her hand into his, trying to draw his attention down to her so she could ease it away.

His crimson gaze flickered to her and back to Grave.

"Thorne," Sable said and he finally gave her his attention. "Rosalind released you of your vow when she came out to help us. I told her to go back inside, reminded her of the vow, and she said that she was breaking it."

Relief beat through him but it lasted only a second before he was frowning at Grave again.

"Who took her?"

The vampire rubbed his good hand over his matted dark hair and grimaced, grinding his teeth together. Red ringed his irises and then gradually faded.

"I saw her separated from the others while you dealt the deathblow upon the Fifth King. The demons she was battling seized her upon seeing their king fall and shortly afterwards they teleported." Grave's pale irises flickered crimson again and he squeezed his eyes shut.

One of his men came to him, stopping close enough to assist him if he needed it but wisely keeping his distance too. Grave glared at him, issuing a silent challenge. Sable willed the vampire to do the wise thing and take a step back from his commander. The man obviously wanted to assist him if he needed it, but as far as she could see, he was in danger of committing suicide.

He edged further away from Grave but remained within lunging distance.

Grave returned his cold gaze to Thorne.

Thorne stared him down. "You saw them seize her and did not attempt to help her? You did not think to go after them?"

Grave stepped closer to Thorne and narrowed his eyes on him, the edges of his irises turning crimson again. "The witch was a fair distance from me and I had my hands full with the demons, and unfortunately I do not possess the ability to teleport."

He slid his glare towards Loren and curled his lip, exposing one fang, before returning his attention to Thorne.

"And besides... the uninitiated should not head into battles such as this one."

The vampire glanced at Kyal as he hobbled past them, assisted by Kincaid, badly injured and covered with blood.

And nude.

Sable stared at her feet.

Thorne growled. "By the gods' good names, put some clothes on."

"If you are quite done interrogating me about the fate of a single female, I have matters that require my attention." Grave stepped back and sauntered down the aisle between the beds, heading towards the other end of the infirmary.

Kyal growled as he passed them.

For once, Grave ignored him, his focus locked on the end of the room where some of his men lay wounded and recuperating.

Olivia gave her a strange look and led Loren away, leaving her alone with Thorne. Her friends were clearly conspiring against her now, seeing her need to speak with him and wanting to give them some privacy.

Sable looked up at Thorne, unsure what to say as her thoughts collided, tangling together in her mind and leaving her uncertain of everything.

"Thorne," she whispered and he looked down at her. "We'll find Rosalind."

He frowned. "We?"

Her heart flipped in her chest and she blew out her breath, trying to expel her nerves with it.

She nodded. "We."

He sat beside her again and took hold of her hand, his beautiful dark scarlet eyes locked on hers.

"But your mission here is done. You will return to Archangel."

She hated the certainty with which he said that and looked away from him, catching Olivia's gaze across the room.

Sable closed her eyes to shut everyone out and focused on why she had come here.

She had come to the Third Realm to prove herself as a hunter and finally achieve the rank of commander, a position she had desired ever since she had joined Archangel, but so much had happened.

She had learned part of the truth about herself and it was going to be a long time before she could come to terms with it. If she returned to Archangel now, after her men had seen her fighting the Fifth King and had witnessed what she had done to him, she would have to face Mark and the other senior members. They would want to know about her powers.

She didn't know about them herself. How was she meant to tell them about something even she didn't understand yet?

Thorne's hand gently settled on the silver cuff around her wrist and she opened her eyes and looked up into his. His soft gaze held hers, his tender emotions travelling through the link between them and speaking to her heart.

"I will be there with you, Sable, at your side for all eternity, no matter what happens or what decision you make. I will always be yours, and you will always be mine, and we shall always have each other."

She gave him a shaky smile.

"I want you to know that you have a place here with me... and I do have an opening for a commander. You are welcome to it." He smiled at her, beautiful and enchanting, bringing hers to life.

Before her was a man who would do anything for her.

A demon king who loved her with all of his heart.

And had claimed hers.

Sable stared deep into his eyes, seeing all his love in them and knowing that she could never bring herself to part from him. She didn't want to leave Archangel behind but she had a new purpose now and this was where she belonged, with Thorne.

He would do all in his power to help her discover the truth about her family and how to control her abilities, and she loved him for that and for being there for her.

She would return to Archangel to report on her mission here in the Third Realm, but she would also tell them that she wasn't staying. Her mission wasn't over yet. She had lost too many of her men in the war and she refused to give up on the others who had been captured by the dragons. She would track and slay every single one of the shifters to free her huntresses, beginning with Anais.

That mission to rescue her huntresses would also give her the time she needed to put her life with Archangel to rest and to learn more about herself. Then, she would be ready to embark on her new, eternal life with the beautiful demon watching her intently, studying her face as he held his breath and waited for her to speak.

Sable reached up and brushed her fingers across his cheek, holding his gaze and keeping it locked on hers even as it wavered, his nerves getting the better of him. She smiled to alleviate them and let the words flow freely from her soul.

"I knew in my heart the moment I gave it to you that I would leave my life at Archangel behind one day so I could be with you… whether that's as your commander or your queen."

Thorne grinned. "Or both."

"I can do both." Sable chuckled and he pulled her back onto his lap and wrapped his arms around her, his expression turning deadly serious, making her flutter inside. She pressed a kiss to his cheek and then another, and whispered against it, "Queen Sable, commander of the legions of the Third Realm… it has a nice ring to it, don't you think?"

Thorne's relief flowed through her as he fingered the holes in the back of her black t-shirt, stroking her sensitive skin. Shivers skittered down her back and along her arms and her gaze grew hooded as she lowered it to Thorne's mouth, already imagining the searing kiss she felt coming.

"You are not queen yet, Little Female," Thorne husked and edged his lips closer to hers, his slowness tearing at her and making her wriggle as frustration tightened her stomach.

"But I am *your* queen," she murmured with a smile and hooked her arms around his neck. "And you are my king…"

Sable slid one hand down his bare chest, feeling his muscles flutter beneath her light touch, and settled it over the hard bulge in his leathers. Hunger flooded the link between them, desire that matched the ferocity of her own, and he groaned.

"And my king needs."

Thorne crushed her lips under a kiss that seared every inch of her, setting her aflame with need and claiming every part of her, right down to her soul.

They would be each other's forever.

And the whole of Hell would know that King Thorne of the Third Realm had been claimed.

Claimed by his angel queen.

The End

ABOUT THE AUTHOR

Felicity Heaton is a New York Times and USA Today best-selling author who writes passionate paranormal romance books. In her books she creates detailed worlds, twisting plots, mind-blowing action, intense emotion and heart-stopping romances with leading men that vary from dark deadly vampires to sexy shape-shifters and wicked werewolves, to sinful angels and hot demons!

If you're a fan of paranormal romance authors Lara Adrian, J R Ward, Sherrilyn Kenyon, Kresley Cole, Gena Showalter, Larissa Ione and Christine Feehan then you will enjoy her books too.

If you love your angels a little dark and wicked, her best-selling Her Angel romance series is for you. If you like strong, powerful, and dark vampires then try the Vampires Realm romance series or any of her stand alone vampire romance books. If you're looking for vampire romances that are sinful, passionate and erotic then try her London Vampires romance series. Or if you like hot-blooded alpha heroes who will let nothing stand in the way of them claiming their destined woman then try her Eternal Mates series. It's packed with sexy heroes in a world populated by elves, vampires, fae, demons, shifters, and more. If sexy Greek gods with incredible powers battling to save our world and their home in the Underworld are more your thing, then be sure to step into the world of Guardians of Hades.

If you have enjoyed this story, please take a moment to contact the author at **author@felicityheaton.com** or to post a review of the book online

Connect with Felicity:
Website – http://www.felicityheaton.com
Blog – http://www.felicityheaton.com/blog/
Twitter – http://twitter.com/felicityheaton
Facebook – http://www.facebook.com/felicityheaton
Goodreads – http://www.goodreads.com/felicityheaton
Mailing List – http://www.felicityheaton.com/newsletter.php

FIND OUT MORE ABOUT HER BOOKS AT:
http://www.felicityheaton.com

Printed in Great Britain
by Amazon